THE
STANTON
SUCCESSION

THE

STANTON
SUCCESSION

by

WARREN KIEFER

DONALD I. FINE, INC.
New York

Library of Congress Cataloging-in-Publication Data
Kiefer, Warren, 1929–
The Stanton succession / by Warren Kiefer.
p.   cm.
ISBN 1-55611-282-3
I. Title.
PS3561.I34S7   1992
813'.54—dc20   91-58658
CIP

Manufactured in the United States of America

10   9   8   7   6   5   4   3   2   1

Designed by Irving Perkins Associates

For Dorothy Olding

"The prince of darkness is a gentleman."

SHAKESPEARE: *King Lear*

CHAPTER ONE

THE LAW. If Colin Draggett's life was about anything it was about the law. The law's great gift, he would say, was to tempt people with solutions. Although the solutions seldom satisfy the litigants, they have to satisfy the law. Colin Draggett even tended to think of the law as a metaphor for life, an orderly series of briefs summarizing the one big case he was certain to lose in the end.

Why, then, did he flout and betray the law the first time the chips were down? Perhaps, as the old songs say, you always hurt the thing you love. But that is too facile a description of his behavior, and doesn't really explain anything. As he saw it, greed and panic got the better of him. But in fact he was being too hard on himself. Colin being what he was, his conscience troubled him. He felt he should make amends to some as he got even with others, and he wanted to set the record straight for the rest.

His running battle with Adam Walsh could have been called *Draggett vs Walsh*. Colin Draggett, attorney-at-law, pitted against Adam Walsh, big-shot corporation executive. But the file would have had to include Ken Fairchild and Brian Redfern, whose ambitious scheming affected Colin's better judgment and decent instincts from the start, and made the *People vs. Redfern* possible.

Colin Draggett was not a criminal lawyer, and that was a criminal proceeding in more ways than one. Justice is blind, they say, but often so are the judge, the jury and the public. In the *People vs. Redfern,* justice of a sort was served, no matter who thought Redfern was guilty and in spite of those who swore he was innocent, starting with Redfern himself. In democracies presumed innocence is the rule and guilt the egregious exception. Then there was Redfern's case. He wasn't innocent, but he wasn't guilty either.

When Colin Draggett finished law school he wanted to do some good in the world. He was offered a chance of going with the district attorney's office or joining Cranmer, Fisher & Cleves on Wall Street. The D.A. promised glamour, excitement and the chance to get his name in the papers. Wall Street offered a degree of respectability and prestige not to be found in a prosecutor's office. It was world-class, top-of-the-line corporate law, and for a poor boy from Bay Ridge, the access to power was as irresistible as the certainty that anyone with half his brains could get rich. One of the partners lulled him with the comforting message, "Make your fortune here, and then you can do whatever you want to further your ideals."

When Colin was hired by Cranmer, Fisher & Cleves, the senior partner told him that in the hundred-year history of the firm he was the first.

"The first what?" he asked.

"Why, Irish Catholic," the old gentleman explained in a hush, as if the two words together were not to be spoken in polite company. Such an attitude surprised him, because a number of prominent Irish lawyers like Wild Bill Donovan and William Casey had practiced law on Wall Street. And ten years had passed since the country had elected an Irish Catholic President.

Colin was Harvard Law Review, and had gone through school on scholarships. His father, a gentle, kindly man who owned a bar and grill in Bay Ridge, had one refrain: "You get a good profession like law, Colin, they can't do nothing."

"Do what, Pop?"

"If you're a lawyer you can tie them in knots."

These conversations occurred when he was helping his father clean glasses and sweep up behind the bar.

"Who, Pop?" Colin had fought Italians and Blacks around the Brooklyn schoolyards and he enjoyed a certain prestige because he was tall, tough and fast. He was also at the top of his class, so he often became a mediator among the different ethnic student groups.

"Colin, you know what's happening in Belfast? They're killing Catholics. The only ones they leave alone are professionals."

Colin loved his father and knew that in most things the older man was hardly stupid. But he was a little cracked on this subject and honestly believed if his son studied law it would exempt him from discrimination or persecution by the Protestant establishment.

"It's how you get ahead," his father said. When Colin failed to give such sermons his undivided attention, his father would take a fall-back position and say, "Don't break your mother's heart, Colin boy."

Contrary to all the myths of motherhood, Colin's mother Maisie had no heart to break as far as he could ever tell.

A quarter of a century later, she was still going strong, sustained by her unfathomable fascination with herself and her grudge against the world, living in bourgeois splendor at her son's expense, no longer on speaking terms with his only sister and eager to tell him her manifold troubles whenever he gave her the chance. Colin's father was the one with the heart, but his gave out before Colin became what he so ardently desired in a son.

"You mean I'm the only Catholic in the firm?" Colin asked the senior partner of Cranmer, Fisher & Cleves.

"By no means. Some of our best clerks are of that faith and we also have one Jew," he said without embarrassment. He then explained that Colin had been taken on for two reasons. The firm always tried to corral somebody from Harvard Law Review and that year it was he. The other reason was a burgeoning number of liberal-minded clients who were a little nervous about a firm that included nothing but Wasp attorneys. Great deliberations had taken place among the partners before Draggett was offered a place.

Soon he had risen to a position of eminent obscurity, making no waves but his first million-dollar fee with a surprise upset victory in a major utility-rates case. He became a Wall Street hero overnight, giving out advice clients could have gotten for a tenth the price from any struggling midtown attorney.

But he was not a little bored by the work, and he got rid of his frustration on the squash court. Twice a week he journeyed uptown to the Harvard Club to play. When his regular opponent failed to appear one day, he took on Avery Stanton, a man twenty years his senior. The older man lost but they began a very special friendship which lasted until his death. The Stantons of Park Avenue, Saratoga and Newport were Old Wasp New York, while the Draggetts of Canal Street, Bay Ridge and Bronxville were Lace Curtain Micks, but that never got in the way of the two men.

Avery Stanton was a brilliant metallurgical chemist with big ideas who was teaching at Stevens Institute at the time. Colin took credit for getting them both out of a rut when he offered to find the venture capital Stanton needed to start a company. Colin put up every dollar he had and took his fees in stock. He also talked various clients into bankrolling the rest until Stanton's struggling company got its first major defense contract.

With Colin's legal and financial skills and Avery Stanton's inventive imagination, the firm of Stanton Technologies soon became conspicuously successful. Avery Stanton astounded the competition with patents on electroplating techniques, silicon ceramic laminates and base metal alloys that revolutionized the metallurgical industry. Without him America would not have gotten to the moon when it did or developed the non-stick frying pan.

They located the main plant near New London, Connecticut, because Colin got Stanton a tax break under a local industrial promotion law. New London was also convenient because Stanton had become a subcontractor to the shipyards building America's nuclear-submarine fleet only a stone's throw away.

Colin meanwhile brought Stanton into Cranmer, Fisher & Cleves as a major client and was rewarded with a partnership. Now, as senior partner, he occupied the office of the old man who hired him. For Colin the commute from Manhattan to the beautiful Connecticut shore was a refreshing change three or four times a month.

Twenty years went by like that, and although his squash days were over, Avery Stanton talked on the telephone regularly with Colin. They golfed together occasionally and saw one another at board meetings.

After one such meeting shortly before his death Stanton asked Colin to join him for dinner. He had slowed down a lot and was looking pale and drawn, but Colin attributed it to the fact that he had only recently recovered from a bout with the flu.

Over the meal Stanton confided the real reason. In a routine medical checkup the doctors discovered a cardiac arrhythmia, and further tests showed a serious problem. It could be helped by surgery, but they also recommended he retire.

"What are you going to do?"

"I'm sixty-seven years old," Stanton said. "If they cut and I quit, they tell me I've got ten or fifteen years left."

"And if not?"

"The pump could founder anytime."

"What are you going to do?"

At first Colin didn't think his friend had heard his question. He wasn't looking at him, and Colin was about to repeat it when he turned back. Tears glistened in the older man's eyes and for a moment he couldn't speak.

"I don't want to die, Colin," he said.

Colin covered Stanton's hand with his. "Ave," he said softly, "I don't mean to sound frivolous, but heart surgery these days is just like an appendix used to be, almost a status thing."

"Good old Colin," the older man said. "I'm a rotten Christian, you know. The worst kind. I only pray when I'm desperate and then I want it all at once."

"So who doesn't?" Colin said. "You think I'm a good example? I don't even pray when I'm desperate, but I do surely piss and moan a lot."

Stanton smiled sadly. "So what the hell do I do?"

"Exactly what the doctors suggest," Colin told him.

"Thanks, old friend, I guess I will. I'm all out of good ideas anyway. Can't keep up with you younger guys."

"Bullshit."

He laughed. "The problem is who takes over?"

"Hunt Benson?" Colin referred to the company's executive vice-president, only a year or two younger than Stanton.

"Hunt is one of the best engineers in the industry," Stanton replied. "But he still comes in every morning expecting me to tell him what to do. There's no way he could ever be number one."

Stanton Technologies had gone public a number of years earlier, but the company was still being run by Avery Stanton, who had an idiosyncratic, hands-on executive style, always acting on instinct and impulse. In the laboratory and on the drawing boards this style served him well. In executive management, however, the results could sometimes be a mixed blessing.

Stanton's critics pointed to examples, such as the way he promoted his son-in-law Kenneth Fairchild through the Stanton sales hierarchy, and his hiring of Brian Redfern right out of business school, then pushing him over the heads of more seasoned executives to the top of Stanton International.

But few knew the truth behind one of his more eccentric hiring hunches when he brought Adam Walsh into the company. After meeting Walsh socially on the golf course and knowing him only a few weeks, Stanton had been so dazzled by his personality and background as a market analyst that he appointed him marketing director.

Like most of Avery Stanton's gut reactions, this one seemed to have paid off handsomely. Walsh was brilliant, and Stanton soon made him a vice-president. Within three years of Walsh's joining the company Stanton stock had soared, mainly because Avery had followed all of Walsh's recommendations for rapid expansion abroad and gone after a larger share of the consumer market at home.

"Suppose you tell me who you have in mind."

As Avery Stanton saw it, there were only three possibilities inside the company. One was his protégé, Brian Redfern, the bright engineer and Harvard Business School graduate who had been mainly responsible for Stanton International's extraordinary growth and profitability around the world.

The second was Ken Fairchild, vice-president for sales, former All-American quarterback and West Point class of '72, who was married to Avery Stanton's only child Barbara.

The third candidate was Adam Walsh. Redfern was the youngest, a thirty-six-year-old boy wonder. Ken Fairchild was forty-one and Walsh was fifty.

"Each is talented in his own way," Stanton told Colin.

"You don't want me to tell you who to choose."

"I handpicked Brian, as you know, put him in charge of Stanton International, and he's done a fabulous job. But he's a bit abrasive with some people, and no one would exactly call him a salesman."

"Unlike Ken Fairchild?"

"Ken could sell the proverbial fridge to the proverbial Eskimo, his grasp of manufacturing is better than mine, and he's a natural at sales-promotion and advertising. The trouble is he doesn't understand the first thing about finance, and today that's essential."

"Which brings us to Walsh, who is older, as brilliant as Brian and as talented a salesman as your son-in-law. Right?"

"He's also clever with numbers, a genius at promotion and not identified with any faction in the company except me."

"As well as being a scratch golfer."

Avery smiled. "Will the board accept my choice?"

"You know they will, Avery."

"If I name Redfern, I'll have a family crisis on my hands because Barbara naturally expects her husband to take over. Yet if I recommend my son-in-law, apart from the obvious nepotism, Brian will probably feel obliged to quit, and he's one of the brightest and most valuable men on the whole management team."

"I understand."

"If I choose Walsh, members of the board might question his short time with the company, but they'll go along. Redfern will be disappointed but I don't think he'd actually leave. My son-in-law also, but as long as he isn't losing out to Brian, they should be able to get behind Adam and work together."

"What can I do to help?"

"You know I trust your judgment even more than my own."

"That's crap. You just want me to approve whatever it is you already made up your mind to do."

He laughed and for a moment Colin thought it was like years ago on the squash court at the Harvard Club. Stanton must have been thinking something similar because he said, "Remember when you first suggested I quit teaching and form my own company?"

"In the lockerroom, as I recall."

"And I thought, this kid is crazy. I'm a tenured professor, over forty, and I have no capital to start a business."

"Your brain was your capital," Colin told him.

"You convinced me of that, all right. My wife thought I'd lost my mind. Without you, I wouldn't have done it." Stanton became pensive. "My other alternative," he said finally, thinking out loud, "is to bring in some star-turn from outside, but that's always risky."

"It might just annoy everyone and satisfy no one."

"Right. I like to promote from within when I can."

"Ave, why not think of company interest alone?"

"You're reading my mind."

"It was a question."

"Not an easy one to answer," Avery Stanton said. "Each man in his fashion is eminently qualified, but I would have to go with Walsh."

"He's more experienced, certainly," Colin agreed.

"And he has the financial smarts. He's an economist, knows production and understands our labor union situation."

"Then he's your man," Colin told him. "Put the company first and let the chips fall where they fall."

"You agree?"

"Walsh is good."

"Oh, he'll do a hell of a job, I have no doubt."

"If I can soften the blow for Ken and Brian by having a talk with each of them, and even Barbara, you know I will."

"If they think about it," Stanton said, "they'll realize they're still young enough and their time will come."

"I'm sure they'll give Walsh their full support," Colin said, as wrong as he had ever been about anything in his life.

_____ CHAPTER TWO _____

SOME PEOPLE believe in the good times and the bad times, when things go right or everything goes wrong. Colin had never thought much about it until recent years, but he counted himself among the believers by the time of the *Redfern* case. At least he believed in the bad times.

Three years earlier, while he and his wife Joyce were sailing off the Cape, she complained of feeling unusually listless and tired, and Colin suggested she go for a checkup. The initial diagnosis shocked and confused them so much that he rushed her back to New York. But after a little more confusion, specialists in the city only confirmed the worst.

She was suffering from myasthenia gravis, cause and cure unknown, a deceptive yet debilitating disease that could kill slowly by undermining essential parts of the nervous system.

Over the years Colin had made money, but the more he made, the more it seemed he needed. About the time Joyce's illness took hold he had been investing heavily in the market for the first time in his life, subject to the opportunities that sprang up all around him in the mid-eighties.

Cranmer, Fisher & Cleves had been among the first legal specialists in leveraged buyouts, thanks especially to Colin Draggett, and they had helped negotiate several profitable deals for clients at both ends of the business spectrum. Privy to vital market information, Colin was also able to invest minimally and profit quite handsomely.

For the first time since he had gambled on Avery Stanton, Colin once again bet heavily on what he believed to be a sure thing. What went wrong? One could say the system was faulty. Only balloon manufacturers made money from air, a lesson every serious Wall Street punter learned early. Colin was seduced into ignoring this, and when the bottom fell out of the junk bond market, he nearly went with it.

Then Joyce took a turn for the worse and further tests revealed an inoperable, malignant thyroid tumor as well. Joyce had always been pretty, and traces of her beauty were still there in her pale, wasted body. Once an energetic woman who sailed with him in ocean races and played a strong game of tennis, now she could drink only when the nurse held her glass.

She had been unable to have children and therefore lavished most of her affection on Colin. He missed that, and he missed her company socially. Although she remained at home with round-the-clock nurses, and he visited with her every day when he was not out of town, by now even short conversations exhausted her.

In September the doctors said Joyce would be lucky to see Christmas. Lucky? he thought. But was this life, this long, long dying?

After things first started going wrong with Joyce and then with his friend Avery Stanton, it began to seem to Colin as if the whole damned convoluted world around him was coming unstuck. He had already pledged most of what he owned for cash to back his margin calls on the market, and his brokers were asking for more.

Ave Stanton chaired the October board meeting and looked terrible, but Colin was reluctant to ask about his health. Stanton must have realized it himself, however, because he took Colin aside after their customary lunch at the golf club and said, "It's all arranged. They're going to do the surgery a week before Thanksgiving. The annual stockholders meeting isn't until the first week in January, so I should be back on my feet in time to get everything in order, announce my retirement and give Walsh my blessing."

"Have you told anyone yet?" Colin asked him.

"I've been putting it off and putting it off. No matter how convinced I am that it's the right thing to do, I hate like the dickens to hurt people's feelings. Brian Redfern's a big boy. He'll take it all in stride. But my daughter and her husband are a different story."

"You want me to tell them?"

"Not yet. Let me worry about it awhile."

"Have you told Barbara you need coronary surgery?"

"I want to tell her everything at once."

"When? The day before you enter the hospital?"

He smiled. "You know how I am, Colin. I'm the first one to do anything I like, but I put off disagreeable tasks."

"Well, I can't tell you how to run your life."

"That's a laugh coming from you. You've been telling me how to run it since we met."

"Your business, not your life, Avery."

"For me they're the same. I can't imagine one without the other, Colin, but I'll have to get used to the idea, won't I?"

The November board meeting was chaired by Hunt Benson, the company executive vice-president. Avery was down in Houston submitting to some tests the cardiologists had ordered. When Colin called to see how he was feeling after he returned to New London, he said he was tired and fed up and wanted to get the thing over with.

"Have you told Barbara yet?"

"I'm having dinner with her and Ken and the kids this Sunday at her house. I figure that's the time to bring it up. Colin, I want to see you about some personal stuff, too. Before the operation. When can we get together?"

"You tell me."

"I want to update my will and talk a little before they cut, just in case. Can you come up on Saturday?"

"Sure. See you then."

Except Colin did not see him on Saturday. The very next morning Stanton called to ask if he could spring loose immediately.

"What happened?"

"I'll tell you when you get here. I'll send the helicopter to pick you up?"

"I'll be ready. Anything special you want me to bring?"

"Just yourself."

"You okay?"

"I'm all right." His voice was weak. "Just get here."

The Stanton Technologies helicopter landed on the roof of the building housing Colin's Wall Street offices an hour later, and he boarded it while the rotors were still turning, blowing everything around. Then up into the morning haze of Manhattan, skirting office towers like mountain peaks until they passed over the Brooklyn Bridge and the sprawling cemeteries of Queens.

Colin hated flying in the best of times but like most busy men he seemed to do a lot of it. Once his initial panic subsided he found himself gazing down on the slate-hued surface of Long Island Sound, white-flecked and wintery a thousand feet below. The co-pilot of this flying spin-dryer served him coffee, only half-filling the cup so it wouldn't go in his lap.

When they landed on Stanton's New London helipad forty minutes later, the sky above was a darkening overcast and a bitter cold wind bounced and jolted the machine. The pilot said snow flurries were forecast.

Colin went directly to the executive offices, where Stanton's middle-aged male secretary received him with a grave shrug and a shake of the head. "I don't know, Mr. Draggett," he replied to Colin's questioning look, "but something bad hit him this morning. I haven't seen him like this in years."

He touched a button unlocking the door to Stanton's inner office and passed Colin Draggett in. The room itself was cheerful, panelled and cozy, like the library in an eighteenth-century English country house. Old seascapes hung in gilt frames between the bookshelves, and a log fire burned in the fluted marble fireplace.

But none of this had any effect on Avery Stanton. When Colin saw him slumped behind his desk, staring out at the bleak industrial landscape, he was truly alarmed. Avery looked like he needed a doctor more than he needed legal help. His eyes were sunken and his skin matched the gray sky beyond the window.

He didn't even try to fake a smile when he saw his friend, and Colin knew that whatever had happened came under the heading of Major Catastrophe. All sorts of nightmare scenarios flashed through his mind. A takeover bid? A tax audit? Merger pressure? A death in the family? But Avery had survived all these things in recent years and never looked as shocked and drawn as he did this morning.

"Are you all right?" Colin asked.

"Of course not."

"Want me to call a doctor?"

"My immediate problem's not medical, Colin."

"Still . . ."

"I just took my digitalis and a Valium."

"Okay, where do we start?"

He swung around in his big leather chair, turned on an antique brass reading lamp and handed Colin a manila folder.

"Read it and weep," he said.

Colin opened the cover and found several photocopied pages stamped with the seal of the State of Indiana Department of Corrections. On the first page were two color mugshots, front and side views of a convict with a numbered card on his chest. The card read SPF, Terre Haute, Indiana.

"SPF?" Colin questioned aloud.

"State Prison Farm," Avery explained.

The file contained the arrest record, charge sheet, sentencing recommendations, prison report and most recent parole disposition of a convicted felon named Adrian Wadjewska. Colin held it up and said, "Is this a joke?"

Stanton shook his head.

Parts of the record went back more than twenty years. The man had been arrested under various aliases by police in a number of states. Fraud, extortion and forgery were his specialties.

Colin asked, "Who else knows about this?"

"My son-in-law gave it to me early this morning."

"And where did he get it?"

"From the Indiana State Department of Corrections."

Colin started pacing the office, looking at the seascapes, at the sprawling factory outside the window, anywhere except at Stanton, trying to bring his best powers of analysis to bear on this bizarre turn of events. "How come you never suspected anything?"

"I don't know, but I didn't. He was so damn clever."

"Who checked him out? Somewhere something should have tipped you. Don't your personnel people require references?"

"I'm the one who hired him, Colin. The best reference he had was me! But the others were all impeccable as well. Who would question a man brought in by the head of the company? Jesus Christ, I met him playing golf!"

"Who was he working for then?"

"He said he was doing consulting work in Washington for the

Secretary of Commerce. The son of a bitch even has a commendation from the President framed on his office wall!"

"Forged."

"What else? He had to be in prison when he got it!"

"There's no possibility of a mistake?"

"I wish there were."

"Who put Ken onto him?"

"I don't know."

"Let's find out. If Ken has this, someone else might."

Stanton nodded, his breath coming faster with his anger. "How the hell did an ex-convict ever get into the Thames River Golf and Canoe Club, answer me that? He's a Phi Beta Kappa, for chrissake! I mean, he said he was and he even wears the key! My God, he really made a fool out of me."

"But nobody knows it," Colin said, trying to calm him.

"*I* know it! And what am I going to do about it?"

"Have you told him you know?"

"I wanted to talk to you first."

"Good. If Ken keeps quiet, I think it can be contained . . ."

"I want the bastard arrested—"

"No, you don't. I'll tell you what you want. You want him as far from Stanton Technologies as possible. Look at it this way, Avery. Better you found out today than a month from now after he took over your company with your blessing."

"I guess you're right, it's just that—"

"Nobody likes to be had," Colin assured him.

"Ken's in his office. Waiting to hear from me."

"Call him in. The sooner we start, the better the chances of keeping a lid on the whole unfortunate chapter."

While Avery Stanton's secretary called Ken Fairchild's office Colin stared down at the malignant photographs on the desk and thought he detected the trace of an enigmatic smile or triumphant sneer on the face of the one-time prisoner. Adrian Wadjewska, aka Abe Waters, Arthur Whitaker and Archie Wharton, meant nothing to Colin Draggett. Short cropped hair, handsome features and an orange, open collar prison shirt. But the face that mocked them all did not belong to some stranger. It was the familiar countenance of their own Adam Walsh, soon to be named president of Stanton Technologies.

Stanton sighed. "Notice how the son of a bitch always sticks to the same initials? You think it's to avoid changing the monograms on all his shirts and handkerchiefs?"

——————— CHAPTER THREE ———————

THERE WAS always a gleaming, neatly pressed look about Ken Fairchild, vestigial signs of the former professional military officer, perhaps, with everything in place on his rugged frame. Cheerful and accommodating, the handsome, sandy-haired executive moved with the easy grace of the All-American athlete he once had been, a man in full control of himself who flashed a warm smile at Colin in spite of the gravity of the business at hand.

"Good to see you, Colin." Fairchild shook hands and took in the situation at a glance before pulling up a chair. The tension could not have been more palpable if a bomb with a sputtering fuse had been left on the floor in front of them. Stanton pale and drawn, Colin solemn as a hanging judge, and the file open on the desk.

Colin knew Ken Fairchild well enough to recognize that he was a fairly shrewd judge of people and an ambitious player in the career game. If he hadn't married the boss's daughter, it might have taken him a little longer to get where he was, but he would have got there eventually on his own merit.

He understood how devastating the Walsh revelations were, but he was obviously not aware of Avery Stanton's delicate health. Colin felt, though, that he had done the right thing in bringing the whole improbable business to Stanton's attention as soon as he was sure the information was reliable.

If they were to limit the damage the scandal could cause, Colin had to know as much as possible. He started cross-examining Fairchild immediately to find out what made him suspect Walsh. Ken was eager to talk about it. "When Walsh joined the company, Brian Redfern said to me, 'This guy is too good to be true. Phi Beta Kappa, economic advisor to the President, scratch golfer.' And I said, 'He's probably an industrial spy,' and we both laughed. No-body suspected anything, least of all me."

"When did you think he wasn't what he said he was?"

"About six months ago. I was keeping close tabs on a continuing market study we'd asked him for. In order to target my own adver-tising I had to stay in touch with Walsh."

"Or whatever his name is," Ave Stanton added bitterly.

"Anyway, he was out of town a lot. One day I had to reach him about something. His secretary said he was in Washington, but she had no number for him. I called his wife and she confirmed what the secretary said. She also told me her husband had left specific orders that under no circumstances was she to contact him."

"Did she give a reason?"

"She understood his Washington assignment was top secret so she followed his wishes and never tried to call him there."

Stanton interrupted: "When Walsh joined the company he made it a condition that his consulting work with the government con-tinue. I agreed because he assured me it was in the national inter-est and wouldn't conflict with anything here. He also had me be-lieving it would be a valuable contact at the highest level." He shook his head as if trying to get rid of the memory.

After a moment Fairchild continued: "When I tried to reach him at the White House they said the panel he supposedly headed did not exist. The Secretary of Commerce's office had never heard of him. I still wasn't suspicious because I know Washington. So I called an army friend in the chief of staff's office and told him my problem. He promised to use his sources to track Adam down and get back to me. But he drew a blank too."

"Is that when you thought things were fishy?" Colin asked.

"I wish I could say yes," Ken replied, "but I still kept blaming it on the Washington bureaucracy. I mean, Christ, the White House alone has more than three thousand people on its staff, plus God knows how many consultants trooping in and out every day. One economic advisor more or less could easily get lost in the shuffle."

"Did you tell Walsh when he came back?"

"I told him and he laughed. He also gave me a number and an extension in case I needed him again when he was there."

"Some number," Avery Stanton said.

"Fake?" Colin said.

"The number was real enough," Fairchild said, "but it wasn't the

White House or the Department of Commerce. It was an answering service."

"What did you do then?" Colin asked him.

"I'm sorry to say I still didn't suspect anything serious, or at least admit to myself that I did."

"Who else knew at this point?"

"Brian Redfern was in my office when I couldn't reach Walsh in Washington. Brian laughed because he was convinced Walsh had a girlfriend stashed away. That made sense. It didn't occur to either of us that he wasn't anywhere near Washington."

"How did you find that out?"

"By accident," Fairchild said. "I told Walsh that Ave was annoyed because I couldn't reach him, that the answering service wasn't good enough if something came up. We had to know where we could talk directly."

"What did he say to that?"

"He gave me another number but said not to call him there unless it was an absolute emergency. He said it was his private line in the Executive Office Building. Brian had an investigator check it out. It was an apartment in the Watergate."

"And that's when you got suspicious?"

"We still thought he had a woman . . ."

Colin suggested it was time Brian Redfern joined them, and Stanton told his secretary to send for him. Redfern arrived within a few minutes carrying a bulky file. "I thought Colin might want to look at this. These are some of the credit reports and bank records we were able to get our hands on." Colin glanced over the photocopied pages as Stanton got up and paced the room. Redfern's eyes went from Colin to Stanton and back again, then he crossed his legs and leaned his chin on both hands, waiting for the lawyer's reaction.

Brian Redfern was sleek. Thin, almost gaunt, with salt-and-pepper hair and dark Celtic good-looks, he was not quite thirty-six years old. Gray worsted English banker's suit, blue tie and just the right amount of white cuff showing.

Confident to a point just short of arrogance, and spurred on by a relentless ambition, he had an air of nervous impatience that annoyed some people and unsettled others. He seemed to know exactly what he wanted and could scarcely conceal his contempt for those who didn't. He was usually diffident around Avery Stanton, and he could be charming when he wished, but it cost him some effort.

A product of M.I.T. and the Harvard Business School, he had spent his entire career with Stanton Technologies acquiring few friends but a number of admirers, including Avery Stanton and Ken Fairchild. A hard worker and innovative manager, he was the perfect choice to lead Stanton International as it expanded around the globe. He had launched the company's manufacturing operations in Europe, quadrupled Stanton's exports to Africa and the Middle East, and beaten the Japanese at their own game by refusing to license certain Stanton processes to them, requiring instead that they import the genuine article made in the U.S.A. by Stanton.

Redfern did not go out of his way to ingratiate himself with anyone, but because he recognized Colin Draggett's influence on Stanton he was careful to treat him with respect.

"Did either of you say anything to Walsh?" Colin asked.

"No, but we hired the private detective," Ken said, "and that's when we discovered Walsh never went near Washington."

"Why didn't you tell me then?" Stanton wanted to know.

"We still believed it was a love nest—"

"Then where *did* he go?"

"That's what didn't make sense at first. He went all over the map. Seattle. San Francisco. Miami. Phoenix. But on his way back to Connecticut he always stopped off in Indiana."

"Is that why?" Colin pointed to the file.

Fairchild nodded. "In all those different cities, he went to banks. In Indiana he reported to his parole officer."

Stanton sighed, popped a tiny pill and drank some water. "I still can't believe it! Adam Walsh a paroled convict!"

"What was he doing at the banks?" Colin asked Fairchild.

"Making deposits under different names."

"Who gave you those names?"

"Various bank employees provided them when the private investigator showed them Walsh's picture," Fairchild said. "Then I had our regional sales staffs check the bank balances through credit firms."

"Jesus, Ken," Stanton groaned. "You mean our whole goddamn sales force is aware of this?"

"Only Brian, myself and the detective know the details."

"How much money did Walsh take? Can you give Colin a figure?" Stanton's voice was barely a whisper.

"Understand that this may be only the tip of the iceberg," Redfern said, "but so far we've turned up deposits of more than two million over the last year and a half."

"My God! How did he do it?"

"Market research," Colin said, having just learned the answer from his perusal of Walsh's bank records. "According to these, he set up fictitious consulting companies all over hell and gone and then committed Stanton Technologies to contracts for in-depth studies at fees running in the high six-figures."

"Fake market research?" Stanton said. "My God!"

"That's just it," Brian Redfern said. "It wasn't fake. The reports were valid. His information was always top quality."

"Only his companies were fictitious," Fairchild added.

"Where did he get the studies?" Colin asked.

"This may sound unbelievable," Redfern said, "but we're convinced he wrote the reports himself."

"One man couldn't do it all," Stanton said. "Impossible!"

"Incredible, maybe," Fairchild replied, "but not impossible. He works like hell and he's very damned bright. The folks at the Indiana State Penitentiary rated his I.Q. at 175."

Colin addressed himself directly to Stanton. "I can guess how you feel, Ave. You picked him and you feel responsible. But your instincts were right. Whatever else the man is, Walsh is a brilliant economist."

"He never even finished high school!" Stanton protested, slapping the hateful file on his desk.

"Walsh's forecasts and analyses have guided this company for the past three years," Colin reminded them.

Fairchild had to agree. "When he came aboard, Stanton stock sold at seventeen-seventy a share."

"Since then it's been among the star performers on the Street," Colin added. "In itself a serious problem."

"You mean the share price?" Stanton asked him.

"Of course. If the Street gets wind of this man's background everyone will take a bath."

Ken Fairchild nodded vigorous agreement.

"Not to mention what the Securities and Exchange Commission

could do," Colin reminded them. "A full-scale investigation to see how much we've all made from misleading information."

"But it wasn't misleading!" Stanton protested.

"The effect would still be the same," Colin said. "No one would trust anyone in Stanton management after that."

"So what do we do?" Stanton said, and all three men looked at Colin Draggett. For twenty years he had tried to give Avery Stanton sound advice, putting company interest ahead of everything. Now all he could tell him was the obvious. "Knowledge of this mess must be limited to those of us in this room, and Walsh must be got rid of as quickly and quietly as possible."

"What about all the money he's taken?" Stanton said.

"We try to recover it," Colin answered, "but if we can't, the important thing is to separate Walsh from the company."

"You mean let him off the hook?" Stanton said.

"That may not be so easy," Fairchild put in.

"I doubt he'd refuse a decent offer," Colin told them, sounding more confident than he actually was, "if we make it clear that the alternative is a return to prison and prosecution for fraud and embezzlement."

"What do you mean 'decent offer'? I'll be goddamned if I'll offer him anything!"

"Ave, we want him to go quietly."

"What do you suggest?" Fairchild said.

"Confront him and try to make him return what he took."

"Suppose he won't quit?" Redfern said.

"I think he will, but if not, we sweeten the pot."

"You mean give him *more* money?" Stanton sputtered.

"If it comes to that, yes. Consider what's at stake—"

"Over my dead body!" Stanton exploded.

"Calm down," Colin said. "I'm no more anxious to buy Walsh off than you are. I'm only suggesting it may be the best way out of a bad situation. But first we have to talk to him. No use speculating until we know where he stands. Whatever else, the company comes first. We call him in, lay it out and hope he sees the light."

"Colin is right," Ken Fairchild said.

"All right, goddamn it." Avery Stanton buzzed for his secretary. When the man appeared, Stanton said, "Tell Mr. Walsh I require his presence here immediately."

CHAPTER FOUR

WHEN ADAM Walsh entered the president's office, the only one who greeted him was Stanton. "Hello, Adrian," he said.

Walsh looked at Avery Stanton with a quizzical expression, then more thoughtfully at Fairchild, Redfern and Colin Draggett. He gave them the benefit of the same half-smile from the prison photograph, as if they shared a secret. He seemed not the least bit embarrassed or afraid, just vaguely amused.

"It is Adrian, isn't it?" Stanton said, pushing the open file across the desktop to where Walsh could see the photographs. "Adrian Wadjewska?"

Walsh was a distinguished-looking man with graying hair, eyes the color of gunmetal and a ruggedly handsome face. He was very fit, a serious jogger, swimmer and a top amateur golfer. He looked the very model of the modern corporate chief, with an agreeable manner and an air of authority whether in the boardroom or on the golf course. Meeting him for the first time, people were invariably impressed. Accustomed to wielding power and being obeyed, he was relaxed and confident, poised and well-spoken. Neither shy nor overbearing, he was also generous in his praise of others, especially subordinates.

He was expensively tailored this day in gray flannel, and immaculately groomed, with only one concession to personal vanity: in the pocket of his vest he carried an antique gold watch the size of a sand dollar and worth as much as a Mercedes. Attached to it by a gold chain was his tiny but conspicuously visible Phi Beta Kappa key.

Stanton watched him, his barely suppressed rage etching his features more deeply in the yellow light of the desk lamp. He gave the file another push in Walsh's direction. "Read it."

"I doubt that's necessary," Walsh said.

Colin said, "Then you know why we're gathered here."

"No, I don't believe I do."

"You're through," Stanton said. "Tell him, Colin."

"Since you concealed your criminal past when you came here, and since we now know who you are, Mr. Walsh—"

"Or whatever you call yourself," Stanton interrupted.

"Walsh will do," he said calmly.

". . . we don't want you around any longer."

"You're going to fire me?"

"You're already fired," Stanton roared, "and goddamn lucky we don't have you arrested!"

Walsh's smile broadened. It was as if he honestly found the whole scene terribly funny.

The smile only infuriated Avery Stanton more, and Colin raised one hand to placate him while he told Walsh, "No one's thinking of arresting anyone as long as you put back the money."

"I beg your pardon?" Walsh said.

"The money you stole from Stanton Technologies," Brian Redfern said. He held up the bank file but Walsh ignored it.

"We want it all back," Stanton said.

By this time Walsh seemed barely able to conceal his mirth, which sent Avery Stanton into a choking fit. When the seizure passed, he gasped, "Return every penny or we prosecute!"

"I don't know what you're talking about."

"We're *talking* about two million dollars for a start," Ken Fairchild said firmly. "How much more we'll soon find out."

"You can bet we'll run an audit," Redfern assured him.

"You can run as many audits as you please," Walsh said agreeably. "I fail to see what this has to do with me."

"You're a thief!"—Stanton was rising from his chair—"A common goddamn thief! You cheated me and stole from my company!"

"I never received a cent from this firm that I didn't earn."

"Look, Adam," Colin said, "this is painful for everybody and has to be humiliating for you. Return the money and there's no notification to your parole board, no prosecution, nothing."

Adam Walsh not only refused his offer, he greeted it with a short burst of impolite laughter. No one was prepared for his reaction, least of all Colin Draggett, who cursed himself for not having managed the situation differently, except exactly how else he could have handled it he didn't know. The bottom line was that they had no hope of making a deal with Walsh unless they could threaten him with something infinitely worse than the catastrophe they assumed he could bring down on their heads.

"Excuse me," Walsh said, "but prosecution for what?"

"Robbery!" Avery Stanton shouted. "Stealing! Fraud! Forgery! Misappropriation of funds!"

"Calm down, Ave, please." Colin worried about his friend. "You asked me here to handle this and I will." Stanton's color had gone from dull gray to ashen, and he was panting like a pufferfish. "Adam, I suggest you and I adjourn to the boardroom where we can discuss this calmly and arrive at some practical solution."

"Anything to oblige, Colin," Walsh said graciously, "but my time is tight today and I really don't see what there is to discuss anyway. But we could have lunch one of these days, if you like, at the golf club."

These words and Walsh's cavalier attitude literally put Ave Stanton beyond speech. He could only sit there sputtering. Fairchild, Redfern and Draggett saw Walsh's crimes for what they were. Cleverly conceived and imaginatively carried out. His theft was a predictable extension of the man's long criminal career, the latest link in a chain of misprisions, misrepresentations and trespasses that stretched back years. Stanton viewed things in a harsher light. Walsh had personally conned him, tricked his way into his confidence with lies, a thing Stanton could never forgive. And if that were not enough, Walsh had used the privileged status conferred on him inside the company to rob his benefactor and thereby make a fool of him.

Avery Stanton's outrage could not have been greater if Adam Walsh had violated his daughter.

Walsh looked around him, letting his eyes rest on each of their faces individually as if adding up a score. Then he astounded them all by saying, "If that's it, gentlemen, I'll leave you now. I've got a lot on my plate today and a heavy week ahead. Colin, whenever you want to talk, give me a call." And with that he stepped out of the office, closing the door quietly behind him.

Stanton gasped, "I'll be goddamned!"

"We sure as hell called that one wrong," Redfern said. "Instead of caving in, he tells us to shove it."

"And you'll note," Colin said, "he admitted nothing that might incriminate him in case we were recording this little session."

Stanton attempted to speak but began to choke again, and brought on a coughing seizure more violent than the earlier one.

While Draggett loosened his tie and collar and groped in his desk for his pills, Fairchild filled a cup with water.

But this time nothing helped. "Get a doctor," Colin ordered, and Redfern was out the door. The coughing did not subside as Stanton fought for breath and clutched his chest in pain.

The company physician reached the office five minutes later, but by then Avery Stanton was cyanotic. In spite of all the doctor's efforts in the ambulance, Colin's old friend died of a massive coronary occlusion on the way to the hospital.

───────CHAPTER FIVE───────

IT SNOWED the day of Avery Stanton's funeral, a record blizzard that whipped in off Long Island Sound and virtually paralyzed towns along the Connecticut coast. In spite of the weather the overheated church was full and the flowers were heaped higher than the drifts outside. The sickening sweet smell of them nearly overpowered Colin as he delivered the eulogy.

That was Barbara Stanton's wish because Colin was one of her father's oldest and closest friends. She sat veiled in the front pew with her husband Ken Fairchild and their two boys. Hunt Benson, who would be taking over the reins of the company until a new president was elected, sat beside them with his wife. Further down the row were Brian and Fionna Redfern, Avery Stanton's sister with her family, most of the board members, and Adam and Celia Walsh.

His presence was offensive to Colin—he felt Ave Stanton would be alive if it hadn't been for Walsh. On the other hand, the entire hierarchy of Stanton Technologies was present, and if Walsh had not attended the funeral his absence would have been noted. He was one of the company stars, after all, known to have worked closely with Stanton and been his regular golf partner.

Colin's remarks were aimed mainly at Barbara Fairchild and Stanton's two grandsons who were fourteen and fifteen and had enjoyed a close relationship with the old man. He knew that the boys would remember this day as long as they lived, and he wanted to give them some idea of just how important their grandfather was.

Although he spoke of his long friendship with Avery Stanton and what a warm, decent man he was and how they would all miss him, he pointed out that Stanton had been a giant in his field, a pioneer. In a life studded with achievements, he had earned his place in the ranks of the great innovative geniuses whose inventions would benefit the world for generations to come. Colin talked about his contributions to the space program, to national security and to the American lifestyle. Stanton's curiosity was undiminished with the years, Colin said, and his favorite place at work was always the research laboratory.

Colin also referred to his many philanthropies, his scholarships and his generous contributions to charity. "He was the best kind of inventor," he said, "who considered social responsibility a personal obligation, a duty that went hand-in-hand with success."

Fionna Redfern had prepared a buffet lunch at her home, and because of the continuing blizzard, the immediate family and most of the funeral guests went directly there from the church service. Only a handful accompanied the coffin to the snow-swept cemetery.

A canopy had been placed over the grave site and two red-knuckled gravediggers shivered under a nearby oak tree waiting for the minister to finish. They had to use pneumatic drills to break the frozen earth, and great brown chunks of it lay lightly covered by snow beside the grave.

Colin hadn't worn a hat and was hunched like a turtle in his old Chesterfield as the wind drove snow needles against his face. Ken Fairchild and Brian Redfern joined him as the minister reached the end of the interment service and gave the signal for the coffin to be lowered into the ground.

From the other side of the grave Avery Stanton's daughter Barbara tossed a single rose on his coffin and cried, the only woman to brave the weather. Hunt Benson stood on one side of Barbara, but it was Adam Walsh's arm she clung to.

"That bastard has some nerve," Fairchild muttered.

"Better he showed up," Colin said. "If he'd stayed away people would have wondered why."

"Avery wouldn't be in that coffin if it weren't for him," Redfern whispered. "The hypocritical son of a bitch!"

Although it was doubtful anyone could hear them over the keening wind, Colin nudged him into silence anyway.

When the service ended Walsh accompanied Barbara and her boys to their limousine before joining Colin as he was getting into his car. The icy wind still cut at their faces although the snow had finally stopped. Walsh placed one gloved hand on Colin's arm.

"Ave was my friend too, Colin, in spite of what you think," he said. "I was really very fond of him, you know."

"He'd still be alive," Colin said, "if it hadn't been for the shock of finding out about you."

"We both knew he was seriously ill; you should have thought of that before you dropped that file on him."

"He didn't drop it on him," Brian Redfern said, coming up behind them with Ken Fairchild. "We did."

"That explains it then," Walsh said.

"Explains what?" Fairchild said.

"I found it hard to believe Colin would have gone to Avery with that trash about me, knowing the man's condition."

"Are you accusing *us* of causing his heart attack?" Redfern said, his voice menacing as he took a step toward Walsh.

"Back off," Walsh said. "You're the accuser, not me."

"Please," Colin told them, "cool it, both of you."

"It's this son of a bitch I'd like to cool!" Redfern said angrily. The funeral cortege had moved off, but Hunt Benson waited impatiently, stamping his feet and swinging his arms to keep warm. When Hunt saw the others still lingering, he came trudging over just as Walsh turned his back, which was all the fuse Redfern needed to set him off. He reached out and caught Walsh by the shoulder. Fairchild saw it almost before Colin did and reacted instinctively, putting himself between the two of them, facing Redfern.

When Brian tried to push Ken aside to get at Walsh, Fairchild pinned his arms. Brian, smaller and lighter, quickly disengaged himself. When the powerful Fairchild tried again, he slipped and went sprawling in the snow.

What Hunt Benson saw as he reached them looked like Brian Redfern assaulting Ken Fairchild. Benson stepped between them.

"Gentlemen, for heaven's sake! We've just buried a dear friend! What in God's name are you doing!"

Ken apologized as he brushed himself off, but Redfern's attention was still on the retreating Walsh. Hunt Benson would later claim that the bad blood between Brian Redfern and Ken Fairchild went back at least to the day of Avery Stanton's funeral.

Colin was parked near Adam Walsh's company Lincoln, and the two men reached their cars at the same time. In the background, silhouetted against the cold winter sky, the gravediggers worked with a tractor, pushing the chunks of frozen brown earth into the grave.

Colin had the car door open when Walsh came around to where he was standing, about to slide in.

Walsh was smiling, that wry, bemused expression Colin had first noticed in the prison photographs. "Colin, unless you want this whole thing to come down around your ears you better talk some sense to those two. We all have Stanton Technologies' best interest at heart—"

"Do we?"

"I believe so. I don't have to tell you how much money is involved. Stanton is a company with a very bright future. Reason with them. Calm them down. Then we'll talk about what's going to happen in that future."

"One thing I'm sure of is that you're not a part of it."

"Colin, you know as well as I that the only thing you can be sure of"—he raised his gaze toward the brow of the hill where the gravediggers were finishing their work—"is death and taxes."

——————CHAPTER SIX——————

TWO DAYS after the funeral, Brian Redfern, Ken Fairchild and Colin Draggett met at the New York law offices of Cranmer, Fisher & Cleves. It was a bleak November morning, blustery and cold, with a week to go before Thanksgiving. Normally Colin appreciated the view overlooking Battery Park and New York Harbor. He found the orderly world of ships, seabirds and the sea reassuring in any season. When struggling with some tangled legal problem he would often spend an hour staring out at that harbor scene, letting his mind range around it until with sudden clarity some solution would begin to emerge. On other days just a glimpse of the busy tugboats and ferries scurrying about like toys on the bay was enough to lift his spirits. But today his mood was as gray as the sky he contemplated when he reviewed the upsetting business they were there to discuss.

After the amenities Ken Fairchild said, "Have you talked to him, Colin? What's it going to cost?"

"It's going to be expensive," Brian Redfern said.

"How expensive?" Fairchild asked Colin.

Colin was silent, hands in his pockets, thinking.

"A man who's already taken us for two million dollars is not going to leave cheap," Redfern said.

"Colin, what did you tell him?"

"I repeated exactly what Avery said the day he died. I told Walsh he was out, one way or the other."

"And what did he say?"

"It was like the first time. He laughed."

"I could kill that bastard," Redfern said.

"Did he name a figure?" Fairchild asked.

"No. He didn't even say he'd quit. But I get the feeling he could be waiting for us to make him an offer."

"Do it," Fairchild said.

"First, I want to be sure it's in Stanton's best interest. Ave devoted his life to building this company's reputation and we're not going to be the ones who tarnish it."

Colin hated the idea of buying someone off and searched for another way out. But he was equally determined to avoid any mistake that would cause precisely what they were trying to avoid.

"Maybe it would be better to leave him alone," he said. "Clip his wings so he can't embezzle any more funds from the company but not do anything about what's already happened."

"Why in hell would we do that?" Brian demanded to know.

"It's an option," Colin said. "Maybe the quietest."

"Not in my book," Fairchild said. "He can't stay on."

"I'm assuming we share one guiding principle," Colin told them. "That whatever we do about Walsh is best for the company."

"That's the whole point, isn't it?" Redfern answered.

"Do we do this on our own or take it to the full board for a decision?"

"That's the same as publishing it," Fairchild said.

"We don't have a problem here, Colin," Redfern said. "After all, what's best for us has to be good for Stanton."

"We like to assume that because it's convenient," Colin replied, "but that doesn't make it necessarily true."

"What do you suggest? That we all take a loyalty test?"

"All I'm saying," Colin advised them, "is that I feel a deep obligation to this company. I was present at its birth. I've watched it grow and flourish, and it's made me a lot of money. I *owe* a lot to it and to the memory of the man who made it possible."

"But what we're talking about here doesn't go against that," Redfern said. "Whatever we do will be to protect the company."

"And ourselves," Colin repeated. "Don't mix the two."

"Like I said—"

"Colin, I concur with the need to keep this as quiet as the tomb," Fairchild said, "and I'll back whatever it is you want to do because I know how strongly you feel about the company."

"That's part of the trouble," Colin said.

"What are you talking about?" Redfern asked.

"I really don't know yet what we should do."

"Force him out," Redfern said.

"Buy him off," Fairchild said.

"Who can authorize major funds now that Avery is dead?" Colin asked them. "I can't very well go to Hunt Benson. But if I promise Walsh something I'll have to deliver."

"I could probably manage a few hundred thousand out of my budget," Fairchild said.

"What about you?" Colin asked Redfern.

"It turns my guts to give that bastard one more penny."

"That's not what I asked you."

"I've got an advertising budget with some flexibility," he said, "and another for construction of new overseas offices."

"Let's say a million in all?" Colin queried.

"Jesus!" Ken Fairchild said.

"He may settle for less but he may want more."

"No way," Redfern said. "Can't be done. Where the hell would we get that kind of money?"

"Let Walsh himself authorize it," Fairchild said. "He's already paid himself a fortune, so who would know?"

"We would," Brian responded. ". . . I think I'd kill him first."

"Let's hope it doesn't come to that," Colin said lightly. "I'll see what he'll settle for."

"When?" Redfern asked.

"We'd all feel more secure if this thing could be disposed of before the board meets," Fairchild said.

"Speaking of the board," Brian said, looking from one to the other of them, "can you enlighten me about their intentions?"

Ken Fairchild waited for Colin to answer.

"Did you know Avery was planning to retire before this tragedy happened?" the lawyer asked them.

"He never mentioned it to me," Fairchild said.

"We talked about who he wanted to replace him."

"Ken," Redfern said.

"Avery considered you both," Colin said, "then decided that neither was first in line for the throne. He chose a third man. After a great deal of soul-searching."

Both men watched Colin expectantly. Whether they suspected the truth or not he didn't know, but the fact that neither of them had been Avery Stanton's candidate of choice obviously came as a surprise.

"He asked for my advice some weeks ago," Colin said. "Before your little bombshell fell on him, he was planning to name Adam Walsh."

"You *can't* be serious!" Redfern said.

"My God!" Fairchild gasped.

Redfern began to laugh, throwing back his handsome head as he said, "Oh, that's rich! That's too goddamn much, I swear!"

"Did he tell anyone else?" Ken asked anxiously.

"I doubt it, but I don't know. Needless to say, Walsh's candidacy is no longer even a remote possibility," said Colin.

"But suppose Avery did recommend him to other members of the board," Ken said. "How do we handle that?"

"I'll be perfectly frank," Colin said to them. "Even if your disclosure hadn't changed all our thinking in a flash, Avery's death rearranged the numbers. As far as I am concerned, and as far as Hunt Benson and the board are concerned, either of you would make an excellent CEO for Stanton Technologies. If all things were equal, the choice between you would not be easy."

A slow smile spread over Brian Redfern's dark features as he tilted his chair back from the table.

"You're saying all things are not equal?" Ken said.

Brian answered for Colin: "How could they be? At the moment your wife owns the controlling interest."

Colin asked Brian what he would do if the board named Ken Fairchild to replace Avery Stanton as president.

Redfern said, "Come on, Colin. We all know it's settled." His attention moved from Ken to Colin Draggett and back again. "Forgive me for being a little slow on the uptake."

"Nothing's been decided yet," Colin insisted lamely.

"Let me be the first to congratulate you," Brian said to Fairchild.

"Believe me," Fairchild replied, "it's premature."

"You haven't answered my question, Brian," Colin said.

Redfern looked at Fairchild for a long minute. "Before Avery's death I would have resigned. Ken and I have always been too competitive, and I couldn't lose the top job to him and hang around."

"Avery recognized that," Colin said, "which was one of the reasons he decided on Walsh. But since that's over, what will you do?"

"Ken and I worked like hell to ferret out that bastard," Redfern said, "and I'd like to see this thing through. But—"

Fairchild interrupted. "But nothing, Brian. Until this company is safe from predators like him we need each other."

"It's not an easy decision," Redfern said doubtfully.

Fairchild touched his arm lightly. "If the board picks me, you write your own ticket. Salary, title, everything."

Colin Draggett stood and went to look out at the gray scudding clouds and the harsh wintery surface of New York harbor, hoping these two men could put their competitive differences aside and work together. Each in his own way was the kind of dynamic executive a firm like Stanton needed. Colin thought of their Japanese competitors and how they would laugh at such a discussion. In Japan loyalty, continuity and cooperation were the rule. You might die or retire but you never quit. Only American executives thought otherwise.

Redfern was neither a greedy nor a sentimental man, but he

could be reached and Ken Fairchild had found the way. For a moment Brian said nothing, then he asked, "You mean it?"

"I mean it."

"Then you have yourself a deal, hotshot." He leaned across the table to shake Ken's hand.

"Did you hear that, Colin?" Ken Fairchild said.

"I heard it."

"Are you pleased?"

"Very."

"You don't sound like it," Redfern said.

Colin was watching a tug warp an immaculate Swedish freighter into a New Jersey pier on the North River. Little cotton balls of smoke appeared against the gunmetal sky as the tugboat churned and puffed. He turned back to his companions.

"What's the matter, Colin?" Ken Fairchild asked.

"I've got a bad feeling about this Adam Walsh business."

"Who doesn't?" Redfern said.

"One way or another, we'll take care of him," Fairchild said.

"That's part of what bothers me," Colin said.

Redfern looked up sharply. "What do you mean?"

"We agreed with Avery that we had to keep it quiet," he told them, "so getting all heated up about it helps no one."

"Nobody's going off half-cocked," Redfern said.

"No? What do you call that scene at the cemetery the other day? You behaved like an angry schoolboy. Besides alarming Hunt Benson, you must have made Adam Walsh's day!"

"I'm sorry about that," Brian said. "I lost my temper—"

"You'll lose a good deal more if you can't control it."

"The kicker is that Hunt Benson thought I was trying to beat up Ken," Brian said, laughing. "That should amuse everybody."

Colin said, "Gentlemen, we're agreed I'll negotiate an arrangement with Walsh. But I want your solemn word, both of you, to steer clear of him until I've worked something out."

"Just do it, Colin," Brian said, "and we'll behave."

CHAPTER SEVEN

THE FOLLOWING Friday Colin left the office early and drove two hours to Essex, a picturesque colonial village and yachting center on the Connecticut River. Maggie, his secretary, had called ahead to reserve a room at the romantic old Griswold Inn, remarking, "I won't ask who you're spending the weekend with." When he told her Fionna Redfern, she said, "Go for it, Mr. Draggett!"

"Except her husband will be with her, Maggie."

Unlike other recent encounters, the evening with Redfern was mellow and relaxing due to a lack of business talk and the presence of his beautiful wife. Fionna Redfern was lively and charming, the Niantic Bay scallops were delicious and Brian appeared to be less tense than usual, perhaps because he anticipated that Colin would wrap up the Adam Walsh affair the following day.

COLIN HAD never been to Walsh's home, but when he called Walsh to arrange a meeting, Walsh suggested he come on Saturday morning. Walsh lived in a sprawling Victorian farmhouse that overlooked the Oyster River and the broad tidal wetland that stretched between it and the Connecticut. According to the financial records assembled by Ken Fairchild, Walsh had paid two hundred thousand dollars cash, while the Old Lyme Savings & Loan held a five-hundred-thousand-dollar mortgage on the place. The house had been meticulously restored by a local architect while Walsh added a few touches of his own. Next to the small pond in front of the house he had laid out a putting green and built a greenhouse where, according to Fionna Redfern, his wife grew prize orchids.

Celia Walsh, a pleasant, rosy-cheeked woman in smock and gardening gloves, met Colin at the door. Her husband was in the barn, she said, and she would show him the way. Colin had a fleeting vision of Adam Walsh pitching hay and watering the stock.

The house itself was cozy and comfortable with hooked rugs on polished hardwood floors, bow windows, fireplaces and overstuffed chintz furniture. But the big red barn was the real surprise. From the outside it looked like the usual kind of conversion to guest house or a Sunday painter's studio. There were frame picture windows, a huge skylight, a wrenhouse and an antique weather-vane at the roof peak. But inside was a sauna, an enormous exercise bay with every kind of physical fitness toy and a sparkling heated swimming pool directly under the skylight that would be the envy of any luxurious midtown health club.

Although the day was as gray and bleak as any other in November, the clever indirect lighting, warm humid air and profusion of greenery inside the barn put Colin in mind of a Caribbean resort. Wonderful potted trees and exotic shrubs, trailing vines and lush, colorful flowers were everywhere. A macaw eyed him haughtily from a perch inside the door.

"Adam," Celia Walsh called out, "Mr. Draggett is here."

Walsh appeared from behind the scrim of greenery, tanned and fit looking, dressed in black bathing trunks and carrying a copy of Barron's he had been reading. "Nice to see you, Colin," he said. "Would you like something to drink while we talk?"

"No thanks, Adam. A bit early yet for me."

"We'll have lunch at one," his wife said. "You will stay, Mr. Draggett? It's low cholesterol, high fiber."

He thanked her but said he had to return to New York as soon as they finished their business.

"If you change your mind there's lots," she said. He was trying to remember what Redfern had said about her. Widowed or divorced before she married Adam Walsh two years before.

"Swim?" Walsh asked him. "There's a dressing room over there and a selection of swimming trunks."

"I'll stay as I am."

"Suit yourself, Colin, but if you want a serious talk the only way we're going to have it is stripped down at the poolside."

"You think I came wired?" Colin said.

"The idea did cross one's mind."

Walsh meant what he said, so Colin changed into an ill-fitting bathing suit and sat in a canvas chair by the poolside, feeling exposed and vulnerable, and sure that was exactly how Walsh wanted him to feel.

"If you'd like a drink the bar is behind you," Walsh told Colin.

"Just help yourself." He laid the copy of Barron's aside and sat on the edge of the pool, letting his feet dangle in the water.

"Nice place," Colin said.

"We like it."

"I'm sure you do."

"I presume you're here to make me an offer of some kind. The Bobbsey twins want to work out a settlement, right?"

"We want you out of the company. I daresay the board would want you jailed if they knew."

"Why?"

"Please, Adam, if that's your name, don't insult my intelligence. In view of what we know about you there's no possibility of your staying with Stanton Technologies one minute longer than necessary to wrap up this whole rotten business."

"Interesting. So what's your offer if I resign?"

"I'm authorized—"

"By Redfern and Fairchild?"

"I and they are the only ones who know about your background."

"And you will all keep quiet about it, I suppose?"

"We will do that if you cooperate."

"What kind of cooperation did you have in mind?"

"First, you return the money taken from the company and deposited in your various accounts around the country. I believe it's at least two million dollars."

"That might be awkward."

"We can devise a way."

"You're very helpful, Colin."

"In return, Stanton Technologies will pay your salary for six months, which should give you time enough to find another job."

"How kind of you."

"The company will give you a reference. In fact, now that Avery is gone you have the perfect excuse to be looking for another place, having been passed over for the top job."

"Works out neatly for you, doesn't it? What else?"

"A substantial severance. With your extra salary the total would come close to a million dollars."

"And no doubt you consider this a generous offer."

"In view of the circumstances it's a grand gesture."

"And if I refuse this 'grand gesture'?"

"We notify your parole board that you're in violation of your parole and you'll be returned to Indiana to serve the rest of your sentence at the Terre Haute prison farm."

"That's it?"

"I would advise Stanton Technologies to seek an indictment for fraud, forgery and grand larceny so you can be prosecuted here."

"Colin, if I didn't know you better I'd think you'd been sniffing glue or something. No one's going to prosecute anyone. Did you and Redfern and Ken really expect me to go for this?"

"You don't have to give me your answer today."

"I'll answer right now. No."

"You don't have much choice."

"You obviously haven't thought this through or you'd see that it's you and the Rover boys whose options are limited. In fact you have none except the ones I offer."

"And what might they be?"

"Colin, old fellow, let me clarify the situation for you. Since I joined Stanton three years ago the company has prospered. And although your two snoopers are upset because my analyses and reports were passed off as prepared by outside firms, that doesn't make them any less valid. I've worked my ass off at Stanton, and my contribution put millions into everybody's pocket. Profits of one hundred forty-seven million last year on sales of one point two billion. Not ten companies in the Fortune Five Hundred have that good an earnings ratio."

"And you're claiming personal responsibility?"

"No one man is responsible but my contribution was critical. Avery Stanton made practically all major decisions in manufacturing and marketing based on *my* research. You can take my word for it."

"I'm not likely to do that, am I?"

Walsh laughed. "Without me this company wouldn't be where it is today. Three years ago it was standing still. Like a lot of firms that expand too fast, Stanton stock was underpriced and overhead was rising while earnings and market share were down. I showed Fairchild where to trim until his industrial-division profit went up twenty percent. And my studies for Stanton International opened Redfern's eyes about the Far East so he was able to exploit markets ahead of competitors."

Walsh's recital did not help Colin's case. It was all true. More than once Avery Stanton had told him the same thing.

Walsh watched Colin as if reading his mind. None of this was going as planned, or hoped for. Either Walsh did not take the threats seriously or he simply had no fear of prisons or the law.

"Colin, I'll tell you something else," he said, smiling. "I was Avery Stanton's choice to succeed him as president."

"Is that right?"

"You knew but you're wondering how I found out. Avery told me over lunch a few weeks before Redfern and Fairchild got to him. He also mentioned he had spoken to you about it and that you agreed I was the best choice."

"I didn't know then what I know now."

"And what is that, really? I'm still the same man."

"Except that now we know who that man is. You implied you had a counteroffer for me. Let's hear it."

"I have two options for you. The first is the simple one. As a director and company legal counsel, Colin, you're in an excellent position to do us both a favor. I'd like you to nominate me to succeed Avery as president."

"That's impossible, ridiculous."

"Think about it. I will certainly keep silent about my past and I'll even see that half the money is returned. The other half I intend to keep because I earned it."

"You are one arrogant bastard. You know you can't remain on the payroll in any capacity—"

"Then I'll tell you about my retirement plan. As president of Stanton I could reasonably expect to put away a million dollars a year over the next fifteen years, with salary, bonuses, stock options and all. After taxes."

"But you won't be president of Stanton."

"In that case I'll be fifteen million dollars poorer unless I can make it some other way. Now I've just offered to stay on and earn it, but you say you're against that idea. So I'll tell you what my other proposal is."

"More money, I imagine."

"You imagine right, Colin. I'm willing to take as severance pay the fifteen million I would have earned, and walk. I'll even make it easy on you. Stanton International can pay it to overseas accounts

I'll name. And I'd take it over three years. It wouldn't even be missed."

"We could never take such a demand seriously."

"Colin, the stockholders meeting comes right after the first of the year, only a month away. I want your answer within the week. Either you and the others back me for the presidency or you agree to the fifteen-million-dollar payment. Otherwise I have a surprise for you."

"You're crazy. I *might* be able to persuade Fairchild and Redfern to go a little higher than the amount I've offered, but fifteen million is not even remotely possible."

"I've been invited to address the Wall Street securities analysts association at their annual dinner next Friday. Unless I have your guaranties beforehand for one of my two proposals I may use that forum to reveal the truth about myself and Stanton Technologies. I don't have to elaborate the disastrous consequences my revelations would have for Stanton on the stock market."

"You're bluffing."

"Am I?"

"You wouldn't say a word because you'd go to jail."

"I wouldn't go to jail, but you and your two friends would once I testified how you threatened me with exposure if I didn't help you rig the market on Stanton stock with my fake reports."

"You bastard—"

"If everyone is *reasonable,* Colin, nothing nasty need happen. If I become president we can all work together harmoniously. And if you force me to retire gracefully on fifteen million, well, what the hell, I've had a pretty good run for my money already."

CHAPTER EIGHT

BARBARA STANTON's marriage to the ex-All American Ken Fairchild was not a very happy one because Ken liked to play around. Not just the usual Las Vegas sales convention hanky-panky but the occasional fling at a serious relationship.

Avery Stanton had confirmed this to Colin Draggett three or four years earlier after he and Ken had gone to the mat about a beautiful young Ph. D. in Stanton's research laboratories. The girl got pregnant, refused to have an abortion, and when the research director fired her she went over everybody's head to the old man, identifying Ken as the father.

First Ken denied knowing her. But when she pointed out that tenants in her apartment building could identify him, he admitted one or two visits. In the end he acknowledged that he paid the rent on her flat, bought her a car and had recently spent a week in Barbados with her.

All the girl wanted was to keep her job and collect some child support from Fairchild. Since Avery Stanton was determined to spare his daughter any pain, and Ken seemed contrite and Barbara knew nothing about the affair, Colin was called to negotiate a settlement.

The pregnant woman was decent, honest and independent, but what she wanted Stanton refused to give her, mostly on account of Barbara.

In the end she agreed to leave in return for a research job at the University of Chicago on a permanent grant from the Stanton Foundation. The sum of two hundred thousand dollars was put in trust for the child's education, and Avery told his son-in-law to keep his pecker in his pants or find himself another place to work.

Barbara was a woman in her early thirties, not a beauty but attractive, a fine tennis player and an avid golfer. She had the same open, optimistic view of life as her father, and was determined to make the best of her marriage to Fairchild. She was not cut out to be a martyr.

Eventually Barbara did find out what had happened through some "well-meaning" friend, and the pain was devastating. Although she was not unaware of some talk around the club about Ken's dalliances, she put up with it. But if she was not cut out to be a martyr she was also no masochist. This was different, this was the worst thing that had ever happened to her. Hurt turned to anger, and anger to an understandable desire for revenge.

But Barbara was also a sentimental young woman, and Ken was a very persuasive man, especially with someone who deep down wanted to be persuaded. So he won Barbara back, and if her feeling for him was not what it had been, she still had every intention of remaining his wife. She had always found him physically attractive and she admired his talent for business. She also very much loved her children and fully expected her husband, their father, to take over in the natural course of things as president of Stanton Technologies. With Avery's death, Barbara had also become immensely rich in her own right, and had asked to see Colin about some of the details concerning her inheritance.

After leaving Walsh's house that fateful morning, Colin knocked back two scotches in the bar of the Griswold Inn, picked at a broiled lobster lunch and then took the turnpike to New London. He turned off just after Waterford, taking the old blacktop road to Crescent Hill, the Stanton-Fairchild estate.

Built in the 1920s by an eccentric New York theatrical producer, it stood on ten forested acres overlooking Fishers Island Sound. Stanton bought it as a wedding present for Barbara in the late 1970s, frustrating a local developer who planned to cut down the trees, demolish the mansion and build pricey summer homes. The house was an imposing, two-storey structure of weathered limestone, with slate roof and mullioned windows. Its indeterminate, vaguely Palladian lines suited the surroundings.

On the land side a small terraced formal garden led up to the porticoed main entrance where Colin parked his rented car next to Ken Fairchild's black Lincoln. Although a Mercedes or a BMW might have seemed more appropriate for a rising corporate star like Fairchild, it was Ken who had arranged a cut-rate lease-back deal on an entire fleet of Lincolns for Stanton sales executives. Avery had joked about them looking like a Mafia crime family or a car-hire service, but he couldn't resist the bargain either and took the first car for himself. Fairchild kept one and Walsh drove another. Only Brian Redfern rejected such uniformity, preferring to drive his Porsche turbo.

A maid showed Colin to the glassed-in terrace overlooking the Sound, where a cheerful fire had been laid in the stone fireplace. Barbara was with Fionna Redfern, who told him, "You just missed the men. They're at the boatyard." Redfern owned *Ghost*, a sixty-foot swordfishing boat.

"Do you want to see these now?" Colin asked Barbara, holding out the file containing her father's will and documents.

"I didn't want you to come all the way up here from New York just for me, Colin. There's no hurry."

"I'd like to say I did come just for you but it would be a lie. I had to see Adam Walsh this morning and I still have some business with both your husbands before I head back to New York."

"You know how Daddy was, Colin," Barbara said. "He explained things a dozen times but it's the little bequests I was concerned about."

"Everything's yours," he told her. "Keys to the castle, fish in the pond, doves in the dovecote and deer in the park."

Fionna said, "Since when have you had deer in the park?"

"Legal jargon," Colin said, smiling, charming. "All goods, chattels and assigns, and everything that pertains to them, including documents and testaments, liniments and condiments, belong to the sole heiress."

That got a laugh from Barbara. "Oh, Colin!" She turned to Fionna Redfern. "You know how lawyers are supposed to be so dry and stuffy? Not Colin. He's been making me laugh since I was sixteen!"

"Not much to laugh at lately," he told her.

"God knows," Fionna agreed, "but life goes on." Fionna had no children and spent her time being beautiful. But she was loyal to friends like Barbara, and gave generously of her time and affection. She, more than anyone, had been at Barbara's side throughout the sad ordeal of her father's death.

"I'm glad to have a little time with you before Ken arrives, Colin," Barbara said. "I mean, the day of the funeral you spent the whole time with Ken and Brian huddled in the study like three conspirators, murmuring and muttering."

"It's hard for everybody without Ave Stanton," he said.

"Daddy wouldn't want to hear you say that. He always claimed there was no such thing as an irreplaceable man."

"Your father was the great exception."

"Ken says Hunt Benson is so frightened of putting a foot wrong that nothing gets done. Is that true, Colin?"

"Hunt always did exactly what your dad told him to and he's sort of at sea now," he said. "But that will change with the annual meeting."

"Isn't that just after the holidays?" Barbara said.

"January sixth."

"Brian doesn't tell me everything that's going on," Fionna said, "but at least he doesn't complain."

"Do you think Ken tells me?"

"He should, darling. You're the owner."

"All I can say is that since Daddy . . . passed away . . . Ken's barely had a night's sleep."

"Brian's the same."

"Ladies, ladies," Colin said. "Would you like me to leave? I feel I'm eavesdropping."

"Colin, it's true," Barbara said.

Although the problem of Adam Walsh might have kept Ken Fairchild and Brian Redfern from getting a decent night's sleep, it had taken a different toll on Colin Draggett. He found himself inattentive to clients, forgetful of appointments and unable to concentrate on briefs that demanded his full attention. Although his secretary protected him, some of the younger partners were beginning to wonder if premature senility had overtaken the senior member of the firm even if he had yet to celebrate his forty-sixth birthday.

"Everybody's under a lot of pressure," Colin suggested.

"Brian's so stressed," Fionna said, "he's even started to smoke again, which makes me furious!"

"It's been a tough year," he said, "and it's not over."

Fionna sighed. "At least they have Adam Walsh."

Colin nearly gagged on his tea.

"Daddy always said Adam was some kind of a genius, but Colin knows more about the company. I wish you were closer, Colin," Barbara said.

"They don't want me underfoot," he told her, "and I'm as close as the telephone for any legal advice they need."

Ken Fairchild arrived a few minutes later, followed by Redfern, and soon afterward their wives left them.

As soon as they were out of earshot, Brian said, "Did he go for it, Colin?"

"Which do you want first, the good news or the bad?"

Both men answered simultaneously. "The good news."

"No, he didn't go for it."

"Oh, shit!" Fairchild said. "What *else*?"

"He wants me to propose him to the board for president."

"The man's crazy," Brian Redfern said.

"On the contrary, he's eminently sane."

"You told him no, of course."

"I told him no."

"And?" Fairchild said.

"And he mentioned what he'd settle for instead. As a consolation prize he only wants fifteen million dollars."

For several moments neither of them made any comment at all. Finally Fairchild was able to articulate the germ of a bad idea, although Colin did not recognize it as such at that moment.

"A fellow like Walsh has to be afraid of some damn thing. The law. Being sent back to prison. Something."

"He's not afraid of exposure," Colin told them, "and he thinks he can call the shots because we sure as hell are afraid about what happens to this company if he's exposed."

"But Ken's right, Colin," Brian said. "Adam Walsh's got to have his softspot too."

"What is it? Pain? Violence?" Ken said.

"What in God's name are you talking about?" Colin said.

"If he thought somebody would kneecap him," Ken said, "he'd change his tune. People like Walsh are cowards."

"Well, nobody's kneecapping anyone," Colin said, "and I don't want to hear another word of that kind of talk."

"Let's just elect him president then," Brian replied with heavy sarcasm. "What the hell? Who cares if he's an ex-convict . . ."

Fairchild exploded then: "Goddamn it, Walsh just killed Ave Stanton and there's no damn way we can let him do us and this company in too!"

Colin said, "Whatever solution we work out, we're agreed there's no place for him in Stanton Technologies."

Fairchild and Redfern both nodded emphatically. "Which puts us back to square one," Ken said. "Unless we're prepared to cough up fifteen million dollars of company money."

"That's not going to happen either," Brian said, "although . . . Walsh is right about one thing. That money could be siphoned off from Stanton International over a three-year period and cause only a very slight dip in earnings."

"Would anyone else have to know?" Ken asked.

"Not if we do it the same way he did," Brian said. "Set up fake firms and have our foreign companies pay for services—"

"And become worse criminals than Walsh?" Colin said.

"Talk about square one," Brian said quietly.

"Okay, the two million's down the tubes," Ken said, "but it galls me like the devil to give him another penny."

"Don't imagine it gives me any special pleasure," Colin told them. "I'm the one who has to listen to him dictate terms."

"I ran a projection on the computer to see what losses we might be facing if the word got out," Brian said abruptly.

"More than fifteen million?" Ken asked him.

"Substantially more. In fact, within the first week of such an announcement the decrease in stock share value could be expected to wipe out all gains for the last three years."

"Exactly what kind of numbers are we talking about?" Ken asked impatiently. "Give me a range."

"It's an educated guess only," Brian told them, "but at the very least it would represent a three- to four-hundred-million-dollar net loss to shareholders."

"Christ!" Ken said. "That's no loss, it's a disaster!"

"On a personal basis," Brian continued, "I'd be down at least a million and a half dollars. Colin, who holds five percent of Stanton, would take a twenty-million-dollar beating, and your wife, Ken, who currently owns or controls about thirty percent of the outstanding common and preferred shares, would drop well over a hundred million dollars."

A long silence followed Brian's declaration until Ken broke it by saying, "So you're saying fifteen million is cheap?"

"It's still extortion," Colin reminded them.

Ken said, "What if we doubled the offer we made the other day. Would he go for that?"

"You heard Brian's loss-projection," Colin said. "Do you think Walsh hasn't come up with similar figures? He'll never accept a dollar less than he thinks he has to."

"Only one way to find out," Brian said.

"If he seems the least bit interested we could even go to half," Ken Fairchild said. "Tell him he can keep what he has and we pay him out a million a year over five years. That would get him out for seven. What do you think, Brian?"

"It kills me, but . . . I guess I can live with it."

When Colin still looked doubtful, Ken said, "Try it, Colin."

"I'll have to see him away from the plant. He's too shrewd to speak on the telephone or in anyone's office."

Actually Colin had very little confidence that Walsh would even listen to a lower offer. He had made it clear that they either make him president or pay what he demanded. And no matter how many times Colin turned it over in his mind, he always arrived at the conclusion that eventually they would have to deal with Walsh on his own terms.

They were foundering, that much was clear. Colin said nothing after they failed to come up with a satisfactory alternative to Walsh's proposals, but he was convinced of two things. A solution eventually would be up to him, and it would be frighteningly expensive.

AFTER COLIN left, the conversation took an unfortunate turn. Had he remained a while longer perhaps the desperate ideas that surfaced then would not have been taken seriously and the whole terrible chain of events that followed might never have happened.

Ken and Brian were standing awkwardly in the entrance hall of Ken's house waiting for Fionna to get her coat when Ken quietly said, "I wasn't exactly kidding about violence—"

"I know."

"I think I'd kill him before I'd give him fifteen million of this company's money . . . well, I don't mean actually kill him, but at least work the bastard over so he gets the word . . ."

"It would have to look like an accident," Brian, the M.I.T. and Harvard graduate, said, "but I'd want Walsh to know he was set up."

Ken shook his head. "Who?"

"We know people who know people."

"For instance?"

"What about Petrey?" Brian replied. Dominic Petrey was the New York private detective hired by Ken Fairchild to gather the evidence against Adam Walsh.

"What makes you think he could deliver?"

"He came recommended by that fellow you knew in the army who runs the New York security service. He worked as an undercover cop for years. If Petrey doesn't have the right contacts, who does?"

"Maybe you're right," Ken said. "Maybe he does."

"I'll bet he can arrange anything for a price. And that he comes a ton cheaper than that goddamn crook Adam Walsh."

CHAPTER NINE

THERE WAS no point in going straight back to New York Saturday evening, although that is what Colin told everyone he was going to do. The weight of Adam Walsh's perfidy and his refusal to negotiate depressed him terribly. If he was going to come up with any solution to the dilemma, he needed time to think without distractions.

He returned to the ancient bar of the Griswold Inn for a nightcap among the old ship prints and steamboat schedules framed on the paneled walls. The Griswold had been run as an inn for more than two hundred years, and the place was warm and welcoming. Already he felt better as he sipped his whiskey and listened to a cheerful crowd of football fans arriving from New Haven.

His peace was not to last. "Colin! Colin Draggett!" sounded above the din, and Hunt Benson, president pro tem of Stanton Technologies, bustled across the barroom to greet him. He had last seen Benson the day of Avery Stanton's funeral.

He was with the football group, all Yale alumni, including two Stanton directors. They all laughed when one, a Hartford bank president named Howie Livingston, said they almost had a quorum. They wanted Colin to join them for dinner. He begged off but had another drink with them before they were called into the dining room.

"What brings you up here on a Saturday night?" Livingston asked Colin. "Certainly not the Yale–Princeton game." That got another laugh because they all knew Colin was a Harvard alumnus.

He explained that he had some Stanton family legal matters to tidy up and the weekend was the only time he had free. His reference sobered them all for a moment and their faces became grave and solemn.

"I miss that man more every day," Hunt Benson said. "I can't tell you how much we all depended on him."

Colin nodded, thinking of the comments Avery Stanton and

other company executives had made about poor Hunt Benson. Most of them agreed Benson was a fine technical man and a wonderful guy, but not the man to make executive decisions. Even trivial ones. The day of the funeral Colin had seen him agonizing over the seating in the church until Avery's secretary took over. The sooner Hunt Benson retired, Colin figured, the sooner Stanton Technologies would start to move forward again.

"What do you think, Colin?" Livingston asked.

"I beg your pardon?"

"Of his chances?"

"Sorry, I didn't hear the question. Whose chances?"

"Adam Walsh's. Maybe it's an indiscreet question, but here we are. Four company directors. One third of the board."

"Chances of what?" Colin said, but of course he knew what they meant.

"Of getting the top spot?"

"I wouldn't say they're too good," Colin answered, trying to nip this one in the bud.

"There's a lot of support for Adam on the board," the other director, Lydell Cummings, said. He was chief investment officer of the Hartford Commercial Insurance Bank and frequently played golf with Walsh.

"I have no doubt there is," Colin replied. "He's clever and he's popular, but I think you're overlooking something."

"He was also Avery's choice," Livingston said.

"Oh?"

"I'm sure he must have spoken to you about it." When Colin said nothing, he continued, "The last time he was in Hartford, he told me he was retiring and was going to recommend Walsh as his successor."

Hunt Benson came into the conversation then, saying, "The board would certainly want to follow Avery's wishes in the matter." That kind of back-up was precisely what Colin did not want to hear. How many people had Avery spoken to about Walsh? It was beginning to sound like he had kicked it around with everyone except his daughter.

Colin said, "While Ave was alive, that possibility existed. He was also considering Brian Redfern and Ken Fairchild."

"But Adam was his choice," Livingston insisted.

"At one point he was," Colin said, maneuvering now, "but not at the end. I was with him when he died, you remember."

"You mean he changed his mind?"

Colin thought, If you only knew. "Yes, he did," he said.

"Why?" Lydell Cummings asked.

"Family reasons," Colin lied. "Also bear in mind that Avery's controlling interest now belongs to Mrs. Fairchild."

"You're saying she wants Ken as president?"

"What do you think?"

"And that's what Avery wanted too?"

"His greatest wish was to please his daughter. After all, he only had two children." They looked startled at that until Colin said, "Barbara and the company. He was father to both."

"One must try to respect a man's last wishes," Hunt Benson said. "By all means, I'm sure you can count on us, Colin." He looked inquiringly at the other two.

Cummings seemed doubtful and Livingston shrugged. "I'd like to hear more debate on it before I decide. Avery was quite positive he wanted Adam. He was also explicit about why he did not want Redfern or his son-in-law."

"What were his reasons?" Cummings asked Livingston.

"He was sure Redfern would quit if he named Ken, and he considered Brian a valuable member of the management team. I'm not sure I altogether agree and I told him so. Look what happened at Avery's funeral. He took a poke at Ken, and Walsh had to pull him off. The man's smart, all right, but that sort of behavior . . ."

Gossip like that made Hunt Benson squirm even though he was the original source of it. He looked to Colin for help, but when the lawyer ignored him, he managed, "It's over and all things are possible among men of goodwill."

When their table was called, Colin made his escape and went directly to his room, thinking he had more than enough problems. Now he would have some recalcitrant board members to bring into line. How many more were there beside the Hartford bankers?

He decided he would call on Walsh again Sunday morning and give it one more shot, trying to secure an agreement on the basis of a seven-million-dollar offer. He told himself the man would be a fool to turn it down. It was far short of the fifteen he was demanding, but even he had to see that the demand was unreasonable and difficult if not impossible to meet. Seven million was still a lot of money, and Colin hoped that Walsh might just go for it if he made it sound like the absolutely best possible settlement under the circumstances.

If he were in Walsh's position, Colin reasoned, he would . . . but he could not imagine himself in that position.

Tomorrow, he thought, maybe. As he turned off the light the urgency of it crossed his mind. It wasn't just Walsh who had given them an ultimatum. Agree to a deal within the week, Walsh had said, or I'll spill everything. Colin did not really believe he would do it. What he feared more was that the story would surface some other way before they could contain it. Through some fissure no one was even aware of. The sooner they reached an agreement and got him out of the company, the less chance of disaster.

At ten the next morning Colin parked his car in the blacktop lot of the too cutely named Foreplay Golf Driving Range in Niantic and walked along the row of empty stalls until he found Adam Walsh practicing chip shots with a five iron, dropping one ball after another on the green. He glanced up when the attorney appeared but didn't speak.

His concentration was focused entirely on the tiny white ball. He flexed his knees and leaned on his club for an instant before lifting it gracefully in a slow-motion backswing. For the smallest fraction of a second he tensed, absolutely still, with the golf club raised high and motionless in the air. Then he brought it down like a swordstroke, sending the ball arcing above the green, to bounce once and roll to within a few inches of the cup.

"Stress doesn't seem to affect your game," Colin told him.

"On the contrary. I function best under pressure."

"So I've noticed."

Walsh selected another ball from a small bucket behind him, leaned back, swung, connected and put it within a foot of the previous shot. "So which offer have you decided to accept?"

"Neither."

"Oh?" Walsh peered at Colin over half-glasses. "I thought you might have reconsidered and decided to nominate me."

"Your staying on at Stanton is out of the question."

"So you said, although it seems an ideal solution."

"We've agreed on an offer."

"Go on."

"This is very painful for me, all of it," Colin told him. "First I lose one of my closest friends and—"

"Now you stand to lose a fortune unless you cut a deal."

"You would put it that way, Walsh . . . Fifteen million is out, as you knew when you suggested it. On the other hand, something between five and seven might be possible."

Colin waited for some reaction, but Walsh said nothing; merely teed up another ball and hit it.

"The way it would work," Colin said, "is that you keep the two million you stole and we will pay out a million a year for three to five years, the best we can do, anywhere you want it. We are all just as anxious to end this business as you are."

"And where will this million a year come from, Colin?"

"What do you care as long as you get it?"

"From Ken and Barbara Fairchild's family holdings? Or yours? I doubt that. And Redfern doesn't have that kind of money."

Walsh's eyes remained on Colin. "I'll tell you where it will come from. Stanton International. It will be embezzled from the company by these two honest stalwarts, with your knowledge and connivance, to buy me off."

"Listen, Walsh, hard as it may be for you to understand, there's not just personal greed at work here. I love this company and you're threatening to destroy it—"

"I at least gave good value for the money Stanton paid me, but this sounds like common theft. I'm surprised that a lawyer with your vaunted reputation for rectitude would be a party to such a plot—"

"Cut the sanctimonious bullshit!" Colin hissed at Walsh. "I'm trying to make this as painless as possible for the several thousand stockholders you defrauded—"

"How very considerate of you, as always, Colin."

"Yes or no?"

"Yes or no what?"

"Do we have a deal?"

"Colin, either you're deaf and dumb or just plain obtuse. No, we don't have a deal. I said fifteen and I meant fifteen."

"You also implied you'd negotiate."

"And I will. But in view of my asking price, an offer of five million plus the right to hold onto two million you seem to think I already collected . . . that's not negotiating, Colin, that's not even close. It's insulting."

"All right, look, this has to be settled. Give me your lowest figure and I'll go back to them. But it's got to be substantially less than fifteen."

"Colin, I've agreed to make it easy and take a three-year payout. I'll even lower my sights a little and give you a bottom-line figure. But all negotiations end there. Don't come back again unless you're prepared to accept it. Do we understand each other?"

"Only too well."

"That's some kind of progress anyway. Now that we're on the same wavelength. I'll lay it out for you, Colin. I keep what I have and I get an additional four million a year for three years. But I must have an immediate deposit of good faith, say a million, with the second million paid before the annual stockholders meeting. No discounts, no rebates, *and no more discussion.*"

"They'll never go for it. Bring it closer to what they're offering and I *might* persuade them."

"Sorry. My pants are down as far as they go."

"But it's still too fast a payout and too high a figure."

"In that case why don't you all join hands and take the fall-back position? Make me president of Stanton Technologies and let everyone live happily ever after."

"They'd see you dead first."

"Indeed! Then you and your pals better be prepared to take the consequences, Colin."

—————— CHAPTER TEN ——————

DOMINIC PETREY was not surprised when Brian Redfern asked to meet with him, but he thought the head of Stanton International could have picked a better place than the shabby workman's bar in downtown New London five miles from the main Stanton factory. It was the kind of cruddy joint Petrey hated yet had spent his life in, a dim limbo of chrome fixtures, cracked plastic, blue neon, and flickering fluorescent light. The place reeked with the smell of slopped draft beer and cheap whiskey and Petrey ordered both while he waited at the bar.

In his late fifties and looking older, the private detective was heavy-set and slow-moving, with the sad skeptical eyes of a veteran skirmisher. Petrey had made betrayal his profession as an undercover cop for too many years, and now his body was betraying him. A hernia and hemorrhoids had already been taken care of by the police surgeon, and an incipient ulcer was next. The Seagrams Seven hit his gut like battery acid until the beer chaser and a Maalox tablet calmed the stabbing pain. Half Petrey's household budget went to laundries and dry cleaners to keep him neat for his work, but his natural color was gray and his natural state a little seedy. He resembled an ageing bloodhound, appropriate to his calling, all jowels and folds and sagging skin. He had no wife anymore and he liked to eat, but had trouble digesting practically everything.

Dominic Petrey always recorded conversations in his office to avoid later misunderstandings with clients about his fees or what they expected from him, and when he talked to them in the field he wired himself. Each tape was slugged with the name, the date and the place of the meeting.

The only other patrons were a blonde muttering to herself near the rear of the bar and two repairmen drinking beer and watching a soap opera on television.

It was eleven-fifteen in the morning when Brian Redfern arrived, brisk and immaculate in his navy blue pinstripe. He peered around the dreary lounge for a moment, then ordered a scotch as he motioned Petrey to a nearby booth.

"I won't waste your time," Brian said. "I need some people to do a job and I hope you can find them."

"Always happy to oblige."

"It requires absolute confidentiality."

"I got no problem with that."

"I want a man . . . beaten up."

"Come again?"

Brian, who had had no courses at the Harvard Business School in the jargon appropriate to such negotiations, sounded foreign even to himself. Sort of fake tough. He pushed on nonetheless. "You heard me."

"Worked over?" the amazed detective said.

"Yes. I want him thoroughly spooked."

Dominic Petrey gave a light laugh and whistled.

"What's the matter?"

"You have to admit it's an odd request coming from a man in your position, Mr. Redfern."

"I've got my reasons."

"If he's messing with your wife, why not just put his lights out?"

"Who said anything about my wife?"

"Nobody, but I assumed—"

"This is straight company business, Petrey, and there's no way I can be connected with it."

"I'm strictly legal, Mr. Redfern, and what you're asking sounds extralegal to me."

"I'm not asking you to do it yourself. A man in your line must know plenty of people who can take care of this kind of thing."

"Oh, I guess I do."

"I'll pay them well."

"Lemme get this straight, Mr. Redfern. You don't want this guy killed or anything, just roughed up, right?"

"Roughing him up should change his mind. If it doesn't . . ."

"Don't tell me you want him snuffed?"

"What? Oh . . . I just want him out of circulation."

"Those things sometimes get out of hand, Mr. Redfern. Some guys get off beating up on people and go too far."

Brian said nothing, but was thinking that that would solve the problem, and a little shocked that he could have such thoughts.

"I'm sorry, Mr. Redfern. I'd like to help you but I don't do that kind of work."

"There's five thousand in it just to put me in touch."

"I couldn't help you there either because of the illegality. Recommending someone would make me an accessory."

"Only if you're caught, and that won't happen. Give me a name, a telephone number. You won't even enter the picture."

"It just ain't my line, that kind of stuff."

"Then where can I go? Who can I talk with? What would you do if you were in my position?"

"Forget the whole idea. You're talking about the real world in Connecticut, Mr. Redfern, not the Hoboken docks or some goombah Mafia place. You been seeing too much television."

"Name your fee, Petrey. Ten thousand? Twenty?" If it was a question of money, Brian was once more on firm ground.

"Sorry, Mr. Redfern."

After Brian Redfern left the bar angry and embarrassed, Petrey ordered another whiskey with a beer chaser and swallowed two more Maalox tablets. The adhesive tape holding the tiny recorder in the small of his back itched, so he reached under his damp shirt, disconnected the wire, and pulled off the little device, wondering if he was becoming allergic to that particular brand of tape.

When the drinks came he loosened his tie and dropped the little machine into his jacket pocket, thinking about Brian Redfern. Not a bad guy. A gentleman who always paid promptly. Married to a great looker and probably taking home a few hundred thou a year. Shame how guys like that got themselves into trouble. If it wasn't someone messing with his wife, Petrey reflected, it was probably blackmail with a gay angle or some kind of kinky sex. Redfern didn't look the type, he told himself, but who could tell these days?

Petrey sat thinking about the offer of twenty thousand dollars just for a name, and he had to smile. He knew a score of names, any one of which he could have passed on to Redfern. Men who would even kill for a few hundred dollars and think nothing of it. Spaced out mostly, dumb and clumsy and easy to catch.

It was a shame. Petrey could use the money. He was still supporting an ex-wife and two teen-age kids as well as a small habit at the track. But he recognized Redfern's naiveté as inherently dangerous if coupled with some druggie willing to take on the job. The sleaze would bungle it, get caught and point to Redfern, who would finger Dominic Petrey as the guy who put it all together. Goodbye license, goodbye business, goodbye livelihood.

Petrey looked at his watch and saw it wasn't even noon yet. Time to lay his bets on the day's races. Then he drained his glass and regretted not having at least asked Redfern for the name of the man he wanted "out of circulation."

_____ CHAPTER ELEVEN _____

BEING AN attorney on Wall Street put one in the way of making big money on a regular basis, and Colin knew that only a great fool would come away after twenty years without well-filled pockets. But he had become that fool and, unknown to anyone except a couple of Wall Street brokers, when the Adam Walsh affair overtook him he was teetering on the threshold of personal bankruptcy.

One might ask how that could happen to a smart New York lawyer in his position? Besides his stock in Stanton Technologies, worth almost forty million, he drew a seven-figure annual income from Cranmer, Fisher & Cleves. He owned several choice real-estate properties, and over the years had accumulated a portfolio of other securities for a total net personal worth of close to fifty million dollars. Not bad for a poor scholarship student out of Harvard, he told himself, but . . .

One got overconfident. Colin had always been prudent in his buying and was rarely burned by a bad investment until he became enamored of junk-bond trading. It began when his firm presided over the first in a number of leveraged buyouts, and he saw that capital raised with junk bonds was the same color as any other so long as people had confidence in the face behind the bonds.

He stepped out of his usual role as arbiter and invested heavily in a couple of these enterprises. His net worth on paper was soon two or three times what it was now. At one point a year or two earlier he could have written a personal check for one hundred million dollars and the bank would have honored it. The rub was that he had pledged all his Stanton shares as security.

Now his entire estate was mortgaged against a forty-million-dollar debt, and the interest, plus the astronomic cost of his wife's illness ate up most of his income. The men he owed wouldn't break his legs or throw him in the river, but they would liquidate him in other ways. Colin had already had some very unpleasant conversations when his interest payments arrived late. So contrary to Brian

Redfern's notion that exposure of Adam Walsh's background could cost Colin twenty million, it could literally wipe him out. He would be forced into personal bankruptcy and asked to leave the firm, an unheard-of disaster for a Wall Street lawyer.

Redfern had been right when he said the money could be siphoned off Stanton International's worldwide operations without being missed. But Adam Walsh was right, too, Colin realized, when he accused him of being a party to "common theft," whatever the good reasons.

Fairchild and Redfern could justify the appropriation of funds for this purpose as much as they wanted. They could rationalize their intentions by saying they were diverting a little of the regular company cash-flow in order to save all the stockholders from monumental losses. But Colin worried because whatever they called it, they would still be stealing money from Stanton International even if they were not putting it into their own pockets.

To cover up Walsh's unsavory background, they were already engaged in a conspiracy to defraud the company and had allowed themselves to become parties to extortion and blackmail. If that were not enough, Colin knew that the moment they diverted their first payment from Stanton to Walsh they were, technically, embezzlers.

There was also the possibility of a disaster even worse than the one they faced. Suppose they paid a few million dollars to Walsh and then the truth came out, including the fact that they had paid him? Suppose, in a word, he was setting them up?

Corporate scandals were nothing new in business, and more than a few had come too close for comfort. Insider trading, tax evasion, bribery, cornering government securities markets and other crimes and misdemeanors were not simply things Colin read about in the newspapers. Wall Street was a small world, and several of his clients had actually been involved, though he had no idea of it at the time.

Colin asked himself a thousand times if they might not be overreacting, exaggerating the damage Walsh's story might cause if it got out. He doubted it, but he wasn't sure. What he did know was that it could cost a fortune to Stanton, its shareholders and himself to find out.

Among other things, he studied Brian's computer projection on the estimated stock-market loss and concluded that Redfern had probably been too conservative. The damage to the company would be at least as bad as Redfern envisioned, and very likely worse. No, the price was simply too high. As risky as their chosen course of action would be, it was preferable to the prospect of the shattering consequences.

Colin was in remarkable physical and psychological shape and had always enjoyed splendid health. So he was surprised to discover at this stage of his life that the mere thought of going broke could make him almost physically ill. This whole deal with Walsh was against his grain, but . . .

They all decided that they had to act, to decide, to finish the ugly business as quickly as possible. Meet Walsh's terms and move on. But before doing that, Colin needed more information. Were any others in on Walsh's secret besides them? Just how great was the possibility of some leak exposing them before they neutralized the man?

There was also the other question Ken Fairchild had raised. Perhaps, as he had suggested, Adam Walsh might be afraid of something they knew nothing about. If he was and they could discover what it was, such a discovery might save them all a great deal of grief and money.

Colin decided to delve a little more deeply into Walsh's background before he came with Stanton Technologies. He poured over the prison file Avery Stanton had first shown him. It said a great deal about superficial aspects of Adrian Wadjewska, but it told him nothing pertinent about the inner man.

Besides some compulsive need for impersonation or intrigue, and a powerful desire for money, what made Adam Walsh tick?

Colin Draggett was a careful person, and in his private safe he kept a very private journal listing favors received, favors given and favors owed in order not to forget an obligation. As a Wall Street fund-raiser with friends on national political committees, he had a long list of names as well as access to a number of senators and congressmen. More importantly, he was known in certain state-houses around the country, and particularly in Albany.

The Monday following his unsuccessful meeting with Adam Walsh at the driving range he telephoned a New York state politician on his list. He had once helped keep the man in office with needed campaign funds, and the marker had not been called in.

He responded favorably to Colin's request, relieved and happy to retire that particular campaign debt so cheaply. He called back later in the day to say he had arranged everything through his counterpart in Indiana.

On Tuesday Colin flew to the state prison farm in Terre Haute for a private meeting with the warden and the prison system's consulting psychiatrist. On the table before them was a comprehensive file on Adrian Wadjewska, aka Abe Watkins, Arthur Whitaker, and A. Lawrence Waters. Colin did not mention the current alias of Adam Walsh. For the purpose of convenience they referred to the former convict as Wadjewska during the meeting.

Colin's first surprise came when they told him that Walsh had been released from parole only weeks before, which meant he had theoretically paid his debt to society and was no longer liable to be returned to prison.

The warden, a burly, likeable man in his fifties, was the most forthcoming. He told Colin, "Unless he pulls another stunt in our state, we've seen the last of him."

"One of the most fascinating cases I've had in twenty years of dealing with criminal recidivists," the psychiatrist said. He was a balding, fussy fellow who played with his eyeglasses and jiggled one leg incessantly throughout the interview.

"From what I understand," Colin said, "he managed to fool an awful lot of people over the years."

"Could I ask what your interest is in Wadjewska, Mr. Draggett?" the warden said. "Has he applied for a job with you?"

"I'm merely checking him out for a client. I really don't know why, but they're interested in knowing everything."

"An amazing man," the warden said. "I never actually thought I would miss a prisoner, but I miss Adrian. Do you know he put this farm on a paying basis? Except for custodial salaries, the place hardly costs the state a dime."

Colin was not interested in Adam Walsh's contribution to the prison economy, but he listened politely. According to the warden, in the years Walsh had been at Terre Haute he had organized the farm so efficiently that it not only became self-sustaining but provided food to other facilities in the state prison system.

"A genius," the warden said in honest admiration. "A man who could have been whatever he wanted to be in life."

"And more often than not, was," the psychiatrist put in. "He's passed himself off as a lawyer, accountant, economist, you name it.

Unfortunately he never bothered to get the necessary degrees or licenses for his various impersonations."

"Tremendously well read," the warden went on. "You find that with some prisoners. They become experts on certain things. But Adrian was an expert on practically everything."

"A deeply disturbed sociopath," the psychiatrist said, "with a compulsive need to prove his superiority over others."

"He had charisma," the warden added wistfully. "Always cheerful and dependable. And completely non-violent."

"But still a threat," the psychiatrist insisted. "A moral vacuum, an intelligent man who knows the difference between right and wrong and couldn't care less."

"Tell me this," Colin asked the doctor, "in your opinion would he ever sacrifice himself to destroy others?"

"An interesting question. I would have to say yes, he's quite capable of acting against his own best interest if things don't go his way. He did it here."

"If you ask me," the warden said, "it wasn't his fault."

"What happened?"

"When he was close to release," the psychiatrist said, "I recommended another inmate to replace him as farm supervisor. He didn't approve and made a scandal that almost cost him his parole. Claimed the other fellow would trash everything he'd built."

"He got a little out of hand," the warden acknowledged. "You'd have thought he was the warden, not me. Adrian's brilliant, as I said, but I couldn't sit still for that."

"Luckily we were able to head him off before any real damage was done," the doctor said proudly, "and he backed down."

"Only after I agreed with him and appointed the convict he wanted," the warden said, smiling, "otherwise Adrian might have pulled time for bad behavior. He's got a helluva big ego, no question about that."

"Is he . . . afraid of anything?" Colin asked them.

"What do you mean?"

"I'm not sure."

"Doc would know more about that," the warden said.

The psychiatrist nodded portentiously. "An inmate with his particular pathology rarely shows fear. But that's deceptive. His whole life is a mask, and masks are mainly used to cover fear, or at the very least, deep insecurity. So yes, one could say he is afraid . . ."

Colin pushed. "But of what?"

"Well, you could say he is afraid of failure," the psychiatrist said. "Yes, I'm sure we could say that." He seemed pleased with his answer, although Colin found it specious.

"Excuse me, Doctor, but that's true of virtually every successful professional person and executive I know," Colin said. "I mean the fear of failure is what makes most of us succeed."

The warden chuckled. He obviously was accustomed to deferring to the psychiatrist, but he enjoyed seeing him made uncomfortable. "I'd sure call our guy successful," the warden said. "He was the aristocracy around here. Expert forger. World-class embezzler. Artful extortionist. Brilliant devil, Adrian could talk on any subject and hold your attention."

"But suffering from a very deep fear of failure," the psychiatrist persisted, determined to make his point after his feelings were ruffled by Colin's rebuff.

Colin was convinced by then that his trip had been a waste of time, and he only wanted to extricate himself gracefully. "Is there anything else of any significance you can tell me about him, anything at all?" he asked them.

The warden thought a moment before he said, "We probably have the only prison golf course in the world. Adrian designed and built it. Only three fairways, but six holes. You play three holes in one direction, then three in the other. He taught the other prisoners to play. You play golf, Mr. Draggett?"

"Occasionally."

The doctor had no interest in golf and did not like to be interrupted. "Anything else you wish to know?" he said, his crossed leg jiggling a mile a minute.

"Thank you, Doctor. I appreciate your help."

The warden escorted Colin to the gate of this minimum-security facility, where a local taxi was waiting to take him back to the airport. The only indication that the place was a prison at all were two unoccupied guard towers on either side of the entrance.

When the warden noticed Colin looking at them he suddenly remembered something. "I don't know why I didn't think of it before, but there was one thing that scared Adrian shitless."

"What?"

"Heights. What the hell do they call that again?"

"Vertigo?"

"I mean he wouldn't even climb a ladder to pick fruit."

"He must have got over it," Colin said, "because for the last three years he's been flying all over the country."

"That's different. The doc says inside a plane they don't relate to the ground but to the cabin floor." He pointed to the railed platform at the top of the guard tower. "It's only looking down from something high up that gets them."

─────CHAPTER TWELVE─────

LAWYERS ARE used to sorting out and reconciling different versions of the same story, and Colin Draggett was better at it than most. He recognized that the true record of any event is seldom more or less than the sum of the available points of view. Witnesses keep a crime alive, he often said, not victims.

Oddly enough, nothing Adam Walsh ever told Colin except his original great impersonation was ever proved false. Colin was forced to admit that inside his elaborate construction of lies Walsh gave the appearance of being honest. This was ironic in view of the way Brian Redfern and Ken Fairchild altered the truth to accommodate themselves and the company. A further irony was that nothing they lied about—always for good and sufficient reasons— ever helped either of them when disaster finally struck.

Colin maintained almost daily contact with them, and he assumed they were informing him of everything they were doing. But from the start there was a certain reluctance on their part to broach ideas they knew he would disapprove of as a lawyer and a man. Like the business with Dominic Petrey, although in Petrey's case, the former policeman was too sensible to be drawn into any scheme of Brian Redfern's.

After Petrey failed to come through, Ken Fairchild had another brainstorm a day or so later. It was the week Colin had gone to Indiana and when the three were feeling their most desperate. He and Brian met in the titanium-plating room of Stanton's New London plant, where the noise level was equivalent to a squadron of jets taking off and where they could talk without risk of being overheard. Ken was accustomed to visiting the facility on a regular basis whenever some large government order was going through, putting on his hardhat and chatting with the floor supervisors. The plating room was in a vast, high-ceilinged building where the heat built to an uncomfortably high degree even in cold weather, so the two men were in their shirtsleeves and perspiring.

Brian would recall later that he had said to Ken, "This place reminds me of what hell should be like. Baths of steaming acid and molten metal. People condemned to spend eternity in it." He could not have imagined then how close to the truth he was.

As they talked, electric cranes whirred and rumbled above them, and huge steel sheets bumped and clanged on their way to the various baths of acid and metal oxides.

Brian told Ken that Colin had drawn a blank in Indiana.

"It figures," Ken said.

"A shrink at the prison told him that Walsh is capable of divulging everything if he doesn't get his way."

"Do you really think he's that suicidal?"

"Something about ego. Anyway, who can afford to take the chance? . . . If that asshole Petrey had come through, Walsh would be in traction now and this nightmare would be over."

"Or not," Ken said.

"One way or another," Brian told him.

"But there have to be plenty of other Petreys," Ken said. "We'll find one."

"We better, or I'll take care of him myself."

"Somehow I don't see you as a mugger."

"We'd stand a better chance of success if I ran him over with my Porsche."

Fairchild smiled at such tough talk from his number-crunching friend with the Harvard MBA.

"Let me ask you hypothetically," Brian said. "If you could do it and be sure of not being suspected, would you do it?"

"I don't know." Ken shocked himself now.

"What would stop you? Conscience?"

Fairchild gave an embarrassed laugh. "What stops most people? Maybe conscience and, I suppose, fear of getting caught. I don't know."

"You killed people in Vietnam."

"That was different."

"All right. Second question then. How would you feel about putting out a contract like they do in the Mafia? You don't even know the man who does it. You just deposit a payment someplace and it gets done. Would you do that?"

"Maybe . . ."

"I want to know how serious you are, Ken."

"Let me put it this way then," Ken said. "If Adam dropped dead, I would not be sorry. In fact I'd be very happy."

"You're begging the question."

"No," Ken said, "the question is whether we hand over a fortune to shut him up or whether we find another way."

"I'll tell you where I stand," Brian said. "I'd see the son of a bitch dead before I'd pay what he's asking."

"So you've said. Not smart."

"Colin is in favor of going along for the whole twelve million."

"I agree with him on everything but paying that," Brian said.

"The bastard wants his answer by tomorrow or else."

"I'm not suggesting we actually pay him, Ken."

"What choice do we have until we get our act together?"

Brian didn't answer.

As they talked they were watching one of Stanton's newest processes, the electroplating of graphite, which created a feather-light metallic material called Graftite used for aircraft and rocket construction. When Brian saw some laminates entering the plating room to be dipped in a titanium solution he led the way up a metal stairway to a narrow catwalk overlooking the operation.

Twenty feet below, acid vapor rose from glistening baths of metal salts. As they waited, an overhead crane came toward them carrying a half-ton cast-aluminum valve.

The operator failed to see them from his cabin as the crane glided by, and if Brian had not shoved Ken out of the way the valve would have knocked him from the catwalk.

Unfortunately, he slipped and lost his balance anyway, through no fault of Brian's. He teetered dangerously, nearly going over the guard rail before Brian caught him. For several seconds the two men stood clutching each other like two boxers in a clinch.

"Stupid blind bastard!" Brian said about the driver.

"Our own fault," Ken said. "They don't expect anyone to be up here except the men on the shift."

But Brian was studying the metal plates beneath their feet and the rail that had saved their lives. "This damn thing is built like a tinkertoy, held together with cotter pins. Jesus Christ!"

"That's so they can move it," Ken said. "For really big jobs they have to swing the catwalk out of the way."

Brian gazed at the shimmering bath of golden metal below. "Perfect place to give Walsh a shove. And it couldn't happen to a nicer guy," he added as they began to descend.

"Who talks to him this time?" Ken asked, not disagreeing with Brian's characterization. "Colin?"

"According to Colin, Walsh wants a million dollars up front now as a token of our good faith. Then he wants a second million before the annual stockholders meeting in January."

"Two million in one month? Can we hack it?"

"It won't be easy keeping it confidential . . . There'll be a paper trail I'll have to account for later."

"But can it be done?"

Brian nodded. "Once I've set it up. I've got to go to London and Hong Kong, and Luxembourg and the Bahamas. But Colin thinks Walsh will give us more time than he says. Colin hopes the first million will shut him up for now if he's convinced we're actually arranging the follow-up payments abroad."

"Do you have that kind of cash on hand?" Ken said.

"By emptying various current accounts I can muster seven or eight hundred thousand. Can you come up with the rest?"

"Not without alarming a few branch managers," Ken said. "But I suppose I can invent some excuse."

"Do it first thing. If Colin is prepared to make the deposit when they talk again, he'll sound that much more credible . . . Meanwhile, think about where we find the man we need."

"We already know someone."

"Who?"

"The man who recommended Petrey," Ken said. "The one that served under me in Vietnam. He was a career sergeant until he retired. One real bad-ass mother if you're on his wrong side."

"And you think he'll know some other bad-ass mother who'd be willing . . . to do it?"

"I'd say those are about the only kind of mothers he does know."

CHAPTER THIRTEEN

KEN FAIRCHILD always relaxed on the trip down the Connecticut Turnpike to New York. He enjoyed the anonymous luxury of the Lincoln and remembered Avery Stanton with affection every time he drove it. Rich as Stanton had been, he loved to cut a corner. The low-cost lease-back arrangement Fairchild had negotiated for a dozen company Lincolns had delighted him.

Even though Ken sincerely regretted his father-in-law's passing, the old man's death had opened the way for him to succeed to the top spot at Stanton. In a way he probably owed Adam Walsh a favor, although in his heart he knew better. If ever a man deserved to head a company, Ken Fairchild felt he did. Actually he had always excelled, always been ahead of the pack. At West Point, in the army, and at Stanton Technologies he was the one they followed, looked up to, talked about.

Since he had taken over Stanton's domestic division and established a series of incentive programs for his people in the field, sales were up, costs were down and profits were higher than ever. There were those who gave much of the credit to Walsh, but Fairchild knew where it really belonged. He had learned his lessons well in the army. The best staff planning in the world—and Walsh was a staff man—was worthless without inspired leadership in the field, and Fairchild was that kind of leader.

If things worked out, the nightmare of Walsh would soon be over. And they had to work out. An ex-con near the top of a Fortune 500 company was ridiculous!

Fairchild visited the city regularly on company business, and when there was no business, he invented it in order to pass the night with Nora Hallowell, a spectacular, recently divorced brunette. Nora worked as art director at Stanton's advertising agency, where she had helped develop one of his favorite projects, an industrial exhibit consisting of models, music and effects that would fill the entrance hall of Stanton's New London headquarters. Ken planned it as the equal of anything at Epcot Center.

But he had other matters on his mind this trip. When he came off the Triboro Bridge, instead of taking the East River Drive south to Nora's eastside apartment he headed crosstown on 125th Street into the heart of Harlem.

It was early evening when he descended into Manhattan, blustery and cold with the feel of snow in the air. The crosstown traffic was light, and when he reached Lenox Avenue he turned north, counting the streets to 138th Street. Ken had rarely ventured into this part of the city, and as he paused for the first traffic light, he punched the button locking the car doors.

The world outside his windows seemed a hostile, foreign land, not a white face anywhere. Boarded-over windows, burnt-out tenements and graffiti abounded, and Ken wondered if the Sanitation Department ever passed this way. Not since Vietnam had he felt quite so exposed, alone, and vulnerable.

This was their turf, and he saw them bebopping along, eyeballing the car and the interloper inside as he eased forward in the traffic, trying to make all the green lights while looking for a garage.

He was already beginning to wonder if he wasn't on a fool's errand, but he'd come this far, and the cool, supremely arrogant image of Adam Walsh spurred him on. It was too bad Brian had lost time with Petrey, but Ken was sure now that he was on the right track. With a little luck they could take Walsh out of circulation and frighten him thoroughly.

When Ken had called the New York number for former sergeant Luther Yancy, a woman answered who said she was his sister.

"Luther isn't here right now."

"Would you tell him Major Fairchild called, please."

"He be real glad to hear from you, I'm sure, Major. Luther hang out a lot with his Vietnam friends."

"I'm looking forward to it, too. He's still at the same address, isn't he, ma'am? On 138th Street?"

"Luther own the building," she said.

It was only after hanging up that Ken decided on impulse to go directly to New York. A personal meeting with Luther would convey his sense of urgency far better than any phone conversation. Ken called Brian to tell him, but Redfern was away from his office. Ken left a message saying he would reach him later.

There was no garage near the 138th Street address Ken had for

Luther but he finally discovered an outdoor lot at 146th Street and reluctantly left his black Lincoln like a drab plant in a garden of pink, yellow and purple Cadillacs.

An eight-block walk down Lenox Avenue and then half a block in on 138th Street would put him in the safe haven of Luther Yancy's home. Almost anywhere else in Manhattan, Kenneth Fairchild would have been just another faceless pedestrian. But here he stood out like Day-Glo in the dark.

He knew it was a bad idea the minute he started down Lenox Avenue and felt the hostile eyes on his back. He saw shuffling and muttering, saw people looking his way. Rap music blasted from a dozen portables, and he looked in vain at the passing traffic for any sign of a police cruiser. But Ken Fairchild was big and tough and could handle himself, he was certain of that.

Ahead a group blocked the sidewalk, teenagers jiving around in dude caps and identical white satin jackets. On his right was Sugar Ray's Bar outlined in blue neon, with a pay telephone visible inside the front window. He paused, saw the group taking his measure, and went into the bar. No white faces there either, just white eyes turned in his direction.

Ken dug in his pocket for change and dialed Luther's number. On the second ring Luther picked it up.

"Major, how are you! Where are you?"

When Ken told him, he couldn't believe it.

"Stay right there. I'll come and get you!"

"No, it's all right." Why did he say that when he knew it was not all right? It was terrible, in fact, and real dumb. But he talked Luther into waiting for him.

Leaving the bar, he saw that the sidewalk group in the white satin jackets had moved closer. They were waiting for him. Either he would have to step into the street to get around them or head back in the direction of the parking lot. He decided to return to his car.

He willed himself not to look back. He would do what he should have done earlier, get back on the East River Drive and have Luther meet him downtown at Nora's place. Then he heard laughing behind him, much closer, and a shouted: "Hey, you, man! What's your hurry?"

He ignored them. The parking lot was only half a block more,

just off Lenox Avenue, and because it was brightly illuminated he
began to think of it as a refuge.

But they were quicker than he thought. Between the Avenue
and the parking lot there was no light, no shops and no people.
Two suddenly appeared on either side of him and a kid about
fifteen came around in front, walking backward.

"Hey, man! You got a permit to walk here, man?"

Great laughter. Six or seven circling him now, another one in
front break-dancing expertly in his Reebok high-tops. Ken
Fairchild tensed under his three-piece suit, flexing his arms and
clenching his fists, ready to tangle ass if it came to that. Kenneth
Fairchild, West Point '72, All-American quarterback; once-upon-a-
time martial-arts expert but lately more of a barroom golf-and-
tennis person.

Hearing the others laugh at the antics of the break-dancer, Ken
felt a wave of relief. He'd read too many newspaper stories and was
getting paranoid. Poor kids was all they were, undernourished and
undereducated, maybe interested in the purses of old women but
no threat to a fit forty-year-old like him.

LUTHER YANCY went looking for Ken Fairchild when he failed to
show after half an hour. Luther himself was careful. He knew most
of the gangs in the immediate neighborhood, the pushers and the
pimps, and they knew him. Partially disabled but still in top physical condition just short of his sixtieth birthday, Luther Abdullah
Yancy had retired from the army to run a lucrative Harlem security
service. He had invested his earnings in local real estate and was
by now a man of comfortable means.

Ken Fairchild had been Yancy's Special Forces company commander in Vietnam, and the two men liked and respected each
other. But this was a different jungle, and Yancy thought the major
must be getting careless in his old age.

At Sugar Ray's the bartender confirmed to Luther that a white
man had been in to use the telephone. "Which way'd he go?"

The bartender jerked a thumb in the opposite direction from
which Luther had come. "Some Devil's Angels were following
him."

Luther hurried along the route Fairchild had taken, and when he reached 146th Street he saw the parking lot halfway up the block. The attendant knew Luther and told him, "That's his wheels over there. He a friend of yours, Luther?"

———— CHAPTER FOURTEEN ————

COLIN WAS leaving his downtown office that same day, as frustrated as he had been since the Adam Walsh affair began. He needed to walk and to get his mind off it, and one way to make sure he did was to visit his mother. The idea bordered on masochism, but it worked.

She was seventy and lived in a charming garden apartment fronting on Gramercy Park. At a cost to him of something over fifteen thousand dollars monthly, she had a string of charge accounts, a full-time companion, a part-time cook and a daily woman in to clean. Crazy Maisie, Colin called her, but not to her face.

His long-suffering father, whom he loved, was dead these twenty-five years, the bar and grill in Bay Ridge long since sold off, but his indefatigable mother went marching on.

People say about the elderly that if they're lucky they enjoy good health. Colin's mother showed every sign of living to be a hundred, but her perverse character did not allow her to admit enjoying anything, not even her good health. She was one of the most amazing people he had ever known, totally dedicated to her own self-interest.

One of Colin's chief memories of boyhood was his father saying, "Have patience, Colin. She doesn't mean it. She loves you and she's good." By the time he was ten he had concluded that both were untrue. His mother loved only herself. She tolerated Colin and his sister and she made his father's life a hell on earth. The sister hadn't spoken to Maisie half a dozen times since he had died.

Colin walked briskly, his mind on Walsh, Redfern and Fairchild, passing the Ladies' Mile with its clutter of glitzy boutiques and trendy shops all gaily lighted and decorated for Christmas. At Union Square he cut over to Park Avenue, and fifteen minutes later found himself in front of the Gramercy Park house. Maisie's companion let him in, a plump, cheerful Italian woman in her fifties named Mrs. Lombardi.

"Oh, Mr. Draggett, how good of you to come! She misses seeing you so much. She won't admit it but I know!" This was the kind of indulgence that had protected his mother all her life. Normal people simply couldn't accept the fact that she was what she was, and they always made excuses for her.

There's a lesson there somewhere, Colin decided. His father spent his life apologizing for her to his children, to his customers, to their neighbors and to relatives on both sides of the family. Colin didn't know whether his father actually believed it or if he simply couldn't accept the idea that the mother of his children was without discernible redeeming qualities. In the beginning his sister made excuses too. "You don't know, Colin, maybe she's arteriosclerotic or it's the menopause." But it was neither and the mother—daughter relationship was finally buried with his father.

"Hi, Maisie, how you doing?" A small peck on the cheek.

"You should ask?"

"Mrs. Lombardi told me you had a cold."

"How would she know?"

"Is she taking good care of you?"

"I could die and nobody'd know."

"Mrs. Lombardi would know. And she'd tell me."

"People don't tell you everything."

She had a point.

"Has your friend Mrs. Kleineman been to visit lately?" Mrs. Kleineman was one of her few friends as far as he could determine, a fat, asthmatic pouter pigeon of a woman who seemed to revel in his mother's abuse. She came on weekly visits from Queens, her plump, corseted figure panting up the ten steps at the entrance, and the two would play gin rummy all afternoon. Sometimes they went to Atlantic City to gamble.

"You know what that Esther Kleineman did now?"

"What did she do, Maisie?"

"Well, last March she went to Disney."

"Hmmm."

"By herself. I mean, give me a break. A woman her age going to Disney by herself? And she met somebody."

"Good for Mrs. Kleineman."

"An actor."

"Even better."

"And she's moving down to Florida."

"To be with him?"

"Why else would she move to Florida? A woman her age."

"Lots of older people move to Florida."

"Not me. I'm stranded here."

"You can go to Florida any time you want."

"You'd like that, wouldn't you? Get me out of the way."

"Only if you wanted to go."

"You're just like your father. He stuck me in Brooklyn and now you want to send me to the other end of the country."

"Maisie, Florida is not the other end of the country."

"Did you come here to visit or to argue?"

"I only meant it's less than three hours on the plane."

"There was a crash in India last week. Two hundred people fried to a crisp. And you want me to fly!"

"I didn't say I wanted you to fly. Flying has nothing to do with what we're talking about."

"No, you'd rather keep me locked up here."

"You went to Atlantic City last week, didn't you? But Mrs. Lombardi says she can't even get you to walk in the park."

"And get mugged?"

"You won't get mugged in Gramercy Park. It's private. You even have a key to the gate."

"What good's a key if he's got a knife?"

There came a point of pure surrealism in every conversation with his mother when Colin simply gave up. That did not mean, however, that she let him off the hook.

"They shoot up in the park, you know. Drugs."

"That's Central Park, Mom, not Gramercy Park."

"Park, schmark!"

He tried to keep what was left of the conversation going by replying, "Maisie, Gramercy Park is safe."

"That's what you say," she told him. "He says he's a diabetic!"

"Who?"

"Mickey Mouse."

"I beg your pardon?"

"Esther's actor friend."

"Why do you call him Mickey Mouse?"

"That's what he is. The head mouse."

"He plays a mouse at Disneyworld?"

"Not a mouse. *The* mouse! He's the oldest, been there twenty years. Trained all the other mice and the Donald Ducks. Diabetic, ha! Give me a break!"

"Tell Mrs. Kleineman I wish her all the luck."

"Who knows what goes on inside that mouse mask?"

"I'll call you next week."

"Don't call me, I'll call you. Ha, ha!"

"Right, Maisie."

After a few reassuring words to the long-suffering Mrs. Lombardi at the door, Colin fled into the chilly evening.

But the visit to his mother accomplished what he desired. A session with lovable old Mom always helped him to look at real life again with a certain bemused detachment.

ACCORDING TO what Ken Fairchild recounted to Colin later, the Devil's Angels launched their attack on him at approximately the same time Colin was leaving his mother's Gramercy Park apartment.

The little break-dancer struck first, but Ken saw the move coming a split second before it arrived. The mugger's knife flicked to slice across the lapel of Ken's eight-hundred-dollar suit. His reflexes saved him, but his quick step backward put him against a wall of white satin where arms grappled for a hold.

He shook them off, swung at the dancer and missed. He whirled and dropped the nearest kid with a place kick in the groin that lifted him three feet in the air. When another got too near, Ken decked him with a karate chop to the ear. For a moment he thought he'd make it. They were light, all of them, weighed nothing. They fell before his blows like paper.

But they were a pack fighting as a pack, and like wild dogs intent on their prey, they knew how to parry and feint before going for the kill. A bicycle chain was Ken's undoing; slicing out of the darkness from behind, it caught him across one side of his head, opening his scalp from eye to earlobe.

Groggy from the blow and half-blinded by blood, he was no match for them after that. The dancer wanted revenge and he sliced him neatly on both arms and across the chest. He was about to stick him hard in the throat but the leader stayed his hand. They stomped him when he fell and kept stomping him after he lost consciousness. They kicked his face and his testicles and his kidneys. They took the forty dollars cash he carried and his watch and cuff links and credit cards.

"Hey, man, platinum!" the dancer said, waving the wallet at the others.

The attendant at the parking lot had seen it all. When Ken did not move after five minutes he dialed 911 and told the police operator, "Guy got mugged. Lying in 146th Street near Lenox." Fifteen minutes later a patrol car arrived. The policeman passed his flashlight over Ken Fairchild's inert body, saw he was white and said, "Asshole." Then he called in for an ambulance.

At the hospital where Luther finally found him, Ken was conscious but so heavily sedated that Luther couldn't get any sense out of him. Stitches were taken in his head where the bicycle chain connected, and more where the dancer stabbed him in the left arm. His other wounds were superficial but he was passing blood in his urine and the emergency doctor diagnosed some kidney damage and a concussion.

"Your friend's tough," the doctor said to Luther. "He'd be a lot worse off if he wasn't in such good physical shape."

Luther formally identified Ken for the hospital records and listed himself as next of kin. Then he took the Lincoln keys and returned to the parking lot.

"My man, this car belongs to my friend like I said. I leave it here another day and you pretend it's mine, you hear?"

"I hear, Luther."

"I don't want to find nothing missing, nothing dirty, nothing scratched and nothing dented."

"I'm only on the night shift, Luther."

"You tell the day man too, hear?"

"Okay, Luther."

"Not 'okay Luther.' You responsible, hear?"

"Sheee!"

"My man, if this car don't pass inspection when I come back, you be one unlucky mother."

When Luther told his sister what happened she said, "Is he one of those crazy Vietnam boys, Luther, that I read about?"

"No, the major isn't crazy."

"You sure? White man walking alone down Lenox Avenue after dark got to have something loose in his head."

After the parking-lot attendant identified the gang as the Devil's Angels, Luther called on the gang leader. An hour later the man returned Ken Fairchild's credit cards and the approximate amount of money that had been in the billfold. Shortly after midnight Luther Yancy was talking to Barbara Stanton Fairchild.

"He's going to be okay, Mrs. Fairchild. He just got mugged and they beat him up some." Luther minimized the injuries, explained where Ken was, gave her his telephone number and said he would look in on her husband first thing in the morning.

"I don't know how to thank you, Mr. Yancy."

"Ma'am, the major and I go back a long way. I'll look after him until you get here, don't worry now. He'll be okay."

Barbara called Colin immediately, and after he reassured her, he telephoned Yancy and heard him repeat what he had told her.

"What the hell was he doing walking around Harlem?"

"Coming to see me, Mr. Draggett. I live in Harlem."

"I see," although Colin didn't see at all. "Look, can he talk? Is there a telephone in his room? Can I call him there?"

"He's out of it, Mr. Draggett. He got beat up pretty bad. And he's in the surgical ward. Nobody's got a phone there."

"What about visitors?"

"No problem, but like I say, the major's not making a whole lot of sense right now. It might be better to wait."

"The major? Did you know Ken in the army?"

"We were in Vietnam together."

"We appreciate what you've done, Mr. Yancy."

Two days later Ken Fairchild was moved by ambulance from Harlem Hospital to a private room at Columbia Presbyterian. He was sitting up, his battered face still swollen and bruised, a large surgical dressing on the side of his head, with smaller ones taped to his chest and arms. The room was filled with flowers and fruit, although he was mainly taking liquids because it hurt to chew.

Barbara had driven down from Connecticut the first day and was staying at her New York apartment, coming to visit him each afternoon. The doctors had told her Ken could leave the hospital in another day if his urine cleared.

Colin visited too, to tell Ken that Adam Walsh was very displeased at not yet receiving his first million dollars. Because Ken Fairchild's three hundred thousand had not been deposited, the full amount was taking longer to arrange than Redfern expected. Colin had to assure Walsh that they'd meet again in a week or so, as soon as he knew when the payment could be made.

The private nurse said later that Brian had come charging in shortly after Colin left, talking to Fairchild in the worst language. "When poor Mr. Fairchild was trying to tell what happened to him," the nurse said, "Mr. Redfern just lost his temper."

"You could have met this guy in a hundred places," Brian told Ken, "all of them safer than Lenox Avenue and 146th Street. You're lucky you're not in a coma. Lucky you're not dead."

"I know it was foolish—"

"It was stupid. Crazy. What the hell did you expect? Just walking into that goddamn hospital ward in broad daylight was enough to scare me. You and I were the only two white faces in the whole damned building!"

"I didn't notice."

"I only want to know one thing. What excuse did you give Colin Draggett for cruising Harlem in the middle of the night?"

"I said I stopped off to see Luther Yancy."

"Why?"

"Old Vietnam buddies."

"Did he buy it?"

"No reason not to."

"Same story to Barbara?"

"Of course not. She thinks it happened in midtown. They were just kids, you know."

"Kids, my ass. They were pretty handy with a tire iron, by the look of the job they did on you."

"The oldest couldn't have been more than eighteen."

"What did your friend say about our problem?"

"Luther? Nothing. I didn't exactly spell it out."

"But that's what you went there for. I mean now that you have a sample of the kind of work they do . . . Adam Walsh is supposed to be the guy in traction, not you. And time is running out."

"I couldn't do it. I mean after it happened to me, I just couldn't find the words."

"What did you tell him? That you decided to take a walk around

Harlem because your post-combat stress syndrome was acting up?"

"He was curious, naturally."

"I'll bet he was."

"I said I'd been under a lot of pressure lately and wasn't thinking too clearly. He believed me."

"So do I."

"That beating did give me a new perspective."

"Next you'll tell me you want to pay Walsh, too."

"Brian, we have to think of something."

"We've been trying to think of something for weeks."

"I know. I know."

"All right. Remember the strike that pipefitters' union tried to pull off in England last year at our Reading plant?"

"Yes . . ."

"I'm going to England tomorrow to talk to the fellow who took care of that strike. I should have thought of him in the first place and not wasted time on Petrey and your pal from the army."

"Have you told Colin?"

"Can you imagine me telling Colin? He'd have a fit."

"Breaking a strike and taking care of Adam Walsh are not the same thing, Brian."

"He's competent and he has some very strong connections in the lower depths."

"So does Petrey but they didn't help us."

"This man is a different story."

"What's your idea?"

"The same as yours with Mr. Yancy, except I don't intend to get myself hospitalized setting it up. He'll choose the people we need. They fly over, do it and fly back."

"I don't know, Brian."

"You're not backing out, are you? I thought military minds like yours thrived on violence."

CHAPTER FIFTEEN

As HEAD of Stanton International, Brian Redfern traveled to Europe and back two or three times a month on the *Concorde*. The company operated factories or sales offices in Paris, Brussels, Dusseldorf, Torino and London, where it also maintained apartments for its visiting American executives after Redfern discovered it was less expensive than paying hotel bills.

Before leaving New York, Brian telephoned Stanton's British managing director to arrange a meeting with Mr. Oliver Quirk at the company's London flat. He planned to be there only one day, Brian said, and would not have time to visit the Reading plant.

"But we've had no reason to call on Mr. Quirk since the strike," the managing director said, misunderstanding Brian's intentions. "And I'm just as pleased. Very unappetizing chap, that."

"Just see that he's waiting tomorrow when I get in," Brian told him. "It's about another matter entirely."

Redfern was certain this time he had found the solution in Oliver Quirk, and finding solutions was what he did best. It was his Harvard Business School training in the so-called case method.

It was no accident that Avery Stanton had hired Brian Redfern straight out of school. The young man had first worked summers in the Stanton plant while studying engineering at M.I.T., and had caught the old man's attention with a suggestion for recovering certain metal salts lost in the production process.

Although Hunt Benson thought the old recovery system was all right the way it was, young Redfern showed that with the installation of a five-thousand-dollar heating unit and a polarizing filter system, metal worth many thousands of dollars monthly could be recovered and reused.

After Redfern graduated at the top of his class, Stanton offered him a permanent job that he immediately turned down.

"Why?" the old man asked him. "You have a better offer?"

"I'm going for an MBA," Redfern told him.

"A waste of time," Stanton told him. "You're a hell of an engineer. Go with that."

"I don't want to be just another engineer," Redfern had said. "And to go all the way, I need the graduate business degree."

"When you've got it, call me," Stanton had said, and a week after graduating from Harvard Business School, Redfern did exactly that.

Impressed by Brian's brass as much as his brains, Avery Stanton hired him as an administrative assistant to work directly under his supervision. But as Stanton spent most of his time in the laboratory Redfern was often on his own.

Stanton disliked travel, considering it time lost from important work, and he particularly disliked travel abroad, becoming irritable and impatient in places whose language and customs he did not understand. Brian Redfern, on the other hand, was happiest jetting from one country to another, hiring people, talking to customers and setting up Stanton offices and plants. Foreign businessmen liked his urbane manners and were impressed by his natural facility for languages. They also applauded his fervent belief in what he called the "irrelevance of corporate nationality."

As Avery Stanton's personal representative he became the man foreign clients and personnel saw most often. When Stanton decided to set up its first overseas manufacturing plant in England, it was Redfern who advised on the location, selected key personnel, and negotiated with building contractors and labor unions.

With that experience behind him, Stanton sent him to supervise the establishment of similar facilities elsewhere. Although Stanton hired others skilled in international sales and administration to run the international operations, it was Brian Redfern he trusted most. Redfern knew this and took advantage of it. Those who clashed with him did not last, and those who lasted made it a point to get on well with the president's assistant.

As international sales grew and foreign profits became significant in the overall Stanton company picture, Redfern acquired power. Most Stanton managers abroad had been selected by him and owed their allegiance accordingly.

For the first few years the title on his business card remained the same—Administrative Assistant to the President—until Avery Stanton received an invitation to serve on a government advisory

panel for international commerce. "You take it," he said to Redfern,
but Brian replied that he could not.

"Why not? You're the one knows what it's all about."

"Aye, the panel consists entirely of presidents or managing directors of international companies. I'm neither."

"But you're running Stanton International."

"True."

"If you were president, would that do it?"

"That would do it."

"Then announce it and take the advisory-panel appointment. I
don't know why you didn't think of it before now. Those things
give us prestige, you know."

So as the first president of Stanton International at the tender
age of thirty-one, Brian Redfern became publicly responsible for a
thousand employees and three-hundred-million-dollars worth of
sales in thirty-one countries. Nothing had changed really. His new
title was merely official recognition of what he had been doing
since soon after he joined the company.

But Brian began to change. If he had been ambitious and hard-
working in the beginning, he now became nearly obsessed. He
made money but he also made enemies. When Avery Stanton was
thinking of licensing his chrome-plating patents to a Japanese manufacturer, Redfern said no. Stanton International would put its own
plant in Japan. But when the Japanese said no it looked as if Brian
had made a costly mistake because a great deal of money was
involved. But after three months of secret negotiations he announced that South Korea's largest automobile-parts manufacturer
was joining with Stanton in the construction of a plant to produce
chrome-plated parts for the entire Asian market. Since the Stanton
process was both cheaper than and superior to any other, this
meant the Japanese would have to buy American from Korea if
they expected to remain competitive.

It was the kind of coup Brian enjoyed most, beating someone at
his own game. But it was also the kind he could not brag about
except to his wife Fionna, who shared every success and hated
failure as much as Brian.

They had met when he was organizing Stanton's English manufacturing operation and she was on a buying trip for Blooming-
dale's. Both were impressed by the other's obvious success at an
early age, and it was with some misgiving that Fionna eventually

gave up her own career to help run Brian's. She was as determined to see him to the top as he was to get there.

He was thinking about Fionna now as the plane decelerated for its approach to Heathrow. For the first time in his marriage he had not told her everything. He had not mentioned the Walsh problem at all, nor had he even hinted at trouble. He was not sure why he had held back but he suspected the reason. He liked to look good to Fionna and feared that before the Walsh affair was over he might come off looking very bad indeed. Either she'd think him a fool for going along with Colin and making a whopping big payment taken from the company, or she'd be shocked because he'd have to play much harder ball than usual. For the moment, it was just better she didn't know.

The chauffeur from Stanton & Co. Ltd. met Brian with the Daimler at Heathrow airport, and an hour later Mr. Oliver Quirk sat facing him over a gin and bitters. Although the purpose of the meeting between Brian and Quirk was exactly the same as the one with Dominic Petrey, the outcome this time would be considerably different.

A natty little man with a red round face, greasy brown hair and a bowling ball paunch, Oliver Quirk cultivated the perpetual smile of the cheerful fool. His too-tight collar, tattersall waistcoat and hand-painted tie were intended to display his imagined status, but Brian knew that virtually everything about the man was bogus, even his name. He called himself a union organizer but hired out as strike-breaker. He professed to be a sports fan but was in truth a soccer hooligan. Part-time drug dealer, former inmate of Borstal and Wormwood Scrubs, rabble-rouser and petty thief, Mr. Oliver Quirk was quite a number. Brian knew only vaguely the details of his background.

"I'll get right to the point, Mr. Quirk," Brian was saying, wanting to get this over as quickly as possible.

"Best do," Quirk said, fixing his hard little shoebutton eyes on Brian while he lit a cigarette and sipped at his drink.

"I need help on a small job in the States."

"Lybor problems?"

"More of a management problem. A man needs some convincing."

"If hit's rough stuff you caime to the raight man. Old Ollie knows just the chaps can teach a man 'is manners or the error of 'is wize. Ollie's boys did nice work in Reading if I do sy so, Mr. Redfern. Werry nice indeed. No more lybor staife there neow, I wager . . . I 'ave a question, though. Why Ollie Quirk? Why not one of your Yank blokes?"

"I know your work."

"First rate, guv'nor, that's raight." He waited for Brian to go on, his eyes alert, his eternal smile in place.

"And I prefer not using someone locally. Shall we talk about the price?" He didn't know which made him more uneasy . . . Quirk, or what he was doing dealing with him. He reminded himself about the *why* of his unsavory mission and felt better . . .

"Let's hear a bit more about the job first, guv."

"What do you want to know?"

"Where is hit comin' orf?"

"A town in Connecticut." When Quirk raised his eyebrows in a question, Brian added, "Two hours from New York."

"How d'you see hit 'appening, guv?"

"I don't. That's your business."

"Any bodyguards?"

"No."

"Guard dogs?"

"No."

"Does 'e carry a gun or keep one in 'is car?"

"No."

"How old is he? Age about like you?"

"A lot older."

"Big man or economy size like me?"

"Average build."

"Piece of cike, aye?"

"It's simple enough, straightforward."

"If 'air's one fing old Ollie learned in 'is business hit's 'air hain't nuffing striteforward. Contingencies and hexceptions is wot interest me, guv'nor, if you get my meaning."

"I'm prepared to cover contingencies, Mr. Quirk."

" 'ow 'igh was you finking, guv, for contingencies?"

"You tell me."

"Oh, no, guv. It's your show."

"Ten thousand and expenses."

"Neow you're jokin'. Pullin' old Ollie's leg, you are. You know better than that, Mr. Redfern. Neow get serious!"

"Twenty."

"Never less than fifty's my motto, never less."

"It's one man—"

"But 'e's important or I miss my guess. No, fifty hit is, guv, or get your Yanks to do it for you on the cheap."

"All right, fifty."

"And ten each expenses for Ollie Quirk and two 'elpers. Mikes 'ighty thousand in all."

"That's outrageous, Mr. Quirk." They never had a course in Oliver Quirk at Harvard Business School. "All right."

"Wif 'arf the fund for contingency up-front and expense money, mikes fifty-five wif the other twenty-five to come when the job's done. Neow that's fair if ever fair was, I say."

"What guarantee do I have?"

"You 'ave the word of Ollie Quirk."

"I suppose you want the fifty-five thousand dollars in cash?"

"Fifty-five thousand quid, not dollars, in cash."

"Pounds?"

"This is England, Mr. Redfern. Coin o' the realm."

"When can you—"

"Soon as old Ollie 'as the details, the deposit and the flights booked. Satisfaction guaranteed, guv'nor."

Brian took a Stanton & Co. Ltd. check from his attaché case and made it out to cash in the amount of fifty-five thousand pounds. He'd figure out later how to explain it if necessary. "I'll call the bank and tell them you'll be coming with the draft."

"Werry nice of you, indeed, Mr. Redfern. A pleasure to do business wif you, I say." He lip-read the check, folded it carefully and tucked it in the pocket of his waistcoat.

CHAPTER SIXTEEN

It was probably only a matter of time before the paths of Barbara Fairchild and Nora Hallowell crossed somewhere around Kenneth Fairchild, and cross they did when Barbara stepped down from her limousine at the Columbia Presbyterian visitors' entrance as Nora was getting out of a taxi directly in front of her.

Barbara noticed Nora immediately, a spectacular brunette in a green minidress. Nora noticed only the limo.

Although Barbara still had the clear complexion and tanned, tawny good looks of her debutante days, she had never really been pretty. Her nose was too thin and her jaw too prominent, her feet too big and her knees too knobby to be considered beautiful. But she was trim and athletic, with a small waist and full breasts, blue eyes and taffy-blonde hair. She had dignity and poise, a warm, engaging smile and the money to make the most of it all.

None of this was enough for her after one glance at the woman in green. As Barbara followed Nora up the steps to the reception hall, she felt drab and awkward by comparison.

Nora Hallowell had no bad angles. Her long brown hair glistened and swirled like a shampoo commercial while she moved with the grace of a prima ballerina. Her dress of green silk jersey clung to all the right places under a white blazer, and her heels beat a supremely confident tattoo as she approached the reception desk clutching a large suede portfolio.

When Barbara saw both their faces reflected in the glass partition separating her from the receptionist, she was dismayed. The same unflattering light that seemed to reduce her own thinnish face to an insipid plane set off Nora's high-cheeked beauty, accentuating her luminous brown eyes and full lips.

The receptionist asked Nora, "May I help you?"

"Could you tell me what room Mr. Fairchild is in?"

Barbara tensed.

"Kenneth Fairchild?" the receptionist said.

"That's right."

"Mr. Fairchild is in four-ten."

"Thank you," Nora said, and flashed Barbara a warm smile as she turned away, revealing even white teeth.

Barbara watched her walk toward the elevator, wondering who she could be. The looks and portfolio said model or actress. She certainly did not work at Stanton Technologies.

"May I help you?" the receptionist was saying.

"What? Oh! No, thank you." Barbara took another elevator to the fourth floor, telling herself it was all very silly, but fear made her heart beat faster. She followed the arrow directing her to room 410, and arrived in time to see the woman enter.

She braced herself, put on her best party smile, and was about to walk in when some sixth sense stopped her. She waited, poised uncertainly outside the half-open door, listening until she heard low murmurs and then a high, musical laugh.

"No, Ken, stop! You're supposed to be *hors de combat*! Darling, really, the nurses . . ."

Barbara saw the woman's back, bent over Kenneth Fairchild's hospital bed. The hem of her green silk dress had been raised above her buttocks by one of Ken's caressing hands while the other circled her shoulder. Barbara turned away, nearly fainted, then backed down the corridor and leaned against the wall. Only an extreme exercise of will kept her from throwing up.

A nurse saw her and stopped. "Are you all right?"

"Yes, thank you."

"You sure?"

Barbara nodded. When she felt able to walk again, she fled the hospital and told her driver to take her home. "To the Ritz, Miz Fairchild?" Her family had kept a suite at the Ritz Tower for years, which everyone except Ken used when in New York.

"Home, I said!" and she broke down in the cushioned comfort of her enormous car and sobbed for the first hour of the trip. After the near scandal with the Ph.D. in the research lab, Ken had promised to behave and he had, so far as she knew. Her feelings had changed, but they had seemed to manage an accommodation, an adjustment. Ken Fairchild was just not somebody you gave up when he was the father of your children and you still had a marriage . . . Until this. The ravishing young woman in Ken's hospital room was not some alleged one-night stand. She was a chic, sophisticated Manhattan career girl of the kind Barbara read about in Vogue and Vanity Fair, and she had just shaken the remaining foundations of Barbara Fairchild's marriage.

Barbara rarely drank anything stronger than wine, but halfway home she opened the bar in the limousine and poured herself two vodkas over ice. The alcohol calmed her but hardly made her feel better. At home she remade her face and closed herself in her room.

She had been heartbroken by her father's unexpected death, but the sickening sense that gripped her now was worse. Nothing matched the gut-wrenching pain and anger she felt as she remembered the green skirt hiked above the woman's rear, Ken's hand cupping the silky pantyhose, his hand with the heavy gold wedding ring she had given him.

In the past she had had her father or Colin to consult, or Ken's shoulder to lean on. Now she had to talk to someone, and she dialed her friend Fionna. The housekeeper said Mrs. Redfern was on the golf course but she would give her the message.

An hour later Fionna called back and when Barbara burst into tears, she told her, "Don't move, I'll be right over."

The two women sat on Barbara's canopied bed, where Fionna Redfern tried to comfort her friend.

"Don't do anything. And above all, don't say anything to Ken about it until it's sorted out in your mind."

"I've got to find out who she is, I can't help it."

"You've still got all the cards," Fionna told her.

"Not all," Barbara said. "You don't know how beautiful she is."

"He's your husband," Fionna said, "the father of your children, the next president of your company, and I believe you still love him."

"No. How could I possibly love him . . . I want to kill her, Fionna."

"One thing at a time. First we find out who she is and what she does."

"She doesn't have to do anything except stand there."

"We learn where she works and where she lives. And once we know that, we sweep her out of Ken's life, and yours."

"How?"

"Lots of ways, darling. You have money and power—"

"For all the good it does me."

"Trust me."

"What do I do?"

"Hire a good private detective."

"I wouldn't even know where to look for one."

"You don't have to look anywhere. Brian used a man recently on some hush-hush company investigation for your father."

"But if Brian knows, Ken could find out."

"Brian won't know, darling, unless you tell him. This detective's number is written down at home. You simply call and say you're

Avery Stanton's daughter and you need his expert assistance, that's all. He's a professional and they have to be discreet."

"I don't like it," Barbara said, "using a private detective to follow my husband around. It only happens in bad movies."

"And the best of families," Fionna reminded her.

"What's his name?"

"Petrey. Mr. Something Petrey."

_____CHAPTER SEVENTEEN_____

ON COLIN'S last visit to Fairchild the day before Adam Walsh was to speak at the securities analysts dinner, Ken announced that he would be out of the hospital in time to attend. He was still a mess, with blue-and-yellow bruises on his face and neck and a swatch of adhesive tape covering the stitches on one side of his head, but he was impatient to leave.

"Are you sure you should?" Colin asked him.

"I wouldn't miss it."

"He sent me an advance copy of his talk."

"And?"

"I hate to admit it, but Stanton Technologies stock should gain quite a few points because of what he plans to say."

"Are you saying you trust him?"

"In a few days he'll be a million dollars richer, thanks to us, and soon he'll begin to see the rest of his blood money. He has accounts in Hong Kong, Montevideo and Vienna. Very well organized, Mr. Walsh, with every incentive in the world to keep his side of this devil's bargain."

"What is he going to tell the securities analysts?"

"His pitch has to be based on his own spurious studies, but you know how credible he always sounds. That's what impressed Ave Stanton in the beginning. Adam Walsh is very believable."

"That's quite an endorsement coming from you, Colin."

"Read the speech. He talks about the new opportunities in Eastern Europe and Stanton's increased corporate income now that those countries are starting to pay royalties on our patents. He speaks of the further consolidation of the Common Market and the anticipated rise in German production because of unification. And he points out that Stanton is the exception to the current American recession not only because of its defense contracts but Japanese dependence on the company's metallurgical techniques."

Fairchild shook his head. "Ironic, wouldn't you say?"

"Worse. If I didn't know what I know about him, he sounds like he'd make some company an excellent CEO."

"It won't be Stanton Technologies."

"We couldn't stop him if he went with a competitor."

"What difference would that make?" Fairchild asked.

"I grant you he's no engineer or chemist so it would be hard for him to steal any of Stanton's technical know-how."

"Exactly."

"But he's got marketing and financial smarts."

"So do a lot of other people."

"None of them has his *inside* knowledge of Stanton."

"You have a point, but we could prevent it."

"How?"

"Make his continued unemployment a condition for collecting the rest of his money."

"You're overlooking one factor," Colin reminded him. "So far Walsh has been setting the conditions."

"That will change, Colin."

"What do you mean by that?"

Ken shrugged as he realized he had almost gone too far. "Just that anything can happen before this is over. My guess is he'll take the money and run. Go off to the south of France or some Caribbean island and live on his ill-gotten gains."

"I don't quite believe it, Ken. Walsh isn't the sort of man to retire gracefully. Too ambitious, too dynamic."

"Whatever he does, we'll need all the help we can get in order to pay the son of a bitch."

"Brian's in London to move some funds now."

"Brian gets the job done," Ken said.

"At least I disabused you both of doing anything rash," Colin said, in part testing.

"That was angry talk."

"With you, maybe, but not with Brian . . . Well, see you tomorrow at the dinner."

"I'll be there, black eyes, bruises and all."

On his way out Colin paused to inspect the colorful arrangements of flowers filling one corner of the room. He pointed to the most elaborate bouquet.

"From Brian," Ken explained. "He has his tender side."

If this was what he sent for a beating, what would he spend on Ken's funeral, Colin wondered.

When Colin arrived at his office, there was a message from Adam Walsh to please call him at his Waldorf hotel suite. Maggie put the call through, and Walsh came on the line immediately. "Colin! Good of you to call me back so promptly. Have you read my speech?"

"I have."

"Like it?"

"Is that what you called about?"

"Writer's vanity, Colin. You know these Wall Street guys. Analysts are as prejudiced and suspicious as hell. How do you think it will go down with them? Is it broad enough? Upbeat enough?"

"It's great if it's all true."

"You know damn well it's true. Every conclusion is based on the best available evidence. I don't warp facts to conform to theory."

"You do when the facts concern yourself."

"I'd like to pretend I didn't hear that, Colin."

"You can pretend whatever you like."

"I asked you for an opinion on the speech. Do you think it will wash well when the market opens Monday?"

"It will wash very well and you know it."

"Good old Colin. You see? In spite of our differences we agree on certain marketing principles. I'm still going the extra mile for Stanton, Colin, putting money in your pocket."

Walsh sounded pleased that Colin was going to attend the dinner and hear his presentation, and listening to him now, all seemed normal, as if nothing unusual had ever passed between them.

At one point he even had the nerve to say, "No other executive ever worked harder to get where he is than I have."

The audacity of the remark annoyed Colin at first, yet he had to admit that what Walsh said was essentially true. The man's capacity for work was as astonishing as his cleverness. Lots of executives clawed their way to the top, but not all of them could back their pretensions with Walsh's degree of talent and performance. And fewer still could conceal a criminal past and prison record as successfully as he had done, or for as long.

_____ CHAPTER EIGHTEEN _____

As SPEAKER and guest of honor, Adam Walsh sat at the dais next to the president of the Securities Analysts Association. But Stanton Technologies had taken two tables near the front for its executives and friends, and Colin sat at one of them with Ken Fairchild and the Redferns.

Even before Colin's wife became an invalid, she avoided these events like the plague, sensible girl that she was. Joyce used to say, "Colin, I married you for better or worse, but worse doesn't include boring business dinners." This one wasn't the least bit boring as it turned out.

When Colin appeared alone at functions where wives were invited, casual acquaintances assumed he was either divorced or a widower. Friends knew differently. His wife had been ill for almost three years and those who knew him well knew that Joyce only had a short time to live. They would inquire after her in tones reserved for the graveside and when he answered with a shrug they would quickly change the subject.

No one was surprised that Barbara Fairchild was missing from the Stanton group. Barbara had always preferred the informal social life of Connecticut to big New York affairs. Fionna Redfern, on the other hand, relished any excuse to dress up and show off her splendid looks in a chic Manhattan setting.

Adam Walsh's wife Celia was also at the Stanton table, seated between Ken and Colin, the same cheerful, placid woman Colin had last seen in smock and gardening gloves, her rosy cheeks glowing with natural good health. According to Fionna, who knew everything about everybody, she and Walsh had only been married a short time and she had a grown son living somewhere in the middle west.

Celia Walsh played some golf and taught a course in modern dance at Connecticut College, Fionna said, but otherwise she was not very social. Fionna also said she had only come to the New York fête because her husband was the guest speaker.

At first the table talk centered around Ken Fairchild's recent mugging and the danger of walking New York streets at night. Redfern and Colin both knew he was in the middle of Harlem when he was attacked, and Redfern knew why he was there, but the others had been given the same story as Barbara Fairchild and assumed it had happened in the midtown theatre district. His bruises were still obvious and his jaw must have bothered him because he gave a little wince of pain whenever he encountered something hard to chew.

Celia Walsh noticed it too, and was almost motherly in the way she clucked over him. She was shy, but with a wry sense of humor, and very proud of her husband. As they chatted during the meal Brian Redfern asked where she and Adam had met.

"Oh, we've known each other since childhood," she replied, and Ken Fairchild nearly choked on his chicken.

Redfern glanced at Colin and then said, "How come you and Adam waited so long to marry?"

"For quite a few years we didn't see one another," she said. "Adam went off to Princeton when I was still a little girl."

"And then they married other people and divorced and met again here," Fionna said. "Isn't it just too romantic?" She saw her husband give Colin a look and misread it. "*I* think it's romantic even if you don't," she said to Brian.

"Oh, it's romantic," he agreed with a straight face. Just too romantic to be true, he added silently.

Colin, taking it in, wondered how much she knew about the money they were paying her husband. Probably nothing, he guessed.

Soon afterward in the men's room Redfern and Colin had a spirited exchange. "She's in it with him," Redfern insisted.

"No, Brian. The woman is straight."

"Then how could she say she knew Adam Walsh since she was a kid? It isn't possible because he isn't Adam Walsh."

"There must be an explanation."

"Sure, collusion."

"I doubt she's lying, Brian. I'd bet she isn't."

"Save your money, Colin," he said as he zipped up and washed his hands. "They're taking us for a ride."

Colin motioned him to watch his remarks even though he saw no one in the stalls. "It's a mystery," he said, "but I believe her."

"Anyway, it doesn't matter," Redfern replied.

Not until much later would Colin discover what he meant.

Adam Walsh's speech took them all by surprise. At first he stuck pretty much to the advance text Colin had read. He mentioned the business opportunities opening up in Eastern Europe and he mentioned Stanton Technologies' increased corporate income now that those countries were paying royalties on patents. He spoke of expansion in the Common Market, and the anticipated rise in German production because of that country's unification.

But then he departed from the text he had shown Colin when he pointed out that Stanton was the exception to the current American recession mainly because of its founder and former president. For five minutes he delivered a ringing eulogy on Avery Stanton, praising "his genius and his vision." Because of him, Walsh said, Stanton Technologies was light-years ahead of its competitors and would always be a world leader in metallurgy. Stanton was on the cutting edge, writing the book on tomorrow's metal technology.

According to Adam Walsh, the world electronics industry was dependent on Stanton patents for the printing of metal circuits on transistor parts and quartz microchips. Also according to him, all automobile manufacturers still paid royalties on chrome-plating processes invented and patented by Avery Stanton a generation ago. The company also held over four hundred patents on metal, graphite and ceramic laminates currently used in sports equipment, shipbuilding, aircraft and space-vehicle manufacture.

Walsh was a first-rate public speaker and he had them sitting up by then, hanging on his words. Although what he said was not exactly news to anyone inside the firm, the way he pulled it all together was impressive.

"And what now?" he was saying. "Where do we go from here? Do we pause and take stock? Rest on our laurels? That was not Avery Stanton's way, it's not mine, and it's not the way of the extraordinary team that makes up Stanton Technologies!"

He lowered his voice. "Scarcely two hours drive from where we sit tonight, in the chill stillness of a special chamber at Stanton's Connecticut research laboratories, a crystal grows in liquid nitrogen at three hundred degrees below zero. This glittering jewel no larger than a pearl will be removed from its cryogenic womb and cut into a hundred microscopic layers by laser. Each tiny filigreed layer, ladies and gentlemen, will be capable of storing data equivalent to the contents of the New York Public Library!"

A hush fell over his audience as he paused.

"But that's not all," he said. "In the same laboratory experiments are being conducted with what we call 'smart' materials, invented by Stanton scientists. One can be heated to five thousand degrees Fahrenheit. It glows but does not melt. And a week later, standing unconnected to any heat source, this amazing material is still too hot to touch. Another is an air gel, 'frozen smoke' we call it, which is the lightest and most efficient insulator ever developed, and which we'll soon have in production."

His audience of hard-nosed Wall Street analysts was spellbound. Walsh's revelations had them whispering, nodding and shaking their heads. Colin looked over at Hunt Benson to see what he thought of these marvels, but his expression of bemusement said this was the first time he had heard about any of them.

Ken Fairchild was as mystified as Colin, but Brian Redfern muttered to him, "What is the son of a bitch up to now? Is he running for president after all?"

"None of these amazing products have names as yet," Walsh was saying, "and I'm sorry I cannot divulge their exact composition until we hear from our patent lawyers. We are molding molecules, rearranging atoms to come up with these amazing 'intermetalics,' as we call them. The miracle crystal is simply called SCX-312, which stands for the number of the Stanton Crystal Experiment, and the remarkable heat-retaining ingot is called the Hot Block."

One of the last inventions to come from Avery Stanton's fertile brain, Walsh continued, was called Graftite, a flexible, feather-light graphite ceramic laminate infused with polymer "whiskers" and covered by an unbreakable film of titanium alloy. "This is a flexible, heat-resistant intermetalic," Walsh said, "one-fifth the weight of aluminum, three times stronger than steel and twice as tough as mylar." Already in production, Walsh predicted the product would reach four hundred million in sales the first year, and within three years could be worth nine billion dollars yearly!

He finished with general remarks about Stanton's glittering earnings prospects—up twelve percent from the previous quarter —and the company's expanding markets—substantially greater than a year ago—before sitting down to thunderous applause.

Reporters and financial writers crowded around him after the dinner as he gave an impromptu press conference. Redfern was right. Nodding and smiling and answering questions cheerfully, Adam Walsh did, indeed, behave like a man running for office.

Meanwhile Brian got to a public telephone and talked to Harold Henderson, Stanton's director of research, demanding to know why none of them had heard anything about the fabulous crystal or the miraculous metal bar.

Henderson wasn't even sure which crystal Number 312 was, he said, because there was a whole garden of them growing at ultra-low temperatures in the lab. He said it was true that some seemed to show a remarkable capacity for retaining digital input, but they cost a mint to produce and so far they all powdered every time anybody tried to slice them with a laser.

The Hot Block was a favorite project of Ave Stanton's at the time of his death, he said. But like the crystals it was expensive to make, as well as uncertain and risky. The amalgams and precious metal laminates used in its composition were very tricky to work with because some were radioactive.

"Radioactive!" Redfern exclaimed.

"Afraid so. It holds heat okay, but the applications are limited because you've got to keep it in a lead box."

"Walsh was talking about putting one in every bathroom to warm the baby's bath water," Brian said.

"You know Adam," Henderson replied, laughing. "Whatever he lacks in expertise he makes up for in enthusiasm."

"He also says Graftite will top four hundred million in sales the first year," Brian said, "and then go into the billions."

"I'm sure he's right," Henderson said.

Redfern pricked up his ears. "Really?"

"Every day we find new uses for it. These intermetalics are the most exciting things we've ever worked with and Graftite is the best of the lot. You can mold it, saw it, twist it, extrude it, anything. It will be the material of choice for airframes, ships, even automobile engines. It's better than any metal, fiberglass, ceramic or polymer compound."

*   *   *

OVER THE weekend Walsh's stories made news apart from the financial and business pages, and on Monday, Stanton shares opened three-quarters of a point up and kept rising until they closed four dollars above the Friday price. Colin wasn't unhappy, but he was uneasy. And he became even more so when Walsh himself appeared abruptly in his offices that afternoon at Cranmer, Fisher & Cleves. At first Colin thought he came to gloat but he was wrong.

He invited Colin to leave his glass-and-concrete tower and take a walk around Trinity churchyard. Once again, he was making certain nothing they said could be recorded. There, among the slabs of weathered marble marking the graves of colonial New Yorkers, he said, "You made yourself some money today."

"Is that so?"

"Be a sport, Colin! Give the devil his due. The forum was perfect. The news was wonderful. They ate it up and the results benefited everybody. I'm used to Redfern's sour face and Fairchild's ill manners, but I always considered you a gentleman."

"What do you want, Adam?"

"My first million, Colin. Where is it?"

"These things take time to organize."

"Frankly, I don't see anybody organizing anything. I see a sullen Brian Redfern flying to London and back, and an angry Kenneth Fairchild battered and bruised by street thugs. I begin to wonder if they're planning to keep their side of the arrangement, or do they have something else in mind?"

"As you said yourself, they don't have a lot of choice."

"You understand that, Colin. But do they?"

"I'll talk to them some more."

"That money is overdue."

"Brian assures me it will be available this week."

"Excellent. Put it through the Hong Kong & Shanghai Bank. Here are the account numbers." He handed Colin a slip of paper with the numbers typed out. "Two checks of three fifty and one for three hundred, made out to Crown Colony Surveys Ltd., Intercontinental Management Associates, and Brisbane Metals Inc. respectively."

Colin jotted down the names and amounts beside the account numbers and showed the paper to him. He nodded and walked on.

"Bear in mind that there are only twenty-one more banking days before our stockholders meeting, and I'm expecting your second token deposit before then, as we agreed."

"That may take a little more time."

"You know, Colin, sometimes I get the feeling from the behavior of your two partners that you're all stalling. Do you blame me for worrying?"

"They're doing the best they can on such short notice."

"I hope so. For your sake, I hope so."

"It's a lot of money, Adam. In order to avoid attracting attention, it must be assembled from small deposits—"

"The details don't interest me, Colin, not in the slightest." Suddenly he stopped and raised both his arms. "Crazy. Really crazy," he said over his shoulder.

"What do you mean?"

"This old graveyard in the middle of the financial district. Imagine what the ground is worth!"

_____ CHAPTER NINETEEN _____

UNKNOWN TO all of them, while Colin stood listening to Adam Walsh in Trinity churchyard on Monday, Brian Redfern's English lackey, Oliver Quirk, was being brought in chains to the United States District Courthouse twelve blocks away to be arraigned on narcotics charges. He had stepped off the plane at Kennedy on Friday and been immediately arrested. By the time he reached Manhattan, however, the courts were closed, so he languished in the Federal Detention Center at Ryker's Island over the weekend.

Redfern had been desperately trying to find him for days, and again on Monday he was on the telephone to England, his voice rising as he spoke to Stanton's managing director.

"What do you mean you can't track him down?"

"I don't even know where to look, Mr. Redfern. His wife says he left last week and she hasn't heard from him since."

"Check the people he hangs around with."

"I've already done that, sir, but you know how those men are. If they know, they're not saying, but I don't think they know."

Brian slammed down the receiver, as frustrated as the day Walsh had laughed in all their faces, thankful at least that he hadn't mentioned to Fairchild the fifty-five thousand pounds he'd advanced to Quirk. Better to keep transactions like that to himself.

But where was the man? If he failed to reach Brian, Quirk was to call Petrey and have him relay the message. Brian couldn't imagine what had happened, but he had a bad feeling about it, a gnawing sense of having been had. He had been a fool to give Quirk more than expenses up-front. That much cash to someone like him was an invitation to disaster. But his judgment hadn't been too sound lately, not since the Walsh business began. He wasn't alone, he thought. No one's judgment had been up to par, not even Colin's, who wanted to pay the bastard off and thought that would do it. And Fairchild? Getting mugged on a Harlem street corner hardly showed clear thinking.

Goddamn Petrey anyway, Brian thought. Who would have guessed the detective could have been such a self-righteous prig? If he had come through they could have put the fear of God into Adam Walsh. It wasn't as if he wanted to hurt the man, Brian told himself, just scare him to death. But Petrey was too dumb to understand something that subtle.

MEANWHILE PETREY had completed three days of surveillance on Nora Hallowell's apartment. Finding out where Nora lived and who she was had been simple enough. One of Petrey's men had been covering the hospital, and the moment Ken Fairchild was released he had made straight for her place before putting on black tie and going to hear Adam Walsh's speech.

Petrey was something of an impersonator himself, in the sense that he carried a dozen business cards with different names, different titles and different addresses. Only the telephone number remained the same so he could be reached whichever card he used. In the space of an hour he might introduce himself to different tenants on the same floor as Dick Steel, a skiptracer, Ron Hicks of Oasis Mutual Life, Harry Rudkin of the Urban Benevolent Society, or Gary Rose of Consumer Protection Laboratories.

Whichever guise he used, his friendly basset face inspired trust, and people usually told him what he wanted to know. When they did not, either he withdrew politely, flattered them, tipped them or threatened them. He had a feel for the work, knowing that a bribe or a threat only worked with a certain kind of person, while compliments appealed to everybody.

"The trick," he once said, "is in knowing how and what to compliment. I mean, say it's a lady and like she's overweight. I want information about her neighbor, say, and if I tell this lady she's thin, right away I'm dead because she knows I'm full of it. So I don't say that, see? I say, 'I'm looking for Mrs. Jones?' and she says, 'That's me,' and I say 'Excuse me but you can't be her.' And she says, 'Well, I am!' And I say, 'But the lady next door'—that's the one I want to know about, see?—'said Mrs. Jones was, well, on the fat side and that certainly isn't you, ma'am.' Right away she hates her neighbor for saying she's fat and loves me for saying she isn't. A minute later I got all I need." Petrey also had his theory about bribes, or *tips* as he called them. "It's gross just handing over a bill, and you don't always get what you want. I got different ways. Polls sometimes."

That was how he got the best information about Mrs. Hallowell, on polls. Like a polygraph. Three out of four questions were innocent but the fourth one mattered. "First you tell 'em it'll take less than five minutes and the company pays ten dollars for each interview. You don't ask name or address, just preferences like what's your favorite breakfast cereal or TV show. Then maybe you want to know where they bank so you ask 'em. Or where the husband works or what kind of a gun he owns. Maybe you ask him what insurance he carries and with what company, or if he smokes, how much. Then you give them the ten bucks, always a new bill in an envelope. If you want a handwriting sample or fingerprints you get them to sign a receipt. For that you carry a clipboard with clean coated paper."

He had polled the doorman at Nora's apartment building, then followed Nora to her advertising agency and polled the receptionist and two secretaries. The information he collected from these people enabled him to get more. He saw a copy of her apartment lease on file at the building-management office with Ken Fairchild's signature on it. He got a retail-credit report on Nora, discovered the number of her checking account and the balance (eighteen hundred fifty dollars), and that she had forty thousand dollars in a money-market fund.

By the time he called Barbara Fairchild and arranged to meet her in New York at the Ritz Tower apartment he knew a great deal about Nora Hallowell. He had established, among other things, that she was a graduate of Chicago's Art Institute, wore a size-eight dress and a size-seven shoe, was fond of sushi and was known by the *maître d's* of at least three fashionable restaurants as Mrs. Fairchild.

True, Barbara rarely came to New York City, but even so, Fairchild's indiscretion was amazing. For a man as experienced and sophisticated as he was, he had conducted this affair with such disregard for the circumstances that it was only a matter of time before his wife found out. Contrary to what one might have thought, a kind of hubris seemed to have overtaken him since Avery Stanton's death and Walsh's blackmail, a self-deceptive sense of invulnerability, as though the worst had happened. At best, he failed to take the time to run his affair with more care. At worst, he appeared to be like those malefactors who subconsciously make mistakes that will insure their capture. Partly what was operative here was that for the first time in a life of not very distinguished philandering he rather liked the idea of people knowing he commanded the love and attention of such a truly spectacular woman.

Barbara confided in Fionna that not only was she through with smiling, she felt like she wanted to kill Nora, she wanted to kill them both. Ken's weakness could no longer be rationalized by her . . . he was "a rotten sneaky bastard . . ."

Fionna was secretly overjoyed. If Barbara divorced her husband she certainly would not want him running the company her father had founded. And that raised the question of who would run it. Because Fionna was not aware of the truth about Adam Walsh, she still believed he might once again be a candidate for company president. But she also knew that Brian would be in the running as well, and she was determined to do everything in her power to help him get the job. If Ken were eliminated, Brian's chances had to be improved.

Barbara was the key. Fionna had to work on her in as subtle a way as she could. She had to campaign with other board members as well. Men like Hunt Benson and the Hartford bankers had to be

convinced that Brian Redfern was the ideal choice to lead Stanton
Technologies in the years to come.

The idea of helping her husband become CEO at Stanton held
tremendous appeal for Fionna Redfern, every bit as ambitious as
Brian and just as determined to see him make it to the top of a
major multinational company. Although he had been Avery Stanton's protégé, this status was no advantage over Adam Walsh, who
had also been personally selected by the old man.

Apart from her remarkable energy, Fionna's great edge was that
she had no children to encumber her, no pets to worry about, and
no serious interests apart from the advancement of Brian's career,
now that she had given up her own. But Barbara Fairchild had her
own priorities, and Brian Redfern's triumphant arrival at the top
was not among them.

The Stanton board was made up mainly of Connecticut businessmen whose reputations were secure and whose wives craved attention. While Barbara seemed to lapse into a kind of bitter apathy
over what she called "the Ken thing," Fionna's ambition translated
itself into frenzied activity. She spent hours networking on the telephone, played bridge with the older wives, paddle tennis with the
younger ones, and she pleased hostesses with her willingness to
be put next to the oldest, stuffiest director at dinner parties.

Having traveled with Brian around the world on Stanton business trips, she knew the appeal of anything exotic or foreign. In
early December she proposed he bring the Stanton managers and
their wives from Hong Kong, Jakarta, Rangoon, Bangkok, Manila,
Delhi and Taipei for a special end-of-the-year meeting.

Brian turned down her idea without mentioning he was up to his
ears with Colin and Ken in the desperate task of containing Adam
Walsh. He already felt like the little Dutch boy with his thumb in
the dike, and the furthest thing from his mind then was a morale-
boosting sales meeting for Far Eastern managers.

But Fionna sat him down on the edge of their bed one night
when he was intent on getting laid. At her most seductive in a
sheer nightgown, she had his full attention. The last thing he
wanted to hear about was business. Placing her palm flat against
his chest, she repeated her idea for bringing in the Asians, and
again he said no.

She told him then about Barbara's discovery of Nora Hallowell,
and Brian said, "Of all the times for that to come up."

"Is that all you have to say?"

"Christ, Fionna . . ." He reached for her but she eluded him.

"Did you know about it?"

"Sure, I knew."

"Why didn't you tell me?"

"Darling, if I reported every one of Ken Fairchild's infidelities we wouldn't have time to talk about anything else."

"This is not just an infidelity," Fionna told him. "It involves the future of Stanton Technologies."

"Ken's done it before and Barbara always forgives him. That's the way they are. He's not going to change."

"Don't you understand what I'm saying?"

He leaned toward her, wanting to spread her legs.

"This *is* different," she said, fending him off. "Barbara's had it. I think the marriage is over. She's so hurt and angry she doesn't know it yet, but that's what's happening."

Again he reached for her, running one hand under her night-gown. She pushed him away and stood up.

"Damn it, Brian! Will you *listen*?"

Anger darkened his expression. "Okay, talk."

"It's finished with the Barbie doll. Done. Since she got a look at his New York tootsie-roll she's been practically catatonic."

That news surprised him. "Where did Barb see her?"

"At the hospital."

"So? Lots of friends came to visit Ken."

"A very popular guy. But how many friends had their pussies massaged while his wife was looking on?"

"You mean he jumped her in the hospital room?"

Fionna shook her head. "He wasn't quite up to that, but he fondled her while poor Barbara watched."

"Barbara saw it?"

"She saw."

Brian got up from the edge of the bed and paced the room, thoughts of making love to Fionna suddenly receding.

"At last I'm getting through to you," she said.

"Who tipped her off?"

"Nobody. She just happened to be visiting."

"Bad luck."

"No, good luck. For you. She's going to divorce him."

"It won't happen."

"Brian, listen to me. I know what I'm talking about. Once she divorces him she'll want him out of the company."

Brian said nothing.

"So you see? That changes the odds."

"She wouldn't divorce Ken just for groping some girl—"

"She's not *some girl*. She's absolutely gorgeous from what I hear, and Ken's paying her rent on a fancy East Side apartment."

"How'd Barbara find all that out?"

"It wasn't difficult. I gave her the number of your private detective and he got the information for her. Petrey."

"You're a regular Helpful Hannah."

"I'm glad you appreciate what I do for you."

"Did Petrey tell her anything else?"

"What else is there?"

"I don't know. Why hasn't she said something to Ken?"

"She'll tell him when she's damn good and ready, and I trust you not to anticipate her by reporting what I've told you. Timing is everything here."

"Suppose Petrey says something to him?"

"Is he likely to?"

"Not necessarily."

"As you see, darling, if Barbara wants Ken out of the company, that narrows the field to either you or Adam Walsh."

Brian said nothing.

"And I intend to see that the board picks you over him, which is why I want you to bring in the Far Eastern managers."

Brian was no longer listening to her words. What Fionna had said changed everything. If it were true and Ken Fairchild suddenly discovered he was going to lose control anyway because of a divorce, what about their plans for Walsh? Ken might even decide to go public himself just to get even with Barbara. No, Brian told himself, he'd never do anything that foolish.

"Well?" Fionna said.

"Well, what?"

"Will you bring them in? It will be the best dinner party of the season. We'll have all the directors and wives. It will show your power, darling. Show that Brian Redfern is obeyed and respected around the world. And we'll give them an exotic little show complete with saris and chem-sans on the eve of the stockholders meeting."

"What the hell," he said, "why not? Does Colin know what's going on with Barbara yet?"

"I'm sure she'll expect him to handle the divorce."

Brian reached for Fionna and cupped her bottom from behind. This time she did not resist.

FIONNA ENJOYED campaigning for Brian and she was good at it. No one yet suspected her real motive because it was still assumed by everyone except Barbara that Ken Fairchild would be taking over the company.

Barbara had not yet confronted him with her knowledge of Nora Hallowell. She told Petrey to continue his investigation.

He said, "There's not a lot more I can find out, Mrs. Fairchild, unless you want pictures."

"I want pictures," Barbara told him firmly.

Fionna, who spent every spare moment with Barbara, said to her one day, "You've got to get your mind on other things, Barb. Stop brooding about him, about Nora Hallowell. Think of your boys, the company. You've got the annual meeting coming up. You're replacing your dad on the board and you'll have to decide how you're going to deal with that."

"I know how I'll deal with it."

"When will you tell him?"

"I don't know."

"But you are going to ask for a divorce?"

"I don't know that either. What does he want most in the world? Her or to be boss of Stanton?"

"It's what you want that counts," Fionna said, and I hope it's Brian, she added to herself.

"No, he'll pay, but I'm not sure about a divorce."

"What do you mean?"

"Getting rid of her without his knowing I did it. You're the one who suggested it."

"Then he'll think he got away with it."

"No. He'll know he didn't if I vote against him at the annual meeting."

It was more than Fionna dared hope for. She had to be careful not to seem too pleased. "God, Barbara, are you sure you want to do that?"

"I don't know, I think so . . ."

"That would be very humiliating for him."

"Not as humiliating as the jumps he's put me through."

"I've never seen you so hostile."

Barbara forced a smile. "Maybe it's about time."

"You're my dearest friend," Fionna said. "Just don't do anything you'll be sorry for."

Tears came into Barbara's eyes. When Fionna put an arm around her and held her, she let go. "*Damn* him, anyway," she said. "If only I didn't know . . ."

Fionna said nothing until she collected herself. "What would I do without you?" she said finally.

"You'd do what's best for you, best for the boys and best for the company. Think positive. If Ken's out, you've got to tell the board who you want in his place."

"I know who."

Fionna held her breath.

"Either Brian or Adam Walsh, I guess," Barbara said. "Right now I don't really care."

Fionna wanted to scream, I care, you silly, selfish bitch. You're trifling with my life. But all she said was, "I know, I know," in a warm motherly tone while her mind searched for a way to guaranty Barbara's vote for Brian.

CHAPTER TWENTY

ONE OF the dubious perks that Colin enjoyed as the senior partner at Cranmer, Fisher & Cleves was membership in the Gansevoort Kaffehuis on Water Street. The Gansevoort is a private club that some say was founded by solid Dutch burghers in 1650. Actually it was started as an expensive joke three hundred years later and simply took the name of the coffeehouse that had once occupied the premises.

Members of the Gansevoort are not called members but "patroons," and membership is limited to one hundred. It is so pricey most of the patroons are embarrassed to reveal the cost. As Colin told Joyce after he was accepted, "Suffice to say, darling, the Internal Revenue Service disallows it as a deduction."

What followed was a good-natured if faintly edged exchange between two people who loved each other.

"Are you really so rich?"

"Richer."

"I'll accept that—"

"Thanks."

"But I'm a little shocked to find out at this late date that my husband is a snob."

"Snob? Me? I come from Bay Ridge, remember?"

"And Harvard," Joyce said, smiling, "and Cranmer, Fisher and Whatnot. Daddy always said there's nothing worse than a convert."

"How would he know?"

"Shall I tell you a secret?"

"Tell me."

"He nearly had a stroke when I told him you'd been invited to join the Gansevoort. He's been waiting thirty years in vain."

But that was the idea. There was no waiting list because membership was by invitation only, and before a new member could enter someone had to die and make room. Money did not guaranty acceptance into the Gansevoort, but one had to be able to afford it.

In forty years no one had ever resigned from the club voluntarily and only two patroons had been asked to leave; one for drunkenly pissing on a potted palm in the entrance hall, and the other after he was convicted of trading in forged stock certificates.

Colin went there several times a week for lunch or dinner—more often since Joyce's illness—usually with a client guest. He visited the barbershop for a monthly trim and tried not to miss the pre-Lenten carnival roast, which was always one of the memorable events of the year. The current chef was an Englishman, but he had been trained in Paris and Switzerland and was paid better than many top executives.

No money changed hands in the Gansevoort and no checks were ever signed. The dues were high enough to cover everything, and if they didn't, the patroons paid a special assessment without question. Was it stuffy? A little. Cigar smoking was allowed. There were billiards, a library and a card room. A fortune in paintings hung on its walls, including some minor Dutch masters, a clever copy or two, and some of the best examples of the Hudson River School. The place was old and dark and male and quiet, except for the bar, which could get very boisterous at lunch. Why did Colin belong? Because he liked good food and cheerful company. And because it meant the boy from Bay Ridge had arrived.

But also because the Gansevoort was unique. When his secretary called ahead on the days Colin was to dine there his favorite dishes were prepared. Belon oysters or beluga caviar. Jellied consommé, steamed clams, corn on the cob, prime ribs, broiled lobster or sometimes even sushi.

A week or so before Christmas Colin invited Brian Redfern for lunch after Brian reported that the first million had been transferred to Adam Walsh's overseas accounts. With that payment there was no turning back. Colin was having an acute crisis of conscience that day. Although he was the one who had urged a settlement as the best solution to a bad situation, now that the reality of it had caught up with him he felt slightly soiled for the first time in his career. He had suggested they meet this time at the club because he could not imagine himself discussing such business in the chambers of Cranmer, Fisher & Cleves. There the gilt-framed portraits of the law firm's founders looked sternly down on each transaction, and Colin knew how those portly Victorian gentlemen would have viewed his solution.

The truth was that he deeply agreed with them, although for the life of him he did not know how else he could have handled things. He had chosen to spend less than fifteen million of company money in order to extricate Stanton from a mess that could cost a hundred million. That was the bottom line, he rationalized, even if the manner of doing it was necessarily unorthodox.

Unorthodox, he repeated to himself as he sat waiting for Redfern. A handy euphemism.

Brian appeared dressed even more conservatively than usual in a dark worsted suit. A discreet red-and-green striped tie was his concession to the holiday season. Not for the first time, Colin thought, he looked more European than American because of his dark longish hair and the cut of his suits. Unlike Colin, who bought most of his clothes off the rack at Moe Ginsberg's, Brian had his suits tailored in Rome or Milan.

Also unlike Colin, who had grown up half a step removed from a blue-collar background, Brian came from a relentlessly middle-class family in a blighted Boston suburb. His goal was to rise to the ranks of the rich and the social upper crust. A clever man who saw the main chance and took it, with the help of such elite citadels as M.I.T. and the Harvard Business School, his capacity for work was exceeded only by his ambition and his love of intrigue.

As a boy Brian suffered because he was small and skinny. He was the last one to be chosen for any team, the cull no one wanted. "Christ, not Redfern!" was a lament he had heard since he was seven. And they were right. He flubbed grounders, couldn't throw to home plate and was an easy strike-out. But he had a memory like a Cray computer and by the time he got to junior high school it began to serve him well.

"Hey, Redfern, what's the capital of Kentucky?"

"Frankfort!"

"I told you it wasn't fucking Nashville."

"Hey, Redfern, who invented rabies?"

"The cure for it was discovered by Pasteur."

"Right, same guy invented milk."

"Hey, Redfern, who's the all-time home-run hitter?"

Someone always shouted, "Babe Ruth."

"Hey, I'm asking Redfern because he knows."

"Hank Aaron with seven fifty-five."

"Hey Redfern . . ." His memory made him a reputation and put him at the head of his class. A poor athlete, he became a sports authority in high school who managed the football and basketball teams, which jobs gave him his first taste of power through service, no matter how hard or long the work.

On a scholarship to M.I.T. at seventeen he suddenly shot up to his full height, learned tennis and discovered that women found him attractive as well as interesting. The cheeky young brain who would impress Avery Stanton was on his way, and the rest, as they say, was history—which Colin knew, at least superficially, very well.

"How's Joyce?" Brian said as he sat down now. "Any change?"

"None, I'm afraid."

"I'm sorry."

"At least she doesn't seem to be in much pain," Colin said. "She's pretty heavily sedated most of the time."

"The chemotherapy isn't helping?"

"The side-effects were so bad she refused to go on with it. She told the doctor that the stupid disease had already taken forever and she saw no reason to stretch it out any more. She has a hundred times more guts than . . ." What could he say?

"It must be terrible for you, Colin."

"It's terrible for her. What would you like to drink? I'm having a vodka martini."

"I'll join you." He made a face. "I've been drinking tea all morning with our Far Eastern managers and their wives."

"Isn't that a little unusual," Colin asked, "bringing your overseas people in just before the holidays?"

"I've got to stroke these guys a little," he said, "so they don't ask too many questions about the money we're planning to borrow from their operations. Some are very sharp."

"Borrow" . . . another euphemism, Colin thought. "Will we be able to make the second payment to Walsh before the stockholders meeting?"

"I was hoping you might stall him."

"He thinks we're stalling now."

"I need time to set the whole thing up properly. Moving that much money without attracting attention isn't easy."

"What kind of problems are you having?"

"Paper trails. My signature is on too many authorizations because of the hurry on his first payment. I had to transfer half a million from Stanton International to a personal account I keep at Credit Suisse. Now I've got to do it again before I can get that money off other foreign accounts and put it back. I can manage it, but it's sloppy and I don't like it. Unless I return the funds pretty fast some middle-level clerk in accounting is bound to pick it up and ask questions."

They discussed this problem for the hundredth time since Walsh had presented his demands, then lapsed into silence and sipped their drinks.

The Gansevoort bar is a friendly place and Colin knew most of the men in it and a couple of the women. Guests were always welcome accompanied by a member, and on any given weekday the place became comfortably full shortly after noon. Several friends stopped by to ask after Joyce, and Jim Chapin, a partner in a major Wall Street brokerage, congratulated Colin on Adam Walsh's speech before the securities analysts.

"The word is out on the street that Walsh could be the new CEO over at Stanton," Chapin said. "Any truth in it?"

"I'm the last one to ask," Colin told him.

"Come on, Colin. If you don't know, who does?"

"I didn't say I didn't know. I said don't ask me."

Chapin laughed heartily and turned to his friend, a luncheon guest like Brian Redfern. "That's Colin Draggett for you. You want caution, prudence and circumspection you'll get it from Colin. That's why he heads the best law firm in town."

"Compliments will get you nowhere," Colin said.

Chapin replied, "Colin, you don't know Adam Walsh like Edgar does. They were at college together." He introduced the man with him as Edgar O'Connell, and Redfern and Colin exchanged glances of surprise.

Brian said, "You're Princeton?"

O'Connell nodded. He was a tall, heavyset man about fifty, with a broad, open Irish face, a linebacker gone to fat.

"Have you seen him much since then?" Brian asked.

O'Connell smiled. "Enough to know if Stanton doesn't put him in charge, one of your competitors probably will."

"We don't have competitors, Mr. O'Connell," Brian said smoothly. "Only a few friendly rivals."

"Brian heads Stanton International," Colin put in.

"Hell of a record your company's racked up," Jim Chapin added, "and great growth potential if you can maintain the momentum without Avery Stanton."

"We intend to," Brian replied.

Chapin turned to Colin. "I don't mind saying we've put the company at the top of our preferred industrial list since Walsh's talk and we are strongly recommending purchase of Stanton common to our institutional investors."

"I'd join the Stanton fan club myself," Edgar O'Connell told them, "except for a slight conflict of interest."

"I'm glad you approve of what we're doing," Brian said.

"But why the conflict of interest?" Colin asked him.

"I'm a cop," O'Connell said, and everybody laughed.

"Edgar's a special investigator with the SEC," Chapin explained.

O'Connell nodded. "So I have to be careful whose stock I favor and whose bonds I buy."

"Would you believe U.S. Treasury?" Chapin said.

"So you're Princeton?" Brian said again. "Well, you're outclassed here by two Harvards." He indicated Colin and himself.

"Poor old Walsh," O'Connell said. "How did he ever fall into such bad company?"

"Don't worry about Adam," Chapin said. "He had that bunch the other night eating out of his hand."

"He's a very persuasive talker," Colin agreed.

"Were you the same class at Princeton?" Brian asked.

"Adam was three years behind me," O'Connell replied, "and normally I wouldn't have remembered him. You know how that is."

"But you did, obviously."

"To tell the truth I remembered his car more than I did Adam. He had the only 1947 Chrysler convertible on campus. One of those fluid-drive cockwagons with the varnished wooden body, white fenders, leather seats and lots of chrome."

"Before my time," Colin said.

"Before mine, too," O'Connell commented. "I'm talking early sixties. The car was already a classic when Adam had it."

"Was he a golfer in those days?" Colin asked him.

"Oh, sure."

"When did you run into him again?"

"Three or four years ago at a Princeton reunion."

"Did you recognize each other right away?"

"People change a lot after twenty-five years. Lose their hair, put on weight, you know?" He patted his ample paunch.

"I've run into people who remembered me," Brian said, "when I couldn't remember them to save my life."

"Oh, I remembered Adam, all right."

"Really?"

"Did he recognize you, too?" Colin asked.

"Not at first."

Again Brian and Colin exchanged glances.

"You know how it is. After I reminded him of a couple of things. The car. A girl we knew in common. It all clicked."

The waiter signaled Colin that his table was prepared and reluctantly he and Brian finished their drinks and shook hands with Jim Chapin and his friend O'Connell, who said, "Give Adam my best." They left the cozy dimness of the paneled bar and moved to the dining room, where two platters of belons on the half-shell waited.

Brian sat brooding while Colin told the waiter to bring a bottle of Montrachet Meursault '75 from his private stock. That was another advantage to the Gansevoort. Apart from the wine the club laid down every year, each member could keep his own cellar.

The waiter brought a little plate of oyster crackers and a bowl of crudités as the dining room filled up. After they began to eat, Colin finally said to Brian, "Is there something I missed? I have that feeling."

"No. You heard it all."

"That's what I was afraid of."

"How do you read that guy O'Connell?"

"Oh, it's simple," Colin said with a half-smile. "They're all in it together. Walsh, his wife, Jim Chapin and the SEC guy. Collusion, I believe you once said."

"All right, I take it back. I can't make any more sense out of this than you can."

"I'm sorry to hear that because I am more in the dark now than ever. If I didn't know better, if Walsh had not admitted it himself, and if I had not seen his photograph in a prison file on the warden's desk, I would assume a terrible mistake had been made."

"No mistake," Brian said. "At least we're sure about *that.*"

"Then explain the wife and O'Connell *both* knowing him."

"I can't, Colin."

The waiter came to say that Colin had a telephone call. It was urgent or he would not have been disturbed. "Neither can I," Colin said as he got up, "but by God, somebody better find a rational explanation before this is over."

He took the call in a private booth adjacent to the bar because the club rules forbid receiving calls in the dining room.

"Mr. Draggett?"

"Speaking."

"I'm Dominic Petrey, Mr. Draggett. Sorry to bother you but I'm looking for Mr. Redfern. Is he with you?"

"He is."

"Can I talk to him, if it's not too much trouble?"

"We're having lunch right now, Mr. Petrey. Can you call later or leave a number where he can call you back?"

"My office. But can you give him a message?"

"Certainly."

"Tell him that a Mr. Quirk called me looking for him. Said he's under arrest and needs bail. Seems he's got a little drug problem."

"Mr. Quirk. I'll tell him."

——— CHAPTER TWENTY-ONE ———

COLIN RETURNED to the table just as his grilled swordfish arrived, wondering whose side everybody was on. The waiter poured another glass of the Meursault while he picked up his napkin and began to eat. He did not resume their conversation.

"Not bad news, I hope," Brian said.

After years of negotiating disputes involving hundreds of millions of dollars, Colin was adept at disguising his feelings. The inscrutable Colin Draggett; the cool, poker-faced dealmaker who could always manage to look the same whether he was outraged, angry, victimized, bamboozled or just so pleased with himself he wanted to dance on top of the conference table. He had also cultivated an irritating—especially to his adversaries—noncommittal smile to mask victories and defeats alike, which he now used on Brian Redfern.

"Having more labor problems in England?" Colin asked.

"No, why?"

"Mr. Quirk."

"Ollie Quirk?" Brian laughed a little too quickly. "A real character. What made you think of him?"

"Heard from him lately?"

"As a matter of fact, no." He looked up when Colin said nothing further and watched him as he continued taking his time with every bite of fish and every sip of the wine. Brian was surely no fool but at times his perceptions were somewhat slow getting through the filter of his ego. Eventually he put the correct interpretation on Colin's silence and said, "That was him just now on the phone, wasn't it?"

"Indirectly."

"I see."

"No, you don't see. If you did, we wouldn't be having this conversation. I thought we were working the same side of the street in this thing, Brian."

"We are, Colin."

"Where does Mr. Quirk fit in?"

"He doesn't really. I mean—"

"Don't bullshit me, Brian."

"Look, Ken and I had an idea about using him but—"

"Why wasn't I told?"

"Colin, nothing—"

"Think before you answer me. Don't make it worse. Either we're honest with each other or we multiply the risks and problem tenfold. I'll ask again. Why wasn't I told?"

"Nothing's happened."

"That's where you're wrong. Your man Quirk's in jail."

"Oh, goddamn. Where?"

"Here in New York."

"But . . . ?"

"On a narcotics charge, it seems. Apparently he used his one telephone call to get in touch with Petrey, who called here looking for you and got me. Why don't you tell me what's going on, Brian?"

Redfern's normal coloring was a little sallow, contrasting pleasantly with lustrous black hair and dark eyebrows, but now he turned pale, and his thin features suddenly seemed pinched and drawn.

"We didn't tell you because you'd torpedo our idea at the start. We wanted to save the company the millions that bastard's trying to extort from us. We all agreed we'd be damned if we'd pay it—"

"Wrong. We agreed it was extortionate. We agreed it was outrageous. But we also agreed to pay."

"Well, Ken and I talked after that."

"And changed the drill."

"We thought, well, we decided to exhaust all our options before we'd give him another damned cent."

"Go on."

"Colin, I'm sorry, but we didn't think you'd understand."

"A moment ago you said you were afraid I'd veto your project. How could I do that if I didn't understand it?"

"You know what I'm saying."

"What was this wonderful idea, by the way?"

When Brian told him at last, Colin had to restrain showing relief that it wasn't worse. After all Redfern's squirming, Colin half-expected him to say they had brought Quirk over from England to kill Adam Walsh rather than rough him up. That he could even consider such a notion showed him how anger and frustration had affected him. To the point of wondering, now that money had actually changed hands, about the wisdom of their original course. What *would* have happened if they had all laughed in Adam Walsh's face and said, "You're a fake, you're a crook, and you're under arrest for embezzling two million dollars of company money!"? Why hadn't he followed his long-time habit of absolute honesty? Except that the danger had seemed real, and it still was, and the need to pay off the man had overshadowed the means they would use to do it. In a real sense, he reminded himself, they were only authorizing the expenditure of funds to defend the company, even if they were doing it illicitly.

Did it matter that he was against the absurd idea of intimidating Adam Walsh with a physical beating? He consorted with those who seemed willing to use violence, and he was as anxious to get rid of Walsh as they were. If he preferred the non-violent solution of paying Walsh off with money taken from Stanton Technologies and sent to overseas accounts, didn't that make him as culpable as those who wanted to rough the man up?

At war with his conscience, Colin also reminded himself that he was not motivated by greed or fear alone. From the beginning he wanted what was best for the company he had helped to found, and this more than anything guided his actions. But being his own severest critic, he also recognized that Colin Draggett, legal counsel and company conscience, was quite possibly wrong and guilty of . . . what, he wasn't sure because he had to be convinced that even if they were doing something illegal he had made a moral choice—done the wrong thing for the right reasons. It helped a little to remind himself of that. A little . . .

Brian was careful to confide only the bare details of his approach to Quirk. The cracks and crevices that counted so much against him later were recounted by others after tragedy brought the chain of events to a sudden halt. What Brian said was that he hired Quirk because "for a very small investment we could scare off Walsh." And while Colin was trying to follow Redfern's reasoning behind this latest blunder and instill some caution in the younger man,

Brian's nimble mind was already leapfrogging ahead to explore ever more violent courses of action.

There was, though, the immediate problem of Quirk, and Brian asked how he should handle it from a legal point of view.

"Handle nothing. Stay away from the man. You don't know him, never heard of him. Forget all about him."

"But I can't very well leave him in the lurch."

"I'll get him a good criminal lawyer, and you should hope that appeases him."

"I don't know what to say, Colin."

"Just cut out the surprises. I'll try to stall Adam to give you time to organize his payments, but *do* it!"

"I'm really sorry about Quirk." He looked at his watch.

"Sorry what? That you hired him or that he got arrested?"

"Sorry. Honestly."

"Let's drop it. Leave Petrey to me. And anybody else you may have been in touch with on this matter."

Brian nodded resignedly, all contrition.

They parted in front of the Gansevoort and went their separate ways. Just how separate they were Colin could not even imagine at that moment. It was nearly four in the afternoon and after he called his colleague Wally Scott to take on Quirk's case, Colin had no other pressing matters at the office. He needed a long walk to help him think.

As he set off north toward home, his mind turned back over the last few hours. The SEC man's college friendship with Adam Walsh puzzled him as much as Redfern's revelation shocked him.

Yet the mystery of Adam Walsh's time at Princeton with O'Connell had to have a rational explanation. Could Colin afford to ignore it for the moment? He hoped so. Priorities had not changed since the day Stanton dropped dead. The vital need still was to get Walsh out quietly. And like it or not, Colin had to persuade him the money would be forthcoming within a reasonable period.

When he reached home the nurse said Joyce was sleeping after one of her bad days with respiratory problems. She was heavily sedated when he looked in on her, the one uncomplaining person who asked for nothing from life except to get it over with. Colin closed the door and retreated to the small library, where he poured himself a drink. He sat alone, recalling happier days when

Joyce would make the drinks for them both and sit across from him waiting to hear about his day. How he missed her!

Colin's love affair with his wife had begun almost twenty years earlier. He was still a novice at the practice of law but he had attracted wide attention by a big upset win in a major utility-rates case. The *Wall Street Journal* wanted to do a story about Draggett, *l'Enfant Terrible,* and the reporter they sent was Joyce. He was so surprised to see a woman financial writer that he invited her to lunch, and lunch turned into a long, lazy afternoon of talk.

She was bright, sassy, pretty and delightful. But when he asked her out a few days later she turned him down. He tried again and she turned him down again. When he asked why, she said she was sort of engaged. By that time, Colin was sort of in love.

"Engaged to be married?"

"That's the idea. We've been going out for two years."

He said, "Then it's not serious," which made her laugh.

"How do you know?"

"Have dinner with me Friday and I'll explain."

"I won't be here Friday. I'm going to Europe."

"With him?"

"With my father."

"Then we'll have dinner in Europe."

"Why not," she said flippantly, playing along. "I'll be at the Danieli in Venice."

"I'll pick you up. About eight, okay?"

"Really, Colin, you're too much."

She flew off to Europe and he thought about her day and night. Then prudent Colin Draggett, careful Colin Draggett, the man who always looked before he leaped, booked a flight to Milan with a connection to Venice arriving Friday afternoon.

When he called her hotel room as soon as he arrived she laughed, thinking he was telephoning from New York. "Ready?" he said.

"You really are crazy."

"If I'm not mistaken we have a dinner date."

"But I'm here and you're there."

"Wrong. I'm here. Downstairs in the lobby."

He could still hear her reaction over all the years, a small cry of delighted disbelief. "You can't be serious!"

"That's the whole point, lady. I have just crossed a very wide ocean to prove how serious I am."

Within three weeks the fiancé was history and Colin had asked her to marry him. Joyce said she'd think about it while she was on an assignment in Washington and told him not to call her there. When days passed and he did not hear from her, his nerves were shredded. Then Joyce's father telephoned and invited Colin to lunch. The older man was a banker, Harvard like Colin, and loved his daughter. But there the similarity between them ended. Over lunch he trotted out some of the reasons why he thought marriage between Joyce and Colin was a bad idea.

"Difference in religion," he said.

"I'm not religious," Colin replied.

"You know what I mean. We're Episcopalians. Difference in age. Joyce is only twenty-three and you're . . ."

"Twenty-eight."

"Difference financially. Joyce has money of her own."

"My share of the fees on that utility case came to nearly a million dollars. Joyce won't starve, sir." Colin did not mention that every penny was already tied up in Avery Stanton's new company.

"She's always been protected."

"I'll protect her."

"I'm advising her against doing this."

"As her father, that's your privilege. I'm advising her in favor. In fact, I'm urging her to do it as soon as possible."

When he stood up to leave, Colin felt as if someone should have said, "Shake hands, go to your corners and come out fighting."

Joyce dropped by his apartment that same evening and with a long, serious face said, "I just had a talk with my father. He told me there are quite a few reasons why I shouldn't marry you, Colin."

"He let me in on most of them, too."

"I just came by to tell you." Still the long face.

"Tell me what?" he said, sure now she was going to turn him down and not knowing what other arguments he could present.

"To tell you yes," she said as a smile broke through and made his heart leap. He took her in his arms then, and in a sense, he had never really let her go.

On their honeymoon, when he said he guessed his stunt of following her to Venice had done the trick, she shook her head. "It made it easier, but I'd already made up my mind I wanted you."

"Really?"

"I had to play my cards carefully. I knew you wouldn't be an easy man to catch."

"*You* were trying to catch *me*?"

"Yup."

"So I could have saved myself the cost of the trip."

"If you'd done that," she said with her special logic, "you wouldn't have been the man I was after, would you?"

They were married and planned to have a family until doctors said she couldn't. Thus began an odyssey from New York to London to Geneva in search of an obstetrical magician as they followed up every new scientific development in the fertility field. Finally Joyce was forced to accept her barrenness as fact. They considered adoption but never seemed to find the right baby or the right legal circumstance. She was even willing to consider one of the radical new rent-a-womb arrangements, where Colin's sperm fertilized another woman's egg so the child would be at least half theirs. But he thought that was going too far so they settled into their childless lives, quite happy most of the time, at least with each other.

Joyce quit the *Wall Street Journal* to free-lance successfully as a magazine writer while Colin's law practice flourished. By chance rather than design they soon became the classic, busy, career-oriented modern couple.

As a student at Harvard Colin had learned to sail on the Charles River, and when he began to prosper he bought the first of several sailboats. Joyce loved sailing, too, and was skillful at the helm. It was on board their boat only three summers earlier that her first symptoms had appeared, the chronic fatigue and malaise that no rest or medicine could cure.

Muscular dystrophy was misdiagnosed and then thyrotoxicosis before the doctors finally agreed on myasthenia gravis. Then came the endless cycles of treatment, remission, hope and relief until the cancer arrived and ultimately took over.

As long as his days were active and busy, Colin could cope, serious though his problems were. But these twilight hours at home were hard. He sighed heavily as he thought of her now, his poor wasted love. The void Joyce left pained him so sharply he often felt there wasn't room in his heart anymore to hold so much sadness.

Cranmer, Fisher & Cleves wasn't closed yet so he called Maggie and listened while she brought him up to date. The messages included a call from Barbara Fairchild that he assumed meant she had some question about one of her father's bequests.

But Maggie said, "She wants you to call her back at the Ritz Tower no matter what time."

"Did she say what was so urgent?"

"No, but she was quite definite about calling her."

It was not quite six when he rang Barbara's apartment and she was out. Half an hour later she called back, apologized for bothering him, and asked if he could please come over.

"Can't it wait until tomorrow?"

"I suppose it can. But unless you have something terribly important, Colin, I'd really like to see you tonight."

"Okay, my dear. I'll buy you dinner. Personal problem or a legal one that can't wait?"

"A little of both," she said. "I'm leaving Ken."

CHAPTER TWENTY-TWO

COLIN WAS putting on his coat to leave when the night nurse said, "She's awake, Mr. Draggett. I told her you were here."

He entered the sickroom. It was actually the dining room of the apartment, which he had converted into as pleasant and comfortable an environment as possible, replete with hospital bed, oxygen tanks, IV bottles and tubes, and all the other depressing paraphernalia of the gravely ill.

Joyce was forty-one and they had been married almost eighteen years. It seemed to him especially unfortunate now that she had been unable to have children. Perhaps if there had been a grown son or daughter around the dreadful business of dying would have seemed a little less unfair to her.

"You look tired," were her first words to him.

"It's the bad light. I'm fine."

"Where are you off to?"

"Taking Barbara to dinner."

"How is she?"

"All right, I guess."

"Trouble with Ken again?"

"She says she's leaving him."

"You think she will?"

"She's been through it all before. I don't know. It depends on the circumstances, I guess."

"And what are the circumstances?"

"That's what she's going to tell me over dinner."

"Some wonderfully helpful friend probably brought her chapter and verse of Ken's latest seduction."

"I get the impression it's more serious than that."

"You think he got someone pregnant again?"

"I have no idea, darling, but whatever happened, Barbara seems to have reached a major decision."

"Do you think she loves him, Colin?"

"Well, he's a successful executive, he's handsome, a former All-American quarterback and a decorated army officer."

"Oh, Colin! Those things mean nothing to a woman."

"All-American means nothing?"

She began to laugh and immediately he was sorry he'd said anything to provoke it. As much as Colin liked to cheer her up, laughter invariably precipitated coughing spells because of the tumor that was slowly strangling her. The nurse came and it was several minutes before Joyce was breathing normally again but too weak to speak. She could only smile at him and shake her head.

Colin was not a demonstrative man, having learned from his mother at an early age to submerge any real feelings or see them thrown back in his face. Joyce had changed all that. If the passion of their early relationship had waned, the love he felt was as strong as ever. He wanted to give her his strength, his own exuberant health by transfusion, osmosis, IV, whatever. And he couldn't. He could only sit there and watch her die a little each day.

"Don't be sad, Colin," she would say. "I hate seeing you sad and I hate being the cause of it. I'm sorry, I really am."

And as likely as not his own tears would come as he took her in his arms, and she would wind up comforting *him,* patting his shoulders and crooning, "It's all right, it's all right, my love. It's going to be all right."

But for Colin it wasn't all right and it would never be all right again. As he saw the pain increase and the once-beautiful body become matchstick thin, her skin translucent, her lovely hair matted and thinned by the awful chemicals, he wished her dead. He would hold her and say to himself, "Die, die, die, my darling!" and then wonder if he'd said it aloud, if she'd heard him.

But it didn't matter. She could always read his mind.

Her lips formed the words "I love you" before he left that evening, but no sound came because that day's strength was gone.

Eighteen years together, the last few grim and full of foreboding as the disease gained a hold on her like some ghoulish rival for Colin's affections. The parade of specialists were as helpless as the patient, and modern science was unable to offer more than nostrums and palliatives, a stall for time.

One day she said, "All of a sudden I understand the value of quacks and holy shrines and miracle cures, Colin. If I found one that worked, I could become the whackiest disciple of all. If eating organic food or saying a mantra or praying to a saint's bones would cure me, I would do them all together."

Mrs. Ryan, the night nurse, said to her, "But surely you believe in God, Mrs. Draggett. He is there, you know, for all of us."

"Oh, I believe in him," she said honestly enough, "I just don't think he's very nice."

Mrs. Ryan was a rather fat woman in her forties, with shiny brown skin and gray hair, whose white nylon pantsuits always seemed two sizes too small. She smiled up at Colin as he was leaving and offered him a chocolate from a box his secretary had sent her. She adored chocolates and Colin made sure she had a steady supply.

She was a knitter, a regular knitting factory in fact, turning out one small sweater after another as she sat before the television set in the hall outside Joyce Draggett's sickroom. When Colin hired her, she told him she was widowed and had a grown son who was a doctor in the army. In the beginning Colin wondered whether she sold her sweaters or was laying them up for a legion of unborn grandchildren. When Joyce told him that Mrs. Ryan gave the sweaters to homeless children looked after by her church in a Harlem settlement house, he told Maggie Caruso to see that her supply of wool kept pace with her chocolates.

"Have a nice evening, Mr. Draggett," she said, needles clicking away, a cheerful smile on her round porcelain face.

"Mrs. Ryan, you have the number where I'll be."

"She'll sleep the night now, no fear."

When Mrs. Ryan first came to work she told Colin she did not mind caring for a dying patient, except children, who were simply too heartbreaking. In fact, she said, she much preferred terminally ill patients to chronic invalids. The latter tended to become demanding and unreasonable and only rarely gave a nurse any satisfaction.

She was also deeply religious, but no prude. Colin especially enjoyed her bawdy sense of humor. She had seen her share of pain and grief in thirty years of nursing. She told him if she could make some sufferer's last days a little lighter, the nights a little easier, she considered it a God-sent opportunity. She sounded too good to be true, and he watched her the first few weeks to spot the flaw, to find her out. But she had been in the house over a year by then, and if she had a defect other than her insatiable appetite for chocolates, Colin had yet to see it.

As he walked down 57th Street toward Fifth Avenue in search of a taxi, Colin thought about life's inequities . . . An ex-jailbird was about to become a multimillionaire while Avery Stanton moldered in his grave. Gentle, loving Joyce lay dying while his shrewish old mother flourished on her bile like some vengeful fury. Mrs. Ryan knit her sweaters for what Maggie Caruso called "some very lucky children." Lucky to be homeless in Harlem?

And what about Colin Draggett, and his temporizing, rationalizing and justifying? What had happened to the young man who only wanted to make his fortune in order to do good in the world? Was the youthful idealist gone, or going? He wanted to think his own moral sense remained intact, even with the years of compromise and negotiation. But they had taken their toll.

Redfern and Fairchild's delusions made him shake his head. Two grown business executives plotting to frighten off a third. Talk about blind ambition. Which made him think of Ken Fairchild's being beaten up in the middle of Harlem. What was Fairchild really doing there? He had said he was visiting his friend from Vietnam days. Only now did Colin wonder about it, after Brian had confessed to the business with Quirk.

A talk with Fairchild's army friend might be a good idea. Colin had his number and made a note to call him. Luther Yancy, retired sergeant.

And Barbara? What should he tell her? Don't leave your husband? Find a marriage counselor? Stick by your man?

Or shoot him? Divorce him? Take his children away from him? Throw him out of the company? Send him packing?

Except who was he to be handing out advice anyway?

___CHAPTER TWENTY-THREE___

AFTER HIS memorable lunch at the Gansevoort with Colin, Brian Redfern telephoned Ken Fairchild at Stanton's New London headquarters and briefed him on Petrey's message, Quirk's arrest and Colin's angry reaction.

Ken agreed they should meet as soon as possible and said he would come to New York that evening. With Quirk in jail, he assumed it would now be necessary to fall back on Luther Yancy.

Brian objected. "We've got to talk first. Don't call Yancy or anyone. I'll meet you at the club bar in two hours."

"How will you do that, fly?"

"Right. In the Porsche."

Redfern wasn't far off on his time estimate. He drove the hundred and twenty miles from downtown Manhattan in two hours and ten minutes, miraculously missing a state police radar trap in Madison because the officer was on a coffee break.

He coasted into the parking lot of the Thames River Golf and Canoe Club at five-thirty, just as it got dark. A few hardy souls who had braved the frigid afternoon to play a round of golf were coming off the links. Others from Stanton Technologies were noisily congregating around the bar, where a large calendar read, "Only 14 More Drinking Days Until Christmas!"

The company controller saw Redfern and reached his elbow before he could join Ken Fairchild. "Just the man I want to see," he said. "Your girl said you were in New York."

"Just got back."

"What are you drinking?"

Brian signaled the bartender. "Dewars on the rocks."

"Maybe you can clear up a great mystery," the man said. His name was Barry Parks, a Wharton School accountant in his forties who wore rimless glasses and a fixed rictus of a smile that masked his total lack of humor.

"Anything to help," Brian said, edging away from him and scanning the room for Ken Fairchild.

"You know we're doing an audit of Stanton International."

"No, I didn't know it." Brian gave the man his full attention. "Why wasn't I told?"

Parks shrugged apologetically, his dead, deadly smile firmly in place. "That's not up to me, you know. Although I assumed Ave Stanton would have said something before he died."

Brian's mind was racing. An audit, for God's sake! That was the worst possible thing that could happen at this time!

"Ave wanted it finished before the stockholders meeting so I called in Booz, Hamilton because I don't have enough staff."

"So what's the problem, Barry?" Brian said, knowing exactly what the problem was and desperately wondering how in God's name he'd ever explain it.

Tact was not among the controller's virtues. "You've authorized the transfer of over half a million dollars cash to private overseas accounts in your name recently," he said, still smiling, "and I find no explanation for the transfers. Got to have something in writing, Brian, over your signature, or those monies go down as overdue accounts receivable."

Redfern rested one hand on Parks' shoulder, leaned toward his ear and told him gravely, "Barry, this is between us, but on my last trip to Albania I took a beating at the casino and had to pay with company money. The rest I invested in a Guatemalan whorehouse and a Polish crack factory." He patted Parks on the back. "Don't worry. As soon as they begin to show a profit I'll put it all back."

The smile had vanished and Parks began to sputter, his pasty, freckled complexion growing paler by the moment. Then the smile bloomed again, hesitantly at first, as he said, "Oh, I get it! You're pulling my leg. Guatemalan whorehouse, ha!"

"Why don't we talk about this tomorrow?" Brian said. "I'll tell you where and why the money had to be moved, and your people can get all their numbers lined up properly."

"I'm really concerned about it," Parks said. "I know there must be some perfectly ordinary explanation but . . ."

Brian started to move across the room to where he saw Ken Fairchild sitting with one of the prettier Stanton secretaries, but Parks followed him, one hand at his sleeve. "There is some perfectly ordinary explanation, isn't there?"

"Naturally."

"I knew it," Parks said with relief.

Redfern turned to him with a reassuring smile. "What do you think, Larry? That I spent it all on my Chinese mistress?"

"It's Barry."

"Right. *Barry.*"

Parks looked around to see if anyone had heard. "You shouldn't joke about things like that."

"Things like what? The mistress or the money?"

"You're pulling my leg again, right?"

Brian gave him a pat, winked and said, "Barry, if I were stealing I'd hardly send funds to my own name . . ."

Parks looked shocked. "I didn't mean to imply anything irregular. It's only that with an audit, you know . . ."

' "Call me in the morning, okay? And we'll sort it out."

"It's a lot of money," Parks said.

"I'm aware of that."

"First thing tomorrow?"

"I'm in before eight," Brian said, and left Parks standing alone in the middle of the room. He joined Fairchild, pulling up a chair between Ken and the secretary, acknowledging the girl with a nod.

Fairchild suggested he'd talk to her later "about that matter."

She shrugged, picked up her purse, and moved off.

"Ever think about if Barbara caught you *en flagrante?*" Brian said.

"It's happened. Hysterics. Run to Daddy. Reconciliation. End of crisis."

"No more Daddy now."

"She's got Colin instead. You say he was upset?"

"To put it mildly."

"That stupid Petrey."

"I imagine he thought he was being helpful."

"What the hell happened with your Englishman anyway?"

Redfern shook out a cigarette and lit it. "He was arrested on a drug charge."

"I don't understand."

"Neither do I. He was supposed to get on a plane and come directly here with two others. Contact me through Petrey."

"Where are the other two?"

"No idea."

"Meanwhile Adam Walsh goes his merry way."

"Exactly."

"What now?" Fairchild asked.

"I've got to get to Quirk and find out what happened before we can do anything. Colin was sending him a lawyer."

"Let Petrey go see him," Fairchild said. "Colin is right. You don't want to be seen talking to Quirk."

"He's not the only problem at the moment."

"What else?"

Brian told him about Barry Parks and the audit. "Apparently it was an order Ave Stanton gave just before he died. Makes sense. He wanted all the company accounts double-checked before the annual stockholders meeting."

"But why?"

"If I had to guess, I'd say he did it right after he found out about Walsh, and wanted his own damage assessment."

"What will you tell Parks?"

"I don't know yet. Any ideas?"

"Not really."

"You're a great help in my moment of need," Brian said.

"Didn't Colin have any suggestions?"

"I told you, Parks just this minute told me. Colin will have a stroke when he hears about it."

"But he'll know what to do," Ken said.

"Parks wants to cover his ass with a memo from me explaining what the transfers were for. What do you suggest I say?"

"Let's call Colin now."

"He will have already left his office."

"Call his house. With Joyce in her condition he doesn't go far."

Brian motioned to a waiter to bring a telephone to their table and in a minute was speaking to the night nurse, Mrs. Ryan.

"He isn't in. Who's calling?"

"Can you tell me where he is? It's urgent."

"I have a number where you can reach him. Just a minute." She read the number, he thanked her and hung up.

"He's at this number," Brian said, reading it out. "Maybe our proper counsel has something going on the side." He smiled at the unlikelihood of that.

Ken reached for the telephone. "That's Barbara's number."

"What's Barbara doing in New York? I thought she didn't like the City."

"Christmas shopping." Or so she said.

Ken dialed but the line was busy. "I'll try again in a couple of minutes," he said uneasily, putting down the telephone.

_____ CHAPTER TWENTY-FOUR _____

"DAMN THAT man," Colin heard Fionna Redfern say as she hung up the telephone and ran to open the door for him at Barbara's Ritz Tower apartment. "Oh, hello, Colin." A warm kiss, the fleeting pressure of a breast and a whiff of perfume. She wore a gold lamé evening skirt and a black silk blouse. The skirt was ankle length but slit nearly to the hip, showing one leg in a provocative way when she walked.

"What man?" he asked her, but she only grimaced.

Barbara appeared after a moment, in sharp contrast to her friend. She wore a plaid quilted robe, no make-up and her hair carelessly tied back in a ponytail. Her eyes were puffy and red but her jaw was set firmly as she poured them each a drink.

Colin raised his glass and asked Fionna. "Out on the town?" When she smiled and nodded, he added lightly, "I won't tell."

"Brian was supposed to meet me at the Dorset an hour ago. We're giving a little welcome party for all his Far Eastern managers and their wives. And now he'll be late, late, late."

"What happened?"

"The usual. Sudden meetings at the plant. Colin, what could be more urgent than seeing his managers after bringing them from the other side of the world?"

"Brian went up to New London?"

"This afternoon while I was at the hairdresser's."

"He didn't mention it at lunch," Colin said, wondering what the devil Redfern was up to now.

"He should be twins. He's so stressed out lately, he doesn't know whether he's coming or going. And I can't find out why."

Better you don't, Colin thought, but said, "A lot of pressure builds in any company at the end of the year, Fionna. And this year, losing Avery has made it tougher on all the Stanton executives."

"I know one who seems to be weathering it nicely," Barbara said. "No stress at all where he's concerned."

Fionna gave Colin a meaningful look as she hugged Barbara to her for an instant and said, "Don't let it get you down, darling. Colin, you're coming to the dinner for the directors tomorrow night? It's going to be Indonesian food. You do like Indonesian?"

"It's my favorite."

"And bring Barbara. She'll only come if you do."

"I told you I wasn't sure," Barbara said.

"Colin, convince her."

"I'll do my best."

"I've got to hurry or I'll be late," Fionna told them.

"You look gorgeous," Barbara said.

"Except for these trashy earrings." She touched her ears. "I meant to pick up some junk at Bergdorf's today but no time."

"Take my emeralds," Barbara said.

"Oh, no, darling! Suppose I lost one?"

"Wear them, silly. They're insured."

"Still, the sentimental value," Fionna said.

"That's a joke. Ken gave them to me on our first anniversary."

The jewelry change was made, and after taking a moment to retouch herself in the mirror, Fionna kissed them both, snatched up her coat and swept out of the apartment. After the door had closed, Barbara said, "Do you mind if we don't go out to eat?"

"Not at all, if you don't want to. But maybe it would do you good. I thought we might go to Twenty-one."

She smiled. "Oh, Colin, remember how you and Joyce used to take me there? One day John Glenn, Lauren Bacall and Billie Jean King were all having lunch in the same room with us!"

"Those were special times, Barbara."

"Having a gawky kid with you? I don't believe it."

"Believe it."

She got up from the sofa and lit a cigarette, but when she tried to inhale she was seized with a fit of coughing.

"Since when did you become a smoker?"

"Damn, I can't even get that right." She stubbed the cigarette out angrily. "Oh, Colin!" She was in his arms like a hurt child, and he patted her gently as he would a child.

Colin poured her another drink and said, "Have you really made up your mind to leave Ken or are you just testing the water?"

"I've made up my mind."

"Because he's playing around again?"

"This time I don't think he's playing."

"Has he said anything?"

"No."

"Have you?"

"To him? No. I hardly ever see him lately."

"Then how do you know?"

"I saw her."

"You weren't following him, I hope."

"She came to visit Ken in the hospital. I was outside in the hall-way. They didn't see me."

"So there's been no discussion between you, no break?"

"Not yet."

"And he doesn't know you know."

"No."

"How long have you been married? About fifteen years?"

"Almost sixteen."

"It doesn't seem like it. I remember the wedding."

"Things were different then. I loved him, I really did."

"And now?"

"No."

"What about the boys?"

"Colin, we've been holding this sham of a marriage together for years just for them. I mean, I've been holding it together. Ken has just gone on being himself. Good old Barbara, she'll put up with anything, but not anymore."

"There's quite a lot at stake," he said, feeling increasingly un-comfortable.

"I want out, Colin."

"Give me time to get used to the idea. You're a sensible woman and I'm sure you haven't reached this conclusion lightly. I'd rather you not leave him, or throw him out, or whatever you want to do, but I'm not you. Still, before you take any precipitate action let's look at some of the consequences."

"I know you want him to take over Stanton, but I don't."

"Why not? Whatever happens in your marriage is one thing. But Ken is a very able manager. Are you trying to punish him?"

She hesitated, then said with quiet honesty, "I guess that's part of it."

"Fair enough. But bear in mind his failure as a husband doesn't make him a bad choice to run Stanton Technologies."

"He's a bad choice for me."

"Ken is smart, experienced, a hell of a salesman . . ."

"You don't have to tell me . . ."

". . . and he worked very closely with your father ever since he joined the company. If you recall, he only left the army at your dad's request because Ave recognized his ability and wanted him aboard. And knowing Ave Stanton as I did, I can tell you he did not make Ken a vice-president to please you. Ken earned it and in my opinion he would make an excellent CEO." Once he learned to be more discreet about his affairs, Colin thought.

As he spoke she was shaking her head with a finality that meant the issue was closed. Although the way Barbara did it was quite feminine, something in the gesture reminded Colin of Avery Stanton. He was the most open-minded man in the world, but once he had made up his mind about something, all hell couldn't change it.

Colin adopted his best lawyer's frown and began to pace the vast, high-ceilinged room. Stalling for time as he mentally catalogued the decor, done at great expense by Barbara's mother when she was in a belle époque phase. Light blue watered-silk drapes and Wedgwood walls, off-white woodwork, a Carrara mantelpiece and ankle-deep Shiraz carpets formed the setting for their little talk, surrounded by a collection of Louis Quinze furniture.

Letting his mind wander to objects or things around him was a way Colin had of getting to the heart of the matter. A little like looking away from a faint star on a dark night. One suddenly saw the star so much better in peripheral vision.

He was focusing now on an ormolu clock that had stopped, when Barbara said, "You think I'm being impulsive, don't you?"

"Your father always put the company first," Colin said. "Even at the very end of his life he had to make hard decisions that went against his grain. Yet he knew they were in the best interests of Stanton Technologies. I rarely disagreed with him because I have tried to follow the same criteria."

She watched him without speaking.

"I don't think personal revenge is a good reason to deny the best-qualified man a chance at the top job in the company, whatever his private derelictions."

"That's just it," Barbara said. "I don't agree Ken is the best qualified man and neither did Daddy."

"Who told you he didn't?" Colin said in surprise.

"Daddy wanted Adam Walsh. Fionna heard it from Brian. Don't tell me you didn't know, Colin. Daddy told you everything."

Colin was beginning to wonder why Avery hadn't published it in the *Wall Street Journal*. Colin would not lie, but he fudged.

"Adam was under serious consideration at one time, Barbara, that's true. There might have been a moment when your father thought of recommending him as his successor, and I won't deny that he talked about it with me. But in the end he decided he wanted Ken and not Adam or anyone else."

"Why?"

"For the reasons I've just given you. He also liked the idea of keeping things in the family. It seems he was mistaken."

"Well, Daddy's not here any more and I vote the stock now. Will you inform the board that I want Adam Walsh?"

"You're putting me in a very awkward position, Barbara."

"Someone else can actually nominate him, Hunt Benson or somebody. Don't do it if it embarrasses you."

"It's not that."

"Then what is it?"

Colin debated with himself about telling Barbara the truth. There was no doubt that as the majority stockholder she had a right to know. But again there was the question of what was best for the company, and Colin was not at all convinced that Barbara could deal sensibly with such a devastating revelation in her present state of mind.

"Colin?"

She was stubborn and impulsive—though God knew she had reason to be furious at Ken—and if she was capable at this moment of sacrificing Kenneth Fairchild as an executive to her hurt and anger, what would she do if Colin told her Adam Walsh was a fake and that Walsh's attempted extortion had virtually killed her father? If she went public with such information, the ensuing scandal would certainly bring the whole fragile structure of deceit down around their ears and ravage Stanton stock on Wall Street.

Those were the reasons he gave himself for keeping silent, and they were compelling ones. But he suspected the truth included the less noble concern that she would also learn what Ken, Redfern and he were planning to do.

"You haven't answered my question," she said.

"Get dressed and let's get something to eat. I'm starved. I'll try to answer your question over dinner."

"Colin, I'm a mess. Look at me!"

"Just a little body and fender retouching around the eyes and you'll be as beautiful as ever."

"I was never beautiful."

"In the eye of this beholder, you have always been beautiful. In fact, if I weren't already taken you'd be . . ."

"You've been telling me that since I was a schoolgirl."

"It's about time you believed it then."

"But no Club Twenty-one. I couldn't bear it. All those sleek fashionable women. I'd feel like a total clod."

"What about Chinese?"

"I'm not that hungry."

"O'Hara's?"

"Where is that? I never heard of it."

"It's an old haunt of your father's and mine. In the West Fifties. We used to go there when we wanted to be alone."

"What should I wear?"

"Slacks and an old sweater." He had no idea what he'd say to her about Walsh when they got there, but between the time she needed to change and the ride to the west side, Colin was pretty sure he'd be able to cobble up something.

She reappeared within a few minutes, her face repaired, her ponytail brushed and tied back with a fuchsia scarf. She looked tired but fetching, a warm and lovable woman in her prime whose self-esteem had suffered a serious setback but whose basic character would, he felt, carry her through.

"Okay?" she asked him. She was wearing a beige cashmere turtleneck and slacks to match. The thought crossed his mind that Ken Fairchild was an idiot to have risked losing a wife like Barbara. Attractive and bright, patient, honest, decent and kind and with a sense of humor. Colin didn't know who Ken had found to take her place, but she had to be inferior to the woman he was probably going to lose. "Colin?"

"Fine. Lovely."

"Then shall we go?"

The telephone rang as they were leaving and the maid had already retired. "Aren't you going to answer it?" Colin said.

She shook her head but waited by the door. On the fourth ring, the answering machine cut in and after the signal tone he heard Ken Fairchild's voice.

There was only the slightest hesitation before Barbara said, "Fuck him," and slammed the door behind her.

___CHAPTER TWENTY-FIVE___

Barbara had tolerated Ken's philandering for most of the years of their marriage, including even his fathering of an illegitimate child. But the day she saw Nora Hallowell in her husband's arms, something snapped. She was more vulnerable than ever following the sudden death of her father, and this latest betrayal was too much.

Petrey's reports on the lovers fed her moods until one morning, as she explained it to Colin, she simply awakened with the certainty that she no longer loved Ken Fairchild. She felt humiliated and angry still, but in a way relieved, because she was not in competition with the beautiful Nora Hallowell after all. That woman could have him.

It was not surrender, Barbara said, anxious that Colin not misunderstand. She was not backing down and giving the field to a rival. She had suddenly discovered she no longer gave a damn what he did or with whom. It had taken sixteen years to arrive at this earthshaking conclusion because she was, she said, a slow learner. But she had arrived, and there was no turning back. The only regret she had was that she had not realized it sooner.

He still asked if she was absolutely sure.

"That I don't love him? I probably haven't loved him for years, but I was a creature of convention *and* my own stubbornness. I couldn't face the fact of losing him until I realized that if love was gone I wasn't losing anything. Do you see?"

Barbara, always a little insecure about her looks, may not have been a beauty like her friend Fionna, but she had a kind of elegance Colin found especially appealing. Thirty-six years old and feeling the butterflies many women seemed to feel when they approached forty, she was not in the best frame of mind to contemplate divorce, but she had indeed decided what she would do, as she made clear to Colin that evening in O'Hara's.

O'Hara had been dead for thirty years, if he ever existed, and the proprietor of the place was a silver-haired, silver-tongued Greek who claimed he married O'Hara's daughter. The head bartender was Irish, there was sawdust on the floor, the walls were covered with autographed pictures of Irish boxers, rowers and Gaelic football players, and the aroma of booze and food was enticing.

A blackboard hung behind the bar with the menu scrawled in chalk. At lunch, when the traffic was mostly bus drivers, stevedores and cabbies, it listed potato soup, lox and Irish stew. In the evening, before the celebrity clientele arrived from local TV studios and other centers of sophistication, the menu would be erased and rewritten. The potato soup became *vichyssoise,* the lox was transformed into *saumon fumé* and the Irish stew was reborn as *bourguignon d'agneau.*

The current O'Hara, whose real name was Nick Gavros, spoke a little of every language on earth, like all Greeks, and circulated among the tables bullying the customers into eating whatever his temperamental cook had prepared too much of.

The grilled sole mentioned on the blackboard was what Colin ordered and Nick immediately said, "I wouldn't give it to the cat. Have the steak and kidney pie."

"Nick, I'm watching my cholesterol."

"So we leave out the steak and kidneys."

Barbara, laughing, ordered the *vichyssoise* and the *bourguignon d'agneau.*

"Where did you find this lady? She's a dream. She's a beauty.

She's the perfect customer. I love her. What taste! What class!" And Nick dropped to one knee and kissed her hand as he ordered a bottle of champagne in her honor.

It was the best possible balm for Barbara's ego, spontaneous and unexpected, one of the reasons Colin thought of bringing her to O'Hara's.

He mentioned to Nick that she was Avery Stanton's daughter.

Immediately the owner planted his great bulk on a chair between them and began to tell Barbara in grave tones, "I cry, my dear, when I hear that wonderful man your father is dead. How many years I know him, Colin? Twenty? Thirty? When you first come in here you tell me buy stock in his company. I don't know, but I have good feeling about my friend Colin and your father. I am rich man today, my dear, because he was such a genius. You know what he invented? He invented my fortune."

"Nick, the food," Colin said.

"Yes, the food will come and it will be delicious as always. My dear, I weep for you to lose such a great father. I weep for myself and for our country. Colin, bring her back, do you hear?"

Nick popped the champagne cork, poured for all of them and toasted Barbara before rushing off to badger his other clients. Barbara said, "Thank you, Colin. You always seem to know what's right for me."

"Nick can be a little heavy with that Greek blarney."

"He's beautiful. Is it true what he said?"

"About getting rich?"

"Yes."

"I guess so. I know he bought into Stanton early and kept buying, so he probably has a pretty good stash of shares by now."

"Because he believed in Daddy and you."

"Because he believed in your father. I had nothing to do with it except to give him good market advice."

"Why do you always sell yourself short?"

"I wasn't aware that I did."

She looked at him thoughtfully and put her hand over his. "You do, Colin, you do. But your modesty has always been one of the reasons I love you. It's a very special strength you have, that we Stantons depend on always."

Little did she know, Colin reflected as she gazed dreamily at him. And better that she should never know.

The dinner was as good as Nick had promised, and Barbara's spirits took a quantum leap upward as they sipped their way through the champagne. By the time coffee arrived she was more relaxed than Colin had seen her since before her father's death. She talked about her boys and eventually she got around to telling him about Dominic Petrey.

"Who put you in touch with him?"

"Brian had his number because the company used him to investigate something or other, and Fionna got it for me."

He smiled. Something or other. It seemed Petrey had tied into a steady source of employment either working for Ken Fairchild or spying on him.

"Is he still on your payroll?" he asked Barbara.

"For a few more days, I suppose. He was trying to get pictures when last we talked."

"Is that really necessary?"

"Isn't it? I mean for a divorce?"

"No. From what you tell me, Petrey already has more than enough to show that Ken is carrying on outside his marriage. If you're determined to seek a divorce, it's in everyone's best interest to go for a quiet mutual-consent decree in Connecticut."

"Will you handle it for me, Colin?"

"No. I'm not a divorce lawyer, not even for you. But I'll send you someone who can deal with it."

That seemed to satisfy her, and for a while he thought she might have forgotten the question she had asked about Walsh. But he was not to be let off so easily. "I'm still waiting," she said at one point, "for the promised answer."

"What answer was that?"

"You're stalling. What about Adam Walsh?"

"As I said, your father decided against him for—"

She never allowed him to finish. "I don't care why Daddy changed his mind, Colin. I want to know why you feel as you do."

"Fair enough. Let's look at Walsh for a moment. Brilliant economist, a bit theoretical but talented nevertheless. Extraordinary feel for market research. Personable, well-liked, articulate and of an age that will allow him ten to fifteen more productive years. All pluses."

"Tell me the minuses."

"Too short a time with the company, only three years. No real understanding of finance."

"He may not be a financial wizard, but look how the stock shot up after his speech to those Wall Street people."

"Any responsible executive saying what he said would have had the same effect on the market. Nothing remarkable in that."

"But he's the one who thought of it and he's the one who said it. Ken told me those research projects had been hanging around for ages, but he never thought to publicize them and neither did Daddy. Adam did and today every share of Stanton common stock is worth several dollars more than it was before he spoke."

"Everything you say is true," Colin agreed, "but it was a one-shot thing. One can't overlook Walsh's lack of background in other areas." He worried that he sounded as stuffy and unconvincing as he felt. He pressed on, though. "The man has only the sketchiest acquaintance with distribution, and no experience whatever in re-search and development, advertising, sales promotion, public relations or personnel."

"But you have good men managing all these functions. I mean, Daddy never worked in any of those departments either."

"But your father often understood them better than the managers. His feel for the big picture made him the exception."

"Colin, I think you're just inventing reasons," Barbara said.

"By no means, no. I haven't even got to the man's most important lack. Manufacturing. This company has always been run by engineers and technicians because its business is highly technical. Your father was a chemical engineer. Redfern is an industrial engineer and even Ken has a technical background from West Point. In fact, most of Stanton's sales force and all of its production executives are qualified engineers, chemists, physicists or metallurgists. Adam is only an economist."

She laughed. "I'd love to see you argue a case in court sometime. You are good, Colin. Well-prepared and well-organized."

"I haven't argued a court case in ages. Well, at least I convinced you."

But Barbara was full of surprises, and the first came when she replied, "Oh, Colin, darling, you haven't convinced me at all, but I can see you'd be very effective in front of some juries. You obviously have your own reasons for not wanting Adam as president and I wish you'd tell me what they are. But since you won't, at least tell me who it is you prefer if I insist it can't be Ken."

"I'd settle for Brian Redfern," he said, wondering if he really would settle for Brian after what he'd seen of his judgment lately.

"That would certainly please Fionna, wouldn't it?"

"I suppose any wife would be happy to see her husband head of Stanton Technologies, present company excluded."

He was rewarded with a smile. "Do you suppose we could have some more champagne? This bottle seems to be empty."

As Colin ordered the second bottle he marveled at the two-hour transformation from the unhappy wife in her frumpy robe to the calm but gently determined woman who sat across from him. The champagne had done its work, and Barbara's eyes already held a dewy, dreamlike glint that hadn't been there earlier.

Nick Gavros's exaggerated attention and the warm ambiance in O'Hara's had helped, as well as having Colin listen patiently while she unburdened herself of some of the pain, bitterness and frustration of these last weeks.

"Do me a favor?" he said to her.

"Of course. What?"

"Hold off."

"On the divorce?"

"For the moment."

"I can do that, until after Christmas anyway. It isn't as if I see that much of him, and I don't worry about his trying to convince me."

"Longer if you can."

"But he'll know what's going on, Colin. The annual meeting is the first week in January and Ken expects to be elected president. When he isn't he'll know I stopped him. Then what?"

"Believe me, Barbara, there are sound reasons why I don't want to see any extra strain on Ken right now. Or on Brian or Adam either, for that matter. I would prefer to postpone the election and ask Hunt Benson to remain in place for the time being."

"Can you do that?"

"Under the bylaws, yes."

"But why should I hold off, Colin?"

"Because I'm asking you to."

Again Barbara smiled. "For reasons you can't tell me."

"Not yet."

"When?"

"As soon as I'm satisfied there's no possibility of any loss of confidence in the firm."

"Is there such a possibility now?"

"Anything's possible, Barbara, when the founder and main asset of a company dies suddenly."

"But surely Adam Walsh's talk to the brokers helped, didn't it? I mean, what better vote of confidence than a jump in the share-price on the stock exchange?"

"The fastest way to erase that gain would be for the rumor to start on the Street that you and the likely future CEO of the company are engaged in a scandalous divorce action that could involve Stanton in costly legal battles and settlements."

"But I wouldn't do any such thing, Colin. I'd never involve the company in my personal affairs."

"You're doing it now, Barbara . . ."

"But . . . yes, I suppose in a way I am without meaning to."

"Ken might, too, if you made him angry enough."

"But how would the company become involved?"

"You involve it by voting against him. Your divorce might seem straightforward enough, but the custody fight for Stanton Technologies could make a lot of lawyers rich and a lot of stockholders poorer."

"You are serious, aren't you?"

He nodded.

"I still don't understand, but I know you wouldn't say this if it weren't true. Darling Colin, I'll do as you say."

"You won't regret it," he told her, hoping he was right.

It was midnight by the time they finished the second bottle of champagne and headed back to the Ritz Tower. In the taxi Barbara clung to him. "I love you so, Colin." She was a little light-headed by then, almost euphoric. "Kiss me, please. Hold me."

He held her and kissed her lightly on the forehead. But she wrenched his face around with both hands and kissed him hard on the lips, then more softly. He tried to act as if it was the most normal thing in the world between them, which, of course, it wasn't. It was warm and sensual, a little drunken perhaps, but passionate nevertheless, and Colin was not a stone. It had been many months since he had held Joyce in his arms like that, and he responded.

They disengaged only after Colin realized the taxi had been stopped for at least a minute and the driver was waiting for his fare. As he said goodnight, they both tried to pretend that everything was the same as always.

But it wasn't. They had crossed a line as surely as if they had gone to bed together.

It troubled Colin, but confusion would have better described his state of mind when he got home that night. In the years he was married to Joyce he had watched Barbara grow from an awkward schoolgirl into an attractive, sophisticated young woman. Although the age gap between them was less than ten years, in a way he felt like one of those people one read about, the horny uncle or the "close family friend."

But he also felt like a man who had just shared an extraordinary moment with an extraordinary woman. And although he remembered thinking he would not go out of his way to make this happen again, neither would he go out of his way not to.

——— CHAPTER TWENTY-SIX ———

WALLY SCOTT was the criminal lawyer who had agreed to take on Quirk's case in federal court, and before leaving for the office early the next morning Colin called him at home for an update.

He laughed. "Where did you find this guy, Colin? I haven't had such a colorful client since the Subway Slasher. You got to admit, this guy's weird for a Cranmer, Fisher & Cleves client."

"Wally, can you get him out?"

"Out is easy. Off, I don't know. The judge wants a two-hundred-thousand-dollar bond and surrender of his passport."

"Why the high bail?"

"Based on the cargo. What's this bird to you, Colin?"

"He did some labor relations work for an international client of ours. They wanted to help without getting involved."

"Colin, he got caught with a bag full of ganja."

"What the devil is ganja?"

"I keep forgetting what sheltered lives you dudes live down there on Wall Street. Ganja, my friend, is the shit they smoke in the West Indies and some parts of Queens. Mr. Quirk was carrying a commercial quantity with a street value of two hundred thousand dollars. Not much as drugs go but enough to earn him three-to-five unless we cut a deal."

"Such as?" Colin hated this, and couldn't help blaming Brian for creating the situation.

"Don't know until I research the subject. If Quirk's got interesting friends he's willing to talk about, I might get him a suspension in return for a guilty plea. But no guarantees. It'll also cost you a lunch at the Gansevoort one of these days."

After he hung up Colin dialed ex-Sergeant Yancy's office and left a message. Then he called Petrey and explained that he wanted the detective to baby-sit with Quirk.

"I'm pretty busy at the moment."

"You're not as busy as you thought you were, Mr. Petrey. Mrs. Fairchild has agreed to call off the chase."

"She say that?"

"You can confirm it with a phone call."

"If she doesn't need me, then I have some time."

"Can you drop by my office this morning?"

"Eleven okay?"

"I'll expect you."

Lauren Jewett, the day nurse who relieved Mrs. Ryan at six in the morning, joined Colin for a cup of coffee. "Mrs. Draggett had a bad night and she's shooting a temp again this morning," she said. "I've asked the doctor to come."

He had looked in on Joyce earlier but she was sleeping. "What can I do before I go?"

"Nothing. If you want, I'll call you at your office after the doctor's been to see her."

It was still early when Colin reached his office and only old Anthony Shattuck, the senior clerk, was there. Invariably the first to arrive and the last to leave, Anthony was reputed to have taken his one and only vacation sometime in the fifties.

A tall, courtly man with white hair, neatly trimmed mustache and an encyclopedic knowledge of the law, Anthony was considerate of everybody. Joyce used to say he gave the law firm its only human touch, the saving grace that she called "Anthony's divine Dickensian image."

Now he handed Colin two message slips indicating Brian Redfern had called the night before, and then brought a coffee to his desk. His own wife was dying from arteriosclerosis, and when Colin asked how she was he said, "Sometimes she knows who I am but can't remember my name. Like the first time I asked her for a date."

Anthony had attended Yale and wanted to become a lawyer but had never made it. After the 1929 stock-market crash wiped out his stockbroker father he was forced to drop out of school and came to work as a junior clerk at Cranmer, Fisher & Cleves. By the time Colin joined the firm he had already been there thirty years and looked much the same as he did now, approaching his eightieth birthday, his step still firm and his mind clear.

"You're going to have to think about retiring one of these days, Anthony," Colin had told him recently.

"I'll think about it," he said, "if you promise not to make me do it."

Colin laughed. The truth was that Joyce was right. Without him, Cranmer, Fisher & Cleves would be just another law firm.

The telephones did not ring in Colin's offices. They emitted a soft intermittent glow on the clerks' desks, or flashed discreetly where the secretaries worked. At a quarter to nine, before anyone else had arrived, Brian Redfern was on the line.

"Morning, Brian. What's up?"

"Major problem. Did you know Ave ordered an audit of Stanton International before he died?"

"Are you sure?"

"Barry Parks nailed me on it last night."

"But Avery would have said something."

"I don't think he got the chance."

"Everything's in order, isn't it?"

"Not quite."

Colin waited.

"You remember I told you there was a paper trail. I authorized a half-million-dollar transfer from Stanton International's New York bank to an offshore account in my name. Parks wants it explained today or the transfer will be flagged when it goes to the board."

"How had you planned to handle it?"

"Malaysian warehouse construction."

"Can't you still do that?"

"Not in one day. You know how auditors are, Colin. They need contract copies, receipts, all the goddamn accounting details."

"How soon can you have them?"

"I need at least a month, but the audit has to be ready for the board before the annual meeting, and that's early January."

"Send Parks a memo stating what you just told me."

"But without the back-up, the audit will make it look like I'm making loans to myself with company funds."

"Your memo will explain that and I'll be at the board meeting to answer any other questions. Delays in the paperwork due to war, pestilence, Malaysian customs."

There was a silence on Brian's end before he said, "If you back me up, I suppose there shouldn't be any question."

Colin was thinking that there probably wouldn't be any question anyway. Brian Redfern did not suspect it yet, but the members of the board would probably be congratulating him by that time on his election as president of Stanton Technologies.

If Barbara was still determined to keep Ken out of the president's chair, and Adam Walsh wasn't a candidate, they had to find someone else. Although he had suggested the compromise of asking Hunt Benson to remain another year, Colin doubted Hunt would do it. He had complained every time they met recently that he hated the responsibility and was counting the days until retirement.

Colin wasn't certain of anything, but he did feel the odds would favor Redfern when the day of the meeting came. If absolutely necessary, he could tell Barbara the truth about Walsh and get her to go along. She was angry and inexperienced in corporate politics, but she was not a fool.

"I'll write the memo," Brian was saying, "but I'll have to do it again to get the funds for the second payment."

"Then say so in the memo. Tell him the five hundred thousand is only the first instance. In order to have cash available, say, to take advantage of fixed prices on construction materials. Mark the memo confidential for Parks and Hunt Benson's eyes only."

"It all seems simple the way you lay it out."

"It is," Colin reminded him. "But because you see it through a scrim of guilt, you imagine complications."

"What are you talking about? Guilt is Walsh's turf."

"You know what I mean, Brian. Must I spell it out?"

At nine on the dot, Maggie Caruso entered Colin's office with more hot coffee and a pile of correspondence needing his attention. Maggie was used to seeing him come in early since Joyce's illness.

"Did Mrs. Fairchild reach you last night?"

"I took her to O'Hara's."

Maggie was mildly scandalized.

"What's wrong with O'Hara's?"

"Well, nothing. I grew up around guys like Nick. But, I mean, the Four Seasons would have been more appropriate."

"You've got the wrong idea about Barbara, Maggie. I've known her since she was a child."

"So you've always been at pains to point out."

Colin looked up sharply. "What do you mean by that?"

"Only what you make of it." Never indiscreet, Maggie was no-nonsense direct in the privacy of the office.

He had thrust the taxi scene of the night before from his mind and her remark brought the guilt back. It was as if she had seen them in their embrace and read his mind.

"You always pretend not to see Barbara as a woman," Maggie said. "She is what most women would like to be."

"Rich? Sure."

"Not only that. I mean poised, pretty, sophisticated, but nice, too. Sort of like Katharine Hepburn."

"You should tell her that. Her self-esteem has taken a pretty heavy beating lately."

"Lately? If they punished mental cruelty in the courts, she would qualify as a battered wife!"

"I suspect you're about to tell me something verging on gossip and you know what I think of that."

"Mr. Draggett, everybody knows about her husband. I wouldn't say this to anyone, but he's even made moves on me."

"Shows he has good taste."

"Don't change the subject. We paid off that girl Mr. Stanton banished to Chicago, remember? I prepared the Stanton Foundation check for the baby's trust account and you signed it."

"Maggie, it's probably about time you married Cranmer, Fisher & Cleves so you can't testify against us in court."

Maggie laughed, a lovely trill up the scale. "Do you really think the firm can afford me, counselor?"

"Why not? Name your price."

"Careful, I might just bankrupt you guys." Again she laughed, brightening his morning. "What you don't know is that most of us would pay to work here."

"Don't disappoint me and go soft and sentimental. I'm only comfortable with tough New Yorkers like myself."

"That's a laugh. Colin Draggett, tough guy. If the opposition only knew. Well, you keep my secrets and I'll keep yours."

"I didn't know you had any."

"A nice, middle-aged Catholic career woman? No secrets? My whole life is secrets. You probably still think my great ambition is to marry a retired life-insurance agent and go live in Riverdale. But after twenty years with tough Colin Draggett, all I'm good for is drafting legal briefs and answering correspondence."

"I'm glad to hear that because that's exactly what we're going to do for the rest of the morning."

Sixty-two attorneys worked for Cranmer, Fisher & Cleves, and twice as many clerks, paralegals and secretaries. There were nine partners, of whom Colin was the senior, an administrative director, and seven in-house accountants. Yet it seemed to him that most of the workload was carried by Maggie Caruso, Anthony Shattuck and himself.

Maggie, as she liked to be called, had entered Colin's office almost twenty years earlier by mistake when she got off at the wrong floor. He was looking for a secretary and hired her because she was intelligent and disarmingly honest. She had wanted to study voice, but girls in her limited Bronx circle were expected to work as secretaries if they did not become nuns or marry immediately. When the nuns failed to recruit Maggie, her family made sure she took typing and shorthand.

Meanwhile her two policemen brothers had guarded her virginity so zealously that she remained single long past the age when girls on Fordham Road usually got married. As she told Colin, most of the men who came around her house were either shy cops or rough construction workers anyway.

She thought she loved one boy in high school because he was so sensitive. She didn't mind that he never tried to kiss her. Then one day she understood why after she overheard her brothers laughing because he had been arrested for soliciting a vice detective in a public men's room.

Most of the girls Maggie knew when she was growing up loved Mick Jagger and wanted a good time. Maggie's idea of a good time was to hear Maria Callas at the Metropolitan Opera. She wanted "Something Else" from life.

While the others got married, had their kids and went to Mass in Riverdale, Maggie went to work on Wall Street, looked after her mother and gradually scuttled her dreams.

She was the only person who could turn Colin's chaotic desk into a model of order, and the only one besides Joyce who could get him out of occasional fits of melancholy with her smile alone.

The successful corporate attorney doesn't need a great mind or even a strong stomach like a criminal lawyer. But the work does demand an attention to detail that can sometimes be as maddening as it is boring. In a complicated lawsuit it is easy to get lost among the trees while looking for a way out of the forest, and more than once Maggie saved Colin from costly mistakes. She was fast, smart and instinctively alert to the nuances of complex cases. Because of this, she eventually became the highest paid secretary in the firm.

Colin recalled her in the beginning as being angular rather than round, and skinny as a garden rake. But she filled out, and made up at forty what she had lacked at twenty-five. She dressed conservatively and well. She had exquisite skin, lustrous dark hair with even darker eyes, and an impish, dimpled smile that won everybody's heart. Although Colin always found her attractive, Maggie considered herself a dead loss in the body department and had learned to joke about it.

"But you have nice breasts," Joyce once told her when she was putting herself down.

And Maggie answered, "Sure, if you can find them."

When her mother finally died, Maggie sent all her furniture to auction and sold the Fordham Road house over her brothers' protests. Then she bought a condo in Brooklyn Heights with a spectacular view of lower Manhattan and the offices of Cranmer, Fisher & Cleves.

ANTHONY ENTERED at one minute before eleven to say, "Mr. Petrey is here to see you, Colin."

Maggie gathered her papers to leave just as Petrey arrived, and Colin was surprised to see they knew each other.

"Her brother and I worked out of the same precinct," he said. "I knew she worked for some downtown lawyer," Petrey said, "but I never made the connection. Nice lady."

Petrey settled himself into one of the leather club chairs in front of Colin's work table. "Mind if I smoke?" He smiled gratefully when Colin pushed a brass ashtray toward him. "Been trying to quit since nineteen-seventy. Even had needles stuck in my ear but all I got for that was an ear infection."

Heavyset, rough-hewn, lumpy and rumpled as an unmade bed, he had a steady hand and eyes that registered every detail of Colin's office. Dominic Petrey wanted to appear friendly and easygoing, and perhaps he was when he was young, but in middle-age he was more gruff than amiable and seemed better suited to handcuffing felons and cracking heads than to other kinds of cerebral police work. But he was as smart as he was tough, and as honest as he was thorough.

Street-wise and cautious, he had been respected by his colleagues as much for his phenomenal memory as for his courage. He was famous among two generations of petty thieves, dope pushers and muggers who believed with reason that the file of names and faces in Petrey's head equaled anything in the NYPD's central computer. His superiors had always acknowledged that he had a nose for the work. He could enter a crowded bar, study thirty or forty hostile, sullen faces, and suddenly collar the one man in the place who had an unlicensed automatic and three hundred grams of nose candy in his pocket.

Once, so Colin had heard, Petrey had seen a store-front preacher haranguing a crowd in Harlem, stopped his car, jumped out and arrested the man for murder. While half the black community went running to City Hall in protest and Petrey's superiors waited nervously, ready to suspend him for screwing up, a fingerprint check showed the sidewalk preacher was wanted under another name for killing a prostitute in the Bronx seven years earlier. When asked how he had known it was the same man, Petrey only shrugged and said, "It sounded like him."

His lack of polish and political skill coupled with his forthright and disarming honesty denied Petrey any important promotions beyond first-class detective. So after twenty years he took his re-

tirement, got a divorce and set up business for himself. He worked
hard, paid his bills and dropped whatever he had left at the track
on weekends. His friends often said if he could pick horses like he
picked people he'd be a rich man.

"I talked to Mrs. Fairchild and you were right," he now said to
Colin. "I'm off the hook, but I charge three hundred a day plus
expenses, five hundred if there's night stakeouts, with a fifteen-
hundred-dollar minimum."

"Oliver Quirk, the man who telephoned you yesterday from jail,
will be out on bail today. Wally Scott is his attorney."

"I know Scott."

"Quirk did some labor work for Stanton Technologies in England and was supposed to do something for Redfern here. I don't
know exactly what. Do you mind telling me why he called you?"

"Mr. Redfern gave him my name. I guess he wanted somebody
he could trust as a cutout between him and the Englishman."

"I don't have to tell you, Mr. Petrey, that Quirk's arrest on a
drug charge came as a pretty big shock, and for obvious reasons it
is important to keep as much distance as possible between Quirk
and Stanton Technologies."

"Which is why you want me to keep an eye on him?"

"In a sense, yes."

Petrey chuckled. "It's a little late, don't you think? I mean how
much more trouble can this dipshit get himself into?"

"Amen," Colin said. "He's still a potential problem, however, until his case is disposed of. I'd like you to put him up somewhere
outside New York, impress on him the need to keep quiet and stay
clean while he's out on bail. Check on him once or twice a week
and keep in touch with this office."

"Who'm I working for, you or Stanton?"

"Bill this firm when you report on Quirk."

"That's all? You could save yourself money by letting Maggie
handle this. With her around, you don't need me."

"Let's say your professional authority is what we're paying for.
With a man like Quirk, that may be critical."

Petrey laughed. "You got a deal. I'll call Scott's office and find
out when he's springing Quirk."

"Before you go, I want to ask you about another matter."

"Ask away, sir."

"Recently you did some work for Mr. Fairchild investigating the background of a Stanton executive."

"That's right."

"You turned up some rather surprising information."

Petrey shrugged.

"I'm sure Mr. Fairchild stressed the need for maintaining absolute confidentiality about your findings.

"He didn't have to. It's the only way I work."

"I've seen your full report and I'm intensely curious about one thing. Recently I've run into two people who know this man now and also claim to have known him by the same name years ago."

Petrey was thoughtful, staring down at rough knuckles for a moment before he shifted in his chair and shook out a fresh cigarette. "Could be mistaken identity. It happens sometimes. They think they knew him before, only it was somebody else."

"One of the people is his wife."

"You believe her?"

"Yes."

"How do you know she's not in on the scam?"

"I don't know, but I doubt it. The other one's a special investigator for the SEC—absolutely unimpeachable bona fides—who says he knew this man in college."

"I don't know, Mr. Draggett, but I'll look into it some more if you want. Maybe the SEC guy knew the real what's-his-name and not the guy impersonating him and was taken in."

Maggie appeared at the door then to say that Lauren Jewett, Joyce's day nurse, was on the telephone.

"I'll call her back."

"She says it's urgent."

____ CHAPTER TWENTY-SEVEN ____

COLIN LEFT Petrey and Maggie to work out the details of Petrey's assignment. As he was putting on his coat, Anthony Shattuck said Mrs. Fairchild had just called.

"What did you tell her?"

"That you were on your way home. She said she would call you there."

"Thank you, Anthony."

"Is there anything else I can do, Colin?"

"Not at the moment, thanks."

THE DOCTOR was waiting when Colin arrived, a cadaverous Hindu whose English locutions required some patience to follow. He was substituting for the regular American specialist who was taking a month's sailing holiday in the Bahamas.

The news was all bad. Joyce's fever had remained high during the morning as she kept drifting in and out of consciousness. Just before the doctor arrived she had been vomiting and then went into convulsions. Although these had subsided by the time Colin got there, the doctor wanted her moved to the hospital, something Joyce had made Colin promise he would not do.

"She is being stable for the moment," the doctor said, "but unless we take her into hospital, there is no guaranty for how long she is remaining in this precarious stable condition."

"I know."

"I am calling ahead and reserving the room, sir."

"She's not going to any hospital, Doctor."

"But we must be moving her, I insist. In hospital are the finest facilities which in no way you are duplicating here."

"If you can tell me there's some hope she'll recover, even partially, I'll carry her there myself."

"I am not telling you such a thing because it would not be the true medical story or prognosis."

"Then she stays here, Doctor, and I would appreciate it if you could make her as comfortable as possible."

"I can not be taking the responsibility for this patient unless she is moving to hospital. It is there, I repeat, that it is easier to be caring for her."

Colin was getting angry. "I don't give a damn how easy it is for you to take care of her, and no one asked you to assume any responsibility for her remaining here. Just cut her pain and help her die in peace, for God's sake! That's all she asks and that's all I'm asking of you!"

The man was greatly offended by Colin's words and his tone. "I am not being shouted at, sir. I am a medical doctor and I am not being shouted at. I am not being insulted."

"I'm sorry. I'm sure you're doing your best, but I made her a solemn promise, Doctor, not to let her die in a hospital."

"She is not dying. I have announced to you her stable condition and unless you admit her I am leaving in this moment."

"What do you mean, you're leaving? My wife is desperately ill!"

"I am not being responsible."

"No, you sure as hell are not!"

"Good day, sir."

He was reaching for his coat and muffler when Colin caught him by the arm. "Do you mean that?"

"Exactly as you hear me."

"You're just walking out?"

"That is correct, sir." And out he went, closing the door behind him. In his anger, Colin shouted that he'd have him disbarred if it was the last thing he did.

A moment later the nurse called in a stage whisper from the doorway. "She's awake. She wants you, Mr. Draggett."

Colin stepped into the dimly lighted sickroom and crossed to Joyce's bedside. He took her hand in his and said, "I'm here, darling."

"I know," Joyce said in a voice so light and whispery he had to lean close to hear. "I heard you shouting. Colin?"

"Yes, darling."

"How can you disbar a doctor?" She was smiling weakly as she said it, and he wondered how in God's name she could keep a sense of humor on her deathbed.

"The nurse is calling for another doctor."

"If it's easier for you," she said, "let them take me to the hospital. It really doesn't matter anymore."

"I'll do whatever you want, my love. But unless you tell me to take you to the hospital, I'll keep you home with me."

She squeezed his hand in what he could only presume was agreement and then her eyes fluttered closed and she drifted off again.

He slowly disengaged his hand and stood, turning away from the bed. He was nearly at the door when he heard her sigh, "You know something, Colin?"

He went back and leaned down close so she would not have to force her voice. "I know I love you," he said.

Again she squeezed his hand. "I dream a lot," she said. Then after a long silence, when he thought she was sleeping once more, she said, "I would so like to do it all again, Colin. It was such fun, with you."

"It was fun, my love."

"I'm sorry . . . for putting you through this, poor sweetheart. Colin, do you love me?"

"I love you."

"Again."

"I love you."

"Remember . . . Venice?" And she closed her eyes. When he was sure this time that she was asleep, he tiptoed from the room.

LAUREN JEWETT spent the next hour calling various medical services and doctors and nurses to find a replacement physician, but without any success. While she was looking up another number, Barbara Fairchild telephoned.

"Colin, I've been trying to reach you. What happened?"

"Joyce took a turn for the worse."

"What can I do?"

He told her about the quack from Calcutta quitting and Barbara said she would call a physician she knew immediately.

The man appeared later that afternoon and introduced himself as Dr. Brenner, a pleasant, elderly man with the cheerful bedside manner of an old-fashioned country doctor. He was a retired professor of internal medicine on the Cornell Medical faculty and rarely accepted patients anymore, but he had once attended Barbara's mother and came now as a favor to Barbara.

He studied the charts that Lauren showed him, examined Joyce gently without waking her, ordered one or two IV solutions started and then motioned Colin out into the hallway.

"You know, of course, what's happening here," he said.

"My wife is dying."

"The quadrant indicates a metastisis, although I can't be sure without further hospital tests . . ."

Here we go again, Colin thought. Should I give in? Maybe she would be better off in a hospital.

". . . but I understand you are against taking her there."

"She's already been hospitalized several times and made me promise not to take her back again."

He nodded as if he understood, then said, "In that case we'll do what we can here. For the time being she's not in pain."

"I understand. I'm grateful you came."

"I'll look in on her again first thing in the morning. The nurse has my telephone and I'm only a few blocks away. My advice to you, Mr. Draggett, is to go back to work or find something to occupy yourself. There's nothing you can do for her here."

There was nothing Colin could do for himself either except sit by her bedside in the foolish hope that if the pale, ghostly figure that was Joyce awakened again, she might feel better knowing he was there. But she did not stir. Her breathing was so light at one moment, he thought it had stopped, yet a small green cathode screen above the bed still showed the rhythmic blip of her heart.

Twilight deepened the shadows in the room as Lauren checked the IV's and recorded Joyce's vital signs. When she had finished she asked if he would like a cup of tea.

"No, thanks. In a while I'll have something stronger."

He told himself he was sitting this vigil for love of his dying wife, but it was something else as well. Guilt because of what had happened with Barbara. Fear because so many safe moorings in his life seemed no longer to be where they had been.

Redfern was feeling pushed to enlist strong-arm methods to clear the way for his ambition. Fairchild, talented, attractive, was careless in his handling of his affair with Nora Hallowell, which could have no end of costly, unforeseen consequences for all of them.

And Barbara's sudden interest in him? She was, he reminded himself, more vulnerable than most after the ego-assault Fairchild had given her. His newest infidelity coming so soon after her father's death had, perhaps, disoriented her. Was that what had happened to them all? Disorientation. A collective spell of sorts brought on by the bizarre Walsh affair and Avery Stanton's sudden disappearance from the scene. It could have caused Barbara to confuse his friendly image with the male protectors she had lost in her father and in Ken Fairchild . . .

Neat, but what jury would buy it? Did he?

Joyce made a small sound then, almost a whisper. Colin moved quickly to her bedside and spoke to her. "Joyce? It's me, do you hear me, darling? Joyce?"

He thought . . . What did he think? That he could bring her back from dying? That she would suffer less knowing he was by her side? His mind started playing tricks. He had the sudden, awful impression that the pale, wasted person in the bed wasn't Joyce at all but someone else. He had been duped. Adam Walsh wasn't the only impostor. A switch had been made when Colin wasn't looking and the woman he loved had been stolen from him.

It was a measure of the fragile state of his own emotions that seconds later tears came as he looked at her and had to bury his face in the bedclothes to stifle the sound. The wave of honest grief was followed by an anger so fierce he had to keep from shouting. It was ridiculous, he knew, but he felt he had failed to protect her, to keep her alive. He loved her and he had let her down.

In those moments he understood every man who ever cursed his fate and the gods who cheated him. He understood every poor devil's frustration at being powerless to fight back or get even. He could avenge himself on nothing. He could only grieve helplessly at the implacable fact of her dying.

If he loved her so much why had he kept that love at arm's length when the doctors pronounced their sentence? If he could not bear to lose her, why then had he distanced himself from her suffering? Did his guilt come from helplessness, or from a gnawing suspicion that once she was lost to him, he was ready to abandon her for another? He wanted to think he was better than that, but perhaps everyone has something of the monster lurking inside. We give it cute names, he told himself, like "self-protection" and "the survival instinct" which makes us sound less treacherous.

He left Joyce's bedside and went into the library to pour a whiskey and try to think of happier days, but he could not shake his depression. He must have dozed because suddenly the telephone jarred him awake and he saw that it was after seven.

"Colin? It's Anthony. Sorry to bother you."

"No problem."

"Are things any better?"

"I suppose they're stable, Anthony. That's the best I can say." He told him about the change of doctors. "What's up?"

"Fionna Redfern telephoned about her dinner party."

"Can't make it."

"Mr. Petrey also called to say Mr. Quirk is out on bond and in a Howard Johnson Motel up in Stamford. You want the number?"

"I'll get it tomorrow. Anything else?"

"Maggie said Adam Walsh was trying to reach you. He seemed anxious about something and will call you."

Colin wanted to laugh. I'll bet he's anxious, he thought. The days slide by and his second million hasn't been deposited yet. "Walsh can wait," he said.

"He was upset when Maggie told him Joyce was worse. He wanted to know if there was anything he could do. A very kind man," Anthony said. "Very considerate."

Christ! Was Anthony mocking him? But Colin kept forgetting that others were not acquainted with the man behind the clever Walsh facade, the con artist extraordinary, forger, embezzler and extortionist. He recalled the warden saying he missed his favorite prisoner. The way Anthony talked they'd soon be building a statue in Walsh's honor.

"He said he'd pray for Joyce," Anthony added, and Colin wanted to shout, "Has he no sense of decency!"

___ CHAPTER TWENTY-EIGHT ___

MAGGIE CARUSO thought her family name was appropriate. Her rich contralto voice was her pride, and as a child when people would say, "Caruso? Any relation to the opera singer?" she would answer, "I *am* the opera singer."

Her brothers were immensely proud of her. She made more money than both of them together and had earned two degrees taking night classes at New York University and the New School. Improving herself, she called it, getting "Something Else" out of life as she always said she would. It was how she spent much of her time.

Apart from friends at work, those close to her included singers, actors, musicians and a few passionate music lovers like herself with whom she shared the joys of Lincoln Center and Carnegie Hall.

At the time of the *Redfern* case, Maggie was forty-two, still unmarried, but financially secure. There had been affairs along the way with struggling lawyers, impecunious music students and aspiring tenors, but nothing durable and few even worth recalling.

Maggie grew more interesting and attractive as she aged. According to old Anthony Shattuck, she would have left Cranmer, Fisher & Cleves ages ago if it had not been for Colin Draggett.

It was appropriate therefore that when the time came Maggie would be the one to attend to the details of Joyce's funeral. Not long after Joyce had been told that her tumor was both malignant and inoperable, Maggie asked Colin what he wanted to do.

"About what?"

"The arrangements for Joyce."

"What arrangements? Everything's arranged. We've got nurses around the clock and she refuses to go to a hospital again."

"I meant the funeral arrangements."

He couldn't believe his ears. If she was joking it was in the worst possible taste, yet Maggie would never joke about death. He told her to do nothing. It was too ghoulish. Joyce might be incurably ill but there was always the chance of a miracle.

Maggie said, "I know how you like me to organize your life and I thought I'd take some of the unpleasant tasks off your hands now so you wouldn't have to do them later."

"Such as what? Getting comparative prices on coffins? Working up the invitation list to the graveside?"

"I am sorry, Colin," she said. Maggie only called him Colin about twice a year, when she was either angry or feeling sorry for him.

"I know you mean well," he told her. "But I'm still not used to the idea of losing Joyce."

They did not speak of it again and he tried to put it from his mind. What he did not know was that Joyce had telephoned Maggie herself and asked her to come to the apartment when Colin was out of town. The two women then discussed the grim details of death and burial. Joyce decided what sort of funeral she wanted and where. Quiet, with only family and friends, at the old Grace Church down on Hudson Street. She asked Maggie to arrange for the music, parts from the Mozart *Requiem* and a short Bach organ piece she had always loved.

Maggie told Colin afterward that they had laughed at the undertaker's discomfort when selecting the coffin from a catalogue he brought to the apartment. Joyce chose a modest gray model with what she called art-deco handles. They cried too, and Maggie said maybe it was hard to understand, but their shared irreverence in the face of something so awful made it easier for Joyce to cope. Joyce knew it would kill Colin to have to do it, and she was right.

She sent Maggie to Connecticut to buy the cemetery plot and order the stone. She made arrangements for donations to go to Mrs. Ryan's church shelter for homeless children. Finally she called in one of the younger partners at Cranmer, Fisher & Cleves and redrafted her will, leaving a substantial fortune to charities. That was ironic because the money would have paid the interest on Colin's junk-bond debts. But Joyce knew nothing about that debacle, or about the Walsh situation. She thought her husband was rich.

All of this had been completed without his knowledge shortly before she lapsed into coma the day the Indian physician quit. For the next few days there was no change in her condition. Dr. Brenner, the internist Barbara had sent, was marvelous, but he could only do so much. The nurses, too, were at their very best, serious and caring. And they had all had been attending Joyce long enough to become her friends.

Maggie came and went. In the morning Colin would get up early and wait until after Dr. Brenner's visit. Then he would usually walk the forty blocks to his office and try to concentrate on other matters. There was no shortage of crises demanding his attention, although for reasons he did not fully trust or understand, the Adam Walsh matter had receded a little.

At least Walsh was not on the telephone to him every day. And Ken Fairchild and Brian Redfern seemed slightly less strung out. According to Barbara, she hardly saw her husband, which was how she wanted it. She had kept her promise to Colin and said nothing to him about what she intended. He was back and forth between Washington and Stanton's New York offices, and she assumed he was spending most of his nights with Nora Hallowell.

Meanwhile, Brian was holding sales and marketing meetings with his foreign managers when he wasn't ordering cash transfers from Bangkok to Hong Kong to the Cayman Islands in order to cover the rest of the second million for Walsh. He had managed to establish four new companies as fronts and buy two existing ones in places like Brunei and Buenos Aires, where he eventually would be able to justify and adjust the expenditure of funds, all in the name of the overall cause of deflecting the disastrous consequences of Adam Walsh going public or getting the presidency.

Evenings Fionna kept him jumping between black tie appearances at important benefits, concerts and intimate dinner parties where he could mingle with the rich and powerful and impress select directors. And impress them he did, with the help of Fionna's skillful social management.

Although she had abandoned her career as a buyer in the fashion industry when she married Brian, Fionna had never left the many friends and connections she had acquired through her work. While Brian's social contacts were mainly with Stanton people around the world and some of the company's bigger customers, Fionna's social circle extended across a broad sector of New York's financial and cultural life.

Her beauty and charm had always endeared her to men, and now that she was sensibly married to the handsome and successful head of Stanton International, she was embraced by a good many of their wives as well. She was an acknowledged fashion and beauty authority and she was popular because she shared whatever she knew with her friends. Fionna networked constantly, keeping in touch, flattering a little here, chiding a little there, but almost always half a step ahead of everyone.

It was she who knew the season's "in" designer months before his or her collection appeared in Vogue. And it was she who regularly wore that designer's latest creations to well-publicized functions at no cost to Brian. Fionna could recommend the most extraordinary clairvoyant in Connecticut, the most exclusive fat farm in the Carolinas or the most effective hormone cream. She always seemed to know which Brazilian surgeon was the best at tummy-tucks, which Bulgarian clinic had a surefire cure for impotence, and which drug-and-alcohol-treatment center could keep a family secret.

At the time she married Brian, Fionna was not in love, at least not with him. For two years she had been deeply involved with a French textile executive who spent a week of each month in New

York. He was the most attractive man she had ever met, fifteen years her senior, divorced and apparently in love with her. Until the day he called from Paris to say he was marrying someone else and wouldn't be seeing her again for a while.

"What do you mean 'for a while'?" she said in shock.

"Your know, *chérie,* a few monz perhaps. Until ze bloom is off ze rose?"

She slammed down the telephone, cried for a day, and a week later met Brian on the plane to Europe. She was still smarting from her cavalier treatment at the hands of the Frenchman, and by contrast Brian seemed refreshingly honest and aboveboard. He was handsome enough, articulate, and somewhat more urbane than most American executives she'd met. Although she never actually fell in love, she was very much impressed by his suave manners, his elegant tailoring and his elevated position in a major multinational company.

Brian in turn was dazzled by her tits, her smile, her legs, her eyes, and finally her shapely bottom as she rose from her aisle seat to make her way to the lavatory. Only much later, after they had been to bed a few times, did he discover that she also had a keen mind and a purposeful character, but by that time he was hopelessly in love.

Each discovered in the other the thing they appreciated most, however, an ambition that transcended all else. And rather than compete, after a certain time Fionna decided to merge her dreams with Brian's. To her surprise she found it gave her both more freedom and more satisfaction than her own relatively narrow goals had provided.

And now that they were poised for the biggest leap of all, with Brian still years short of his fortieth birthday, she grew almost giddy with anticipation. She planned, she schemed, she orchestrated and she dreamed. She coached him relentlessly and she drove him as hard socially as he drove himself on the job.

When she arranged a Bergdorf fashion show followed by a reception at the Metropolitan Museum of Art for some of the Hartford wives, she was in her element. But an unorthodox evening suggested by Maggie Caruso turned out even better. Maggie got front row seats at a Rangers–Bruins hockey game for the entire contingent of foreign managers and the directors. Most of the foreign guests and all the wives had never seen a hockey game before, and found it as exotic as a bullfight.

Fionna called Colin the following morning to rave about the game and say it was the most successful social program to date.

"I'll make Brian take me again. Absolutely the most thrilling blood sport I've ever seen!"

Blood sport indeed, Colin thought. She should see what her husband does, thinking of Brian's planned mayhem with Quirk. But then again, the Stanton playoff was worth more than the Stanley Cup. The only antisocial behavior Colin Draggett had ever known was on the cement playgrounds of his boyhood. He had never fought in a war or been caught in a riot, never been mugged or assaulted, never even seen a car wreck. Nor had he known anyone who had any firsthand experience with violence until Ken Fairchild's indiscreet ramble down Lenox Avenue.

Which was why he was so upset by Redfern's confession about his intended use of Oliver Quirk. He found his idea of roughing up Adam Walsh not only brutal and stupid, but shocking. That such a plan could come from the mind of an outwardly civilized business executive appalled him, never mind the rationalizations for it.

If he had known what was really on Redfern's mind by that time, he would have had a fit from sheer outrage.

He should have been more suspicious, he would later tell himself, or at least more alert. Particularly in view of an unusual visitor who called on him.

It was mid-morning, a slate-hued frosty day with a wind chill factor of ten degrees. Colin had just arrived after another dispiriting talk with Dr. Brenner. Christmas was a week away and Joyce had been ten days in a coma with no change while Colin foundered in a depression not even Maggie's smile could dissipate.

She came into his office to say, "There's a man to see you who says he's a friend of Mr. Fairchild's."

"What's his name?"

"He said you'd know. According to him, he met you when Mr. Fairchild was mugged, but he looks kind of scary."

"Now, Maggie . . ."

____ CHAPTER TWENTY-NINE ____

LUTHER YANCY extended a powerful hand to Colin. A tall, broad-shouldered man with a bald scalp that glistened in the subdued light of that winter morning, he moved with the self-confidence and casual ease of someone long accustomed to being obeyed.

He was dressed in a well-cut gray flannel suit with a pale blue shirt, striped tie and the tiny rosette of some military decoration in his lapel. When Colin moved away from his desk and indicated they sit in the leather armchairs by the window, he saw that Yancy walked with a slight limp. When he sat down he adjusted something on the side of his knee.

He caught Colin's glance and knocked on his thigh with his knuckles to produce a hard, hollow sound. "Most people don't see it's fake," he said, "but you picked up on it right away."

"I thought it was a brace."

"Nope. It's a hundred percent artificial. But it gets me around pretty good even on the golf course. You play golf?"

Colin nodded.

Yancy apologized for not calling first, but said he decided to take a chance on catching Colin in. "Ever since you called I been meaning to come see you, but my workload around Christmas is unbelievable with store security. We had to put on a hundred temporaries because so many New Yorkers got light fingers."

"I'm glad you found the time, Mr. Yancy."

"I been wanting to talk to somebody about the major, and when I got your message, I figured you're the man."

"You and Ken Fairchild go back a long time."

"He was my boss in Vietnam."

"Is that when you lost the leg?"

"I stepped on a mine, the kind explodes only when you take your weight off. I'm standing on the damn thing crapping down my pants leg when the major catches up and says, 'Outstanding, Luther, you dumb sumbitch, look what you done! You going to get us both killed.'" Yancy smiled at the memory. "He has the patrol roll a big old log between him and me and tells me to dive behind that log and do it the fastest I ever done anything in my life. I got lucky. Goddamn mine took the leg but didn't total me. He got hit, too, but it only pickled his backside some."

"It was a brave thing to do."

Yancy nodded. "Foolish, too. The medevac got us out that day. They give him a medal and he chews my ass for walking into Charlie's minefield." He laughed as he said, "But I didn't come here to talk about that. I figure you got something more important on your mind."

"What was he doing in Harlem the night he got mugged?"

"What did he tell you?"

"Not much. He said he was looking for you."

"Did he say why?"

"Only that you were friends from the war."

"Right. Well, this is how it started. He phoned and said he wanted to see me about a job. I told him why would I need a job when I got my own security agency with a hundred-forty guards on the payroll, and he said not that kind of job. My sister thought he was one of them whacko vets from the center where I counsel. Which is a laugh because the major was always about the most together guy I ever knew. But what he's looking for is a pair of dudes for some heavy work he had in mind."

"Did he tell you what the work was?"

"No, he got beaten up."

"Didn't you ask him in the hospital?"

"That's what didn't make sense to me. He laughed it off. Said he was under a lot of pressure and he'd changed his mind."

"Did you believe him?"

"Yes and no. Me and the major get along real fine, like I said. He saved my life and I owe him for that and a lot more. I wouldn't have my own business if it wasn't for him."

"Why is that?"

"When I retired from the army I wasn't sure about my plans. I didn't have enough capital to start my business alone so Major Fairchild told me about a bank. The banker said what collateral you got? I said thirty thousand in savings and my army pension. And you know what the banker said?"

"He probably said no."

"I guess you know bankers, Mr. Draggett. So I say what I had in mind was one of those small business loans the government guarantees, and the banker says he don't mess with them. So I say even I'm a disabled veteran?"

Yancy leaned forward and tapped his artificial leg. "He said they can't insure a handicap like that, I say it wasn't exactly my idea and he says if they can't insure me they can't make me a loan. I tell him, I'm also black as he may have noticed, and I read there were special affirmative-action loans for black people. He tells me he doesn't know where I read that, but anyway its got nothing to do with his bank. As I'm leaving he says if I was to get some solid citizen to guaranty my loan . . ." Yancy laughed as if the joke was on him. "Until I met this banker honcho I considered myself a pretty solid citizen. Funny how a man can make a mistake like that. Anyway, I call the major who's even solider than me, and when I tell him what happened he goes straight up."

"And he guarantied the note for you?"

"Didn't have to. He must have landed on that bank like the Eighty-second Airborne. When I went back there all I had to do was sign Luther Yancy to a paper and walk out with a hundred thousand dollars in credit. I paid it back in a year and now they're on the phone all the time trying to loan me more."

"Did Fairchild ever tell you what he said?"

"No, but I can imagine. He and I aren't exactly what you'd call regular drinking buddies, but I know him. Where we were, you learn the best and the worst about a man. On a scale of ten, I'd rate the major about fifteen."

Maggie arrived with a coffee tray and left.

"What bothers me, Mr. Draggett, is what's he up to anyway? Here he is. Rich, fancy job, nice wife and kids. So what's he doing messing around in Harlem?" A capricious shaft of sunlight burst upon the room at that moment and startled them both. It glinted and danced beyond the windows, shot the surface of the harbor with pointillist flakes of gold and silver, and reached a square of carpet by Yancy's feet that made him look up and smile.

Colin poured some coffee. "It's true he's been under a lot of pressure. Did he get in touch with you again after that or ever give you a clue about what he wanted these men to do for him?"

Yancy shook his head, sighed, got up and went to the window to look out at the harbor. "Nice," he said, turning back after a moment. Colin was thinking what a gentle man he was, big and powerful to be sure, and with a feline grace that enabled him to dissimulate the prosthetic leg. The gentleness made what he had to say next all the more unsettling.

"I probably know fifty ways to kill a man, and I've used most of them. But it's frustrating not to be able to help a friend when he needs you."

"Maybe the need passed."

"Always possible, but I doubt it. I think he just had second thoughts. Big football hero. Big army career. Big business success. But one weakness. Lotta heart, lotta courage. Fine officer. A regular boy scout, you know. Mine wasn't the only life he saved in Nam. But . . ."

"One weakness, you said."

"Women. They fall all over him and he can't resist them. Lock up your wives, they used to joke, Fairchild's in town. You know what I think, Mr. Draggett?"

Colin waited.

"I think he's in some trouble about a woman. Maybe shaking him down or blackmail, the way he likes the ladies. And he's kind of naive about them. Doesn't figure what can happen to him. I don't know who's trying to get him or for what. But I think he came to me because I know people who can solve problems quick. I believe somebody's after him and he wanted them off his back."

Luther Yancy's perception was only a little short of the truth. And as Colin listened he was thinking of Brian Redfern's abortive attempt to employ Oliver Quirk. Ken had undoubtedly been up to the same kind of mischief and changed his mind.

Yancy was watching Colin for a reaction, so he said, "Believe me, Mr. Yancy, I'm sure it's nothing like that."

"I guess you'd know better than I, being his lawyer, but what about the major's wife?"

"What makes you think his wife is involved?"

"She hired a detective to track him after she found out he had himself a new girlfriend."

"Who told you that?"

"The dude she hired is a pal of mine, Dom Petrey."

"I know Mr. Petrey."

"So he said."

"Mrs. Fairchild's no longer using his services."

"No, but you are."

"I was under the impression Petrey was a professional who kept confidences. It seems I was mistaken."

"Dom only told me because I put him in touch with the major in the first place to take care of a company investigation. I only told you because we both want to help him."

"I see."

"Dom was a little surprised when Mrs. Fairchild called. At first he wasn't sure he should take the assignment." Yancy returned to the chair opposite Colin and sat down. "He asked me what I thought he should do."

"And you told him to take it."

"Petrey's paying out a lot of alimony and he's got a weakness for the ponies, so he needs the money. I saw no conflict."

"Did he tell you what he's doing for me?"

"No. And I don't care because it's got nothing to do with me. But if the major's in trouble, if somebody's after him and you know about it, I'm hoping you'll tell me because I might be able to do something."

"I'm sure he's not in that kind of trouble."

"It'd be a goddamn shame if anything bad happened to him I could have stopped."

"You're not suggesting he can't take care of himself?"

Yancy laughed. "I have to say his track record in that particular department lately is not outstanding."

_____ CHAPTER THIRTY _____

CHRISTMASES WERE happy times for Joyce and Colin until her illness intervened. For years they chartered the same ketch out of the British Virgins, flying down around the twentieth and returning the day after New Year's. Just a mellow winter interlude, a chance to bask in the sun and each other's company snorkel the coral reefs and be caressed by gentle breezes as they sipped their rum punch. Joyce never said as much, but he knew that during a holiday season that was essentially arranged for children, it also took her mind off the ones they lacked.

Now Christmas was something to be got through. At Cranmer, Fisher & Cleves the halls were decked with holly a week before the twenty-fifth, and by popular demand the firm joined virtually every other law office, insurance company and brokerage house in the Wall Street ritual of holding a party on the premises.

Maggie tried to explain it to Colin. "The annual Christmas party is the only chance we have to reverse roles and turn the world upside down. The girl in the typist pool gets to dance with you, the senior partner. The mail boy can tell the obnoxious new Harvard Law brain where to put it. Barriers come down, masks fall away and everybody discovers that we are all real live human beings after all." Before she dropped the subject she also got a commitment from Colin to attend this year's party barring any emergency at home.

Three days before Christmas, for reasons neither Dr. Brenner nor anyone else could explain, Joyce improved dramatically. She regained consciousness and remained awake for half an hour at a time. Although she was terribly weak, she asked for Colin, who felt a small surge of hope each time she held his hand before she drifted off to sleep again.

He remained at home the entire day, looking in every little while only to see her sleeping. On one of his visits late that afternoon he leaned down and kissed her lightly on the lips.

She opened her eyes and smiled. "Just like the movies," she said in a voice as light as air. "The kiss of the handsome prince breaks the spell of the wicked witch."

"Just like the movies," he agreed, stroking her hair. "Can I bring you anything?"

"You already have. Are you playing hooky from the office today?"

He nodded.

"When is Christmas?"

"In a couple of days."

"We should be in the Islands."

"I was thinking that myself this morning. Next year."

She looked away with the barest shake of her head. "Don't start that, please."

He felt his throat tighten.

"But you could make me a promise."

"Okay."

"Not 'okay.' Promise."

"I promise."

"Go back next year and take somebody with you. Some nice lady . . ."

"Oh, for Christ sake."

". . . who knows how to sail. I don't want you moping, Colin. You're no fun when you mope. And you can be fun, counselor."

They were both silent for a while as he held her hand, still stroking her hair. "Talk to me," she said finally in a barely audible whisper. "Tell me what's going on. It's hard to speak but not to listen."

"Things are pretty quiet downtown. I've got to go to New London after the New Year for the Stanton stockholders meeting."

"Is Ken . . . ?"

"Going to be president?"

She nodded.

"Barbara's made up her mind to divorce him and she's dead set against his taking over from Hunt Benson. So the job's up for grabs at the moment."

She pointed at him.

"Me? Take over Stanton Technologies?"

She nodded.

"I'm a lawyer, not a manager," he said. "And apart from having no interest in a career change at this late date, I'm not qualified to run a high-tech company."

"What about . . . ?"

"Brian? He's the logical choice . . ."

She shook her head.

". . . or maybe Hunt Benson can be persuaded . . ."

She continued to shake her head. "Walsh?" she whispered.

"Impossible." He took a deep breath, shifted his weight on the edge of the bed and then said awkwardly, "I haven't told you about this before because . . ." Still he hesitated.

"If it's a secret," she said faintly, "I won't tell."

"Not only is it a secret, my darling, but I'm not exactly happy with my role in it."

She patted his hand, and with that slight encouragement he began to tell her what they had found out about Walsh and about their decision to deal with him following Avery Stanton's sudden death. He mentioned the amount and the source of the money they were paying Walsh to leave quietly, and the reasons Colin was using to justify his action.

He was not sure she had understood everything until she smiled mischievously and said, "No wonder you didn't tell me before."

"Why do you say that?"

"Poor sweetheart. How did you paint yourself into such a corner? What about the wife . . . and the man who knew him in college?"

"That's what I'd like to know. What about them?"

"You think they're telling the truth?" she whispered.

"I'm afraid I do."

"Wonderful . . ." Joyce sighed, squeezing his hand. "I love a mystery." And she closed her eyes again.

Later, more buoyant and hopeful than he had been in weeks, Colin told Lauren Jewett that perhaps a change for the better might be taking place in Joyce after all. He did not use the word "remission" but it was in his mind.

The nurse answered, "They rally sometimes, Mr. Draggett," in a tone that implied he should not be encouraged by the change.

That evening Colin invited Anthony Shattuck to dine at the Gansevoort, where they talked law. It was the kind of outing Colin enjoyed with the old man, whose legal experience went back more than fifty years and whose total recall seemed to include every case the firm had ever handled. He had known the famous and the infamous in his time as a top Wall Street law clerk, and his store of anecdotes was inexhaustible.

As the waiter served them a lemon sorbet after the Beef Wellington he said, "Colin, may I ask you an indiscreet question?"

Colin smiled at that. The idea of Anthony Shattuck being indiscreet about anything was almost preposterous.

"What is it?"

"Hunt Benson called yesterday to see if I had put together your agenda for the Stanton stockholders meeting. It's ready, by the way. He says some of the directors are very keen on Adam Walsh taking his place when he steps down next month."

"What's the question?"

"Why aren't you?"

"Why aren't I what?"

"Keen on Adam Walsh."

"Who said I wasn't?"

"You mean you've changed your mind?"

"Not at all. Walsh is a clever fellow. But I'd prefer a man with a technical background for the top slot."

"There's a rumor going around that something other than lack of an engineering degree might hold Walsh back."

"Oh?"

"Does he have any skeletons in the closet, Colin?"

"Anthony, you would probably find a few old bones rattling around everyone's closet if the facts were known. Except yours. Who passed this rumor on to you anyway? Hunt?"

"He asked me what I knew. He also wanted to know if you favored Walsh or not for the presidency."

"What did you tell him?"

"That I didn't know how you felt."

"Did he say what it was that marred Walsh's past?"

"I don't think he really believed there was anything to the story. He was very vague, to tell the truth, but you know how gossip goes round when a man is being considered for a high position. Caesar's wife and all that sort of thing."

"There's bound to be a certain amount of speculation."

"Did you see the squib in this week's Forbes magazine touting Brian Redfern as Stanton's new Mr. Wonderful and mentioning Ken Fairchild as an also-ran. That should thrill Ken."

"Everybody seems to have their favorite," Colin said.

"Except you," Anthony replied, "or am I wrong?"

"You want me to tell you?"

"No, Colin, but I do believe Hunt Benson and the other directors would like you to tell them."

"Anthony, the Hartford Commercial Insurance Bank owns fifteen percent of the stock in Stanton. That gives Howie Livingston and Lydell Cummings each a seat on the board. The First Boston owns ten percent and also has two directors. I own five percent, Barbara Fairchild now holds roughly a third of the outstanding shares, and the other third is spread around."

"But the trustees vote Barbara's shares, Colin."

"What? Ave Stanton voted them."

"He had their proxies, Colin, but with his death the three directors appointed by the Foundation vote her shares."

"I'm sure you're mistaken, Anthony."

"Colin, you set it up yourself years ago. Don't you remember? All inherited family shares are voted like that for tax reasons."

Anthony was right, of course. Although Colin had not forgotten the elaborate cat's cradle of stock ownership he had established for Stanton when Barbara was still a schoolgirl, he had overlooked the detail of who would actually vote the stock in the event of Avery's death.

As the waiter poured their coffee Anthony didn't say a word. He was tracking Colin. "Doing sums?" Anthony said finally.

Colin had to laugh. "Right. Avery, Redfern and Fairchild made up the executive committee on the board. With Avery dead, Benson takes his place and he favors Walsh for president because he believes Ave wanted him."

"Didn't he?"

"Not at the end. He wanted Fairchild."

"What changed his mind?"

"It's a long story."

"Worth telling?"

"Not tonight."

"So who do you favor?"

"I, too, would like to see Ken Fairchild take over."

"Would Redfern?"

"He'd go along, but Barbara's against it."

"I heard there was trouble there," Anthony said.

"Has Maggie been telling tales out of school?"

"There are no secrets inside Fisher, Cranmer & Cleves," Anthony said. "There better not be any from me, at least. Maggie's thick with the private investigator Barbara hired to watch Ken. So things trickle back to my desk."

"I hope that's as far as they trickle."

"Maggie speaks only to me, and I speak only to God. In this case, you."

"Then you probably know that Barbara wants a divorce and she's going to ask for it soon after the first of the year. She's definite about not wanting her husband to take over Stanton."

"Who does she think should get the job?"

"Walsh."

"Interesting."

"But I think I persuaded her otherwise."

"To back Ken?"

"To back off. I said I would try to persuade Hunt Benson to stay on another year until she sorted out her marital mess."

"And she agreed."

"More or less. But I don't know if Hunt will."

Anthony smiled. "I doubt if the intrigue in the inner circle of Henry the Eighth's court was more interesting to follow."

"Maybe. But Tudor politics were at least a little more deadly. You could lose your head if you weren't careful."

"And what makes you think that can't happen at Stanton Technologies?"

Colin was almost ready to agree as he thought of his lunch in this very dining room with Brian Redfern and the call from Petrey about Quirk.

"You're not telling me quite the whole truth about Adam Walsh, are you, Colin?"

"Not quite."

"Any reason?"

"In the military they use the phrase 'need to know.'"

"I was never in the military. Anyway, what I don't know is why you would withhold anything unless there was a compelling reason, such as some truth in the rumor Hunt Benson was asking about."

"I don't want Walsh as president of Stanton, and as long as I can do something about it I will. Let's leave it at that."

"Fine, but what can you do about it? Benson wants Walsh, you say, and I presume Cummings and Livingston do too."

Colin nodded.

"Deke Peabody and Rog Devere of the First Boston Investment Fund will vote with Cummings and Livingston. That's five for Walsh against you, Redfern and Fairchild, with the three Foundation directors looking on. Who will they vote for?"

"If Hunt Benson agrees to stay, they'd confirm him."

"But failing that, won't they follow Benson's lead if he's for Walsh? I hate to be the devil's advocate but—"

"You're right. Hunt Benson's the key."

"Would you support Redfern if Hunt won't stay?"

"Yes."

"So maybe Forbes magazine is right."

"Let's not get ahead of ourselves."

Colin knew perfectly well that the directors representing the Foundation had backed Avery Stanton's recommendations in better times, which was why no one paid them any attention. They rarely came to board meetings but left permanent proxies in Avery Stanton's hands. Now they would want to do the right thing, and that presumably meant following Hunt Benson's lead.

One was a New London newspaper publisher, one was president of an Ivy League women's college and the third was a retired navy admiral. A collection of outsiders who could very well decide the fate of the company.

"Perhaps it doesn't matter," Anthony said. "Boards have a way sometimes of making the right choice instinctively."

"Not this time. Not if they go with Adam Walsh."

"I'll take your word for it. What happens now?"

"I'm not sure. Until a moment ago I was under the impression that Barbara would cast the deciding vote on my advice."

"I'm glad you got that straight before the meeting."

"As always, dinner with you has been instructive, Anthony. Tomorrow I'll start networking these guys to see if I can avoid unpleasant surprises."

"These guys include one lady college president."

"So I'll charm her first."

"You know what surprises me? Why you don't back Walsh and save all the hassle. Is it really worth the push and shove to put Redfern in and keep Walsh out?"

"It's worth it. You'll have to take my word on that."

———— CHAPTER THIRTY-ONE ————

HUNT BENSON's lifelong devotion to Avery Stanton was little short of worship. Although no one ever called Hunt stupid, neither did the world glimpse any spark of imagination or ambition behind his round, agreeable features and self-effacing manners. Yet those who assumed there were no surprises in Hunt Benson were wrong.

In his own plodding way he had great strength of character and was fiercely loyal to those he admired, qualities which congealed after Avery Stanton's death into a stubbornness that caused Colin no end of trouble.

If it hadn't been for Ave Stanton, Benson would have finished his career as an obscure middle-level engineer with the giant aluminum manufacturer where he had started out. Instead Stanton had recruited him as production chief when he founded Stanton Technologies, and Hunt had become his acolyte.

For twenty years he followed Stanton's orders, teed off with him on the golf course and carried his briefcase on business trips. With little life of his own, when Avery Stanton died and Hunt inherited the president's title he had precious little notion of what to do. Death only confirmed Stanton's elevation to sainthood in Hunt Benson's mind. This fact and Hunt's obstinate refusal to follow anyone else's lead helped prepare the ground for precisely the struggle Colin was seeking to avoid.

The day after his dinner with Anthony Shattuck, Colin left New York at daybreak and drove to New London. Hunt Benson and he sat in the same executive suite Avery Stanton had occupied, with its dark oak paneling, subdued light and gilt-framed seascapes, reviewing the agenda for the January stockholders meeting.

There had been one conspicuous change in the office since Colin's last visit. At the entrance, dramatically lit by a halogen spot, was a large globe painted like a blue-and-white marble similar to photographs of the earth taken from outer space. Nearby were models of space craft, rockets, submarines and planes that were dependent on materials produced by Stanton Technologies.

"Like it?" Hunt said, his voice vibrant with pride.

"Very handsome," Colin agreed, "but shouldn't you put it at the building entrance where more visitors would see it?"

"Oh, Ken Fairchild's working on a whole futures concept display for down there in time for the annual meeting. And he's got an outfit from Canada making a 3-D movie people can watch while they wait."

"Since when is Ken involving himself directly in things like this?" As he asked the question, Colin answered it in his mind. Nora Hallowell was the most likely source of inspiration, with her advertising job and intimate access to the Stanton vice-president.

"Colin, Ken comes up with more good ideas in five minutes than our advertising department gets in a year."

"I daresay."

"How do you like this one?"

The globe was about two feet in diameter and looked heavy, but to Colin's surprise Hunt picked it up and bounced it easily in the air before tossing it to him. It was lighter than a beach ball and Colin assumed it must be made of some foam plastic.

But Hunt said, "This is solid, molded Graftite, the titanium graphite product that Adam was talking up at the New York dinner. You can stomp it, burn it, hammer it or shoot at it. But you can't hurt it. He generated so many orders we can't cope with our current plant capacity." He sighed, then confided, "But that's a problem for Stanton's next president to sort out, not me."

"That's something I want to talk with you about, Hunt."

"Ken's way ahead of us on that. He already has people working on cost estimates for the required plant expansion."

"I don't mean that. I mean about your staying on."

"Oh, I'd never dream of it. I'm moving to Florida as soon as we sell our house. I bought a condo on Eslamorada."

"I hope you'll reconsider."

"I'm flattered you want me, Colin, but I've done my part here, held up my end, so to speak. It's time for new blood to take over. I never expected this job and never wanted it. You know that."

"I'd like to submit your name to the board anyway."

"But why?"

"These are uncertain times, Hunt, with Avery gone and the country just pulling out of a major recession. You represent continuity, which translates into stability and market confidence."

"Kind words coming from you, Colin, and I appreciate them, but I'm not the only one around here who inspires confidence. Look what happened to the share price after Adam's speech."

"It was smart, Hunt, but you and I know you can't pull that twice and get away with it. The Dow dropped forty points last week and the market's in the doldrums."

"But Stanton stock is still up almost seven dollars over the day Avery died." He retrieved the globe and set it on its pedestal. "Graftite is only part of the story. We've got those frozen crystals that Walsh raved about and the Hot Block. I had the R&D people send me an update on everything they're doing. You wouldn't believe some of that stuff. Talk about Star Wars!"

"All the more reason to hang in there another year, Hunt. You're part of the old guard, like me, and that counts."

"Colin, I'd never want them to say I didn't know when to step down and make room for the next fellow. No, sir."

The bland obstinacy of the man was infuriating, but Colin knew that the more he pushed, the more Benson would resist. So he stroked him a little before he said, "I'll be sorry to see you go, Hunt."

"No reason to be sorry. I thank the good lord that Avery worked it all out before he died."

"Worked what out?"

"Choosing the right man to succeed him." He leaned closer to Colin and lowered his voice as if someone else was within hearing distance. "You know what I was afraid of, don't you?"

"I don't believe I do, Hunt."

"That he'd want Redfern. Ave always had a weakness for Brian ever since he came to work here summers as a college kid. Oh, I'm the first one to recognize the job he's done for Stanton International, and he's a damn good engineer. But he can be arrogant and that rubs a lot of people the wrong way. The head of a huge company like ours has to get along with everybody from the union steward on the shop floor to the man in the White House."

"Brian just needs a little seasoning," Colin said.

"Maybe, but who can tell him anything? He never consults me on a single thing, just goes on his merry way, writing new rules to suit himself."

"It seems to me that was one of the main things Ave always liked about Brian," Colin suggested.

Benson grunted. "He wouldn't like the loose way he's been transferring company money around, but I put a stop to that. Otherwise the auditors would never finish. I don't expect strict conformity, but Redfern gets so wrapped up in all his great schemes he doesn't even take the trouble to be civil."

At least not to Hunt, Colin thought. Brian had never made any secret of his contempt for Hunt Benson, whom he regarded as a sycophant and time-server fit only to carry Avery Stanton's briefcase. Benson knew this and it was a measure of his own sense of fairness that he did not criticize Brian even more harshly.

"What was I saying?" Benson said. "Lost the thread. Oh, yes. I'm sure he told you who he wanted, Colin, knowing you'd agree."

"We talked about it, but he had more than one candidate in mind, trying to second-guess what was best for the company."

"Stanton always came first with Ave," Hunt said.

"He didn't expect to die," Colin said, "even though he knew he'd have to step down. In the last days he gave the matter of a new president his full attention."

"That was Ave's way," Hunt agreed. "He never went off half-cocked. Always so careful how he studied a problem. Adam Walsh is a lot like that. He reminds me of Ave."

Colin almost choked. "Indeed? How?"

"Dedication, to begin with. I don't have it, never did. I'd rather go fishing any day. You don't have it either. You'd rather be sailing your boat than sitting talking business with me."

For Hunt that remark showed uncharacteristic insight. As he rattled on, Colin waited to hear precisely who it was he thought Avery Stanton wanted to head up his company.

"Nothing impulsive about Ave Stanton, and I knew him better than anyone. A careful, prudent man, by God."

As Benson recited this litany Colin marveled at how Hunt could have worked so closely with Stanton for so many years and not known him at all. Hunt Benson did not realize that only his own pale virtues were reflected in his memory of Ave Stanton.

What was the real Stanton like? He was eccentric, unpredictable and more than a little manic-depressive. Like many geniuses, he lived his whole life on impulse, adrift in a sea of indecision. He could brood for days about nuclear waste, the ozone layer or over-population, and convince himself the world was coming to an end. Then he could snap out of his funk, turn to some pet laboratory project and work around the clock. He rarely spent any effort on routine matters. In his impatience Avery Stanton would leave them for someone else. It was as if he knew he had only so much time to set down his ideas and he refused to devote his attention to anything that vexed him. He passed his life following hunches, and it was his special talent for finding innovative solutions to chemical puzzles that forever separated him from the Hunt Bensons of the world.

Colin did not tell Hunt that his portrait of Stanton was way off or that he was projecting his own tepid values onto his idol.

Hunt confused and irritated Colin even more with his talk of Ken Fairchild's amazing cleverness and Adam Walsh's understanding of everything from the national economy to the inner workings of a new electro-plating machine.

The more Hunt had to say, the less Colin was sure who he favored, until at last he said, "Ave was anxious to please Barbara, too. That's why he wanted Ken Fairchild, and that's why we have to see that his wishes are carried out."

As relieved as Colin was not to hear another vote for Walsh, Benson's endorsement of Fairchild hardly helped matters because of Barbara's intransigence and his concern for her. Besides, she was still a force, no matter who technically voted her stock. Colin had to persuade Hunt to stay on at all costs or make the directors do it for him.

THE ANNUAL stockholders meeting on January sixth was only two weeks away. Avery Stanton had always made it a media event with the announcement of some new product or process. But this year whatever Stanton Technologies was ready to talk about, Adam Walsh had already publicized in his speech to the securities analysts.

Hunt Benson's plan was that the meeting would take place in the employee cafeteria, which could seat a thousand people in relative discomfort. It would begin at ten in the morning with Hunt and the rest of top management onstage. After his introductory remarks, Hunt Benson would turn the floor over to the different vice-presidents. A tour of the Stanton plant would follow and then the stockholders would be treated to a buffet lunch in the cafeteria. After lunch, the board of directors would hold its meeting to elect the new president of Stanton Technologies.

"We start here at headquarters, then divide them up into groups, with a company officer at the head of each group," Hunt told Colin. "I want Adam Walsh to guide the first VIP bunch, who are all investment bankers and money-market reps. Then Ken will lead the second, then Redfern and then the others. Take them to the raw-material reception docks, the rail spur, the wharf, the warehouses and then to the laminate preparation bays. It's damned exciting." The laminate preparation bays had been designed by Hunt Benson and were about as exciting as the cafeteria hot tables.

Benson listed the acid-storage tanks, truck-dispatch sheds and maintenance shops before passing to the plating rooms them-

selves, the place that might indeed be called interesting. Most of
the work in the plating rooms was done by white-coated operators
in remote Plexiglas cabins high above. The tour guests would also
view it all from overhead as they passed directly over the metal
baths on narrow steel catwalks.

"How about walking through the tour with me before we eat
some lunch," Hunt Benson said with enthusiasm.

"Thanks, but I've seen it, Hunt."

"Not the laminate preparation bays!"

"Those, too. Hell of a job you did there, Hunt."

"Not bad. One of the last things Ave and I worked on together,
in fact."

"It shows," Colin said, knowing Avery had him supervise the
design job in part to get him out of his hair the previous year.

"But you haven't seen the Graftite electroplate setup," Walsh
said, "it was just installed."

He had him there, and Colin agreed to look.

"I'd like you to speak to the stockholders, too, Colin," Benson
said as they left his office and crossed the windswept lawn that
separated the headquarters building from the main plant.

"To say what?"

"The same sort of thing you told the mourners at Ave's funeral.
Talk a little about the old days, about how we all started out like
the Three Musketeers. Ave, you and me. Tie it into today, you
know. Challenges are different but just as great. Back then we
were all trying to put a man on the moon."

Inside the main electroplating complex the din was tremendous.
Every time Colin set foot in the place he wondered why nobody
ever took the acoustics into consideration. A worker must go deaf
after a few years in this high-decibel echo chamber where great
sheets of metal were constantly clanging and banging like the cym-
bals of the gods.

Hunt Benson happily led the way through this orchestrated
chaos, keeping well clear of the machinery. The heat and the acrid
odors were on the same level as the noise, and the humidity had to
be close to a hundred percent with wet slippery floors everywhere.
But the workers they saw seemed cheerful; most tossed a friendly
salute or a thumbs-up as they recognized Benson, while his plump
florid features wore the contented smile of a man at home in such
an environment.

When the two men reached the vast shoulder-high tanks of glistening titanium salts, Benson paused and led Colin to one side, shouting in his ear, "Graftite!" A continuous roll of what looked like tar paper was coming off a huge spool at one end, passing through the bath and emerging from the other end like cloth of gold. Other nearby baths of titanium shimmered in hot suspension under infrared light as huge castings were put through the plating process. Dipped, retrieved and dipped again.

"Only two-millionths of an inch thick," Hunt shouted, "then back to the resin room and the graphite presses again."

"Incredible!" Colin shouted back, which pleased Benson.

He pointed overhead at a giant crane dangling what looked like a monster bomb. "Rocket nose cone!"

"Fantastic!" Colin continued, looking up, prepared to duck as it came by, but the thing cleared them by fifty feet.

"That's where our tour goes!" Benson pointed to a narrow catwalk high over the baths. "Great view! Of course, one must be careful. Want to go up?"

Colin shook his head and pointed at his watch.

——— CHAPTER THIRTY-TWO ———

NATHANIEL SAWYER, editor and publisher of the New London *Post-Advocate,* could trace his family roots in the town back more than three hundred years. Sawyers had been soldiering and governing and preaching and doing business in Connecticut since the English first put a settlement at the mouth of the Thames River.

Even before the colony existed it was a Sawyer who surveyed the local hills when they still belonged to the Wampanaug Indians, and another who laid out the streets of colonial New London.

Nathaniel was a gaunt, vigorous man in his sixties with mouse-brown hair, a widow's peak and a long thin nose bequeathed by a dozen generations of stern New England preachers, scholars and seamen. He was one of the few men Colin Draggett knew who still wore bow ties, and the three-piece houndstooth suits he favored were invariably shiny in the seat and elbows.

An ardent yachtsman, the collection of silver cups and salvers in his office testified to his skill. Colin knew him on the water as a shrewd competitor, cunning, knowledgeable and unyielding.

Outwardly taciturn, he nevertheless had a marvelous dry wit, an open mind and a pithy way of expressing himself that made him a most agreeable companion once a few drinks thawed his Yankee reticence. Colin discovered this the first time he beat him over the finish line in a race when Nathaniel said, "Most of us fuck up eventually."

His newspaper occupied a crenelated Victorian brick building near the old railroad station, and his office was a modest second-floor cubbyhole with a single window that looked out on a cenotaph commemorating Captain Isaac Sawyer, a Revolutionary War hero killed when the Redcoats attacked New London.

"What brings you to this end of town?" Sawyer asked Colin. "Come to take out a classified?" He selected a pipe from among those on his desk, tamped the tobacco and lit it with a wooden match.

Colin had learned from experience that the best approach to Nathaniel was direct. "I'm trying to persuade Hunt Benson to remain as president of Stanton for at least another year."

"Why?"

He outlined the same vague reasons he had used on Benson. Stability, bla-bla, confidence bla-bla, Dow-Jones bla-bla.

Listening patiently as he puffed away behind a layered smoke-screen of sweet-smelling tobacco, Sawyer finally said, "Colin, the Foundation directors always voted with Avery. Even now, in his absence, we'd still want to go with him."

"I respect that, Nathaniel."

He took his time, and for a minute all Colin heard was the gurgle of his pipe. It had gone out and the editor struck another match and puffed until he had it going again. "Don't misunderstand me, Colin. Hunt and I are friends and everybody says he's a fine production man. But he's no more equipped to run that company than my twelve-year-old grandson." He peered down his long nose. "So why keep him around?"

"I'll put it this way. Whoever takes over next will decide the company's future for some years to come, and I'm not yet ready to choose that man. I'd like Hunt to hang in there long enough to give the board time to find the right person."

"You mean bring somebody from outside?"

"Not necessarily, but it is a possibility to consider."

Sawyer concentrated on his pipe. "Have you talked to Hunt about staying on?" When Colin nodded, he said, "And?"

"He's got Florida on the brain, so he needs convincing."

"I'm certainly not the one to convince him."

"We have to gang up on him, Nathaniel. I think he'll do it if we can make him realize it's in Stanton's best interest."

"Why are you so sure it is, Colin? I don't want to sound critical of Hunt, but he's not exactly famous as a fireball."

"Precisely why he's in the saddle right now."

"Frankly, I expect Ken Fairchild should succeed him. Ken's on the board, he's sales chief, and being married to Stanton's only child puts him in line for the throne."

"I'd rather not force that issue with Barbara right now."

He looked up. "Trouble in paradise?"

"Let's say they're going through a squally spell, so she is not his greatest fan at the moment. I'm sure they'll work it out."

"Meanwhile, you'd prefer Hunt Benson running the store?"

"I prefer it to our making premature decisions."

"Have you talked to any of the other directors?"

"I came to you first."

"The job should go to Fairchild, no doubt about it. But if we have to keep old Hunt at the tiller a little longer to make sure, you can count on me. The others will go along. But you'll still have to convince Benson. When will you see Long John Silver?"

"This afternoon, I hope." Long John Silver was Nathaniel's nickname for retired Rear Admiral G. Wesley Scheutter, his fellow director and also a trustee of the Stanton Foundation.

"Good luck," Nathaniel said as Colin left with some of his optimism restored. His vote, together with Fairchild's, Brian's, Barbara's and Colin's, gave them five out of twelve. If Colin could get the admiral and the lady college president on his side they would have a clear majority and Benson could hardly refuse a draft. There would be no more rash talk of making Adam Walsh president. Colin also hoped that by the time they had settled accounts with Walsh, perhaps Barbara would have cooled down enough to accept Fairchild at the helm.

He reached the admiral's wife by telephone at lunchtime. They lived in Groton, a short distance from the Stanton plant. Scheutter was out Christmas shopping but would be returning soon, she said, and invited Colin to come at five for tea or a drink.

REAR ADMIRAL G. Wesley Scheutter, U.S.N. (Ret.), had once been Admiral Hyman Rickover's chief troubleshooter during the development and construction of America's nuclear submarine fleet. In his capacity as procurement officer he had steered many complex and profitable contracts through the Pentagon maze for Avery Stanton. Upon retirement he was made a trustee of the Stanton Foundation and rewarded with a directorship in the company.

New London is a navy town, a submarine town, and Wes Scheutter was in his element there. He lunched daily at the officers' club on the sub base, played bridge and golf with other retired officers and worked on his memoirs, which he had shown to Nathaniel Sawyer. The editor once told Colin in a rare moment of whiskey-induced candor that Scheutter's memoirs were among the most amazing documents he had ever read.

When Colin showed surprise—the admiral impressed him as a man of limited expression and even more restricted vision—Nathaniel smiled wryly. "I said they were amazing. Not interesting or particularly literate or in any sense publishable."

"But how are they amazing?"

"Colin, Wes' memoirs are a detailed record, a diary more meticulous than a ship's log, of *every* day of his life from the moment he entered the Naval Academy."

"You're joking."

"He filled over four hundred lined notebooks during his career and he kept them all. The memoirs are a transcription of thirty years."

"But what are they about? Vietnam and—?"

"He never got near Vietnam, never heard a shot fired in anger, never actually had much sea duty. It's true he was present during the formative years of our nuclear navy, but you'd never know that from reading his diaries. Anything of interest was either classified or perhaps beyond his field. Most of his career was spent in a series of offices, where he recorded every thermostat reading, typing error, coffee break and piss call between nineteen fifty-three and nineteen eighty-three when the navy mercifully retired him. If Proust had been assigned to the Pentagon or James Joyce to the Naval Annex, they might have come up with something of comparable length and detail. But only a stonecutter could produce anything as weighty."

Nathaniel's description had everyone at the yacht club bar laughing. "But why did he show it to you?" one asked.

"He was giving me first crack at publishing them. I have read seed catalogues that moved me more. Gas bills that were funnier, funeral announcements with more suspense."

"But are you going to publish them?" someone asked.

"I suggested Wes have them serialized in the Naval Institute Proceedings. I believe he's in touch with them now."

"Do you think they will?"

"If they do," Nathaniel replied, "it will be the worst setback for the American navy since Pearl Harbor."

THE ADMIRAL himself received Colin at the door of his modern single-storey ranch-style home. In the driveway a sleek power launch with two massive outboard motors sat on a tarpaulined trailer.

"Mr. Draggett, what an unexpected pleasure! When Maude told me you were coming by I said, 'The wind's up, Maude, and the glass is down, or Colin Draggett wouldn't be making this a port of call.'"

"Not quite that, Admiral. I wanted to consult you on a couple of things and thought the best way was just to drop by."

"Four-oh!" the admiral said. He spoke a nautical jargon any seagoing man would be embarrassed to use except at sea, probably overcompensating for his landlocked career as a glorified office boy. He invariably announced the time in bells or so many hundred hours, and if he changed his mind about something he would say, "Belay that!"

He took Colin the length of the house to an enclosed veranda done up like a battleship wardroom. One of his rare overseas assignments had been at a Polaris base in Scotland, where he had acquired the habit of afternoon tea. Mrs. Scheutter brought it on a tray with wafer-thin sandwiches, fresh baked muffins and an assortment of sugar-dusted cookies. She seemed as fragile as one of her tea-tray confections, a sweet woman whose leftover beauty had become brittle with the years.

As she poured the tea, Colin took in the room. Windows on three sides with a broad wintery view of the Thames River submarine pens. The remaining wall was covered with pictures of Wes Scheutter interspersed with paintings and photographs of nuclear submarines. The picture gallery showed Lieutenant Scheutter in 1961 with Admiral Rickover and President Kennedy, Commander Scheutter ten years later with Rickover and President Nixon, Captain Scheutter with Henry Kissinger and President Ford, and Rear Admiral Scheutter with President Reagan at Rickover's funeral.

"You've certainly had a colorful career, Admiral," Colin said, remembering Nathaniel Sawyer's comments on it.

"I can't complain," the admiral replied. "Not every man gets a chance to do what he likes in life, and I sure did."

In one corner of the room near the windows was a magnificent antique telescope mounted on a stout, varnished tripod. Its polished brass fittings gleamed. Standing near it, Scheutter looked the salty part he liked to play, a broad well-built man, not as tall as Colin Draggett, but solid. His features were weathered-looking, with crow's-feet at the eyes and mouth, believably a face that might have battled nor'easters for thirty years instead of fighting indigestion in an air-conditioned Pentagon office.

He noticed Colin's admiring glances in the direction of the telescope. "It's a beauty, isn't it?"

Colin went to get a closer look.

"They don't make them like that anymore. English. Cooke lenses. Look at the inscription."

He did. The brass plate on the gimbaled head of the tripod was beautifully engraved in a flowing script that read: "To Capt. A. T. Mahan U.S.N. in grateful appreciation. H.R.H. Edward, Prince of Wales. 1885."

"That belonged to Alfred Thayer Mahan," the admiral said proudly, "the same Mahan who invented the doctrine and wrote the bible on modern seapower. It was a gift to him by Queen Victoria's son, who later became King Edward."

"It's really something!" Colin said in honest appreciation.

"Adam Walsh gave it to Wesley," Mrs. Scheutter said.

The admiral laughed guiltily. "Funny how it happened. One day we were watching a sub tie up and Adam told me, 'Admiral, you need a glass on your bridge to see them come and go, and later he dispatched this. Naturally I couldn't accept it, although I wanted to. So he jury-rigged a deal where it goes officially to the Naval Academy when I die."

"Wonderful," Colin muttered, wondering how many other directors Walsh had suborned with "jury-rigged" presents.

"While we have you here, Mr. Draggett," Maude Scheutter said, "I'd like to invite you to our open house on Christmas Eve. Wes and I have made it a kind of tradition here and there will be many Stanton people."

"That's very kind of you, Mrs. Scheutter, but I'll be back in New York by then."

"How silly of me. I forgot you lived there."

After tea and the telescope Colin didn't have to broach the business of keeping Hunt Benson on as president. Admiral Scheutter brought it up himself when he said, "I've been expecting to hear from you, Mr. Draggett, to tell us how to vote at the meeting."

Colin smiled, not knowing if he was being facetious. But his open, honest face was so sincere that Colin believed him. "I would never tell you how to vote," Colin said, and that made the admiral smile.

"Mr. Draggett, I accept being told what to do. That's a naval officer's duty. On board ship if everybody didn't do what he was told, well, I don't have to tell you. I look at corporate responsibility the same way. One man has the conn and the rest are along for the ride. So who has the conn now that Ave Stanton's not around? Hunt Benson?"

"At the moment, and I would like to see him keep it."

"But I hear he wants to quit."

"If the entire board got behind him, I'm sure we could persuade him to stay on another year."

"You think he's that good? I've got nothing against Hunt, but he's not what I'd call command material."

"Avery Stanton left him in charge," Colin said, "as a reliable caretaker until the board finds the right man."

"But we've got the right man. Why not vote him in now?"

That was exactly what Colin did not want to hear. If this pseudo-sailor intended to pay for his spyglass by voting for Adam Walsh, they were all in trouble. Even if the college president agreed with him, it would only give them six votes against the other six who would presumably vote for Adam Walsh. Hunt Benson would feel honor-bound to vote for Walsh, and in a tie Nathaniel Sawyer might switch to break it. Barbara, too, for that matter.

"If you ask me," the admiral was saying, "we owe it to Ave to give Ken Fairchild our blessing now. Don't you agree?"

——CHAPTER THIRTY-THREE——

BEFORE RETURNING to New York Colin met with Brian Redfern at the main Stanton offices to check on how his fund-raising was going. Walsh had been behaving as Colin predicted and was not pressuring him about the second payment since he received the first one, but they were still committed to getting it to him on or before the day of the stockholders meeting.

"Can't do it," Brian told Colin when he asked. "Not while they're running this damned audit."

"Did you send the memo I advised to the company controller? With a copy to Hunt Benson?"

"The day after we talked. But I told you it wasn't simple, not with the way accountants think. Barry Parks—he's the controller— went to Benson and said he couldn't guaranty the accuracy of the audit if I kept doing this. So Benson ordered that no more funds be diverted to anyone's personal account until after the board meets in January. My hands are tied!"

"Is all this in writing?"

"Yes, why?"

"Get me copies so I can show them to Walsh."

"You think he'll go along?"

"Why shouldn't he? We've demonstrated our good faith. He'd be cutting his own throat to go public now."

"But that's always been the case," Brian said grimly.

"Except now he's got another reason for behaving."

"What?"

Colin filled him in on the fact that several directors were enthusiastic about Walsh because they believed he was Avery's choice.

"So you see, he thinks he stands a chance. If Hunt stays, our problem is solved."

"Wouldn't it be better if Barbara knew about Walsh?"

"If I can't convince Hunt, we may have to tell her."

"How else can we be sure, damn it? Colin, if you don't sort this out before the meeting, Walsh could actually get in."

"I'm aware of what can happen."

"We can't take that chance, goddamnit!"

"What do you suggest? That we notify the police? Publish his curriculum vitae in Nate Sawyer's newspaper?"

"I know, I know. But I think Barbara would understand what we're trying to do if you laid it out for her."

"That's wishful thinking. She might understand, but I doubt she'd agree with our handling of it."

"What a wonderful Christmas this is going to be."

"Enjoy it, my friend, and think what a Christmas it would be if Walsh's story *had* got out."

"What are you going to do now, Colin?"

"Go home. Hunt Benson, Wesley Scheutter and you in the same day are all I can deal with. And tomorrow is Christmas Eve and I have an office party I promised to attend."

"Do you want me to talk to Hunt?"

"God, no. The more you push a man like Hunt, the worse he gets. And apart from that, he doesn't like you very much."

"No reason he should. I've told him he's an idiot."

"He hasn't forgotten."

"How could he? I reminded him as recently as today."

"Brian, we're trying to get the man on our side."

"Sorry. But did you see his tour plans for the stockholders meeting? Adam Walsh guiding the investment bankers and mutual-fund guys around our production facilities? That's all we need, Walsh leading the parade, courtesy of Ma Benson."

"You better just hope he postpones that retirement long enough to help us win."

Redfern walked Colin to his car, braving the freezing early evening in his shirtsleeves. When Colin suggested he would die of pneumonia without a coat, he said he had to pass by the plating rooms to check on an overdue order for Taiwan going through the plant. "And it's hotter than hell in there."

He was shivering by then and Colin motioned him to get out of the cold as he closed the car door and started the engine. Colin saw him still in the rearview mirror as he pulled away, a solitary figure outlined against the night, jogging toward the sprawling building that housed the plating baths.

It was that evening, Brian would admit months later, when he got the idea that was supposed to take care of Adam Walsh once and for all.

For the first hour rolling down the Connecticut Turnpike Colin hardly noticed the miles peeling away. Like a chess player trying to extrapolate future moves by studying the pieces on the board, his attention was so concentrated that the car seemed to be driving itself . . . Redfern, Fairchild, Barbara and Nathaniel Sawyer would vote with him for Hunt Benson. Wesley Scheutter would, too, as soon as he saw that's what Fairchild wanted. Six votes. Howie Livingston and Lydell Cummings would support Walsh, Colin had no doubt. As would the Boston directors and Hunt Benson. Five for Walsh.

So the key was the single woman director, Louisa Mae Barton, president of Cathcart College, America's oldest institution of higher education for women, nestled in the wooded hills of Fairfield County, Connecticut, forty miles from New York City. Ms. Barton was not aware of it yet, but her vote could decide the uncertain fortunes of Colin Draggett as well as the future of Stanton Technologies.

The night had become exceedingly cold and Colin turned the car heat to high. What little traffic there was came from the other direction, people driving up to New England for the holiday weekend. Outside, the black vaulted sky was studded with stars, clearer and brighter than at any other time of the year, like great cosmic clusters of Christmas lights.

The exit signs ticked by his headlights: Old Saybrook, Branford, New Haven, Bridgeport, Stamford.

Stamford brought him back to the present. Quirk was at a motel in Stamford. Colin remembered the address as he slowed the car and moved into the right-hand lane. This was as good a time as any to call on him. Colin was curious about a number of things that might possibly compromise them with Walsh, details he did not especially want to get into with Quirk's attorney, his friend Wally Scott. If Quirk was in, Colin could see him now, alone.

The Howard Johnson's Motor Lodge that Petrey had put him in

resembled an orange tepee from the highway. Colin turned off and circled around it to the parking lot. According to the night clerk, Quirk was in his room.

A girl with spiked purple hair, purple stockings and inch-long purple nails answered Colin's knock. "You're not the pizza," she said. Her skin belonged to a child, but her dull, sullen eyes were ageless.

" 'Oo is it, pet?" came a man's voice from the other room. " 'Ave him bring hit in. The money's on the tyble."

Colin stepped into the suite, a large, overheated, sterile-looking place with two queen-size beds, a television set and armchairs upholstered in purple plastic.

Quirk appeared, as pink and round as Colin remembered him, with a motel towel knotted about his bulging middle. " 'Oo are you? Do oy know you? Ra-ight! Redfern's solicitor. To what do I owe, Mr.—?"

"Draggett, Colin Draggett."

"We thought you was the pizza boy, di'nt we, darlin'? Oh, Mr. Draggett, this is Susan."

"Sue-Anne."

"Whatever your nyme is, pet, call that place again, will you? If they don't come wivvin five minutes we eat free. Sit down, Mr. Draggett. Want a drink? Pink gin? Beer?"

"I'd like to talk to you for a few minutes," Colin said.

Quirk called the girl over to him and whispered something in her ear. She made an exasperated face, picked up her purse and went out the door. Quirk called after her to let him know when the pizza arrived.

"Mr. Quirk," Colin said when they were alone, "no one knows I've come to see you and I would prefer to keep it that way. I've spoken to Redfern and know why he had you come to the States."

"That puts you one up on Ollie then."

"I beg your pardon?"

"You know why he sent for me. I don't."

"Come on, Mr. Quirk. You don't expect me to believe that."

"What do you want from me?"

"I want you to tell me what Mr. Redfern offered you when he hired you in London. I want to know why you went to Jamaica and I want to know what you were doing bringing in narcotics."

"Why should I tell you?"

"Because I'm the man looking out for your best interest. I sent Wally Scott to get you out of jail and I sent Petrey to put you up here until your case comes to trial."

"What's in it for you?"

"I represent the Stanton company," Colin said. "It's in our mutual interest, let us say, for me to help you. But I must know the truth in order to do it."

Quirk turned this over in his mind as he dropped the towel, pulled on a pair of jockey shorts and striped trousers. "Mykes sense," he said at last. "You picking up the ticket for this lawyer Scott?"

Colin nodded.

"What's in it for me?"

"The more I know, the better I can help. If you're lucky, Scott will get you off on the drug charge."

"No guaranty, though, is there?"

"No."

He popped a can of beer and again offered Colin one. This time he accepted, which seemed to please Quirk. "I'd like a guaranty," he said. "Then I'd feel more like talking."

"We're paying your hotel and food."

"Whot the 'ell," he said. "Whot 'ave I got to lose?" and he began to tell Colin his story.

After cashing Brian's check for fifty-five thousand pounds he took a long weekend to plan his action. But as he explained to Colin, Redfern had not given him the name of the target. That was to come when Quirk arrived in Connecticut ready to do the job. He put two of his friends on standby in London and got on a flight to Jamaica.

When Colin asked him why he went to Jamaica instead of flying directly to New York, he eyed him suspiciously before apparently deciding there was no harm intended by the question. As usual, he referred to himself in the third person.

"Ollie was on a roll, 'e was, guv'nor. Grite opportunities droppin' in 'is lap like Mister Redfern and then the werry next day a black gentleman nyme of Stomper Bill Hicks 'oo was kind enough to put Ollie onto a likely connection, a nuvver Jamaican bloke nyme Sugarpop Muggs lives on the island, you see."

"So that's why you went to Kingston?"

Another long look as he pulled an electric-blue turtleneck over his head. Like the rest of his clothing it was too tight and made him look a little like a neon knockwurst. Then a brisk nod from the pink pudding of a face before he decided to tell his story . . .

He had stepped down from the British Airways jet, had taken one look around and hated the place on sight. The damp tropical air gave his cigarettes a moldy taste and the heat shimmering off the tarmac made him dizzy. It was even worse inside the terminal because the air conditioning had shut down and none of the windows could be opened.

A man in a wrinkled linen suit and no shirt held up a card lettered in red saying, "Mr. Quirt." They left the sweltering terminal and after a long walk arrived at a battered old Austin with broken springs and sagging fenders. A sign lettered in the same red ink was stuck to the inside of the windshield and read, "Imperial Limousine Service."

By the time he reached his destination, a tin-roofed shack near Spanish Town at the end of a winding, hilly road, Quirk in his wool suit was certain he was dying of thirst, dehydration and heat stroke. A nearby radio blared reggae as he staggered from the car. At the entrance to the shack a thin black man stood barefoot and clad only in frayed khaki shorts. The man's hair was a swirl of greasy dredlocks and he smiled a greeting from a mouthful of gold teeth.

"Drink," Quirk gasped, and the man led him inside to a kind of bar where a kerchiefed woman ladled some watery fruit juice from a galvanized tub. Quirk drained his glass four times before he felt ready to talk.

"You bring the money?" the man asked.

"Show me," Quirk said.

The man brought a jute sack and took out four plastic-wrapped packages. He opened one and cut some of the ganja with a clasp knife, molded it expertly into a small porcelain pipe. Once he had it going he passed the pipe to Oliver Quirk, who savored the sweetish, heavy smoke and felt better.

After half an hour and two more glasses of fruit juice, Quirk took ten thousand pounds from his imitation Gucci briefcase and replaced the cash with the drug. There was little small talk between them because Sugarpop Muggs understood even less of Quirk's cockney than Quirk did of the man's island patois.

Quirk checked into the Ramada Inn in Kingston, repacked his luggage, bought a pair of luminescent fuchsia bathing trunks that hung to his knees, and got wet in the hotel pool. The driver from the Imperial Limousine Service had offered to show him the town that night, but he said no, just send a girl by the hotel around seven.

She was young, with corn-rowed hair and pointy breasts, a sparkling smile and musical laugh. She wore a sequinned miniskirt, gauzy blouse and no underwear. Quirk got it over with quickly.

He had booked an early morning flight to New York, where he hoped to complete his business, but the moment his New York plane reservation was confirmed his name was fed into a police computer to join a list of other passengers staying in Jamaica less than forty-eight hours. This list existed because the U.S. Drug Enforcement Administration and Jamaican police had discovered that people passing too quickly through the tourist island tended to be drug couriers.

Quirk's name and British passport number were flagged while he slept and sent via satellite to Scotland Yard whose own computer replied that Oliver Quirk was a shady fellow indeed, and although not currently wanted by the British authorities was an ex-convict who had been known to deal drugs.

He was almost saved by a case of the runs that kept him up most of the night and left him wrung out and exhausted at dawn. He cursed Sugarpop Muggs and his watery fruit juice but did not cancel his plane reservation.

The New York Customs and Immigration inspectors were polite, and just as he thought he was in without a full-scale luggage inspection two DEA agents appeared with a dog.

"Cruel wot thay do to the poor dumb beasts, mykin' 'em into slobberin' haddicts just to catch the likes of ol' Ollie."

"What did you do?" Colin asked him.

"Do? Got frog-marched off to the fookin' clink."

"Is that when you called Petrey?"

"Not that day, I din't. Rang him up on a Monday. Felt like a bloody fool, too. Shopped by the narks for ten key o' ganja! 'Oo'd bloody believe it?"

"It wasn't very clever of you, Mr. Quirk. You must have been aware of the high risk involved."

"Easy for you to sye, guv, but when there's a wifc and kiddies to feed back in London, every li'uhl bit counts."

"What happened then, Mr. Quirk?"

"I troyed to expline 'ow ganja's connected wi' my religious conwictions, guv, but it din't wash wi' that lot."

"I'm sure it didn't."

"The bloody beggars violated my civil raights, thay did, treatin' ol' Ollie like some tupenny nigger pimp."

"They can be unfeeling, no doubt."

"When 'e freatened the bloody book, I rang your friend."

"And Petrey called me."

"Neow whot?"

"Has Mr. Redfern been to see you?"

He seemed uncertain how to answer. " 'E wants 'is money back, 'e does."

"What did you tell him?"

"We myde a deal, I said, a contrack's a contrack. I'll still keep my part of it if 'e tells me where, but no refunds."

"And what did he say?"

" 'E'd get back to me."

Colin was afraid of that.

_____CHAPTER THIRTY-FOUR_____

As a boy Colin never understood why Christmas Eve began in the morning, and he remembered arguing the matter with another twelve-year-old expert on the Christian holiday calendar. "You can't say 'This morning is Christmas Eve.' You have to call it Christmas Day or just plain Christmas."

"That's tomorrow, dummy."

"But it can't be an Eve until tonight," Colin had insisted. The other boy agreed with his logic but said he was wrong. He conceded it could be called "Christmas Eve morning" but that sounded even dumber. Colin's friend was Lutheran and eventually told him that Catholics were incapable of grasping the finer points of the Protestant faith.

Colin couldn't make a lot of sense out of Catholicism either, but he didn't admit it and resented being singled out for something he didn't understand.

"I am not a Catholic," he would announce, and friends who knew better would reply, "Okay, so what are you?"

"An atheist." He had discovered atheism, or at least the idea of it, at fourteen. His closest friend, a Jewish boy, said he was an atheist too but he was still a Jew. That, of course, carried the two boys into the deeper waters of theological choice as influenced by ethnic difference. The Jewish boy said being an atheist made some sense but it wasn't much fun. Colin nodded sagely and gave that up too.

When Colin was very small he believed in Santa Claus and the Easter Bunny. Easter for his sister and him meant a trip to 34th Street for new clothes, then an afternoon at the Central Park Zoo or a ride on the Staten Island Ferry. These outings were always with his father, and ended with a big supper of milk shakes and hamburgers at the nearest White Castle.

Christmases they went to Macy's toy department where they stood in line to present their wish list to Santa Claus. It was all magical, all believable. Then by bus to Rockefeller Center where they would eat hot pretzels from a street vendor and watch the skaters. Colin's father always had tickets to the Radio City Music Hall, where as part of the special Christmas matinee the children would see dancers and jugglers, a magician or a dog act.

Colin was twelve or thirteen before he made the connection between Easter, Christmas and religion. Later on at Harvard he read a lot of history and philosophy. He added rationalism and humanism to his quiver. He thought he understood music, art, mathematics, physics and poetry, but the more he learned about religions the more incomprehensible he found them. Early in their marriage, Joyce and he discussed this, and Colin discovered that her point of view was far more sophisticated than his. "You're missing the point, darling," she would say. "Religion is *supposed* to be incomprehensible. Mysteries of the faith and all that. The need for priests to interpret."

"How can you believe in something you can't understand?"

"Colin, if anyone really understood a religion, he'd never believe in it. They're like operas. Just listen to the music and don't pay too close attention to the plots."

"But they're all based on a fear of death," he would say, trying out his latest profound analysis on her.

"Operas?"

"Religions."

"That's a reasonable fear, darling, if you ask me."

"But each religion claims to be the owner of the truth, each one got it straight from the horse's mouth. The same for Jews, Moslems, Christians, Hindus, everybody."

"You're ignoring religion's main advantage. Identity. Belonging."

"When you're a minority that's no advantage."

"In some circles it is. Just the simple act of belonging solves so many stupid problems. It doesn't matter what you believe, darling, if you belong. You belong to the Law Review, to Harvard, to a club, to me, a political party, a law firm, whatever. Then you're free to devote yourself to other matters."

"Such as?"

"The eternal truths," she would say with a giggle. "The gut issues of life, like why dogs have wet noses or whether the light goes off when you close the door to the fridge."

So many happy years together, and yet so few. All this was passing through his mind on Christmas Eve morning as he sipped his coffee. Joyce had been awake when he visited her earlier. She smiled when he said her name and turned her head toward him. He liked to think she knew who he was, but her eyes seemed already focused on something beyond the room.

Had he ever really settled anything? he wondered. He thought he was rich enough to live happily ever after until the junk-bond market collapsed. He thought he had an almost perfect marriage until a cruel cancer intervened to steal his love away. And now whatever influence, position or prestige he enjoyed in his profession, Adam Walsh was threatening to topple into the mud.

Maggie was on the telephone before nine to ask if he was coming in to the office.

"In a little while."

"And to remind you about the Christmas party."

"I haven't forgotten. Anything happen yesterday?"

"Barbara Fairchild called you. Mr. Scanlon from your brokerage. And a Mr. Dimitri."

"Who's he?"

"He said it was about your mother."

"What about her?"

"Apparently he's having some sort of problem."

"With my mother, everyone has some sort of problem. What is he, a department-store manager, or what?"

"That's all he'd say, but he left a number to call."

"Anything else?"

"Only things requiring your signature, including all the bonus checks to be handed out at the Christmas party today."

"I'll see you in an hour or so." After Colin hung up and got his coat he looked in on Joyce one more time. She was sleeping and Mrs. Ryan said, "Dr. Brenner called to say he isn't coming today, Mr. Draggett, but if we need him he'll be at his daughter's."

Unless it was raining or snowing or he was in a hurry, Colin walked downtown and back each day. The round trip was about six miles between his Turtle Bay apartment and Wall Street. He varied the route to avoid boredom and he got some of his best thinking done. It wasn't as aerobic as a good jog but it was better than standing in a stuffy subway car or listening to some angry Nigerian cabbie expound on the mayor's latest outrage. But today it was raining—sleeting, in fact—and he hailed the first cab that passed.

The driver was not an angry Nigerian. He was a sullen Haitian. The native New York cabdriver seemed as extinct as the dodo bird these days, but cabbie grievances against the mayor, the police and the city itself never died. This morning's driver was especially incensed because the mayor had publicly endorsed a gay rights protest and marched with gay demonstrators.

"Haul zee aids have zeeze people not Haiti people!" he protested. "But 'e blame Haiti people because haul black people!"

"But the mayor is black, too," Colin said.

"Zat eez why 'e blame Haiti people!" It was a logic only the driver understood, and he treated Colin to a dozen variations of it all the way downtown.

They came off the FDR Drive at the Brooklyn Bridge and headed south. The sleet had turned to snow and Colin had enough of his complaining so he got out at Fulton Street and walked the last few blocks to his office.

Maggie was busy arranging some holly sprigs in a vase on his desk. "That was fast," she said. "Did you run all the way?"

"Taxi."

"Not feeling well?"

"It's snowing."

"A white Christmas."

"Bah, humbug!" He started signing checks when she went out and after about fifteen minutes the light on his desk flashed.

Maggie's voice sounded. "It's Mr. Dimitri."

Colin picked up the receiver. "You don't know me, Mr. Draggett, but I'm Max Dimitri, Esther Kleineman's friend."

"Whose friend?"

"Esther Kleineman from Queens."

Who the hell was Esther Kleineman from Queens? Colin wondered. "My secretary said you called about my mother?"

"I was wondering if we could possibly get together today. I'm working a party at a bank in your neighborhood at one o'clock and I could drop by your office beforehand."

"Suppose you tell me what it's all about first, Mr. Dimitri. Today is a busy one for me."

"It's better discussed in person, Mr. Draggett."

"That may be, but let me be the judge."

"Well, Esther invited your mother . . ."

"Oh, that Esther!" Colin almost blurted. Esther Kleineman from Queens who played pinochle with his mother. Esther Kleineman, one of his mother's rare friends.

". . . and she said she couldn't because you were against the idea and Esther thought it best if you and I could talk."

"Come on by, Mr. Dimitri," Colin said. "Between twelve and twelve-thirty will be fine."

As soon as he hung up Maggie said, "I'm holding Mr. Scanlon on the other line. Are you available?"

"Put him on."

"Colin, how are you? Merry Christmas."

"Same to you Malcolm."

"I hate to bother you, Colin, especially at this time of the year, but we've got a little problem over here with your account."

Colin's stomach knotted. He owed Scanlon's brokerage a substantial fortune but so far his pledged holdings in Stanton Technologies and his prompt payment of the interest had been enough to keep them off his back. "What's the problem?"

"You see, Colin, a court decision came down yesterday on the bond redemption value, and the judge . . ." What he then told Colin was the worst possible news. One of the companies whose bonds he had bought went into reorganization under Chapter Eleven and the judge handling the case had just ruled that the current value of its bonds should be determined by the market.

Until now the value had been theoretically determined by inflating the company's remaining assets, in this case about a third of face value, which was to say a hundred-dollar bond was carried on the books as being worth thirty-three dollars. The company assets were sufficient to make the bonds worth half that, or about sixteen dollars. On that basis Colin would take a beating, having bought the bonds for as much as thirty dollars. But he would still get out solvent.

Scanlon's news changed all that. By ruling that the bonds were worth only what they could currently fetch on the trading floor, the judge had put Colin in a bind. The judge had also displayed a costly ingenuousness, because the bonds were selling for six dollars, and there was no shortage of speculators willing to snap them up, certain of a killing once the reorganization was complete.

Colin knew that as soon as the company's assets were published, the bonds would indeed command something around fifteen dollars on the market. But that could be as much as a year away. Scanlon was proposing that he sell off a substantial block of his Stanton stock immediately to cover the shortfall. This had to be done quickly, he warned Colin, or the brokerage would be acting illegally by carrying his account with an insufficient cash margin.

"Let me think about it and get back to you," Colin said.

"Pardon me for saying this, Colin, but there's not a lot to think about. We have to cover the difference."

"Look," he said, "the ruling was announced yesterday."

"That's right."

"And today is Christmas Eve, so the market closes early."

"What's your point?"

"You're not in violation of anything yet because it's a short trading day. Tomorrow is Christmas and the Exchange is shut down. Then we have Saturday and Sunday and the market doesn't open again until the twenty-eighth. I'll let you know by then."

"That's cutting it a bit fine," Scanlon said. "We're talking about approximately ten million dollars . . ."

"I know what we're talking about, Malcolm, please bear with me."

"First thing Monday morning?"

"I'll call you the moment I've decided."

After Colin hung up he did some rapid numbers on a pocket calculator. If he sold two hundred thousand bonds Monday, with some luck he'd take out a little over a million. If he sold the same number of Stanton shares at thirty-eight dollars a share he'd have another seven million six hundred thousand. Still short a million, but close. But in order to solve one problem he would be creating others. If he sold that many bonds on Monday, so soon after the judge's ruling, the trading price could easily drop a dollar or more, so instead of counting on six dollars he might have to sell another hundred thousand to average out at four and reach a million cash. Not to mention the effect of a two-hundred-thousand-share block of Stanton stock suddenly appearing on the market. The Wall Street watchbirds would want to know why somebody was unloading and they would begin to ask around to find out who. A clerk or a runner for Scanlon's brokerage could make a succulent tip by revealing that the seller was Colin Draggett taking off profits. Would they then recommend that their clients do the same? After all, Colin Draggett was practically a founder of Stanton Technologies, so if he was selling he must know something all the others didn't.

The Internal Revenue Service would pounce on the sale within hours, their hands out for the government's share. Next year he could deduct some of the bond losses, but he would have to pay through the nose now on his Stanton profits. Enough. He'd sleep on it.

"Maggie, get me Brian Redfern, please."

"In New London?"

"If that's where he is."

A minute later Brian came on the line. There was considerable background noise and he had to shout.

"Where in hell are you?"

"In the plating room!"

"Brian, I have to talk to you. Can you call me right back from a pay phone?"

"It'll take a while."

"Soon as you can."

He was on the line again within ten minutes, but he had no change so he gave Colin the number to call him back.

"Where are you?" Colin asked him.

"Company cafeteria."

"After I left you last night I stopped in Stamford."

"So I heard."

"What the hell are you up to with Quirk?"

"Look, Colin, nothing to worry about."

"The man claims he's still willing to fulfill his part of whatever devil's bargain he made with you."

"He's history, Colin, really."

"We had an agreement, Brian. You were not to go near him again."

"I was only trying to get some of our money back."

"How much did you pay?"

"Look, I'll cover it, Colin. It was a London check."

"On Stanton International?"

"Stanton & Co. Ltd., our English subsidiary."

"To whom? Oliver Quirk?"

"Colin, I'm not that stupid."

"That's a matter of opinion, Brian, and on the strength of your recent performance I'm inclined to disagree with you." Colin's anger was great, but even then he knew a lot of the spleen he was venting on Brian Redfern had been generated by his reaction to Malcolm Scanlon's call. "How much?"

"Fifty-five thousand pounds."

"Signed by you. How do you explain that to an auditor?"

"I'll take care of it."

"You better, Brian."

"Colin—"

"Just find the money for Walsh, will you, and stop trying to be a one-man hit squad or you'll have us all in jail."

___ CHAPTER THIRTY-FIVE ___

COLIN GAZED out his office window at the veil of snow falling on New York harbor. Instead of cheering him, as white Christmases were supposed to do, the gray scrim overlaying the skyline only added to the depression pressing in on him. What Joyce had always called his "Irish melancholy" was taking over. The phone light flashed and he picked up the receiver. "Who is it, Maggie?"

"Mrs. Fairchild."

He picked it up. "Barbara?"

"Hi, darling," she said, and suddenly his spirits soared. "Colin, you never return my calls."

"Sorry, I just got in."

"Maggie has invited me to your office Christmas party. Do you mind if I come?"

"Of course not. But why aren't you in Connecticut?"

"At the last minute their father decided to take the boys skiing in Vermont. He seems to know something's up, although we still haven't discussed it. But rather than spend the holiday alone at home I decided on New York."

"I'm delighted."

"I don't believe you. You think I'm being pushy."

"I'm still delighted."

"Oh, Colin!"

"See you in a little while then."

"You're sure you don't mind? I've never seen the senior partner of Cranmer, Fisher & Cleves in his natural habitat."

After he hung up he sat staring at the pile of unsigned checks, the sweet sound of Barbara's voice lingering in his mind. He wanted her to come to the party and he didn't. He wanted to see her and he wanted to avoid her.

He told himself it couldn't be love because he was still in love with his dying wife. Yet the night at O'Hara's was still with him, the kiss in the taxi, all of it. He was excited by just the sound of Barbara's voice, and he had to admit he liked the way she had started to call him darling. He wondered how he could feel this way about a woman he had known since she was practically a child. Yet thoughts of her were almost enough to dispel the depression inspired by Scanlon's call and to bring a smile to his face.

At that moment Maggie entered. "Well?"

"Well, what?"

"Did you tell her she's welcome?"

"She knows she's welcome. You invited her."

"That lady needs every bit of Christmas cheer she can find, Colin, and so do you. Why not just sit back and enjoy?"

"Maggie, when I need your advice—"

"I know, you'll ask for it. But that won't stop me from giving it unsolicited. By the way, Mr. Dimitri's here."

Over the course of the years, all kinds of people had passed through the offices of Cranmer, Fisher & Cleves. Rich men, poor men, beggarmen and thieves. But this was the first time Santa Claus ever paid them a visit.

Maggie opened the door to admit him and he came bounding across the room to shake Colin's hand. He was not big and fat and imposing as Colin remembered him from the Macy's visits of his childhood. He was small and wiry and bounced on the balls of his feet as he talked. He was so small, in fact, that Colin decided he must be one of Santa's elves and not the great man himself.

His red velvet suit was immaculate, as were his shiny plastic belt and spats. His silky white wig overflowed his collar and his nylon beard curled around very red lips beneath an equally red nose. He took a visitor's card from one pocket and snapped it as he handed it to Colin with a flourish. It read "Max Dimitri—Actor, Impersonator, Liaison" above a Kissimmee, Florida, address.

"How do you do, Mr. Dimitri."

"Max. Call me Max, please. Terrific office. Terrific view. If you like New York. I was born here. Couldn't get out fast enough. You know Florida, Mr. Draggett?" When Colin nodded, he said, "Terrific state. Terrific climate."

"About my mother, Mr. . . . . Max?"

"Terrific woman. Fantastic sense of humor."

"How long have you known my mother?"

"It seems like years. I mean when your mom and me get going, Esther's rolling on the floor breaking up. We worked up some routines would knock your socks off. Terrific talent, your mom."

"You don't say."

"Esther and I, we're going to tie the knot. I'm retired sort of, but I still work a lot of gigs, kiddy parties and that. I do the Mickey, the Donald, the Goofy and the Dumbo. I can't do Cinderella or Snow White, ha, ha, ha, because I'm not a female impersonator, ha, ha, ha. I got a terrific house in Florida with a pool, hot tub, the works."

"I see."

"Trouble is, Esther won't leave Maisie."

Colin found it hard to imagine what his mother had done to inspire such fierce loyalty. "I'm sorry to hear that."

"Oh, no, it's terrific! Esther's like that. If she likes somebody, you can't tear her away, and she likes your mom. So I say terrific, bring her with you. And Esther says you mean it? And I say would I say it if I didn't mean it?"

"To Florida."

"So we talk to Maisie and she wants to come. But she's into reincarnation, and Renata, her past-life medium, lives here."

So Crazy Maisie was off again and running.

"You know how mediums are. Like being with a shrink. Then there's you and your sister she don't want to leave neither."

"But she hasn't seen my sister in years."

"Once a mother always a mother."

"Mr. Dimitri . . ."

"Max."

"Max, believe me, there is nothing to prevent my mother from moving to Florida. In fact, I have often suggested it."

"Terrific. I thought if we could sort of talk to her together, you me and Esther, maybe we could convince her. At least to come down for a month or two. She can always come back."

"I think it's an excellent idea."

"That way I get Esther down there."

"I'll be happy to talk to my mother and try to convince her. But are you sure you want to do this? Why not concentrate on persuading Esther to go without her?"

"I couldn't do that. The truth is, your mom is terrific. I mean you never seen me act, but I'm pretty good." With that, he went into a squeaky Mickey Mouse imitation, then a sputtering gurgle like Donald Duck. "See what I mean?"

"Very convincing."

"You got to see me and your mom, you want to see something. I mean her improv material's so far out. All I do is play to it. Remember George and Gracie on the radio? Or Easy Aces? No, you're too young. Well, we do a turn like them only funnier."

"It's hard to imagine my mother funny," Colin said.

"She cracks me up. Who writes your stuff, I ask her, and she says my children, they hate me. And I say I don't believe it, what'd you do they should hate you? She says if you only knew, you'd hate me too, and I say no I wouldn't because I'm not your kid and she says thank God for that! Esther says we're better than TV."

Colin agreed to meet at his mother's apartment on Christmas day and try to persuade the great comedienne to take her act on the road, at least as far as Florida. Max Dimitri bounced out of his office doing a little quickstep, doffing his Santa cap to the delighted secretaries and clerks in the outer bay, calling, "Merry Christmas! Merry Christmas to all! Merry Christmas!"

Old Anthony Shattuck arrived at that moment with Barbara in tow, her mouth open in astonishment at the sight of this tiny man in his red suit dancing through the offices of Cranmer, Fisher & Cleves. Before Dimitri disappeared, the entire staff applauded.

Barbara preceded Colin into his office. "What was that all about?" she asked.

"Just one of the gnomes of Wall Street doing his annual Christmas dance. They're all over the place this time of the year. Don't tell me you never noticed them before. Actually he's part of a new comedy team. He thinks my mother's funny and wants to take her to Florida with him."

"That's wonderful, Colin." When he didn't answer immediately, she said, "Isn't it?"

"Having my mother in Florida would suit me fine. Having her in Tasmania or Bangladesh would suit me even better."

"Oh, Colin, you don't mean that."

"You haven't met my mother."

"But you said that little man thinks she's funny."

"That's what he told me."

"Is she?"

"I could think of a hundred adjectives to describe my mother, but 'funny' would not be one of them. Either she's changed since I saw her last or that dancing dwarf needs his head checked."

Barbara looked around the office, a simple, almost spartan place where Colin worked at a large teak table. Behind it was a computer console, telephone, reference books, and a recording device which could tape meetings and conferences when needed.

The only decorative touches were a nineteenth-century painting of a grain barque rounding Cape Horn, photographs of sailboats Colin had owned and a picture of Joyce. The real attraction was his enormous window with its breathtaking view of New York Harbor.

It was snowing quite heavily by then, and Barbara stood watching the storm while he finished up the bonus checks and other papers Maggie had left for his signature. At twelve-thirty she called over the intercom, "Mr. Draggett, the offices of Cranmer, Fisher and Cleves are officially closed as of now and your presence is awaited by the wassail bowl on the floor below."

"Coming, Maggie."

The staff occupied four floors in the building; a fifth floor was devoted to the law library, one of the best outside any university law school. For several years Colin had a team of specialists cross-indexing and feeding this library into a computer data base so that much of it could now be summoned at the touch of a button. In a profession that only recently abandoned the quill pen, it gave the firm a considerable advantage over the competition when cases came to trial, and also served as public relations since Colin occasionally opened it to federal and state prosecutors who had no equivalent facility of their own.

The wassail bowl Maggie referred to was actually a huge tropical fish tank Anthony Shattuck had commandeered for the occasion. Two of the junior attorneys were already ladling punch out to the waiting staff as they lined up with plastic cups.

"This shouldn't take too long," Colin said to Barbara.

"I hope it does, Colin. It looks like fun." Most of the women had come to work that morning dressed for the party. There was a profusion of new hairdos and gaily colored dresses among the sombre flannel and worsted suits of the men.

During the first hour Colin shook a good many hands as he munched sandwiches and sipped punch. There had been a time when he prided himself on knowing everyone in the firm by name, but no longer. Half the faces in the room now he did not recognize, and quite a few belonged to people who had been with them for years but who worked in offices he rarely visited. Maggie knew them all and stayed by his side to keep him out of trouble.

Colin introduced Barbara to the partners, helped pass out the bonus checks and even made a little speech. As the punch level in the fish tank dropped, the noise level rose, and by three o'clock the hallowed halls of Cranmer, Fisher & Cleves reverbrated to hard rock as desks were pushed back to make room for the dancers. Colin was going to quit after he danced with Barbara and Maggie until a pretty young attorney grabbed his arm and kept him on the dance floor. She claimed she had read about him in law school.

"I don't believe it," he said, flattered anyway.

There were other guests besides Barbara. He saw his colleague Wally Scott deep in conversation with Anthony Shattuck and wondered what brought him downtown. Two lawyers from the New York County D.A.'s office competed for Maggie's attention while a State Supreme Court Justice got quietly plastered with one of the partners.

The lawyer from the Securities and Exchange Commission whom Colin had met barely a week before at the Gansevoort was crossing the room toward him. Colin tried to put a name to the face. MacDonald? McConnell? O'Connell, that was it.

His handshake, like everything else about him, was strong and hearty. "Just had lunch with some clients of yours," he said.

"Really?" Colin had to raise his voice above the music.

"Malcolm Scanlon and my old college buddy Adam Walsh with his boss Hunt Benson. I gather from them that Stanton's fourth quarter earnings will break all records. Adam wants to know why I don't quit the government and come to work for him."

"Are you considering it?"

"The money would be nice but I'm doing what I do best. I couldn't do what he does, but I couldn't imagine him working as a fed either, could you?"

"I doubt they hire people with his background."

"Only because there's no incentive. The SEC would give anything to get its hands on a guy with Adam's track record."

"I'm sure they would," Colin said with a straight face.

"It probably sounds like sour grapes but it's not," O'Connell said. "I admire guys like Adam."

"A lot of people do . . ."

"He's in his element at Stanton," O'Connell said, "and the transition from the old man to Benson to him should be smooth."

"Is that what he said?"

"No, but it is going from Benson to Walsh, isn't it?"

"I'll tell you the same thing I told Jim Chapin."

"But I understood from Hunt that it's settled."

"There's heavy pressure for him to stay on."

"He never mentioned it."

"Too modest."

"Walsh didn't bring it up either."

"Too personal."

"Adam is always discreet about sensitive matters," O'Connell said. "I've never known him to lead a conversation."

"It's a lesson every smart executive learns," Colin said. "Don't commit until you know who's got the power."

O'Connell smiled. "I also see it in people we indict, but that's because they're afraid of self-incrimination."

"Do you think that's Walsh's problem?"

He laughed. "No way. Adam's too clever to break the law, so he'd never have to worry about incriminating himself."

"Don't you think people said that about Boesky and Milken and some others before they got caught?"

He looked at Colin sharply. "What are you suggesting?"

"Nothing at all," Colin assured him with a smile, "but it strikes me that every white collar criminal is eminently respectable until he's found out. Look at Keating, a decorated war hero and multimillionaire who stole more from his Savings and Loan than Jesse James, Dillinger and all the bank robbers in history."

"That's what I love about my work," O'Connell said. "I get to match wits with some of the best-dressed crooks in the world."

"I can see where you'd get a lot of satisfaction in seeing justice done," Colin told him.

"There's that," O'Connell agreed, "but the real pleasure comes from beating them at their own game. You know something else?"

Colin waited.

"The higher they fly, the harder they fall. We were talking about it today at lunch and I pointed out that in almost every case I've prosecuted, hubris is what does them in."

"The 'I am Untouchable' syndrome."

"Exactly. If they didn't get so cocky and think they're above the law, most of them *would* get away with it."

"How successful are you at catching them?"

"Not great, frankly. On a scale of ten, we're probably about a six. But prosecutions are time-consuming and expensive."

Colin wondered how much Walsh's scam would shock O'Connell if he knew the truth, yet he himself was still confused about what was the truth. At least the whole truth. O'Connell's knowing Walsh in college simply wasn't possible, and Petrey's explanation did not wash. But what made sense? That O'Connell and Walsh's wife were party to his impersonation? Speculation of that kind verged on paranoia.

"Every time you think you've seen the limit," O'Connell was saying, "somebody tops it."

Don't tell me, Colin thought, wondering how long some things could be kept confidential if his broker was having lunch with O'Connell *and* Adam Walsh. Talk about hubris! Walsh was really pushing it.

"Luckily," O'Connell added, "the need for violence never arises in white collar crime. These guys are greedy but they're not killers."

CHAPTER THIRTY-SIX

BRIAN REDFERN had been taking uppers for two days to stay sharp but his nerves were shredded. In an angry frame of mind he had gone to the Stanton plating room to find out why a large export order of Graftite was behind schedule. According to the division superintendent, the delays were unavoidable because several domestic orders had been given a higher priority.

"By whom? This Taiwan order was supposed to be shipped two weeks ago and it's still piled up in the preparation bay."

"Sorry, Mr. Redfern. Orders from the top."

"What top? Foreign orders have always come first around here. Who changed the rules?"

"Take it up with Mr. Walsh."

"Since when is Mr. Walsh in charge of production schedules?"

The superintendent opened his desk drawer, shuffled some papers and found a memo sent to all division heads over Hunt Benson's signature. Dated three weeks earlier, it ordered all Graftite production priorities cleared through Mr. Adam Walsh's office.

Walsh again, like a malevolent spirit hovering over Stanton corporate life. Brian's life. He stormed out of the superintendent's office and started to cross the plating room, dodging forklifts, heading for the exit on the opposite side of the building. Suddenly an earsplitting horn sounded and one of the white-coated workers put his arm out to stop him. "Hold it right there!"

The horn sounded again, followed by a whooping siren as Brian looked up, puzzled.

"Just be a minute, sir," the worker said. "Can't cross yet. There's a stoppage on Number One bath and restarts cause splashes. You don't want to go home gold-plated for Christmas."

Brian waited impatiently as the clanking din died down to a muffled racket. When the siren sounded once more, the clanking began again as an overhead crane fished a chain of turbine blades from the main bath. Moments later the chain slipped and the blades fell back into the bath from a height of fifteen feet. Great splashes of molten metal and acid slopped out of the bath and hit the cement floor near where Redfern stood, a few drops even spattering the cuff of his trousers and burning his shoe leather with a smoking hiss.

He jumped back.

"You okay?" the worker said. Brian nodded. "Better move a little further. They'll have it out in a minute."

While Brian watched, they rescued the blades again and this time they did not fall into the bath. Above him on the catwalk a foreman was directing the operation with a walkie-talkie. That's where the stockholders tour would pass, Brian was thinking, led by Adam Walsh. A good shove and he'd hit the metal bath like those turbine blades. Splash. A tragic industrial accident. End of Walsh, end of problem. If only there was a way to do it, he couldn't help thinking.

"It's okay, sir."

"What?"

"You can cross now."

It was then that Colin's call found him and he went to the company cafeteria to call back from the pay telephone. After they had talked he was still seething about Walsh, about losing the money to Quirk, about Colin too. Lawyers had their place, but lawyers could also be losers . . . His mood did not improve after he called Ken Fairchild only to discover he had already left for a skiing weekend and would not return until the following week.

Brian Redfern felt very much alone, weighed down by the responsibility of raising the money for Walsh not only to save himself and the Stanton share price, but all of them. He was angry and he was harassed. Fionna had not let up. "Brian, you must do this, you must do that," she would tell him. "We have the Scheutters' open house on Christmas Eve and we've got Nathaniel Sawyer and Tricia on Wednesday and the Junior League ball on . . ."

"For god's sake, Fionna, I'll be in Nassau Monday."

"Well, you better be back by Tuesday in time to go to West Hartford because the Cummingses have asked us and the Livingstons to dinner. That's two votes, Brian. Lydell Cummings is in hand and all you have to do is ice the cake. He's Harvard, by the way, and has a lot of influence with your Boston directors. Two more votes."

"I appreciate what you're doing, Fionna, but—"

"No, you don't. You haven't the faintest idea what I'm doing or what it costs me. But it doesn't matter. If they vote you in it will have been worth it."

"I still don't believe—"

"Do you think I enjoy sucking up to these old bags? Who took care of Tricia Sawyer's darling Siamese cats when she had the breast tumor operated on? Me, for which she's forever grateful."

"I do realize what—"

"And the Livingstons' daughter? That no-talent girl wants to work in television and I found her a job through a friend."

"Fionna, really, I appreciate—"

"Just get your butt back from Nassau in time, Brian!"

Stanton headquarters closed at noon on Christmas Eve, and when Brian called Benson's office the secretary told him Hunt had already left to attend the company Christmas party in the cafeteria.

Redfern was not about to appear there. He called Fionna and listened to his own voice on their answering machine. Then her recorded voice saying she had a three o'clock appointment at the hairdresser's in the Waterford Mall and to please pick her up. He left a message saying okay and he would be having lunch at the club.

Then he slumped into his Porsche and headed for the Thames

River Golf and Canoe Club, intent on brightening his world a little with a pre-Christmas drink. The snow was falling heavily by then and the back roads were slippery. Twice his heart skipped as he nearly lost control of the car taking curves too fast. He felt the skin prickle on the back of his neck when the Porsche entered a skid and fishtailed slightly before recovering its grip on the road. Actually it was exhilarating, riding the fine edge like that. For a change he felt in control of his life again.

Although Brian had been accustomed to pressure he had never endured anything as harrowing as these weeks before Christmas. Neither his tough M.I.T. engineering course, his Harvard graduate studies nor his rapid climb within Stanton had ever placed so much concentrated stress on him. Not a day went by without one of the auditors requiring an explanation of this transfer or that withdrawal. He had got the money together for Walsh all right, but to do so quickly he had been obliged to violate every rule in Stanton's books. It was true that they could patch it over later, as Colin had said, but meanwhile it was he, Brian Redfern, who was holding the bag. He had to cut down on his drinking, his smoking and the pills he was becoming used to. But later, when it was over, when the pressure was off . . .

The club lounge was full and friends called his name when he entered. "Hey, Brian! Over here!" They made room for him at the bar. "The best Tom-and-Jerry in the state of Connecticut!" someone shouted, and handed Brian a warm creamy cup pungent with the rich smells of nutmeg and rum.

Until recently Brian had never been much of a drinker. An occasional glass of wine or a cold beer in the summer was his limit. Soon the hot rum seemed to be reaching his nerve ends, loosening him up, pleasurably tingling the tips of his fingers, dissolving his anger and leaving him momentarily at peace with the world. The talk was cheerful, the room was cozy and these men were his friends. A few were from Stanton Technologies like himself, others were retired naval officers or local professionals or executives from the Electric Boat Company, which built the nuclear subs.

Nathaniel Sawyer puffed his pipe as the men around Brian debated the merits of different kinds of rum. An accountant from Stanton Technologies insisted a dark Haitian rum was the best, while others argued for the light golden Jamaican product.

When Sawyer asked Brian's opinion on rum, Brian held up his cup and said, "Whatever's in this has to be the winner."

A ripple of laughter and Brian smiled, surprised by their reaction and pleased with himself. I can work the room, he thought, I can do anything I want. Someone filled his cup for the third time. By then he was detached, floating and surprised at how little it took to have them in his hand, how droll and amusing they found his slurred, boozy exchanges. But he was also somewhere else, on a rarefied level of existence only he could understand. That was what none of them would ever appreciate.

They were talking around him, to him and with him. He answered their questions, flattered their egos, made them smile at his rum-sharpened wit. He had them roaring with laughter more than once, but he could not remember for a minute what he said that was so funny. They were hanging on every word. Even Nat Sawyer, who was considered the local poker face, even he seemed amused.

"Why don't you let me drive?" one of them was saying.

"I'm fine, fine. Going to get Fionna at the hairdresser's. Don't know what they serve there but it's her favorite hangout."

"Brian, let Bob take you home. I'll follow in my car."

"I'm okay." An exchange of doubtful, meaningful looks in the parking lot. One of them shrugging, as if to say, It's out of my hands, as the freezing wind blew and the snow swirled around them.

Brian got the Porsche started and then stalled it as they watched. But he started it again quickly and peeled out of the snow-covered parking area as one of them asked the other, "Do you really think it's right to let him go like that?"

"No, but who's going to stop him?"

The road was icy beneath the powdery snow, but Brian felt he had total control of the Porsche, knowing its bad habits, steering it back to the center of the road each time it tried to swerve toward the shoulder. "No, you don't," he would say, and the little car would growl its own high-powered answer and once more do as it was told.

The mall parking area was vast but filled with the cars of last minute Christmas shoppers. He drove down the aisles for several minutes before he finally found a vacant slot near the mall entrance. Only after he parked the car and locked the door did he see the wheelchair symbol reserving the place for the handicapped.

He looked around guiltily to see if anyone had noticed, but the snow was coming down so hard by then, everyone's visibility was limited. Satisfied that no mall cop would come out in this, he set off for the entrance, to pick up Fionna, head down, chin tucked inside his collar as snowflakes swirled about him, glazing his dark hair white. Shoppers came out in a relentless stream, laden with bags and packages. A desultory Santa Claus rang a bell just inside the door.

Brian stood back to let a large woman pass, her shopping bags crammed with brightly wrapped presents. Behind her, his arms also full, came none other than Adam Walsh, who did not see Redfern.

Brian stopped dead. The sight of the man was enough to rekindle all the rage and frustration that had been temporarily dissipated by the golf club rum. His eyes followed Walsh's back until it faded beyond the curtain of snow.

"I'll kill him," he muttered to himself, and wondered why he hadn't decided to do it sooner, the idea seemed such an obvious solution. The combination of anger, frustration, drink and speed had been fused by the catalytic appearance of Walsh in the shopping mall. With murder in his heart, Brian started back through the blizzard after Adam Walsh. It was as though fate had delivered Walsh to him for execution. He actually felt that way in his moment of derangement. He ran back to his car and drove to the exit just in time to see Walsh's black company Lincoln pull out of the parking lot. He stayed well back, going very slowly, because the going was slick. After a while all he could see were the two red pinpoints of Walsh's tail lights.

He followed the car for two or three miles, with no specific plan in mind but convinced beyond all doubt that the only solution to his dilemma was to kill the son of a bitch. There was no reason to pay Walsh one more cent, or to worry about his being elected president of Stanton, or to think about frightening him. Dead, he collected nothing and threatened no one. It was as if the possibility had been somewhere in his mind the whole time and he only needed a glimpse of Walsh's face to turn it into an obsession.

Suddenly he felt free, no longer angry or frustrated but elated, almost giddy with a desire to put an end to the man, *remove* him from their midst forever. Whatever had provoked his sudden realization didn't matter. It was as if the whole scene had long been written and all he had to do was play his part.

He followed the Lincoln onto the turnpike where the roads had been sanded, and they both picked up speed. Walsh did not turn off at his usual exit but kept on going. Eventually the Lincoln turned at the Oyster River exit to take the blacktop road leading north. Brian followed, still without a plan, but he felt like a hunter stalking his quarry. Something would occur, and he felt protected by the snowfall.

The Oyster River Road bisects a very lightly populated area and appears on maps as a secondary country route. It winds through large stands of fir, maple and scrub oak, skirts a tidal wetland covered with sawgrass and meanders by some small farms and two or three development tracts before it connects to the old Middletown road. In severe snowstorms the plows and sand trucks seldom pass there until they have taken care of the more heavily traveled highways. The Oyster River is not really a river at all but a tidal estuary about fifty yards across. The narrow iron bridge which spans it is only fifteen feet above the high-water line, just enough to allow medium-size powerboats and very small sailing craft to pass. It is dangerous in bad weather because the approaches are steep, and on one side the road angles sharply to the right just before it reaches the bridge. Caution signs are posted to warn motorists that the surface is slippery when wet. In all weathers it clatters like a giant suit of chain mail every time a car crosses.

Remaining ten or twelve lengths behind the Lincoln, his windshield wipers beating a steady tattoo against the snow, Redfern followed. Both drivers were taking the curves cautiously and rarely braking. As they approached the Oyster River Bridge, Brian suddenly thought he knew exactly what he had to do.

The hill was steep, the turn was sharp, the rail was low, and the river was deep. As they reached the crest and began to descend he could see through the scrim of falling snow the broad dark ribbon of water ahead.

He gunned the Porsche and heard the comforting whine of the engine as the car shot forward and streaked down the hill behind the Lincoln. The Porsche felt almost like an extension of his body at that moment. He knew that what he wanted had to be a precision move, a surgical strike, as they called it. Inflict maximum damage to the enemy and get away unscathed . . .

He checked his rising speed as the distance closed. He must overtake the Lincoln as it reached the bottom of the hill, not one second sooner. He would ram it a glancing blow in the left rear, sending it crashing through the guard rail and into the ice-fringed Oyster River while the Porsche hurtled on over the bridge and disappeared.

When he was barely fifty feet from the rear of the Lincoln he aimed his sports car at the tail light and floored the accelerator. But a split second before he struck the other vehicle, the Porsche began to slide. By the time he recovered he had lost momentum and changed direction slightly. Instead of striking the Lincoln on the left rear, he missed completely and sideswiped it along the door on the driver's side.

He wished he could see Walsh's expression as he swept on by in that instant, fighting to control the Porsche. He would have given anything to see that smirking face transformed into a mask of fear when the man presumably knew for a certainty he was about to die.

The bridge rattled as Brian veered into a long crabbing slide and only managed to straighten out on the far bank of the river. In his rearview mirror he saw a fiery comet of sparks as the Lincoln skidded the length of the bridge on its side before smashing through the guard rail and plunging to the water below.

___CHAPTER THIRTY-SEVEN___

BY FOUR o'clock in the afternoon on Christmas Eve the offices of Cranmer, Fisher & Cleves had more in common with a Soho disco than with any temple of corporate law. Cups and crumpled paper napkins littered the corners, great trays of smoked salmon, ham and caviar hors d'oeuvres lay in ruins on the secretaries' desks, and the fish tank had been filled and refilled with a mysterious mixture that now seemed to be equal parts vodka and brandy poured over ice.

With foresight and Colin's authorization, Anthony Shattuck had earlier laid on several vans with professional drivers to take people home safely when the party officially ended at six. Three vehicles would be going to Westchester County and Connecticut, one to Long Island and two to New Jersey. Those who lived in town could fend for themselves with taxis or the city transit system.

Over the din of the music, Colin said to Barbara, "Anytime you're ready, we can leave," and she replied that fresh air was exactly what she craved after all the punch and the dancing.

They made the rounds briefly, wishing a Merry Christmas to those near at hand, and then they slipped away. The storm had not abated as they came out of the overheated building, and the chill hush of the city took them both by surprise. Barbara shivered and clutched his arm as they walked along Water Street toward Wall. It would soon be dark and there was barely any traffic. Several inches of snow had already fallen and some cars spun their wheels on the icy incline.

The few taxis Colin saw were taken, but Barbara said not to worry and tugged him after her. Parked on Pearl Street two blocks from Colin's building was her own car and driver.

"You mean to say the poor guy's been waiting out here in the snow all afternoon? For shame, Barbara."

"How long have you been here, Edward?" she asked him.

"Ten minutes. I got here at four like you said."

"How's that for timing?" Barbara grinned.

"Maggie couldn't have arranged it better."

"Where shall we go, Colin?" She wanted to add, My place? Yours?

"What would you like to do?"

"You'll laugh."

"What?"

"I'd love to go to Rockefeller Center. The tree should be beautiful in the snow and they'll be skating. Do you skate?"

"It's been a few years."

"Me too. When I was little I didn't want to be a Hollywood star or a ballet dancer, I wanted to be a champion figure skater. But when

I discovered how much I'd have to practice I decided I'd be just an ordinary figure skater."

"And that's what you became?"

"I was better than ordinary but not really competitive."

As it grew dark they drove slowly uptown to Herald Square, where the traffic became heavier. Macy's shimmered behind the falling snow, its facade sequinned with thousands of tiny lights that sparkled like diamond chips against the night. Continuing up Sixth Avenue past Bryant Park at 42nd Street, their car slowed to a crawl because of the sudden increase in traffic and poor visibility.

"I can't remember when I've seen it snow so hard in New York," Barbara said. "Do you think it's the ozone layer?"

"Or burning down the Brazilian rain forest," he replied. "You can bet one or the other will be blamed."

She was snuggled up against him by then, her head against his shoulder and her hand in his. When they descended from the car at Rockefeller Center they did so arm-in-arm and walked to the rail overlooking the skating rink. The hundred-foot Christmas tree was indeed a spectacle, glittering above them in all its glory while a score of hardy souls braved the blizzard to skate on the lighted ice below. The waltz from *Der Rosenkavalier* blared from loudspeakers as the skaters circled the rink in slow, graceful strokes to the time of the music.

"Thank you, Colin," Barbara said. "I'll treasure this," and she squeezed his hand. A light wind had come up and the snow fell at an angle, clinging to her hair and eyelashes and brightening her cheeks. After a while they went down to one of the cafes that faced the rink and had a cappuccino while they watched the skaters. "You really do know how to please me," she said, her eyes shining.

At six-thirty he telephoned his apartment to learn that Joyce had spent a quiet day. She was sleeping, Nurse Jewett said.

When he returned to the table, Barbara said, "Would you like to go home and be with her, Colin?"

"In a way, yes. In a way, no." Actually, it would have been easier just to go, indulge whatever guilts he had, even though he knew very well that Joyce was so heavily sedated that she wouldn't be able to recognize him being there anymore. He knew what Joyce would say, just go ahead, Colin, I want you to. But she was always more courageous and realistic than he was. He knew he didn't need to explain to Barbara, whatever he chose. And realizing that, he decided, still uneasily, to stay with her.

Barbara had sent the car home so they decided to walk awhile in the snow. There were few pedestrians on Fifth Avenue and the vehicle traffic was growing lighter here as well. Barbara held her face to the snow, reveling as the downy flakes caressed her cheeks. "Did you ever try to catch them on your tongue when you were little?"

"I was never little, not the way you mean."

"Did you have an awful childhood?"

"Not awful. Just not much of a childhood. When I was small I was very small. And I was the only Irish kid in a neighborhood divided between Jews and Italians. Whenever they made peace and decided to kick the cat, I was the cat. Lucky for me I grew big pretty quick."

"And got even."

"Not right away. It took three or four years. And by the time I'd carved out my own turf I left the neighborhood."

"For Harvard?"

"Yeah, Harvard."

"Didn't you like college?"

"I lived my first three years in mortal fear of flunking out and losing my scholarship."

"But you didn't."

"I made the dean's list, like a good over-achiever."

"And then you went to law school."

"Then I went to law school."

"Why?"

"To please my old man."

"And was he pleased?"

"He was dead by then but he would have been pleased."

"When did you fall in love with the law?"

"Who said I was?"

"My father always said you were. He said you'd be on the Supreme Court by now if you hadn't spent your talent representing people like him."

"He was a great one to talk."

"Do you think he wasted his genius?"

"He did what most of us do. He got along. But if anyone wasted your father's genius it was me by persuading him to become an industrialist. Your father was a great chemist, an inventor of the first rank. If he'd stayed in the laboratory where he belonged I bet he'd have won a Nobel prize."

Barbara smiled. "You both liked the money, right?"

He laughed. "Guilty as charged."

They had walked eight blocks by then and were facing Grand Army Plaza at the foot of Central Park. "I don't know about you, Colin, but my feet are soaked and frostbitten."

"Ditto."

"What shall we do?"

"Taxi home?"

"Easier said than done." Traffic had thinned since they left Rockefeller Center. The buses no longer seemed to be running as the snow grew deeper and began to drift. Private cars and no taxis. But just then Barbara let out a squeal and ran ahead. On the far side of Central Park South a lone horse-drawn carriage still lingered, one of those that take tourists around the park.

She had the top-hatted driver's full attention when Colin walked up. He was saying, "I don't know, miss. We were heading for the barn . . ."

"Take us to the Ritz Tower before you head for the barn. Please."

He looked at Colin. "It'll cost you. Won't hardly be worth what I'll have to charge."

"The Ritz Tower isn't far," Colin said.

"But the lady wants to go through the park."

Barbara was looking at him. "Game?"

"What the hell, why not? Double pneumonia or nothing."

Before Colin climbed up behind Barbara, the driver whispered in his ear, "A hundred dollars. I can't stay out in this for less."

He nodded. Under the seat there were blankets and a moth-eaten old bearskin rug that covered them.

They were alone after they entered the park, not a car to be seen or a soul on foot anywhere. No traffic noise reached them, and except for the blurred lights of the nearby skyline they might have been passing through some distant northern forest. The air was clear and sharp and the blankets over their laps were rich with the pungent odor of horse. The sound of the hooves was muffled by the snow and they moved to the creak of the ancient carriage and the rhythmic jingle of the harness bells. There was a fairy-tale feeling to the night, a sense of enchantment in the snow-covered trees around them and in the white halo of snowflakes surrounding each street light.

"Okay?" Barbara said at one point.

"And then some. I feel as if we entered a time warp and wound up at the turn of the century."

"I wish I'd lived then. Much more romantic than now."

"I don't know. If you ask me, this is pretty romantic."

"What a nice thing to say."

"Even if we do catch our death."

"Are you cold?"

"Only my feet, but I'm not sure."

"Why aren't you?"

"No more feeling below the knees."

She burrowed closer under the blankets. "Colin?"

"Yes."

"Hold me."

He put one arm around her and she snuggled into the hollow of his shoulder. "Better?"

"Better than better," and they did not speak again until they had left the park and pulled up in front of the Ritz Tower.

_____ CHAPTER THIRTY-EIGHT _____

COLIN KNEW when he went in with her it was probably the wrong thing to do, but by now he was no more capable of resisting than Barbara was. The mood of the evening had been set by the city's hush, the softly falling snow and their ride in the carriage. Neither of them wanted to let it go.

She kicked off her shoes just inside the door, and as he continued on into the drawing room she went to bring him a towel, calling back over her shoulder, "You know where the bar is. Make me a good stiff drink, will you, darling?"

She reappeared wearing a blue silk robe and marabou slippers and handed him a pair of gray wool ski socks. He had prepared two tumblers with scotch on the rocks, and Barbara said, "Let me have your shoes and I'll put them in the kitchen to dry."

They sipped their drinks in silence, he on one of her overstuffed silk divans, she curled up on the carpet in front of him, leaning against his knee. "You know it's going to happen, don't you?" When he didn't answer, she turned to look up at him. "Don't you?"

"I don't know."

"I've already been to bed with you in my fantasies."

"I'm flattered, but I don't believe it."

"Darling Colin, I've been fantasizing about you for years. Since we first met when I came home from boarding school."

"Come on, Barbara. You were practically a child."

"That's all you know."

"And after that you were happily married."

"For a while. But you were my first big crush. I was madly in love with you and tremendously jealous of Joyce."

"And now?"

"I'm not jealous anymore because I love Joyce too. But you're a very attractive man and I love you more. If I could steal you away and have you all to myself I would do it and not look back."

"You might not be getting much of a bargain."

"There you go again. Selling yourself short. I've known you too long, Colin Draggett, and I guess I know my own mind."

"It doesn't have to happen, Barbara."

"Yes, it does. It's some kind of crazy fatalism. Karma, isn't that what they call it? Daddy dying was part of it. And Joyce's terrible illness. Then Ken screwing around again and again. I believe life gets very far out of whack sometimes and bad things happen. People die, relationships fail and the world we took for granted suddenly seems to be coming apart and collapsing all around us."

Colin was thinking that most of what she referred to, except for Joyce's dying and Ken Fairchild's philandering, could be blamed on their mutual nemesis Adam Walsh.

"I believe every so often God gets fed up and gives the world a great shake so things can sort of realign themselves."

"You think that's what's happening now?"

She nodded. "Like your meeting Daddy years ago and my going to your party today. The blizzard and that horse and carriage being there at exactly the right moment just for us."

"All part of God's great shake."

"Don't laugh."

"I'm not. But I like to feel I have some freedom of choice in my life. Do I?"

She smiled up at him. "That depends on what you choose."

He eased off the sofa to sit beside her, his arm on her shoulder, her eyes on his. He kissed her, lightly at first, softly as he drew her to him, brushing her lips with his, her forehead, her cheeks and again her lips. His hands caressed her shoulders, traced the fine line of her throat and fondled her breasts as he kissed her once more, tasting the sweetness of her, the exquisite softness.

When they separated it was only to return to each other again, not so gently this time but with a kind of desperation deeper and more urgent than passion. Their bodies pressed against each other and her hand went to his loins, rubbing, clutching, then running under his shirt and up over his chest as he struggled out of his clothes.

Under her robe she was naked and moist and waiting, and by unspoken mutual agreement they came together with only an inch of Persian carpeting between them and the unyielding parquet.

Afterward they killed a bottle of good Bourgogne and snacked on caviar before finally reaching her bed. There, over the next five hours, he surprised himself by managing it twice more, to Barbara's sweet delight. Once he began, he craved her sex with an appetite born out of long abstinence, a hunger that subsided only when he could no longer sustain an erection. They lay in each other's arms for a long time, dozing, kissing, caressing, reluctant to part but unable to come again. How much of it was love he didn't know, but did it really matter?

In the early hours of the morning he left the bed and dressed as Barbara sat up sleepily and watched him.

"Must you go?"

"I'm afraid so."

"Are you sorry?"

"No. Are you?"

"I'm happy."

"Thank you, Barbara."

"Will I see you tomorrow?"

"I'll call you. The cathedral choir Maggie sings with is giving the *Messiah* at St. John the Divine. Would you like to go? Then later we could have Christmas dinner somewhere."

"Oh, Colin, that would be lovely."

He kissed her one last time, a lingering caress on her cheek. He held her and then he let her go. When he reached the door she called after him, "Merry Christmas, Colin. I love you."

He let himself out and rang for the elevator. The doorman offered small hope for a taxi so he walked the strangely silent streets. It had stopped snowing and the jaded old harridan of a city slept like a queen under her glittering white mantle. Colin was a little proud, but he remembered thinking, Now you've done it, Draggett, added adultery to your list of crimes. But the guilt would have to wait.

_____CHAPTER THIRTY-NINE_____

A STEEP hill on the far side of the Oyster River Bridge probably saved Brian Redfern's life. The speed of the Porsche before he struck the Lincoln was so great that he never could have braked on the snow-slick blacktop without spinning out of control and crashing into the old oaks that lined the side of the road. As it was, he only fishtailed a little, geared down, and the upward slope did the rest. By the time he reached the crest, the speedometer needle had dropped from ninety miles an hour to forty.

He did not stop or look back. What he had seen in the rearview mirror was enough for him. The Lincoln had been on its side, spewing sparks the length of the bridge before it disappeared over the edge. Ten miles down the road he noticed a flicker in his right headlight. He pulled over and got out to see how badly he had damaged the Porsche. The broken light was hanging from its mounting like a loose tooth and the entire right front had been flattened by the impact. Solve one problem and create another, he thought, his mind feverish and racing on ahead. But Adam Walsh was really the only problem, and dead he wasn't even a minor nuisance. Getting the car repaired didn't worry him, he would find a place to do it. Walsh was dead and there had been no witnesses to the accident except the victim, Brian was sure of it. But if there was an investigation he decided to take no chances . . . He didn't know how the state police handled cases if the involvement of a second car was suspected . . . Walsh was dead and—

He was still standing by the car, the falling snow forming a white mantle on his head and shoulders, when the realization that he had actually killed a man burst inside his consciousness like a starshell. No longer giddy or manic or high, but shivering suddenly from the cold and from the numbing fear of what he'd done, he stared at the damaged fender and saw instead a vision of Adam Walsh in the dark waters of the Oyster River, clawing at the door handles trying to get out of the car, trapped and drowning behind the windows.

Brian staggered back from the Porsche as if it were a lethal thing, hearing Walsh's silent scream beneath the surface of the river as the icy waters rose around his face and his palms pounded against the glass.

Brian vomited into the snow, bent from the waist. Minutes passed, but each time he thought it was over, his body was convulsed by another series of spasms as if trying to throw up his guilt. When the dry heaves ceased finally, he felt weak and disoriented. He knew it was only the pills and the Tom-and-Jerries and he should feel better now that he'd cleared his system. But instead he felt worse, and a terrible sense of foreboding overtook him. "What in God's name have I done?" he said aloud, and even thought absurdly of racing back to the scene of the accident to help pull Walsh from the river.

Crazy. Stupid. He never meant to go that far, never would have believed himself capable of such an act. Yet he remembered clearly seeing Walsh come out of the mall, his arms full of packages, as he remembered also the clarity of the decision to kill him. But it was almost as if another person had decided to follow the Lincoln, as if Brian Redfern had been watching someone else do it from a distance. I must have been mad, he told himself now, drunk or high or wired.

His hands trembled on the wheel when he returned to the car, then sat there for half an hour getting a grip on himself, or trying to. He swallowed two dexes and his mouth was bird-cage dry but slowly he began to feel a little better. As the speed took hold, the guilt and the dread faded, and with them, his sense of responsibility. Walsh brought it on himself, he decided as he turned the key and started the car.

Hc followed the old road to Route 145 below Winthrop, then cut south to the turnpike and headed west to New Haven. In East Haven he stopped at a McDonald's restaurant, drank a cup of steaming, watery coffee and thumbed the yellow pages in the outdoor phone booth. A page of body-and-fender repair shops, but several seemed to be located in one section of West Haven.

An hour later he was talking to the paint-spattered owner of one of them in a noisy, tin-roofed garage redolent with acetone and foggy with lacquer spray.

"Nice mess," the man said, running his fingers along the damaged side of the Porsche. "Got sideswiped, did you?"

"Afraid so. Can you fix it?"

The man nodded. "Some kid hit you, right?"

"That's right."

"Goddamn kids got no sense these days. Tried to pass you on the right. I hope you got his license number."

"As a matter of fact—"

"The state police will pull him over if you got his number. Beautiful car like this. It's a shame, goddamn kids."

The body work could be done fast, the man said. But it would take five days if Brian wanted three coats of paint. The light bracket would have to be replaced, but there was a parts dealer in Greenwich and he could have it in a day.

"I hate being without the car," Brian said.

"Don't blame you. Car like that. But we don't do half-ass work here. We do it right."

"Five days, you say?"

"You'll have it for New Year's."

Brian left the Porsche, rented a Chevrolet from Hertz and drove back to New London. It was still only eight o'clock when he pulled in the drive, but Fionna was livid.

"Damn it, Brian, where have you been? You said you'd pick me up at the beauty parlor and you never showed. I waited until six and we were supposed to be at the Scheutters' at seven."

"The Scheutters?"

"Their annual open house. *Remember?* The admiral and his lady give a cocktail party Christmas Eve and he hates people being late. At least three of your directors will be there so get a move on! Where the devil were you anyway?"

"I got tied up."

"I called your office and nobody was answering the phones. Not even a recorded message."

"It's Christmas, Fionna. The plant is closed and the switchboard shut down at noon."

"Where were you so tied up? Not at the club. I heard you left there at three flying high."

"I had a meeting."

"Why didn't you call instead of leaving me stranded? I should have come home with Adam Walsh when I had the chance."

"Walsh!"

"Yes. Nice Mr. Walsh. He offered to drive me home."

"When was that?"

"I guess it was around five."

"Walsh was at the hairdresser's?"

"He was Christmas shopping at the mall and saw me standing like an idiot waiting for you."

"How did you get home finally?"

"How do you think? I called a taxi."

"Look, I'm sorry. I wasn't near a telephone."

"All bars have telephones, Brian. You even have a telephone in your goddamn car."

"Call the Scheutters and say we can't make it."

"At this hour? Are you crazy? We can't beg off now." She followed him to the bathroom and brought him a clean shirt as he stripped to the waist and began to run an electric razor over his face. "You look like hell," she told him.

He was sober now, but wired with amphetamines, and he had a growing headache. "Get me a couple of aspirin, will you? I think I might be coming down with something."

"They're right behind you in the medicine chest, and you're not coming down with anything except a hangover."

"We can use the blizzard as an excuse."

"For being late but not for not turning up. Are you going to tell me where you were or not?" She remained in the doorway, hand on hip, watching him.

"You're positively beautiful when you're mad."

"Spare me the bullshit, Brian. I'm ugly when I'm mad, and I'm going to get a lot uglier before this day is over if you don't explain why you stood me up at the mall this afternoon."

"Actually, I met this spectacular girl . . ."

"Sure, and you fucked your socks off. Sorry, darling, but it's not your style. Leave that to Fairchild."

"Make me a drink, will you? Like a good girl?"

"You don't need a drink and don't patronize me. Move!"

With her fashionable cloth coat and a Hermes scarf, Fionna waited at the door while Brian caught up, still tying his tie. No furs for Fionna because she knew that at least two of the directors' wives who would be there this evening were death on fur. One of them, Tricia Sawyer, was even a vegetarian.

"What's this?" Fionna said when she saw the rented Chevy. "Where's your car?"

"Being fixed."

"We can take my Porsche then."

"No point in taking it out in this stuff. We'll use the rental. It's already warmed up anyway."

"What happened to your car?"

"That's what held me up."

"I thought you were in a meeting."

"After the meeting."

"But what happened?"

"Compression problem. Pooped out on the turnpike."

"What are you talking about? That car is brand new."

"Probably a defective engine part."

"That's ridiculous."

"Fionna, the Germans aren't perfect."

"It's the first time I ever heard of a Porsche blowing an engine with less than ten thousand miles on it."

"It didn't blow an engine." Why hadn't he said he'd run out of gas or had a flat or broken a shock or something? He had forgotten she considered herself an expert on sports cars and actually did know as much or more than he.

"That's what you said."

"I didn't say that. I just didn't want to drive it any further with low compression until it was checked and put right."

"Hmm. Well, you picked a great day for it. Did you have to get a tow?"

"Ah, no. I made it to a garage okay."

"With no telephone."

"Fionna, I'm sorry. I forgot, okay? I had a lot on my mind and I just plain forgot."

"At least that bears some semblance to the truth."

"Resemblance, not semblance. *Resemblance* to the truth or *a semblance of* the truth, but not some—"

"I didn't ask for a lecture, Brian."

"Look, I said I'm *sorry.*"

"And that's supposed to make everything all right? What's so top secret you can't tell me where you were all afternoon?"

"I told you. I was in a meeting."

"Drunk? That must have been illuminating." The blizzard had not let up, and although the snowplows were out by then, the road conditions off the turnpike were extremely hazardous.

"I wasn't drunk. I just had a couple of drinks at the club before lunch. What is this, anyway, the third degree?"

"Exactly. Where was the meeting. Not at Stanton."

"New Haven. I had to see a guy in New Haven."

"About what?"

"What difference does it make? A job interview."

"Were you hiring someone or looking for work?"

"Very funny, Fionna."

"And slow down. You're driving much too fast."

"I know what I'm doing." An icy sheet had formed under the fresh powder as the snow continued to fall, and Redfern squinted against the white gauze that overlaid the night, trying to make out the road ahead.

"Will you slow down, damn it? You lost your license once for too many speeding violations. Do you want them to take it away permanently?" Suddenly the flashing yellow light of a slow-moving sand truck appeared in front of them. Brian braked to avoid back-ending it, but the treacherous surface sent him skidding into the path of an oncoming car as Fionna screamed.

Miraculously the vehicle missed them by the breadth of a snow-flake and flashed by on the wrong side of the road, its horn blaring angrily. "Sorry," Brian gasped when they came to a stop.

Fionna was thoroughly frightened, trembling. "Damn you, Brian, you nearly got us killed . . ."

"You okay?"

"No, I'm not okay! Let's try to arrive in one piece even if we are an hour late. Do you want me to drive?"

"It's just this car, you know. I'm used to the stick shift on the Porsche. These wheels can go right out from under you."

"See that they don't do it again, Brian."

"It's really beautiful tonight," he said to change the subject once they were under way again. "When was the last white Christmas you remember around here?" As they neared the Scheutters' neighborhood he called her attention to the quantity of trees and shrubs brightly decorated with colored lights.

"Please watch the road so we can live to enjoy them."

"They give a prize for the best light display."

"Our host is the one who usually wins it," Fionna said. "He spends weeks stringing lights all over his shrubbery."

Brian said. "The worst is over. You have no idea."

"What are you talking about?"

"Just what I said. It's over! Onward and upward."

"Are you on something, Brian? Why the sudden euphoria?"

"The Christmas spirit, my love. Can't I be happy?"

She eyed him doubtfully. "Be my guest."

"If Barbara's as determined to keep Ken Fairchild out of the driver's seat as you say she is, then I'm in."

"Aren't you overlooking one other obstacle?"

"Hunt Benson wants out before he falls on his face. He's got visions of tarpon fishing in the Keys and—"

"I wasn't thinking of Hunt. I was thinking of Adam Walsh. He's still your only real competition."

Brian, feeling his stomach tighten, said, "If I can't beat the competition I don't deserve the job."

Fionna looked up in pleased surprise. "That's better," she said slowly. "That's more like the Brian Redfern I married."

A great many cars were parked along the street where the Scheutters lived, some of which Brian recognized as belonging to Stanton executives and directors.

"Looks like we're the last ones," Fionna said. "I'll take the blame. You just shut up and play the long-suffering male."

"What do you mean?"

"I mean I wasn't ready and you were, if anyone asks, and you're steaming because your wife made you late."

They rang the bell and were received by a Filipino mess steward borrowed from the naval base for the occasion. He took their coats as they drifted in toward the Scheutters' enormous living room where familiar well-dressed men and women sat, perched or stood talking and laughing, sipping their scotch, Perrier or white wine.

Wesley Scheutter came toward them, hand outstretched. "I was beginning to think you two were snowbound."

"My fault," Fionna said quickly. "Poor Brian's been cooling his heels for hours. My hair, I'm afraid. So sorry we're late."

"Think nothing of it, my dear," the admiral said. "You know the drill here, just help yourself. But come and get a drink."

A waiter handed Brian the light scotch and water he ordered as Wes Scheutter whisked Fionna off to the other side of the room where the Livingstons and the Cummingses were listening to one of Nathaniel Sawyer's dry Yankee jokes.

Thank God we came, Fionna told herself. The score was higher than she had calculated. Five directors instead of three, if one counted Hunt Benson, who was deep in conversation near the fireplace with a uniformed naval officer she recognized as the commandant of the Coast Guard Academy.

Brian crossed the room in Fionna's wake and took a place at the edge of the group. "Is it still coming down?" Lydell Cummings asked. When Brian nodded, Cummings said to his wife, "We better get on the road or we'll have to spend the night here."

"There you are!" Howie Livingston said, making room for Brian in their circle. "What do you think of this weather?"

"Great if you're off skiing like Fairchild."

"But what's it going to cost us in highway fatalities and fender benders?" Howie complained loudly.

"A blizzard is no time to be in the insurance business," Cummings agreed.

The guests overflowed into the dining room, where an elaborate buffet *froid* was being served—heaping platters of shrimp, oysters, smoked salmon and turkey surrounded by a colorful assortment of salads, fruit, breads and cheeses.

Fionna was laughing at something Nathaniel Sawyer had said when she glanced at Brian and gasped, "My God, what's wrong? Are you feeling all right? Brian? What's the matter?"

But he couldn't answer. His normally sallow skin had gone white as the snow outside. His mouth was agape and his eyes wide at the sight of the man filling his plate at the dining-room buffet.

Fionna was at Brian's side. "Are you ill? What's *wrong*?" The others looked at Brian too, noticing Fionna's alarm. "Brian, what is it? You look as if you'd seen a ghost."

As indeed he had. Adam Walsh came to the Redferns holding his plate of turkey out like an offering. "Merry Christmas, folks," he said, smiling. "Have some?"

_____ CHAPTER FORTY _____

IF TOO many Tom-and-Jerrys, a little speed, and weeks of angry frustration were sufficient to turn Brian Redfern into a would-be murderer on the highway, the sight of Adam Walsh alive sent him almost totally off the rails.

It was impossible for Walsh to be standing there in the Scheutters' house. He was dead. He had to be. Redfern had seen it with his own eyes, the car turning on its side and going into the long, spark-limned skid before it plunged off the bridge. Walsh had to be entombed in his black Lincoln beneath the ice-encrusted waters of the Oyster River. Yet here he was, alive and smiling, holding out his plate to Fionna a few hours after the accident. Not a mark on him, big as life. No, bigger than life, Brian thought, because he'd come back from the dead. Brian's shock and astonishment were mixed with perplexity and not just a little relief.

"Brian, what's wrong?" Fionna was at his elbow.

"I'm okay."

"Why don't you go sit down somewhere?"

"Can I help?" Adam Walsh said, reaching out to steady Redfern, who pulled back.

"It's a reaction," Fionna explained to Walsh.

"A reaction to what?"

"Four Tom-and-Jerrys and God knows what else," Fionna said. "Brian isn't used to drinking that much. Seldom more than a little wine. And you know what happens on the holidays."

Walsh chuckled. "Indeed. It's more a question of getting through them alive than celebrating. Right, Brian?" He winked at Redfern, who backed away as if he'd been struck.

"That's what I mean," Fionna said. "Brian's just out of training. He overreached himself after lunch at the golf club."

"Overreached yourself, did you?" Walsh said to Brian. "You know what they say, old man. If you drink at a golf club, don't drive. Don't even putt."

Fionna laughed dutifully. Brian did not crack a smile.

Ramona Livingston found Fionna then to thank her for her help in getting the television job in New York. "The salary's half what I made in Daddy's office, but it's great fun, Fionna, fabulous! The characters you meet, you know?"

Fionna led her aside, knowing Brian was in no mood to listen to the girl's prattle. Walsh continued to maintain the same infuriating expression of detached good humor that Brian remembered from the convict mug shots, as if Walsh knew something no one else did, which happened to be the case.

Brian grabbed a scotch from the tray of a passing waiter and gulped it half down. "Easy, boy," Walsh said. "Your wife says you already overreached yourself today."

"What are you doing here?"

"Like you, I was invited by our good friend and genial host, the admiral of the ocean sea."

"How did you get here?"

"It's obvious I didn't walk or take a train or fly. But why should that interest you?"

Brian finished the rest of his drink without answering, certain Walsh was playing some sick kind of game. Then he lit a cigarette and asked the waiter for another drink.

"I didn't know you smoked," Walsh said.

"There's a lot you don't know about me."

"This is a nice party," Walsh said, "no reason to be belligerent. Or is there?"

"You can cut out the act, Adam. We're not exactly friends."

"I'm the first to admit that," Walsh said. "You owe me money and I have serious doubts I'll see it paid."

"We're doing the best we can."

"I doubt that. I don't think your heart's in it."

The waiter arrived with Brian's drink.

"What's this I hear about an outside audit on Stanton International? Don't tell me Hunt Benson doesn't trust you."

"Avery ordered it before he died."

"How about that. So he didn't trust you either."

Redfern glared at Walsh.

"How convenient. Now Colin wants to use it as an excuse for not paying up before the stockholders meeting."

"It's true. Benson's orders. No further transfers of funds in excess of ten thousand dollars without prior approval."

"So you'll have to find another way," Walsh told him. "Not much time left either."

"There's no way we can do it."

"Too bad. Colin asked me for an extension, but in view of what's been happening lately, I'm not sure that's wise."

"What are you talking about?"

"I have a wife to think of, expenses," Walsh said. "If I keep giving in to you, you may get the idea I'm not serious."

"Colin was telling the truth. Getting that much money together before the sixth of January is simply impossible."

"So he said."

"Well?"

"You understand my problem. Do I wait to collect or do I blow the whistle? It's a tough call."

"Blow it on yourself?"

"I meant on you and yours. You've already embezzled a million dollars of company money. Wouldn't that be a juicy scandal?"

"It was only to shut you up, for the *sake* of the company. You damn well know that."

"You'd have a terrible time proving that. There's nothing to connect me with that money. The companies it was paid out to don't even exist anymore." His smile was firmly in place as he gazed at Redfern with a look of mild contempt that bordered on pity.

Brian could have killed him with his bare hands at that moment. He ground his teeth and said in a hoarse whisper, "You'd go down with us. And you've been in prison . . ."

"By no means. I wouldn't be accused of anything because my testimony would be needed to put you three away."

"You slimy son of a bitch—"

"For a Harvard man you're not terribly articulate."

"What do you plan to do?"

"I'll think about it over Christmas," Walsh said. "No hasty decisions. That's your problem, you know? Too impulsive. Not like Colin. He's sensible. Even Fairchild has better sense than you. By the way, why isn't he here this evening?"

"He's skiing."

Walsh found that very funny, so funny in fact that his handsome head went back and he roared with laughter.

Redfern turned his back and walked away, seeking a neutral corner. Fionna motioned him over to where she was stifling a yawn as she listened to Howie Livingston and Lydell Cummings compare casualty insurance losses for trucks, cars and motorbikes.

"Brian, join us!" Howie said. "We're boring your beautiful wife to death."

"Not at *all*," Fionna protested. "It's fascinating."

"Holidays!" Cummings was saying. "Should be done away with. It used to be just Labor Day, New Year's Eve and the Fourth turned murderers loose on the roads. Not any more."

Howie said, "I counted fifteen cars in the drifts on the way down here tonight. Most of them had slammed into each other or a tree or some damn thing."

"Weather multiplies the risk," Cummings said. "If we went out of the automobile-insurance business we'd make money."

"You mean you don't make money now?" Fionna asked.

"I'm kidding," Cummings admitted. "We make a little."

"People never think of Christmas as a killer holiday," Howie said, "but it's almost as bad as New Year's. Did you see that accident on the television news tonight?"

"I didn't watch the news," Fionna replied.

"Some guy went into the Oyster River. A power company crane fished his car out. Cops and firemen all over the place."

"Was he killed?" Fionna asked them.

Cummings shrugged. "He was alive when they pulled him out, but the news didn't say if he made it or not. The hypothermia will kill you in minutes."

"Poor man," Fionna said.

"The TV said a second car sideswiped him on the bridge," Livingston reported. "Some skaters saw it. The police are looking for a small dark car, you know, like an old black Volkswagen beetle or something similar, but the kids didn't get the license number."

"Probably one of their friends," Cummings said.

"God save us from drivers under twenty-five," Livingston said. "Most of them shouldn't be allowed on the road."

". . . What time did this happen?" Brian asked them, his voice low.

"I don't know. Howie, what did the TV say?"

"Just before dark. Must have been around five-thirty."

"What an awful way to die," Fionna said with a shudder.

"Did they say who he was?" Brian asked.

"Man from Branford," Cummings said. "Don't recall the name. His car was full of Christmas presents for his kids."

"Awful!" Fionna cried. "His poor family. Brian, are you all right? You look ill. Do you want to leave?"

Redfern shook his head, although for the second time that day he felt very sick to his stomach. He set down the remains of his drink, excused himself and rushed to the Scheutters' lavatory only to find it in use with the door locked. But the nausea couldn't wait. With one hand covering his mouth, he pushed rudely past several guests and out the front door.

Outside he threw up all over Admiral Scheutter's snow-covered, Christmas-lighted shrubs. Then he continued with the dry heaves until Fionna appeared carrying his coat, and the admiral assisted him down the path to the car.

There Scheutter helped him into the passenger side and looked inquiringly at Fionna.

"We'll be okay, Wes, thank you," she said. "I'm really very sorry. Brian's never done anything like this before."

"Don't worry about it, my dear. It's probably some bug he's coming down with. A lot of it around, you know."

"That's kind of you to say so. You're a dear."

"You're sure you're all right?"

"I didn't even finish my first drink and I'm a good driver. I'll get home all right now that the snow has let up."

As Brian laid his head against the cold glass of the partially open window, Fionna drove very slowly and very silently home. When they got out of the car she said, "Feeling any better?"

"Yeah. Sorry about that. God, what a disaster!"

"Brian, listen to me." She led him into the kitchen and made coffee while he sat with his head in his hands. "It doesn't have to be a disaster if you use your head."

"Well, it was. I should never have mixed scotch with rum. They say never—"

"I'm not talking about your little tummy problem."

"No?"

"It was you, wasn't it?"

"What was me?"

"The car that hit that poor man at Oyster River."

"Are you crazy, Fionna?"

"Look me straight in the eye and say it wasn't. I saw your face, Brian. I saw what happened to you when Cummings and Livingston were talking about the accident. It was you, wasn't it? That's why you didn't pick me up or call. That's why you were so late. That's why you left your car somewhere to have it fixed."

"Fionna, you don't know what you're talking about—"

"You didn't have a compression problem, Brian, you smashed the Porsche up when you ran into that man."

"My own wife!"

"You were drunk."

"So I had a few too many. That was obvious."

"And you ran into him."

"What the hell are you? The Grand Inquisitor all of a sudden? Back off, I don't have to listen to this crap!"

"No," she said calmly, "you don't. But I would listen if I were you, because what I have to say is important. If you lie to me about something as terrible as this, Brian Redfern, so help me God I'll go right out that door and never come back. Tell me the truth and we're in it together. I'll do everything I can to help you. But lie to me and you lose me."

"Fionna . . ."

"The truth, Brian. Please."

"It was an accident," he began, "and—"

"I knew it. Oh, God, I knew it!" Her poise left her then and she broke down, sobbing into her hands. He got up and put his arm around her slender shoulders.

"I'm sorry, honey. God, I'm sorry! I didn't even see him. I was going too fast and couldn't brake. I thought he just peeled into a snowdrift. I didn't think anything bad had happened."

"Why didn't you *stop*?"

"I knew if a cop showed up I'd be arrested for my breath alone. You know how tough they are. So I just kept going. I had no idea he went into the river, I swear."

"If you went to the police now, they'd never believe you. What matters is that no one finds out." She wiped away her tears with a paper towel and sat on a stool opposite him as he disconsolately sipped at his coffee. "Where is the car?"

"New Haven. East Haven, actually, at a body-and-fender shop. It will be ready the end of next week."

"Killing someone in a hit-and-run accident while drunk is about as bad as it can get, Brian. What do they call it? Negligent homicide?"

"No one said he *died.* Maybe he came through it okay. I mean they said he was alive when they found him."

"Leaving the car at a garage right after the accident was not the brightest move you ever made either. Suppose the garage man watched the television news and put two and two together?"

"I don't think so, Fionna. There was a bad storm, remember. Lots of cars get banged up. You heard them at the party complaining about the fender benders."

"What about your insurance?"

"I'm sure as hell not going to report it to the insurance company. I don't want any record of the accident."

"I mean, didn't the garage ask about insurance? They usually have to give estimates for the insurance company to check."

"I said not to bother because they'd jack up my premium."

"Pray they're all stupid at that garage. Pray it all blows over, because if you're even suspected of responsibility for this, you can kiss everything we've worked for goodbye . . . And I'm trying not to think about the Christmas that poor family will have. How awful!"

"They got him out, Fionna. I'm sure he's okay."

"Did he get a look at you?"

"I don't think so. No."

"But you're not sure."

"No."

"Then you better hope he's dead."

"God, Fionna, what are you saying?"

"The truth. You ran into the man and took off, Brian, not I. How could you have done it?"

"It was the booze—what can I say?"

"What were you doing at Oyster River anyway?"

"Trying to sober up. I was really shit-faced when I left the club and I thought if I just drove around awhile with the windows open before I picked you up I'd get my balance back. That's when it happened."

"I hope you've learned a lesson."

He would never forget the momentary manic elation he had felt when he was certain Walsh lay entombed at the bottom of the river. The presumption that he had killed Walsh and singlehandedly released them all from the tyranny of the man's demands had been, for a moment, a headier mix than rum and scotch.

"More than one," he said. But the lessons he was thinking of had little to do with what Fionna was talking about. He was sorry for the man who went into Oyster River, and he would have willed him safely back with his family if he could have.

But as for Adam Walsh, the bottom line was that son of a bitch was still alive and a terrible threat and filling his face and smirking over a drink at the Scheutters' party. It was hard-luck coincidence that two black Lincolns were leaving the parking lot at the same time the snowfall was heaviest and the visibility at its worst. Unless the poor guy from Branford died by mistake, he was off the hook.

Fionna hoped he had learned a lesson and he supposed he had. Adam Walsh was more dangerous to them than ever. Next time, he told himself, he would be more careful.

———— CHAPTER FORTY-ONE ————

CHRISTMAS MORNING. The changing of the guard in the sickroom. Nurse Lauren Jewett arrived with a stunning poinsettia for Joyce, who was awake but too doped up to notice. Mrs. Ryan wrapped her sweaters, toys and candy in bright paper and bustled off to visit children at her church hostel, looking more like a prosperous bag lady than the good Samaritan she really was.

Colin took his time over coffee and the morning papers. Outside, the empty streets remained white and quiet.

There was mail from the day before which he had not seen or opened. Christmas cards mainly, and one that made him clench his fists. It was an elaborate, gilded reproduction of a Byzantine icon of the crucified Christ with the message: "Holiday Greetings and Best Wishes for Happiness in the New Year from Celia and Adam Walsh."

IIe checked the weather. It was overcast and cold but the snowstorm seemed to be over. He put on a viyella shirt, wool tie, tweed jacket and gray flannels, with his old camel-hair polo coat on top. Wind-chill factor about five degrees according to the radio. He walked briskly in the direction of his mother's house, carrying a large box of glazed fruit, a holiday vice she couldn't resist. He had decided this would be a perfunctory visit. If Mr. Dimitri and Esther Kleineman showed up, he would urge his mother to leave with them for Florida.

He intended to get away as soon as possible after lunch, take Barbara to hear the *Messiah* in the late afternoon and enjoy some Christmas cheer and a little turkey at the Tavern on the Green.

He was not prepared for the first scene that greeted him at Maisie's, although he didn't know why not. After knowing his mother as long as he had, he should have been ready for anything.

On the stone steps leading up to her Gramercy Park apartment were two Oriental gentlemen in leather jackets, and between them, giving as good as she got, was his mother's companion, Mrs. Lombardi. When she saw Colin, she cried, "Oh, thank God! Mr. Draggett! I was about to call the police."

"Cawra porreece!" one of the Orientals shouted at her. "Gowan! Cawraporreece! We cawraporreece and rock you awrup!"

The great mediator, arbiter, negotiator and defender of the faith, Colin Draggett, stepped into the middle of this fray and said calmly, "Hold on! Take it easy now! What's the trouble?"

Both men began to talk at once in a mixture of accents, dialects and languages, presumably explaining the problem until Colin finally had to shout, "One at a time! Hold it!" He pointed to the nearest one and motioned for the other to wait while he spoke.

With Mrs. Lombardi's help Colin pieced the basic picture together. They were Korean fruit vendors and they had sold his mother fruit for which they claimed they had not been paid. According to Mrs. Lombardi, however, the old lady swore they were trying to cheat her by collecting the same bill twice.

He explained he was the lady's son. He was an attorney, and if she indeed had legitimate accounts he would settle them.

"Pay now!" one of the men said. He was very rough-looking and built along the lines of a sumo wrestler.

"Cawra porreece!" the second one said, a little man with a goatee. Probably a martial arts expert, Colin thought.

"I want my money!" the wrestler said.

Colin asked each in turn what they were owed. The sumo wrestler presented a bill for sixty-two dollars and the other one claimed forty and change for a rough total of a hundred. Colin said if they would wait five minutes he would write them each a check.

"No checks," the goateed one said. "Money!"

Mrs. Lombardi was opening the door as the big guy grabbed Colin's coat and ripped the belt in the back. "Now just a goddamn minute!" Colin turned on him, the torn belt in his hand. Colin had great patience and long practice in holding his temper, but when someone laid a hand on him he had a very short fuse. It was a holdover from his Bay Ridge boyhood when a reputation for a fiery temper could be worth more than height or muscle in discouraging any would-be attacker.

Colin gave him such a hard shove into his friend that both went sprawling down the steps. He thought, okay, here it comes, but Mrs. Lombardi caught his arm, saying, "Mr. Draggett, inside please," and pulled him and his box of glazed fruit through the door before it closed behind them. On the steps the two men continued to shout and wave their fists.

"Are you all right?"

"Damn right."

"I'll mend your coat while you're with your mother. She's been so upset by all this. And on Christmas of all times!"

He entered the drawing room to find his mother dressed in her Cardin gym sweats, a red Christmas bow in her hair, her face covered with what looked like rubber cement, pedaling a stationary bicycle. What next? She didn't look up until he leaned over, waved his hand in her face and held out the box of glazed fruit.

"Put it over there," she gasped. "I got to do another two minutes." And she kept pedaling furiously.

He went to look out at the snow-mantled square, at the black skeletal trees and high iron fence like an etching against the pristine whiteness of the park. The foreground was less serene where the two Korean men still glowered from the sidewalk.

When he turned around he noticed that his mother and he were not alone. At the far end of the room a dark, gypsy-looking woman sat thumbing a magazine. A bell on the bicycle rang and his mother stopped pedaling, picked up a towel and flung herself on the divan beside the woman, mopping her face.

"You shouldn't overdo," the woman said.

"Hello," he said. "I'm Colin."

"I love your aureola," she told him.

"What?"

"Your aureola. It suits you. Tall men usually don't have mauve with violet. It assures success, power, dominance."

"That's him," his mother said. "My son, the big shot."

He had no idea what the woman was talking about, but that was not unusual in this house. "My name is Renata," she said.

They shook hands and she gave him a crested card that read "Princess Renata Radziwill, Clairvoyant, Clairaudient, Clairsentient, Psychic Development Instructor and Self-Image Improvement Coordinator, Past-Life Regressions, Rebirthing."

"I've been doing a past-life regression with Renata," his mother said. "You can't imagine who I was. You want to guess?"

"Attila? Genghis Khan? Ivan the Terrible?"

"He thinks he's funny," his mother said. "In past-life regressions I was still a woman, thank God."

"Let me guess. Delilah? Lucretia Borgia? Lizzie Borden?"

"My son, the comedian. I'll give you a clue," his mother said. "My last appearance was around two hundred years ago."

"Let's see. Dolly Madison? Martha Washington?"

"That's close."

"I give up."

"Betsy Ross."

"I don't believe it."

"It's true," his mother said. "I was Betsy Ross."

"You can't even sew."

"Not now, maybe. But then I could. Else how could I have made the flag? Think about *that* for a minute."

Renata was nodding encouragement all through this fascinating colloquy, but Colin thought it was time to return from whacko land. "On my way in the front door two men tried to collect—"

"You mean the Japs?"

"They were angry Koreans and they claim you owe them a hundred dollars for fruit you bought."

"You trust them after they bombed Pearl Harbor?"

"Koreans didn't bomb Pearl Harbor, Maisie."

"You weren't even born then. While I slaved at the navy yard your father was out getting the clap on some tropical island."

Colin had heard her version many times but he'd also heard his father's. The tropical island was Saipan, where his father had been wounded. The clap he got from a nurse in a stateside hospital.

But Maisie was not about to let him off the hook. "How do you tell a Korean from a Jap, Mr. Smartypants? Go on, tell us."

"What does that have to do with it? Did you pay for the fruit or not? If you didn't I'll leave Mrs. Lombardi the money."

"How do you tell a Jap? We want to know."

"He carries a camera, Mother. How should I know?"

"Ha!" She punched Renata on the arm. "What did I tell you? Maybe I can't sew but I guess I know a Jap when I see one."

"It really doesn't make any difference," Colin said.

Before this Mad Hatter conversation could go any further Renata suddenly clutched both sides of her head, closed her eyes and began to tremble as if she were having a killer migraine. The old lady looked at Colin sternly and said, "Shh!"

"Is something wrong?"

"Shh!"

The woman began to moan and rock back and forth on the divan. Her mouth was open and at first Colin thought she was having an epileptic seizure as the trembling became more violent. Soon she was jerking and writhing on the pillows like a spastic, and her moaning and whimpering rose until it became a series of shrill cries before she abruptly stopped.

He had gotten to his feet in alarm but his mother motioned him back. Apparently this was not a new experience for her.

When the woman spoke again, her eyes were still closed as she sat rigidly on the edge of the divan, her hands in her lap. Her voice had changed. It was low and husky, almost hoarse, as she muttered gibberish that sounded like *"Abba dabba doo, ibbety-baba-boo. Ibity bibity-dibity-boo."*

"Bibity-dibity-boo!" his mother repeated, transfixed.

"What is she saying?"

"Shh! She's possessed. She'll tell us later."

"What if she swallows her tongue?"

Princess Renata's possession lasted until the doorbell rang and Mrs. Lombardi ushered in Esther Kleineman and Max Dimitri. He danced across the room to throw his skinny arms around Maisie Draggett and jerk her to her feet like an ice-skating partner.

"Maisie!" he said, presenting her to the room. "Say something funny."

"Put me down," Maisie said, and they all laughed except Renata, who was still coming out of her trance.

"You see? What'd I tell you. Isn't she terrific?

"This is my son, Colin," his mother said.

"We've had the pleasure," Dimitri told her. "Old Colin here and I are going to do a number on you, Maisie."

Esther Kleineman said, "I brought you some Christmas cookies, Maisie dear. Fresh from the oven."

"Are they kosher?" Maisie asked, and Dimitri erupted in another burst of laughter.

"Hear that?" he shouted. "Ain't she terrific? Kosher Christmas cookies! Maisie, who writes your stuff?"

Colin agreed they were all terrific. The possessed Renata, hysterical Dimitri, fat Esther and the two Koreans on the sidewalk. Why not a kosher Christmas? Everything else in his mother's house was off the wall. Why should Christmas be any different?

"Max is the actor I told you about," the old lady said, "who did Mickey Mouse and all that down at the Disneyworld park."

"I worked for the most terrific talent in show business," Dimitri said solemnly, "the great Disney himself."

"I thought he was dead when you started," Esther said.

"Not quite," Maisie replied. "Renata's talked to him."

"You knew Walt?" Dimitri asked her excitedly.

His mother nodded agreement. "Renata knows him well."

"But didn't he die years ago?" Esther said.

"That doesn't bother Renata if they're dead," Maisie said, "as long as they're willing to talk."

"I'm a trance medium," Renata explained.

"They froze him, you know, Disney," Maisie said. "Stuck him in a freezer like a chicken. Costs a fortune, but they keep you until technology can thaw you out as good as new."

"Really?" Esther said. "I didn't know that."

"I wouldn't mind seeing old Walt again," Dimitri said. "He was terrific, just a terrific guy to work for."

"It's really wonderful," Colin's mother said. "They say the bloom on your cheeks stays there the whole time you're in the freezer even if it's a hundred years. I'd do it myself when my time comes if old spondulicks here would spring for the money."

"If you believe in reincarnation, Maisie," Colin said, "you don't need a cryogenic vault. You'll come back as someone else."

"You'd like that, wouldn't you?" She turned to the others. "Some son. The only mother he ever had and he's not satisfied. Now he wants somebody else."

"You just finished saying you used to be Betsy Ross."

"Long before I had you, kiddo, I gave birth to the flag. Renata can tell you all about it. She was there."

"I didn't know that," Esther Kleineman said. "That's wonderful! Isn't that wonderful, Max?"

"Terrific," Dimitri said uncertainly.

"I always imagined Betsy Ross as old and wrinkled," Esther Kleineman added. "Was she old and wrinkled?"

"She was no chicken," Renata said.

"You didn't tell me that," Maisie said.

Esther Kleineman giggled and asked Renata coyly, "Who do you think I used to be?"

Renata said, "Sit beside me here. That's it. Relax. Close your eyes." She stood and placed both hands on either side of Esther Kleineman's head before she closed her own eyes and began in a singsong voice, "Escape your body, get in touch with your spiritual self, liberate the inner you, fly from the flesh and free your ethereal memory . . ."

"Great act," Dimitri said. "Terrific!"

Colin thought Maisie would crown him. "It's not an act," she hissed. "It's a past-life regression."

"It's still terrific," he said lamely. "Isn't it?"

"I seeee," Renata said. "I seeee . . . in the mists of time, a form, a woman emerging . . . You must feel it. Do you feel it?"

"Oh, yes!" Esther Kleineman piped up, "I feel it!"

"Emerrrging . . . this woman I see in the mists," Renata intoned. "A beautiful woman. Is it you? It must be youuu . . . so beauuutiful. Your hair, your gown, your breasts like ripe apples . . ."

"It's me! It's me!" said Esther.

"In a great palaaace—"

"I *knew* it," Esther said.

". . . a French palaaace. Your gown is cut so low, so beauuu . . . tiful. Your husbaaand . . . the emperor . . . takes you in his arms."

"Ohhh!" Esther raised her own arms to be taken.

"Jo . . . se . . . phine . . . my darling Josephine," Renata sang in her husky baritone.

"Napoleon! Oh, my brave Napoleon!" Esther shouted before she rolled off the divan in a dead faint.

"That's the end of her," Maisie said.

Dimitri was immediately at her side. "Hey, Esther. You all right? Hey, do something somebody. She had a heart attack!"

Renata quickly knelt beside her and took a small vial from her purse. "Spirits of ammonia," she said as she held it under the unconscious woman's nose. Slowly Esther Kleineman revived as Dimitri heaved an audible sigh and Colin's mother scowled at Renata.

"Oh, Napoleon! Wherefore art thou, Napoleon?" Esther Kleineman said in a hushed whisper as she came out of her faint.

"Right here, baby," Dimitri said.

"Gimme a break," Colin's mother said. "With a body like a turnip how could she ever get to be an empress?"

"I only tell what I see and feel," Renata said.

"If she was Josephine, I'm Greta Garbo," Maisie said.

"You are what you are and you were what you were," Renata said. "I cannot control the eternal wheel of life."

"Is that so? How old was Betsy Ross?"

"About your age," Renata said.

"And not famous for her beauty," Maisie said ominously.

"Maybe she got her mixed up with Molly Pitcher, Maisie," Dimitri volunteered. "It's easy to do."

"Shut up," Maisie told him.

"She probably didn't take such good care of herself like you do," Dimitri suggested. When Maisie glared at him, he asked, "Did I say something wrong?"

"Are you trying to ruin my Christmas?" Maisie asked Renata.

"If you're not happy with Betsy Ross," Renata said, "we can go back further on the wheel and see who you were before."

"I'm not going anywhere on your wheel," the old lady said.

"Oh, go on, Maisie," Esther Kleineman told her. "It's fun. Don't you want to know who you were before?"

"Shut up, Esther," Dimitri said.

"You got your aureolas crossed that time, kiddo," Maisie told Renata. Then to Dimitri: "When are we leaving for Orlando?"

"We figured next week. We'll take our time. Hey, you mean you'll come? That's terrific, Maisie! What about her?" he added under his breath, with a meaningful glance toward Renata.

"You were right," Maisie said. "It was an act."

Colin was blessedly out of it.

———— CHAPTER FORTY-TWO ————

AFTER LEAVING his mother's house Colin went home to check on Joyce. Her eyes were open but she did not see him as he stood beside her bed. Neither did she seem to hear him when he said her name. She lay as still as an effigy in marble, and once again he thought she was dead until she closed her eyes and then slowly opened them. Little icicles of guilt pricked when he thought of how he planned to spend the rest of the day with Barbara.

He asked himself how he could be with another woman when the one he loved lay dying. He didn't have an answer that made any sense. But as Joyce slipped further away from life, he spent less and less time at home. The place depressed him and he rationalized his absences by telling himself she did not know whether he was there or not.

Mrs. Ryan, kind soul that she was, noticed his confusion. "Some folks can't handle it, Mr. Draggett, and some folks can. You're one of those who can't. But it's nothing to be ashamed of."

"Thank you, Mrs. Ryan, but I don't like myself very much these days. You know what I mean?"

"Dying's hard on everybody," she said, "even those folks God keeps alive."

Sometimes Colin would sit by Joyce's bed for an hour or so watching her, no longer feeling anything, barely recognizing the wraith she had become. It was as if they both had changed so much that neither knew the other any longer.

She would open her eyes to stare at the ceiling or occasionally try to focus on the nurse when the bed was being made or when they bathed her. But she rarely seemed to see or hear him.

After such moments he would flee the odor of the sickroom like a drowning man to walk the streets with nothing in mind except to get away from the smell of death and fill his lungs with fresh air. He would try to recall what it was like before this monstrous disease stole her away from him. Sometimes he even played childish games with himself, thinking if he squeezed his eyes closed and opened them quickly this would turn out to be only a bad dream.

Joyce was dying and taking longer than expected. There were times when he wallowed in self-pity, wishing she'd finish with it and stop torturing him and herself. He had a right to a little happiness too, didn't he? There was nothing wrong with him, for God's sake, so why should he suffer? Why should he not go to bed with Barbara? Until then he had always been the model husband. Faithful since their wedding. No sex in almost two years. Until Barbara. Joyce couldn't expect more than that, damn it. A man had his needs.

"You doing the best you can, Mr. Draggett," Mrs. Ryan told him. "Don't be so hard on yourself. She knows you're a good man and you love her. That's all a woman asks."

But she doesn't know about Barbara, he thought, and neither did Mrs. Ryan. Joyce might understand. She was always much too tolerant of what he did. He wondered how far Mrs. Ryan's Christian charity would carry her if he told the whole truth.

"Go on out now, Mr. Draggett, and get your mind off your troubles. You can't help her. Only God can do that."

Which lets me off the hook, he told himself. Let Him worry about it. He's the one started the whole business. You want her, God, take her! But for God's sake get it over with.

THE CATHEDRAL Church of St. John the Divine dwarfs St. Patrick's Catholic Cathedral as well as most other churches in the world. It was conceived, designed and mostly constructed in the late nineteenth century when members of the rich Wasp Episcopalian establishment saw themselves as very close to God and their New York cathedral as visible proof of His favor.

Morningside Heights was no longer the idyllic sylvan glade it had been when the church fathers decided to put their cathedral there. Although the park was still a green oasis with its trees and acres of grass, the church also fronted on St. Luke's-Roosevelt

Hospital, where the emergency traffic was heavy. St. John the Divine, intended as a temple of worship for prosperous white Victorians, looked out on an ethnic combat zone where muggings, arson, drugs, rape and murder defined the social climate.

Only two blocks from Columbia University, the cathedral stood like a besieged fortress in the midst of one of the major battlefields of twentieth-century America. Colin knew that one child in ten born within a mile of the cathedral had AIDS at birth. And according to the New York *Times,* the murder rate in that part of Harlem lying just to the east was the highest in the nation. Yet it was there on that Christmas day that Colin heard the angels sing.

Colin would have agreed that there could be more demanding choral works than Handel's *Messiah.* Bach's *Saint Matthew Passion* possibly, or Faure's *Requiem,* or the great masses of Berlioz or Mozart. But on that particular snowbound Christmas day, in that particular drafty and immense cathedral, he felt about as close to heaven as he would ever get when a hundred voices sang to Handel's glorious music that the Messiah had arrived.

He didn't remember where the orchestra came from or who the conductor was. He did remember Maggie telling him that the choir was drawn from a dozen churches of different denominations. And he did remember his pride in seeing his secretary-and-friend Maggie Caruso singing her heart out in the soprano section.

It was emotionally overwhelming, and he found himself clutching Barbara's hand and saying, "God, Joyce, have you ever heard anything so beautiful? Aren't we lucky?"

He realized the gaffe the instant he made it, but it was too late. He turned to her to explain, apologize, something.

"What a stupid thing to say. I—"

She was smiling. "Yes, Colin, we are lucky."

"I meant to say—"

"I know what you meant to say, darling."

"I'm sorry . . ."

"Don't apologize, please. I understand."

And looking into her eyes, he felt she did.

____CHAPTER FORTY-THREE____

AFTER THE concert Colin saw Anthony Shattuck in the crowd but the old man did not see him or Barbara. When they were leaving the cathedral he watched Maggie catch up with Shattuck, embrace him warmly and go off holding hands. Colin smiled and Barbara said, "What's so amusing?"

"The world."

"Tell me."

"I just saw Anthony Shattuck."

"The charming elderly gentleman from your office?"

"That's right. He left arm-in-arm with my secretary."

"Does that surprise you?"

"He's almost eighty and Maggie is barely forty."

"Maybe he likes older women."

"Barbara . . ."

"Is she married?"

"No, but he is. And his wife's in a nursing home."

"Is that a reason why he shouldn't hear Maggie sing?"

"I didn't mean that. It was the way they kissed and walked out of here that caught my attention. Like lovers."

"What's wrong with lovers?"

"What gets me is why didn't I notice it before?"

"Maybe you're imagining things. Maybe there's nothing to notice except an excess of Christmas spirit."

"Or else I'm a lot more aware of some things now than I was a week ago."

"Oh, oh. I'm about to hear a confession."

"No, nothing like that. It's just—"

"You implied something pretty heavy."

"I didn't mean to, but I am extrasensitive, I guess. And not a little confused."

"About us?"

"Yes."

"Are you sorry?"

"Of course not."

"But you're feeling some guilt."

"I guess. Until the other night I'd been celibate since Joyce was
. . . you know."

"And you'd like applause for being a Boy Scout."

"You know what I mean. I did make the effort until—"

"Until Barbara the Temptress crossed your path, batted her
eyes, wiggled her bottom and crooked her finger. Then you suc-
cumbed to temptation and were immediately transformed into . . .
God forbid . . . an adulterer!"

"That's not what happened at all."

"But it's an interesting interpretation, isn't it? You could probably
call it the Colin Draggett hair-shirt version. But if you believe it
you're being unfair to me and too tough on yourself."

"You're the second person today to tell me that."

"You mean cheating on Joyce is no longer our secret?"

"I *meant* about being tough on myself."

"I also know I made the first moves. I wanted you to make love
to me and I did everything I could to make it happen."

"You think I didn't?"

She smiled. "You were a little reluctant until I told you I've
wanted you since I was sixteen. Remember? You were my big ado-
lescent sexual fantasy. What man could resist that?"

By then it was dark and they had walked several blocks in
search of a taxi. The streets were clear but not the sidewalks,
where patches of ice made the going tricky. The snow had been
plowed and shoveled into glistening sooty heaps melting along the
curb, no longer covering the city's blemishes but an eyesore in
itself.

"How did the reality compare to the fantasy?"

"Better. When a woman talks about a man being well-built she
doesn't always mean strong shoulders, firm muscles and lean hips.
It can also be her way of describing what men call well-hung. A
woman notices the bulge, Colin darling, and she has a special interest in erections. Apart from natural curiosity about the opposite
sex, you can't imagine the extent of our fascination with penises."

"Don't get carried away, Barbara."

"It's true. You were divine and I was glad I'd been carrying the
torch for you all these years."

"I don't believe you. You're inventing."

"Why would I do that?"

"To make me feel better. Take some of the guilt away."

"Everything I said happens to be true. But you're right. I would make it up to make you feel better if it weren't. You see, Colin darling, I don't think what you and I have been up to has anything to do with Joyce. I know you love her and you would be making love to her now and not to me if it was possible. But it isn't. So it's not as if you're cheating on her or leaving her or anything. And it's not as if I'm taking you away from her either, because if she were well and healthy she would still have you all to herself and I wouldn't get a look in."

"That's what you don't understand, Barbara."

"What?"

"I don't know if that's the case."

"What do you mean?"

"I mean the reason I'm so confused at the moment is that I have the feeling this might have happened between us even if Joyce was okay. That's where the real guilt comes from. Don't you see what I'm trying to say?"

A taxi stopped for them then and she gripped his arm tightly as she got in ahead of him. "You know something, Colin?"

"What?"

Her eyes had filled with tears, which he didn't understand. Had he hurt her with something he said?

"Barbara, what's wrong?"

"Nothing's wrong, my darling. I'm touched because that's one of the nicest things anyone ever said to me."

"Then why are you crying?"

"Oh, Colin, you make me so damn mad and happy!"

"It's nothing to cry about then, is it?"

And she started laughing.

They went to the Tavern on the Green where he telephoned Mrs. Ryan, who said everything was the same at home. Joyce was asleep and her day had been quieter than usual. Dr. Brenner had called to check on her and said he would be back on Monday. Mrs. Ryan would stay on duty until Saturday morning when a new nurse would take over for the rest of the weekend, giving her some time off.

"Do you know the new nurse, Mrs. Ryan?"

"Not personally, Mr. Draggett, but he's recommended by the county association and is supposed to be real experienced."

"I'll be back late."

"Don't worry. Have a nice dinner and Merry Christmas."

When he came back to the table the magic touched them once again, as it had in the taxi after their dinner at O'Hara's and on Christmas Eve. They drank champagne, held hands and looked out on the stark white beauty of Central Park at night. They didn't eat much because each was too taken with the other.

They didn't talk much either. Colin had told the truth when he said he thought their affair would have begun anyway, even if Joyce had not been ill. It was a fact he had not dared to face until he blurted it out to Barbara on the sidewalk.

She was telling the truth too when she named him the star of her boarding-school fantasies. When he asked if Ken Fairchild figured in them too, she laughed. "Before we married he did, but not afterward. He was good in bed the first two years or so and I had no complaints. But I didn't see him in my dreams anymore. And after a while I didn't see him in my bed that often either."

They finished the evening at Barbara's Ritz Tower apartment. On the way there in the taxi they sat a little apart, not calm at all but afraid to break the spell. They entered the Ritz without speaking and rode the elevator to her floor virtually without touching. Unlike their first encounter, which had been so tentative and caring, the moment they were alone this time a frenzied recklessness possessed them. It was as if some force had taken over and had to be sexually appeased.

Barely inside the door she rushed into his arms. He held her so hard he hurt her as they pressed their bodies into each other and flung off their coats. The path to her bedroom was quickly strewn with clothing: his tie and shirt, her shoes, bra, dress and jacket as they shed each article, clutching and groping and feeling each other like two insatiable erotic dancers.

Her skin was flawless, her tummy flat, her body lean and rounded but with a hardness in the arms and legs from all those years of tennis. Her breasts were small but lovely and responsive to his touch, still firm and a joy to fondle.

Her bedroom was all softness. The deep pile rugs and downy sofas, the great wide bed with its silken pillows. Wherever they rolled or tumbled or sprawled was cushioned.

They fell across the bed with Colin on top panting and then he knelt and took her from behind. But before either one could climax they were off the bed again and she was riding him as he tossed and writhed around the carpet on his back.

He didn't know when it ended the first time, but he remembered Barbara calling out, "Hold me! Hold me!" Later she said the orgasm went on and on and on. Something similar happened to Colin too, and he didn't remember ever before having reached such a violent and sustained peak as he did that night.

In a moment of calm she asked him to stay and he agreed. When he called Mrs. Ryan to say he would not be home, the nurse was reassuring. "Don't fret, Mr. Draggett. Take your time and get some rest. We're doing fine."

They made love once more before dawn and again in the morning. Barbara brought his coffee, saying, "How do you feel?"

"Sated."

"I was afraid you'd say that." She began to run her hand slowly over his chest and tickle his nipples.

"Christ, woman, you'll kill me if you don't have mercy."

"Christmas Eve, we only made love," she said with an impish smile. "But last night we fucked like rabbits."

"How do rabbits do it on a diet of lettuce?"

"The same way you do. Put it in and take it out."

"I'm talking about stamina, not technique."

"We can run a check on both whenever you're ready, darling." Her fingers were still busy among the hairs on his chest.

He was vaguely aroused and she knew it, but he doubted he could perform again so soon after the last time. His desire, as it turned out, was greater than his capacity to deliver. After several minutes of trying they agreed to wait awhile. "Anyway," Barbara said, "three times in eight hours, not too bad." She smiled when she said it.

"I prefer to think of it as six times in thirty hours," he said seriously.

"Vanity," she sighed. "Why do men keep score? To a woman it's quality that counts, not frequency."

"As long as she's getting laid often enough."

"I prefer to think of it as making love."

"Not banged?"

"Horrors!"

"How about balled?"

"A cliché."

"I give up."

She smiled and the smile turned into a lovely trill of laughter. "It seems you do understand something about women, but you certainly didn't learn about them at Harvard or in the offices of your illustrious law firm."

"All I know or ever hope to know about women I owe to my sainted mother, God bless her and keep her."

He had told Barbara at dinner about Betsy Ross's disenchantment with Renata over the sudden and unscheduled return engagement of the Empress Josephine, née Esther Kleineman.

"I'd love to meet your mother," she said.

"You may have to travel to Orlando to do that."

They passed the morning lazing about her apartment. Barbara called the hotel at Stowe to check on her sons and to hear them say they wanted to come home. When she hung up she was giggling. "I love them so and I'm such a fool."

"Why a fool?"

"When they said they wanted to come home I immediately thought it was because they were fed up with Ken and missed me. No such luck. It's storming and the really difficult trails they like are all closed, so they're bored."

After that they talked and they talked. To Colin's surprise, he found himself telling her openly and in detail about his plunge in the junk-bond market and what it was going to cost him, something he had never mentioned to Joyce.

"But must you sell, Colin, really? Is there no other way to cover the margin call at the brokerage?"

"If I had another two hundred thousand shares of Stanton to pledge I'd be all right and could probably bail out in a few months without a heavier loss than I've already taken."

"What's the downside?"

"You do know the jargon, don't you? Well, the economy could always turn around. Stanton could fall off on the Exchange. A lot of things could happen and probably won't. But the question's academic. I don't have the shares to put up so I face the music on Monday."

"You seem relaxed about it."

"The truth is it makes me sick and it's all my fault, but basically

I've tried not to think about it because it's beyond my control. It took me twenty years with your father's help to put together some real capital. I then reduced it by half in less than a year, thinking I could get something for almost nothing. And now, thanks to an ignorant judge and a panicky broker, I'm facing what they used to call ruin in the old days."

"Well, something must be done about it."

"I have no more collateral to put up."

"Who's your broker?"

"Malcolm Scanlon."

"Suppose someone like Hunt Benson spoke to him?"

"And said what? It's not a question of influence, Barbara. It's a question of cash or a pledge of available assets."

"You mean they'd sit still if they had more stock as collateral?"

"As I said. But I don't have more."

"Couldn't you borrow it?"

"My love, Wall Street doesn't work like that."

"Well, it should," she said stubbornly.

It was five in the afternoon when he left her in bed after their last lovemaking. It had been the perfect complement to the night before, long and lingering, with an extra dimension of feeling that touched them both.

The new nurse would be on duty with Joyce, and would have questions about routine matters of kitchen and household. Prior to Joyce's illness, the only thing Colin had been able to find around the house was a corkscrew or a bottle opener. Since she had been bedridden, however, he learned in self-defense where everything was, from the freezer bags to the vacuum cleaner.

The nurse let him in, a fussy, middle-aged fellow with a heavy beard and weight-lifter looks. He wasted no time listing Mrs. Ryan's shortcomings and describing the general disarray he had found around the patient. Colin decided to straighten him out.

"Look, Mr. . . ."

"Rutherford. Lance Rutherford."

"Naturally there will be differences in approach to—"

"I'm talking about sloppiness. The bedpan in the lavatory instead of its proper place. The bed table stuffed with chocolate wrappers and knitting needles."

"The hours are long, Mr. Rutherford, and Mrs. Ryan passes her time knitting sweaters for orphan children."

He gave Colin the benefit of an elaborate shrug.

"Let's get one thing straight. I know all about Mrs. Ryan's balls of wool and her candy wrappers and I think she is one hell of a nurse. If you want to get along with me, don't knock her!"

Colin looked in on Joyce later that evening and found her sleeping restlessly while Rutherford was busy adjusting her IV feeding tubes. Colin tried to read and couldn't, and sometime after midnight he fell asleep in front of the television.

———CHAPTER FORTY-FOUR———

For the first time in days the sun appeared early Sunday morning and seemed to want to hang around. Colin decided to go for a run along the East River by the UN Plaza.

Before he went out he looked in on Joyce and was surprised to hear her moaning a little, a barely audible whimper. Rutherford, the substitute nurse, seemed unconcerned.

Colin asked if there was a problem.

"Everything is under control, Mr. Draggett."

"Then why is she moaning?"

"She's very ill, that's why."

"But she wasn't doing it yesterday."

"We don't know if she was or she wasn't. I can only assure you I am following doctor's orders to the letter."

"You sure you gave her all the right medicine?"

"I am a specialized oncological nurse, Mr. Draggett."

"No, I mean it. She may be in pain."

"She is not in pain, sir."

"Then why is she whimpering?"

"They do that in their sleep sometimes, but with all the dope she has in her system she can't feel anything."

Lance Rutherford, R.N., put Colin's back up with his superior attitude and patronizing airs even though good nurse Ryan said he had to be competent or the service would not have recommended him. Colin was forced to admit that Joyce's bed did look better than usual. Crisp pink pillow slips and sheets with neatly folded corners. But that didn't make Mr. Rutherford less of a pain in the ass.

"I was looking for tea earlier and didn't find any," he said, "and I don't drink coffee."

"The tea is in a large red tin above the stove. It's Suchon Lobsang or something like that. It's Joyce's favorite."

"I prefer Earl Grey's," he said.

"Afraid we're all out of that."

"And juice? What juice do you have?"

"There's every kind you can imagine in the freezer."

"Nothing fresh or organic, I suppose."

"Sorry about that."

"What about oat bran? That's what I eat in the morning."

"Can't help you," Colin told him, "but there's cereals in the cupboard. Help yourself." And choke, he silently added.

IT WAS a warm sunny morning when Colin hit the pavement. The snow was melting fast, turning the city into a vast puddle of sooty slush. There were the usual dogwalkers, the Sunday *Times* readers lugging their five-pound newspapers home and a few young mothers with small babies in carriages and strollers.

An aerobics class of middle-aged women in designer sweats went by at a fast walk as he was lacing up his Adidas, one of them counting cadence like a drill sergeant. The weekend joggers were fewer than usual and Colin assumed that most were still assembling their children's Christmas toys, nursing hangovers or simply lying low until the holidays ended.

He had been running about twenty minutes when he heard a voice say, "Lawyer Draggett!" and glanced back to see Luther Yancy stumping down the path. Colin slowed to a walk as Yancy said between breaths, "I can't hit your pace with this peg leg, man. Got to go slow or I pay for it later."

"Do you always run in this part of town?" Colin asked.

"Where I live the only time a man runs is when he chasing somebody or somebody chasing him. You live around here?"

"Not far."

"Run every day?"

"Usually only on weekends."

"Me, too. No time during the week. But you look to be in good shape for a man does office work. How old are you?"

"Forty-five."

"I'll be fifty-eight next birthday," Yancy said, "but I run three or four miles a week, pump a little iron and can still get out a couple hundred push-ups without menstrual cramps."

A glance at the man's rugged physique was enough to convince Colin of the truth of that. He was wearing only sweatpants and a tank top, and the muscles in his powerful shoulders stood out like tire treads. On his hip he wore a beeper "to compete with the street pushers," he said with a laugh, but in reality to keep him in touch with the shift bosses of his security service.

They finished their walk at Yancy's car, a black four-door Ford with the rear passenger part caged off like a police car. "That's the idea," he said when Colin commented on the resemblance. Yancy invited him for coffee and they went into a little pancake joint across from the UN. "So how's the major doing?"

"He took his sons to Vermont skiing for the weekend."

"He could have stayed here and done that," Yancy said, looking toward the dirty snow beyond the window. "Did you ever find out who was bothering him?"

"Just business pressure."

"After we talked that time in your office I did a lot of thinking about it," Yancy said, "and the more I thought about it, the more I was convinced I was right. Somebody was out to get him."

"Believe me, you're wrong, Mr. Yancy."

"In the security business you get a nose for some things. Who would it most likely be in the major's case? He didn't want to tell me, but knowing his mating habits, I was a hundred percent sure it had to be some woman or some woman's husband."

"You're wrong."

"I know that now, Mr. Draggett. But I was looking at the obvious so hard I didn't see the not-so-obvious."

Colin waited.

"It never dawned on me somebody in that hotshot company he works for might be trying to break his rice bowl."

"What?"

"In Vietnam a man's job was his rice bowl. There were ten Vietnamese applicants for every decent job, so they schemed and scrambled and when one of them succeeded in taking a job away from another one they used to say he broke his rice bowl."

"Why do you think someone wants Ken's . . . rice bowl?"

"Not the one he has now. The one he's supposed to step into. The man who headed the company died, right?"

Colin nodded.

"And he was the major's father-in-law. So who gets his job? The major looks like the obvious choice, right?"

"Maybe."

"But another maybe is the guy Petrey investigated, the advertising boss or whatever he is."

"Adam Walsh. The vice-president for marketing."

"Okay. And we know he's got a spotty background."

"We know no such thing."

"Don't we? Then why did the major spend all that money with Petrey to check him out?"

"Companies check people out all the time, Mr. Yancy."

"They don't check out vice-presidents after they've been on the payroll a few years. Unless the guy's suspected of taking from the till to play the ponies or pay his girlfriend's rent."

"What did Petrey tell you about him?"

"Diddly squat. It was a confidential investigation and Dom keeps him mouth shut about things like that, even to me. But I can draw my own conclusions."

"What are you trying to say?"

"Is this Walsh capable of going after the major to keep him out of the top job?"

"No. As I said, the whole idea is silly."

"Maybe, but bear with me. Who decides who gets the top job in that company?"

"Indirectly, the stockholders, but in reality it will be the board of directors."

"When?"

"January sixth."

"Who's going to win?"

"I don't know yet."

"You're on the board, aren't you?"

"That's right."

"Well?"

"The selection is still up in the air."

"Is Major Fairchild up for the job or not?"

"The acting president may want to stay on. If that's the case, the board would most likely confirm him."

"You want to know how I see it? I see it complicated by a couple of things a board of directors may not know about."

"Such as?"

"First, what I said. Somebody else wants that job worse than he does, bad enough to want to take him out. And second, his wife wants a divorce, doesn't she?"

"Did your friend Petrey tell you that?"

"He didn't have to. She hired him to make her case. And don't forget. I know the major for a lot of years."

"So?"

"If she gets her divorce, does she want him running her daddy's company? I can't answer that and maybe you can't either. But she'd have no reason to kill him, would she?"

Colin laughed. "Come on, Mr. Yancy."

"I know it sounds crazy but let's hang in there a minute, all right? I'm not from around here originally, you know. I was born and raised in the Virgin Islands."

That explained something about Yancy that Colin had not been able to put his finger on. An important part of his gentle charm was the soft, lilting way he spoke, a West Indian speech.

"I tell you that because where I come from a man saves your life, you responsible for him as long as you live. You a guardian angel, you know?" He lapsed into a real island patois then. "Heavy duty, mon. Tiresome. And anybody hurt him, mon, you become the Avenging Angel. It's the custom there, mon."

"Fairchild's lucky to have a guardian angel like you."

"Maybe not. I can't keep a close eye on him because we live different lives and he don't like me on his back. But whether he likes it or not, I got a deep personal interest in looking out for that man. If he needs me, I'm there, even if he don't know it." He paused, took a deep sip from his coffee, and continued. "So I ask myself who is another possible rival for this top job, mon? The foreign division head, what's his name?"

"Brian Redfern?"

"That's him. Does he want to run that big company so bad he'd lay a heavy load on the major, like a contract?"

"That's ridiculous, Mr. Yancy. Ken and Brian Redfern are close friends."

"What makes you so sure?"

"What are you saying?"

"Why did Redfern hire that Brit hit man?"

Colin laughed. "If you're talking about Quirk, he's hardly a hit man, just a man Brian used once in a labor dispute over there."

"Suppose I told you Redfern contracted this scumbag in England to do a specific job of company business here."

"I'd say that was just a wild supposition—"

"Come on, mon. I thought we were having a serious conversation." Apart from his fiercely loyal dedication to Ken Fairchild, Yancy intrigued Colin because he was such a unique combination of softness and menace. He moved as quietly and gracefully as a cat, and with his strength and condition could obviously break bones if necessary.

Colin remembered him saying that he knew many ways to kill a man and had tried most of them.

Colin liked him instinctively, but could imagine him as implacable as death if he was crossed or angered.

Yancy spread his powerful hands over the tabletop. "Why'd you put up this dude's bail and hire Dom to provide custodial care until his case comes to court?"

"Another confidence betrayed by Petrey?"

"Nothing confidential about the case. The man was publicly arraigned in Federal court. Dom and me trade information all the time, but Quirk was in the newspapers."

"This time you were misinformed."

"Not by Quirk. He's an idiot but he's an open book."

"If he said Brian Redfern hired him to hurt Ken Fairchild," Colin said, "he's lying through his teeth."

"He didn't say that. I say that. All he said was Redfern hired him to muss up somebody."

"He's still lying," Colin assured Yancy. "As I said, the company once used him overseas, that's all."

"He mentioned that. He said that's when he met you."

"I arranged his payment. I'm sorry the company ever used him. I didn't want him dragging Stanton Technologies into his affairs, so when he got into trouble here I offered him legal help and Petrey's assistance to make sure the company stayed out of it."

"So why hold out on me?"

"Believe me, Quirk's deal with Redfern, whatever it was, had nothing to do with Ken Fairchild, you can be sure of that."

"Then who does it have to do with?"

"I can't say."

"Sure you can, Mr. Draggett," he said, getting up, "but you don't want to. Fair enough, as long as it don't hurt the major."

Yancy paid the check and joined Colin outside, where they shook hands. "Enjoyed our little talk. You know how to reach me if I can help. Have a nice day."

THE DOORMAN at Colin's apartment building was new, the latest in a string of men who looked as if they'd been recruited in a Baghdad bazaar. The man did not understand much English and had trouble figuring out the floor numbers, so Colin punched the elevator button for him.

Colin was putting his key in the apartment door when he heard a muffled scream. He froze, dropped the key and fumbled with it again.

As he opened the door, the scream diminished to a whimper. It came from Joyce's sickroom.

Lance Rutherford, R.N., was standing next to her bed.

"What the *hell's* going on!" Colin demanded as he saw his wife doubled up and moaning in pain. Colin pushed the man away from the bedside. "She's hurting, for Christ sake! What did you do, give her the wrong IV?"

"The other nurse had the dosage wrong."

"What do you mean?"

"She was administering five cc's every two hours, which no doctor would ever dare prescribe! The MLD is ten cc's over eight hours. I've reduced the dosage to a safe level, that's all."

Joyce was almost thrashing on the bed now, and she would have been screaming if her strength allowed it.

"Get the hell out of my way!" Colin found the small plastic sachets of Demerol, filled a disposable syringe the way he had seen Mrs. Ryan do it and injected it into Joyce's IV bottle.

"I'm going to report this," the nurse said. "I won't be responsible for killing this patient!"

After about ten minutes Joyce was calm again and seemed to be sleeping. Colin scrawled a check for Rutherford and told him not to come back. At midnight Mrs. Ryan returned, surprised to see Colin alone with Joyce.

"Is everything under control, Mr. Draggett?"

"Yes and no, Mrs. Ryan, but I'm damn glad to see you."

—— CHAPTER FORTY-FIVE ——

COLIN NORMALLY awakened early without the help of an alarm, but on Monday morning he slept until after eight and staggered out of bed.

Dr. Brenner showed up while he was shaving, and when he explained what had happened the day before, the doctor said, "Sorry, my fault. I should have been available."

"He said he'd report it."

"He won't report anything. Legally he was in the right, but medically he was out of line. It is not uncommon for long-term drug users to build up such a tolerance they can withstand several times the minimum lethal dose of some substances. This is especially true of patients who've been receiving graduated quantities of morphine derivatives for months. It is criminal to addict patients with a chance of recovery, but in the terminally ill it is humane. You did the right thing, Mr. Draggett."

"I did the only thing I could when I saw her in pain. Would you like some coffee?"

He joined Colin in the kitchen, saying, "This will soon be over, you know."

"I don't know what kept her alive this long."

"Spirit, love, all the things that keep most of us going," he said. "It's amazing how much punishment we can take."

Colin didn't arrive at Cranmer, Fisher & Cleves until mid-morning to find there had already been two calls from Malcolm Scanlon. "He sounded pretty frantic," Maggie said.

"If he calls again before I'm ready to talk to him, say I'm in conference and will get back to him within half an hour."

Colin needed time to collect his wits. He knew what he had to do
and he was prepared to do it. At Joyce's bedside the previous afternoon he had worked out the numbers on a calculator. He would
not dump his Stanton stock but sell it over a period of two or three
days whether Malcolm Scanlon liked it or not, dribble it into the
market ten or fifteen thousand shares at a time.

The bonds, on the other hand, he would hold off selling on the
assumption they might recover some value once the panic subsided. Apart from the loss, the whole damned business made him
angry at Scanlon, at the judge and at himself for letting himself get
boxed in like this.

He was the one people tended to call when they had major corporate legal problems. Clients paid Cranmer, Fisher & Cleves million-dollar fees so that Colin and his staff could save them millions
in taxes, court costs and fines.

But Colin Draggett couldn't help himself. He had allowed himself to be blind-sided by an ignorant judge and a panicky broker.

Live and learn, he told himself, or perish in the process. Those
that can, do. Those that can't, litigate. But how could one defend
oneself against an appellate judge who understood nothing about
bond markets, capital flow or speculative hedging? The answer to
that was that no defense exists against ignorance, ever.

Meanwhile Maggie had arranged an appointment for him with
Louisa Mae Barton, president of Cathcart College, the last of the
Stanton directors he had to see, and at that moment the most
important to him in terms of keeping Hunt Benson in the saddle.

"She's expecting you for tea at four o'clock," Maggie said. "Anthony laid on a car so you won't have to drive. Up in Fairfield
County there's still a lot of snow."

He thanked her and told her to leave him alone awhile. He
needed to psyche himself up for his call to Scanlon. He had kept
the whole business as far from his mind as possible over the long
weekend, hoping some brilliant idea might occur to him whereby
he could avoid throwing his capital in the street, so to speak. But
all the brilliant ideas were somewhere else on this gray Monday
morning.

He picked up the telephone finally the way a man mounts the
gallows steps.

"I have your mother on line one," Maggie called to him over the
interoffice speaker.

"Who?"

"Your mother. Remember her?"

"Oh, damn it."

"I'm sorry, Colin, but you told me always to tell her you were in if no client was in your office."

"It's okay, Maggie. Bring me a cup of coffee, will you."

"It's nearly lunch time."

"I know what time it is. Just bring the goddamn coffee." He pressed a button. "Hi, Maisie, how are you this morning?"

"I'm off," she said.

After all these years, she's finally admitting it, he thought. But he said, "Is that so? Where are you off to?"

"Florida, where do you think?"

"That's wonderful, but isn't it a little sudden?"

"It's what you wanted," she said. "To get rid of me."

It was going to be one of those conversations. But she is my mother, and I must be kind. "I don't want to get rid of you—"

"Oh, no? Wanna bet? Any other son would be happy his old mother could enjoy her last days in the sun and not freeze her bum off among strangers in this stupid burg."

"Strangers? You've lived here all your life."

"Don't remind me."

"I thought you liked Gramercy Park."

"With the Japs moving in and phonies like Renata? Gimme a break! I would have left ages ago except for your father."

"But he's been dead twenty-five years, Mom. Long before I got you the Gramercy Park apartment."

"You think I don't remember? If that bum had sold more whiskey instead of drinking it all, I'd be a rich widow today."

"I guess he had his reasons."

"Are you saying I was one of them?"

"I didn't say that, Maisie."

"Let me tell you something, Mr. Know-it-all. I worked my fingers to the bone for that bum."

To Colin's knowledge she never worked a day in her life except for her famous shipyard stint during the war.

"When I wasn't slaving over a hot stove . . ."

She had no notion of cooking. They lived on hamburgers and whatever else his father's short-order cook sent from the bar and grill.

". . . I was washing and sewing," she said.

Maisie didn't own a washing machine. All the family wash went to the same laundry that did the bar towels.

"I scrubbed floors on my hands and knees."

He really had to laugh at that. The porter who cleaned his father's bar swung a mop through their upstairs apartment once a week.

"What's so funny, Mr. Wisenheimer?"

"Nothing, Mom. Something that happened here."

"What?"

"Nothing, really. Are you going to Orlando with Mrs. Kleineman and her friend?"

"Who?"

"Esther Kleineman and what's-his-name, Max?"

"Max Dimitri?"

"Right."

"Who else would I go to Florida with? It was his idea."

"That's right. I forgot."

"For a hotshot lawyer I don't know where you keep your brains sometimes."

"Right. Should Maggie get you a plane ticket?"

"We're driving, taking it easy. Maybe we'll book the act on the road. Max knows some clubs and radio stations."

"The act?"

"Max and Maisie. My name should come first, being the woman, but Max and Maisie sounds better. Like Upsa daisy."

"What exactly is the act?"

"Patter. It's hilarious."

"Patter?"

"What did you think I said? You got wax in your ears? We talk in front of an audience and they *double* up."

"I didn't know you had already tried it out."

"We haven't."

"But you said the audience doubled up."

"I didn't say that. I said they *double* up."

"Forget I mentioned it. Break a leg."

"That's a terrible thing to say to your poor mother."

"It's an old show business expression, Maisie. Means good luck. I want the best for you, you know that."

"As long as I'm out of the way, you mean."

"That's not true."

"You calling me a liar?"

"I was only trying to correct a mistaken impression."

"You're still not so big, Mr. Whistlebritches, I can't come down there and wash your mouth out with soap."

"I was only wishing you *luck*. What are you doing about Mrs. Lombardi and your cook and the cleaning lady?"

"The cook quit after the Japs came. Good riddance. She was trying to poison me anyway. And now Lombardi will strip the place because Rose Lynne, my cleaning woman, won't be there to stop her."

"Why do you say such awful things about Mrs. Lombardi?"

"I count the silver every time old Mealy-mouth leaves. On her day off she goes loaded like a camel. Can't make it through the subway turnstile. Has to hire a stretch limo."

"Where did Rose Lynne go?"

"She's taking a sabbatical while I'm away."

"I'm sorry I won't have time to come and see you off."

"Max is loading Esther's junk now, I don't know where the four of us will sit. Max will fit because he's driving, but . . ."

"Who else is going?"

"Walter, who do you think?"

"Who the devil is Walter?"

"You met him the other day. Walter the Firewalker."

"I only met Renata, Betsy Ross and Josephine."

"What a lot of horsefeathers that was. I told you Renata was a fake. What can you expect from a woman eats raw garlic and don't shave her legs?"

"Maisie, who is Walter the Firewalker?"

"Walter Hooponopo. He must have come after you left. He's pure Hawaiian from the islands and could teach you a few tricks. Didn't you get an invitation to his Florida workshop? I told him to send you one. It's in two weeks."

"No," he said, but as he answered her, his eye caught sight of a large pink sheet among the mail Maggie had left open on his desk. Across the top of it he read, *Life Expansion & Firewalking Workshop. Create the Life you want. Transcend your Limitations and develop a More Effective YOU through Life Mastery. Discover why you have been denied Prosperity and Harmony through FIREWALKING. Bring an air mattress or pad to lie on after initiation.*

Or a stretcher, Colin thought. "I just found the invitation," he told Maisie. "Sounds like fun if you wear thick socks."

"You got to keep moving, Walter says."

"Is firewalking part of Walter's act?"

"It's his religion, so don't make fun of it."

"That never crossed my mind, Maisie. What does he do for a living, or is he independently wealthy?"

"He does some rebirthing and past-life therapy. He fixed up Esther the other day after Renata made that mess."

"Oh, what happened?"

"It took Walter about two minutes to get rid of Josephine and find out who Esther really was."

"Who was she?"

"Mrs. Lincoln."

"You mean . . ."

"Abe Lincoln's wife. Squirrel Nutkin."

"That must have upset her."

"Walter knows what he's doing. Not like a lot of them. He's been firewalking since he was a kid. In the Islands they learn that stuff like surfing."

"I hope you're not planning to try it."

"Gimme a break. I'll stick with Dr. Scholl's."

"Where did you meet him?"

"On the boardwalk in Atlantic City."

Before she could say more, Maggie was paging him. "I have Mr. Scanlon on the other line. What do I say?"

He signed off with Maisie and punched a button for the other line, prepared to face the music. "Morning, Malcolm."

"Colin! You sneaky son of a bitch! You really put one over on us, boy. How the hell did you do it?"

"Do it?"

"This is no time to pull my leg, man! How in hell did you ever put together all that collateral so fast? Two hundred and fifty thousand shares, my God! Don't tell me. I know. You had them up your sleeve the whole time!"

"I . . ."

"I knew you were rich, old buddy, but not that rich. You really had us all fooled."

Colin was stalling for time, trying to make sense out of what the broker was telling him. "You know how it is, Malcolm," he said.

"Do I ever! The next time I need a miracle, I won't call the Pope I'll call you!"

"See that you remember that."

"Why didn't you have mercy on my ulcer and at least give me a hint of what you were up to before Christmas? The way you were talking last week we thought you were all tapped out."

"Well . . ."

"Very sly coming up with so many new shares at the last minute. Got to hand it to you, old buddy. You're off the hook and we're pretty happy about it over here I don't mind saying."

——— CHAPTER FORTY-SIX ———

MALCOLM SCANLON rattled on for another five minutes. "I didn't even know you did business with Bear Stearns until they notified us the shares were available this morning."

Bear Stearns was *Barbara*'s brokerage.

"I don't keep all my eggs in the same basket," Colin said, certain now who his rescuer was.

"I said some unkind things to you, Colin, and I want to apologize. But you understand how stressed out we were around here."

Screw you, Malcolm. "I understand," Colin said.

"How about lunch at the Gansevoort?"

"Can't today. I'll get back to you."

"I really do apologize, Colin."

For the next few minutes he sat alone staring into space and pondering his escape from a humiliating financial debacle, and who had made it possible. Barbara's loaning him the stock provided a massive financial life-preserver. It also carried a theoretical risk to her of several million dollars. Apart from his surprise, he was deeply moved.

When he had collected himself a little he called her. "Why did you do it?"

"A hundred reasons, Colin. Was it enough?"

"More than enough. I'm touched by your generosity and awed by your confidence in me."

"Good. You know how you can thank me?"

"Tell me."

"Really, darling. Have you forgotten so soon? It's only been two days since the most wonderful Christmas I can remember."

"You can't imagine how overwhelmed I am, Barbara. I never imagined you'd do anything so crazy."

"Don't forget a bit of history."

"What's that?"

"Daddy told me he never could have started Stanton without your help. So I only did what he would have done."

When he invited her to drive to Connecticut with him that afternoon she was pleased. "Ken won't be bringing the boys back until Wednesday," she said, "so I'm in no rush to get home."

ALTHOUGH FAIRFIELD County is essentially a pricey New York bedroom in the midst of a densely populated area, it appears deceptively rural within a mile of the old Merritt Parkway.

The drive north through Wilton and Cannondale is winding and hilly. The recent snowfall was much in evidence, and high drifts still obscured the entrances to some homes along the way.

Although the stately elms had long since fallen victim to the Dutch disease, oak and maple trees of great age survived along the county roads, as well as stands of fir and pine, and clumps of birches like silvery shadows bordering the snowy fields.

There were a few farms, but owned now as hobbies by people who made their money in other ways. There were palatial estates as well, hidden from the road and marked only by imposing gate houses. And there were tract houses here and there, the sort advertised in the Sunday New York *Times* as "three-bedroom Tudor Dutch colonial" or "Renaissance revival split-level with heated garage, greenhouse, swimming pool and indoor tennis court."

"I'd forgotten how beautiful it is along here," Barbara said as they watched the passing scenery. An hour and a half out of New York they reached the entrance to Cathcart College, one of the nation's last bastions of all-female education, and currently the defendant in a widely publicized sexual discrimination suit filed by a male student applicant who was refused admission.

They talked about it as they approached the school. Barbara said she liked best the fact that the young plaintiff was represented by a woman lawyer while legal counsel for the college was an old fogey in his dotage who had gone to Yale with her grandfather.

Although Cathcart College dated from the first great feminist movement in America after the Civil War, when the very idea of higher education for women was revolutionary, it had only occupied its present site since the end of the Second World War.

Loredana Cunnington Shaw, an otherwise undistinguished alumnus of the school, had married Gabriel Shaw when she was twenty-one and he was seventy-two. Gabriel Shaw, known in sports and political circles as "Soapy" Shaw, had the good fortune to be the sole inheritor of an immense fortune his father had made in shaving cream, shampoo and other personal-hygiene products. Soapy never worked a day in his life, unless polo and poker counted as work, and when he died sometime in the dim past before the Second World War he left his fortune to his beloved Loredana.

Loredana knew nothing about stocks, but she read the newspapers and believed in hunches. So she ignored her broker's advice and invested Soapy's assets in aircraft companies and arms factories on the eve of the war. If she was rich when Soapy died, she was ten times richer five years later.

She became a popular benefactress, and one of her favorite recipients was her obscure old alma mater, Cathcart College for Women, located on the edge of what had become a Bridgeport slum. After her death in a water-skiing accident, she left most of her fortune and the two-hundred-acre Shaw estate near Soapstone Mountain to her beloved Cathcart. The Bridgeport ugly duckling immediately moved from its decayed urban quarters to one of the most beautiful, secluded and best-endowed campuses in New England.

They turned in the gate and drove up a winding tree-lined drive past playing fields, stables and a skating pond. The original mansion had become the center of a Gothic quadrangle of dormitories and classroom buildings where Cathcart's eleven hundred students and faculty lived and studied.

Almost everyone was away on Christmas holidays, so the place was eerily empty when they entered. An elderly security guard directed them to the president's cottage, which looked like part of the stage set for *Hansel and Gretel*.

Louisa Mae Barton, Ph.D., met them at the door, a tall, plain woman about Colin's age, dressed in the Ivy League uniform of pleated plaid skirt, cashmere sweater and single strand of pearls. He knew her from board meetings as a cool lady with a deep voice, a no-nonsense manner and a good sense of humor. She was meeting Barbara for the first time and seemed genuinely pleased.

He addressed her as Dr. Barton and she never once suggested he call her anything less formal. That was fine with him. If a little stroking would get her to back Hunt Benson at the stockholders meeting he'd be more than pleased to do it.

Before coming, he had looked into her background more carefully because, as Pasteur said, success favors the prepared mind. She played tennis, flew a plane, had never married and held a dozen honorary degrees besides the Ph.D. she had earned in chemistry. She understood, it seemed, more about Stanton than most board members.

The first few minutes she eulogized Avery Stanton for Barbara's benefit. She clearly considered him one of the great men of her time and displayed real passion as she described how he had solved a heat-bonding problem that had baffled polymer chemists for years. When she spoke about Avery's work, it was the reaction of a serious scientist to something exciting in her field.

"Do you miss the laboratory?" Colin asked her.

"There's nothing more satisfying than what I do now, but yes, I do miss it. I use any excuse to drop in on the chemistry and physics labs when classes are in session." She poured Barbara's tea and passed the cup. "I did the same thing every time I went to a Stanton board meeting in New London. I always got there early and followed your father around the lab while he showed me what they were up to."

"That's where he was happiest," Barbara said.

Louisa Mae Barton nodded emphatically.

Colin suggested that Hunt Benson might take her in hand now that Ave Stanton was no longer there to do it. "He was Avery's right arm for twenty years, you know."

And that got them gracefully onto the subject of Benson and the company leadership, which, after all, was the reason for his visit.

"Are you suggesting that Hunt Benson is your choice over your husband?" she asked Barbara.

"At the moment, yes," Barbara answered frankly. "I agree with

Colin that it would be in the company's best interest for Hunt to stay on at least another year. Then choose a new president."

"I can see your reasoning," Louisa Mae Barton said. "With so much at stake, no one wants to rush in blindly."

"He'll take some convincing," Colin told her, "but I'm hoping you'll help the rest of us talk him into it."

"How do the other board members feel about it?"

He told the truth, that the board might be evenly divided, but he thought they would go with Benson if she did.

She smiled. "You know, you're the second visitor I've had recently lobbying for Hunt."

"Is that so?"

"Adam Walsh was here last week with the same request."

___ CHAPTER FORTY-SEVEN ___

IF THERE was a prize for deviousness Adam Walsh would win it. Colin said nothing when they left the Catchcart College campus, because he was trying to divine what the man was up to now. What could his interest possibly be in seeing Hunt Benson remain at Stanton as president?

Colin thought Dr. Barton had been charming and hospitable. She asked Barbara about her children and expressed a friendly interest in her life with Ken Fairchild, recalling how Avery Stanton had bragged about Barbara's family. She was full of praise for the Stanton brass and said she was proud to serve on the same board with such a distinguished group of movers and shakers. She also managed not to commit herself on the subject of Hunt Benson. Unlike Sawyer and Admiral Scheutter, she did not say, "You can count on me." She was as much of an unknown card when they left her as she had been before they went to Fairfield County.

In the car Barbara said, "A very bright lady, Dr. Barton. A lot of pleasant chat without promising anything."

"She'd make a good politician."

"She already is," Barbara said. "She didn't get to be president of

Cathcart College and a director of Stanton on her looks. I mean that as a compliment," she added quickly. Then: "How do you think she'll vote, Colin?"

"With the majority."

"Me, too. She's not a chance-taker."

"Is it my imagination or do I get the impression you didn't much take to Dr. Barton?"

"When she wasn't trying to make me feel like an awkward schoolgirl she practically called me a brood mare. All that patronizing tolerance and the bland smile; the combination of fake humility, fake interest in my kids and graceful manners can't mask the ironclad ego that lurks beneath the cashmere and the pearls. She has qualities I avoid in other women. Maybe it's what some of them need to succeed in a man's world, but they make me damn uncomfortable."

"You mean lesbian overtones?"

"I don't know, but I'm terrible about recognizing things like that. She's feminine enough, I guess, but I think she'd cut your throat if there was something in it for her." Barbara laughed. "I sound like a tremendous bitch, don't I?" The laugh took its own time and was delightful. "But I'm not, you know. Unlike Dr. Barton, I'm just an ordinary bitch."

"Remind me to keep off your blacklist."

"No need to worry, darling. Tell me, why do you think Adam Walsh was soliciting support for Hunt?"

"I've been thinking about that."

"And what exactly have you been thinking?"

"He knows I oppose him and will try to block his candidacy if someone on the board nominates him."

"Did you tell him so or is he only assuming that?"

"Believe me, Barbara, we've talked about it."

"I see."

"He also has no reason to be overjoyed about either Ken or Brian taking over the company."

"Why not? What does he have against either of them except that they don't seem to like him any more than you do?"

"There's that."

"Plus the other mysterious reason you won't reveal."

"Let's just say that under either Ken or Brian, Walsh's wings would be clipped so he wouldn't have the freedom he enjoyed under your father or Hunt."

"And you believe that's why Adam prefers having Hunt stay on?"

"Wouldn't you if you were he?"

"Perhaps."

Colin knew that if Walsh was actively campaigning for Hunt Benson it would reinforce his own efforts to keep Hunt on. Yet that could hardly be Walsh's reason. What Colin did not say to Barbara was that Walsh's lobbying also indicated a confidence on his part that he would be at Stanton longer than Colin or the others intended.

All Colin said was, "He knows he can't make it on his own so he'd rather help make sure Hunt stays around."

"How do you see the vote going now?"

"You, me, Brian, Ken and Nate Sawyer for Hunt Benson. Admiral Scheutter too, if he sees that Ken favors Hunt. That's six out of twelve. Livingston and Cummings will vote as a pair for Adam Walsh. The two Boston bankers, Deke Peabody and Rog Devere, will probably vote with them. Plus Hunt Benson himself makes five unless he abstains. If La Barton goes with them, they tie, and Benson's vote counts as two, breaking the tie in favor of Adam Walsh. Or she goes with us, to make it seven to five for Hunt Benson."

"So no matter how you look at it, she is the key to Stanton's immediate future."

"In a sense, yes."

"I don't like that."

"Sorry, but that's the way the points add up."

"Would you be awfully upset if Walsh wins?"

"It won't happen."

"How can you be so sure? You just said—"

"I'm saying that because I don't want it to happen."

"When will you tell me why, Colin?"

"After the meeting. After Hunt is in." And, he added to himself, Walsh is silenced. He hoped. Later Ken and Brian could go at it, after Walsh was disposed of.

As soon as they were on the Merritt Parkway, Barbara dozed against his shoulder while he glanced through the newspapers he had not yet seen that day. The business world loves statistics, and at the end of the year the New York *Times* and the *Wall Street*

Journal become especially enamored of year-end reviews, wrap-ups and summaries.

This particular Monday after Christmas yielded a fair harvest of material directly or indirectly promoting Stanton Technologies. In one *Times* article the company was named as the world's leading producer of gallium arsenide for the semi-conductor industry. Without Stanton, the article implied, the smart bombs that helped win the Gulf War in a matter of days would not have been possible.

In another piece on the financial page Adam Walsh was featured as the star-turn of the year, according to the reporter; the living, visible proof that market research had reached new heights of accuracy, respectability and power.

Once the stepchild of the advertising industry, the newspaper said, market research now commanded huge budgets in most companies where its practitioners wielded tremendous influence at the very top of the American industrial pyramid. Gone was the hit-or-miss guesswork of the Madison Avenue necromancers that had led to such marketing disasters as Ford's Edsel and Coca-Cola's new flavor. Today, "according to Adam Walsh, vice-president of Stanton Technologies, 'market research is to business what astrophysics is to the stars, a way of understanding and predicting forces beyond our control, and of harnessing them so they work in our favor.' " Walsh was always good for a quote.

The article went on to say that Mr. Walsh obviously knew what he was talking about, as the spectacular performance of Stanton Technologies had demonstrated. A chart showing the metals industry in general and Stanton in particular revealed a steep upward curve for the New London firm against the erratic performance of the competition. During Walsh's three years with the company, sales, market share and stock values had all skyrocketed. "Success depends on how you react to the information available," the Stanton vice-president was quoted as saying. "There's no mystery about it. But of course you must get that information, make sure it's complete and then know how to use it."

Beside the market-research article was a three-column box containing the picture and authorized biography of Adam Walsh. Princeton, Phi Beta Kappa and government consulting work were all mentioned, as well as one thing Colin had never heard of. Walsh claimed to be working on a book in his spare time, a text for graduate students about something he called the "fourth dimension" of market analysis based on theories he had developed from his own experience.

Once again Colin was forced to admit that, ex-convict or not, Walsh was among the most brilliant adversaries he had encountered in years of corporate legal work. The man seemed to be leading a charmed existence no matter what they did.

The *Wall Street Journal* was also on Walsh's side, but in an entirely different way. In a long piece entitled "Comers" and dealing with several rising superstars in American industry, Walsh was given the most space. The reader almost got the impression that although Avery Stanton was responsible for the creation of most of the company's products, Adam Walsh had invented the profit.

Stanton was consistently out in front among go-go, hi-tech companies, the *Journal* said, one of the few American firms that continued to keep the Japanese off-balance. But now that the founder was gone, the writer asked, what will happen? "Can the company maintain its momentum and its profits under new leadership?"

Like George Westinghouse and George Eastman from the past, and more recently Dr. Edwin Land of the Polaroid Corporation, Avery Stanton had been that rare American combination of scientist and industrialist so dear to investors. The question asked by the investment community as the year drew to a close, said the *Journal,* was "who has the charisma and talent to pick up where Avery Stanton left off?"

The list that followed included mention of Forbes magazine's recent selection of Brian Redfern, "the thirty-six-year-old whiz kid at Stanton International," as the executive most likely to succeed to the presidency. The *Journal* called him "a superbly qualified favorite." The same article, however, reminded readers that a poll of institutional investors and securities analysts showed the majority in favor of Stanton marketing chief Adam Walsh, whose "dazzling record has received close attention recently from the financial world."

"But according to some sources," continued the *Journal* reporter, "the smart money on Wall Street is behind former football star and war hero Kenneth Fairchild, vice-president in charge of sales, whose wife Barbara Stanton Fairchild became the company's largest single shareholder upon her father's death.

"Current boss Hunt Benson suggested that a further possibility existed if Stanton directors looked outside the company for a new

CEO. 'This would conform to a basic tenet of Avery Stanton's philosophy, which was always to bring in new blood.'"

When Colin chuckled at that, Barbara awakened and said she didn't know the *Wall Street Journal* was famous for its humor.

He read her Hunt Benson's quote and the last part of the article, which described what was at stake in New London on January sixth. "Whoever takes over the direction of this healthy young industrial giant will be well rewarded. According to one source, approximately two and a half million dollars a year in salary, options and other perquisites make up the prize."

"How do they know that?" Barbara asked Colin. "I didn't know that. Where do they get their information?"

"Guesswork. Although it's easy enough for a good reporter to get hold of your father's last income tax return and put two and two together."

IT WAS close to eight by the time they arrived in New York and he called home from Barbara's apartment. Lauren Jewett reported that Joyce had passed an uneventful day, conscious from time to time but no longer responsive. Barbara suggested going to O'Hara's for dinner. A depression had overtaken him again as a result of his phone call, and trying to put a good face on it didn't fool Barbara.

"If you'd rather not, Colin . . ."

"Sorry. I don't mean to be a gloom-puss but—"

"Don't apologize. I understand. You know that."

They took a taxi to the restaurant and Barbara went in ahead while he fumbled for change to pay the driver. He had barely finished the transaction and seen him drive off when she came hurrying out of the restaurant again.

"What happened? What's wrong?" he asked her.

"Do you mind if we go someplace else?"

"I thought you liked—"

"Please, Colin."

"Sure, anywhere you want. Just tell me."

"I don't care, just not here."

They had to walk several blocks looking for a taxi. She said nothing, just kept her head down. He couldn't imagine what could have driven her from the restaurant.

On Eighth Avenue they caught a cab uptown to an Italian place in the Fifties. Barbara offered no explanation, merely clutched his arm in the taxi. By the time they were seated in the restaurant she had relaxed a little. She smiled and reached across the table to take his hand. "I'm really sorry, Colin. I feel like a fool but I couldn't have stayed there."

"I thought you'd seen some kind of ghost."

"I did. The ghost of my marriage. Ken was supposed to be in Vermont until Wednesday. That's what I assumed when I talked to the boys. But he was in O'Hara's having dinner with his friend."

"Nora Hallowell?"

She nodded. "I really do want to divorce him, Colin. You know I would have started the action already if you hadn't asked me to wait."

"Waiting is best, Barbara, believe me."

"Maybe, but why should I be running away, damn it? Why should *I* be trying to hide?"

"You felt humiliated, I guess, although you damn well shouldn't be."

"That's just it. I love you and I don't give a damn what he does, so why do I care?" She reached for her purse as tears glistened in her eyes, then went off to the restroom.

The remainder of the evening was a dead loss for them both. Colin failed to shake off his depression entirely, and Barbara's attempts to compensate for her own turbulent feelings with forced cheerfulness were no help. After toying with their food, they taxied back to the Ritz Tower, where she asked, "Do you want to come up?"

When he shook his head and kissed her gently he had the feeling she seemed relieved. "I'll call you tomorrow," he said, and left.

Mrs. Ryan was knitting when he got home, with the television tuned to an old Bette Davis movie and the sound turned low.

He stood beside Joyce's bed for a few minutes, holding her hand, stroking her arm where a hundred needles had left dark bruises under the translucent skin. She did not stir and again he had the sensation that life had left her body, until he felt the faintest flutter of a pulse, like the touch of a bird's wing.

After a while he went into the study, poured himself a whiskey and sat and brooded. Why, on the very day when he'd been saved from financial disaster, did he feel as if the bottom had dropped out of his life? Joyce was no worse than the day before. Adam Walsh was still waiting voraciously in the wings, as he had been right along. And if he wasn't exactly reassured by his visit to Dr. Louisa Mae Barton, at least she hadn't declared herself against his plan to draft Hunt Benson.

But reason never cured a depression, and Colin was no exception. A second whiskey didn't help either, so he picked up a book he'd started and found himself reading the same sentence over and over again. When he was about to fall asleep something made him sit bolt upright, feeling panicky.

He had seen nothing he could put a name to, nor dreamt anything he could remember, but the feeling remained. A third whiskey calmed him some but sleep did not come.

Mrs. Ryan looked in on him at one point and offered to make some hot cocoa. He thanked her and shook his head, feeling her eyes on him before she returned to her knitting in the other room.

When the telephone sounded he picked it up before the second ring. "You obviously weren't asleep yet," Barbara said.

"Just sitting here," Colin said.

"I had to talk to you."

"Are you all right?"

There was a pause before she answered, "I think I am. I think I'm much better than I was an hour or two ago, but I doubt you'll approve of what I did. I told him, Colin."

"Ken?"

"Ever since I went in that restaurant tonight and saw them, I couldn't think of anything else. Please understand, darling, I don't love him, don't even like him, but I'm human and the thought of him there with her . . . lying to me, to his own children on Christmas so he could be with her. It was the last straw, Colin. I didn't mention it to you earlier because I was too stunned, but the owner saw me."

"Nick?"

"He saw me and he knew exactly what was happening, because he looked from me to them and nearly had a stroke."

"I see."

"I wrote him a letter, Colin, demanding a divorce. I just mailed it. I'm sorry, but I couldn't not do it after . . . that."

A whiskey or two later Colin was still sitting in his chair, thinking that the world was spinning out of control all around him, and for the life of him he couldn't think of a way to stop it.

____ CHAPTER FORTY-EIGHT ____

CHRISTMAS DAY and the three days immediately after were among the worst Brian Redfern had ever spent as he sweated out the matter of another man's life or death. The innocent man he had put into the Oyster River had somehow survived but was on the critical list at the Yale Medical Center in New Haven.

The New Haven *Register* carried the story on Christmas Day next to a photograph of the man's children kneeling by the family Christmas tree with their gifts unopened. "Police are looking for the hit-and-run driver," the article said, "as the victim's distraught children postpone Christmas and pray for their daddy's recovery."

As soon as he knew the man's name, Brian called the hospital repeatedly to inquire about his condition. The answer was always the same. Critical.

"But he is expected to live, isn't he?"

"I'm sorry, sir, we are only authorized to report that the patient is still on the critical list."

"But is he conscious?"

"I'm sorry, sir."

By the middle of the week, the man was off the list and well enough to tell his story to state police investigators. According to the press follow-up, the victim had given a complete description of the vehicle that had forced him off the bridge. In a television interview from his hospital bed for Action News he said, "It was deliberate, no mistake about that. He sideswiped me on purpose. I'm lucky I'm alive."

Redfern had the rest of the week to get through until his car was repaired. Undoubtedly the police would be making a systematic check of body-and-fender shops in hopes of turning up the other car. If they found his Porsche and began to ask questions . . . ?

No way they could prove he was the one, Brian told himself. Obviously no one had got the license number or they would have identified him before now. And no one could have seen his face because of the way the snow was coming down. A thousand times he tried to reassure himself, but he knew he would not be safe until he had the car back with no telltale marks on it and no questions asked.

Fionna had given him the cold shoulder all week. In spite of her protestations that if he told the truth she would back him all the way, she was treating him as if he had a communicable disease, turning her lips away to take his kisses on her cheek, giving him her back in bed and removing his hand every time he tried to touch or caress her.

When he protested she snapped, "I don't feel like it, damn it. I'm not looking for it, Brian!"

"A kiss, Fionna. I was only trying to hold your hand, for Christ sake."

"One thing leads to another, and I don't want my hand held. How can you even think of sex when . . . Oh, to hell with it!"

"Who said I was thinking of sex? You're my wife, the woman I married—"

"Don't remind me."

"What kind of a crack is that? For better or worse, remember? I'm counting on you."

"Come off it, Brian. Let's not turn this into a marital squabble. Things are bad enough already."

"You're the one who's escalating it."

"I'm not the one who got drunk and nearly killed a man."

"How many times must I tell you it was an accident?"

"He says it was deliberate."

"That's crazy!"

"Is it?"

"My loyal wife! Ready to accept anybody's word over her husband's—"

"He's not just anybody. He's a man who nearly was killed because of you. I don't know what to believe anymore."

"You can start with me. Do you think I haven't been out of my mind all week with this damned business?" At least that was true.

"If they find the car, what will you tell them?"

"Nothing. They can't prove anything. And he didn't die, so they won't be trying very hard."

"Don't be so sure. Paint and scratch marks might match up, you know. The police aren't stupid, Brian, and they have technical laboratories. They can do amazing things."

"On television," he said. "But in real life they're slow, shorthanded and—"

"Don't push your luck."

"Suppose they did come? And suppose they could prove it was my car? It doesn't prove I hit him deliberately. And I didn't. It's his word against mine."

"Except you didn't report it."

"I didn't want my insurance premiums raised. I—"

"That won't fly, Brian."

"Okay. What am I charged with?"

"How do I know? I'm not a policeman. Reckless driving? Drunken driving? Leaving the scene of an accident?"

"No one could prove anything, and even if they could, what's the worst they could do? Take away my license again?"

"If that's the case, why are you so worried? Why do you jump every time the doorbell rings or the telephone?"

"I don't need the hassle it would bring. I've got enough to worry about at the plant right now."

"Just don't mess up at the last minute, Brian. Do you realize how close you are to taking over as president of Stanton?"

"Nothing's certain, Fionna."

"Well, it's a lot more certain than it was yesterday. That ridiculous Wes Scheutter was all in favor of Ken."

"You didn't find him ridiculous at his party the other night. You were practically seducing him there in front of me."

"How observant of you, Brian. I didn't think you were seeing much of anything that evening. Just to put your mind at ease, I'd fuck Wes Scheutter all day if that would guaranty his vote for you, but thanks to Ken Fairchild I don't have to."

"What do you mean?" He was so startled he forgot to be offended.

"His incredible television appearance has the whole board screaming bloody murder. Everybody's after his scalp."

She was referring to Ken's televised response on a major news network to a cease-and-desist order issued against Stanton by the

Environmental Protection Agency for releasing certain metal salts
and other toxic substances into the Thames River. Ironically, some
were by-products of the same gallium arsenide production necessary for computer manufacture. The company had a good defense
apart from the fact that their recycling system had broken down,
but Ken had failed to present it.

"I heard he lost his cool with that lady reporter," Brian said, "but
he's been under a lot of pressure lately."

"Haven't we all," Fionna said.

If you only knew, Brian was thinking. Fairchild could blame it on
the stress of the moment—Barbara's letter announcing her deter-
mination to divorce him, his own obsession with Nora, his maneuvering for the Stanton presidency or the nightmare of Adam Walsh
—but that didn't change anything. His handling of the television
interview had been a major blunder.

"It still doesn't get me elected next week," Brian said.

"Did you know that your pal Colin has been canvassing every
board member on behalf of Ma Benson? No, I didn't think you did.
But it was Hunt who failed to play straight with the government
when they told Stanton to stop dumping shit here in the river.
Thanks to Hunt's fumbling management style and his obstinate
stand against the EPA, his stock is no higher than Ken's."

"How do you know all this? I see some of those board members
regularly and nobody's said anything to me."

"God, Brian, sometimes I wonder how you made it past kinder-
garten let alone M.I.T. I talk to their wives, darling, and unlike you,
other men tell their wives everything."

"Gossip," Brian said, his tone contemptuous.

Fionna replied, "God bless gossip and the gossipers. Because
you and Adam Walsh are the only ones in the running now as far
as the Stanton board is concerned, and Walsh seems to be the
favorite."

"Walsh won't make it."

"Maybe not. Barbara says Colin is dead set against Walsh but
won't say why. So why don't you tell me?"

"We don't want him in the job."

"We? Who's we?"

"Colin, Ken and I."

"But why is Colin so vehement?"

"Because he wants one of us in the saddle."

"I didn't ask you who he wanted. I know that. I asked why you are all so hard against Walsh. Does he have bad breath or a lousy Dun & Bradstreet rating or what?"

"Look, Fionna, I appreciate all you're doing, but stop trying to run the company for me, will you? Adam Walsh is a smart guy with a lot of ambition but we just don't happen to think he's the best choice for Stanton right now. I'd accept Ken. I'd even put up with Ma Benson a while longer if I had to. But if Walsh took over, I'd quit."

"You still haven't said why."

"I don't want him, that's all. Enough!"

"At least Colin was honest enough to tell Barbara he'd give her his reasons after the stockholders meeting."

"Good for Colin. I'll tell you then, too. Satisfied?"

"No, but it will have to do, I suppose."

He went to his jacket, hanging over a nearby chair, and rummaged through the pockets until he found a cigarette and lit it nervously as Fionna looked on with distaste.

"Must you?"

"Must I what?"

"Smoke."

"Yes, I must," and he left her angrily and passed through the kitchen to the back entrance hall. She heard him clatter noisily down the basement stairs, and after a while the sound of sawing and pounding came from below. "Would wonders never cease?" she asked herself. "The great Brian Redfern puttering? Mr. Fixit?" Although Brian had a small workshop, he rarely set foot in it, preferring to call a maintenance man from Stanton whenever anything went wrong around the house.

The way his nerves were now, she decided, it was just as well he had found something to occupy himself, although he was hardly the handyman type. Thank God for occupational therapy, she sighed. At least it kept the cigarette smoke out of her house.

_____ CHAPTER FORTY-NINE _____

STANTON'S NEW York offices in the World Trade Center were only a few blocks from Cranmer, Fisher & Cleves, but a hundred floors higher. For some men it was a very dangerous place to work so far above the city, distorting one's perspective and seducing the imagination beyond delusions of grandeur. Above the clouds, one couldn't help but feel a little godlike.

Such thoughts crossed Colin's mind as he waited for Ken Fairchild to arrive for their first meeting since his unfortunate television interview in which he had come across as a corporate monster indifferent to the environment—which, in fact, was not the case. He had been taking heat from all sides, and Colin intended to touch only briefly on the matter to make sure Fairchild clearly understood the Stanton legal situation.

"Not you, too," Ken said when Colin began.

"Right. Me, too. What possessed you to give that marvelous off-the-cuff interview?"

"I didn't believe what I was seeing. What they broadcast bore no resemblance to what I said."

"But it was you talking, Ken."

"How can I explain it? Her original interview lasted maybe an hour. Some questions were tough, but I said we were doing everything possible to correct the situation."

"You mean you were quoted out of context?"

"Not only that, Colin, much worse. What nobody understands is that woman *changed* the questions. In the interview she'd ask a question and I'd answer it. But on the show she'd asked an entirely different set of questions followed by my answers. So when I didn't sound like an idiot I came off like some kind of reactionary goon."

"You're saying they edited to change the meaning?"

"Absolutely! I know better than to say some of the things they had me saying. It's terrifying. That's not me on that show. It's a talking head that the interviewer invented, to make herself look good, I suppose. Can I demand they play it like it was?"

"Afraid not," Colin said. "What we could do, but I wouldn't advise it at this moment, is to sue them for malicious misrepresentation and then demand the original interview be screened for comparison by a judge or jury. But that would only stretch the thing out for months with no guaranty we'd win."

"But I'm telling the truth, damn it."

"I'm sure you are, but you should know by now that the truth is incidental to some people. It could drag on for a year or more, take up time and money and probably end up making you angrier than you are now."

"I was *trying* to be honest," Ken said dejectedly. "At the time I didn't see any harm in giving them the interview. Even my kids had a fit. 'Dad, did you really mean what you said on television?' Try and explain to them that I was edited to make me look foolish."

"Okay. It's done. Let's move on. I assume we're agreed no more personal appearances?"

"You don't have to tell me. You should see the Faxes that came in from stockholders. Not one favorable."

"I've got people working to take the sting out of the case," Colin said, "but it would have been a lot simpler and cheaper if Hunt hadn't ignored those government notices."

"And if I'd kept my mouth shut."

"We still have a more pressing problem."

"Walsh. Do you think I could forget that?"

"Unfortunately, coming just before the meeting, this EPA thing hasn't exactly worked in our favor. It makes Hunt look incompetent and it got you in a pack of trouble."

"I got myself into trouble because I believed that interviewer was on the level. She made me sound like Al Capone."

"It's over, so forget it," Colin said. "I've been worried about Walsh making a run for the top job right from the start, no matter what kind of deal he did with us. He knows we won't tell on him after having paid him a million dollars. And he also knows we're having trouble getting the rest together."

Fairchild shook his head. "That *would* be a coup, wouldn't it? Two million bucks embezzled from Avery, another million extorted from us, and then . . . can you imagine? . . . he takes over the company?"

It was black humor at its best, or worst, except that Walsh was also the current favorite among the directors, as Colin reminded Fairchild, especially since the damage done to his and Benson's reputations by the media after the EPA injunction.

"You're not seriously suggesting that he could—"

"He could."

"But he won't," Ken said. "I swear, if I have to march into the board meeting with his prison file, he'll never be CEO."

"I think we're agreed that's a last resort."

"It's the first resort worries me. We don't have one."

"I expect Walsh will be nominated, probably by Howie Livingston or Lydell Cummings. And he'll have four sure votes."

"Then what?"

"I'll move immediately that elections be deferred for an additional year and that Hunt Benson remain until then."

"Will Hunt do it?"

"A week ago I had my doubts. But since this EPA fiasco he's coming around. He knows he screwed up and I made it clear that he still has a chance to be a hero if he hangs on a little longer. In fact, I suggested he'd be leaving under a cloud if he left now."

"And he agreed?"

"More or less. If the motion carries, he'll go along."

"And if the motion's defeated?"

"I'd be forced to nominate Brian."

"I see. That comes as something of a surprise."

"Because you thought I'd nominate you?"

"Well, Barbara is the majority stockholder."

"Let me explain why." Colin told him that according to company bylaws her stock had to be voted by the directors representing the Stanton Foundation."

"I had no idea."

"I only recently discovered it myself."

"And you think they'd favor Brian over me?"

"I hope we don't reach that point. I'm counting on my motion to keep Hunt Benson around."

"But . . ."

"I believe Walsh would beat Brian one-on-one."

"So what would you do if that happened?"

"We'd have to trust Livingston with our secret, at least the part about Walsh's prison background."

"Then what?"

"Livingston would probably endorsc Hunt and the other votes would follow. Hunt would stay on, Livingston would keep quiet, and a year from now you and Brian could work out Stanton's future between you while Adam Walsh retired on his annuity."

"If that scenario works."

"It'll work," Colin said with conviction. "It has to."

The office they were using in the World Trade Center was like working atop an alp, so high that cloud formations twenty stories below sometimes cut off their view of New York City and the harbor. When Fairchild commented on this to Colin, he conceded that too much time atop this climate-controlled Olympus might give a man a complex about gazing down on lesser mortals.

"But working at ground level can affect your judgment, too," Colin said.

"What's that supposed to mean?"

Colin told him about Brian's arrangement with Quirk and asked if he had known.

"I'm afraid I did, Colin. I'm sorry. We should have told you but we convinced each other that you'd scuttle the idea."

"And you were right. I would have. Let's hope this Englishman doesn't take it in his head to tell some journalist why he really came to the United States."

"He wouldn't do a dumb thing like that, would he?"

"He might if there was something in it for him."

"Is there?"

"I hope not. I'd love to see him jump bail and leave the country, but the judge lifted his passport."

"It was stupid, employing someone like him."

"Better if you'd stuck with Luther Yancy."

"What do you mean?"

"Instead of Quirk. You were going there to hire him when you were attacked, weren't you?"

"Whatever gave you that idea?"

"Yancy."

"Luther?"

"He came to see me. He thinks a lot of you, Ken. He told me how you saved his life in Vietnam by risking your own."

"Luther talks too much."

"Not at all. I found him discreet to a fault. He told me that in the

Virgin Islands when a man saves your life you have a very special responsibility to look after that man."

"Well, this is Manhattan Island, where the rules are different. What the hell did he want to see you about?"

"You. He knows your habits and he thinks some woman or some woman's husband is trying to blackmail you."

"Oh, for God's sake!" Fairchild laughed. "He'll never change, old Luther. That security business has softened his brain."

"He also figures that's why you were looking for his services, then changed your mind after the attack. He's no fool, Ken."

"No, he isn't, but he may be just a little paranoid. Vietnam affected a lot of guys that way, but I thought Luther was tougher."

"He's as tough as any man I ever met," Colin said.

"You know what I mean. More stable or something."

"He cares about you and he's worried. He said if anything ever happened to you, he'd never forgive himself."

"I appreciate that, but the only thing that can happen to me already happened right there in his own backyard. But I don't blame him. That was my stupidity."

"He also said if anything happened to you he would have to avenge it because that's the way the system works. Kind of old-fashioned, but it's good to know there are still men in the world like Luther Yancy, especially if they're on your side."

_____ CHAPTER FIFTY _____

As GLAD as Colin was to see the year end, he was just as reluctant to begin a new one with so many of the old year's problems unresolved. New Year's had always been his least favorite holiday anyway. The idea was okay. Wipe the slate clean and all that. New resolves, fresh starts, new beginnings. But the manic celebrating, the forced gaiety and marathon drinking always put him off.

For years he had passed the holiday with Joyce, cruising the Islands. More often than not they celebrated New Year's Eve in some turquoise bay after a good day's sail, with a swim and a couple of daiquiris, a light dinner and some quiet talk, and a little lovemaking at the end.

But whatever they did had the rich, sweet full flavor of the life they shared, a life that was lost now. It was their great good fortune to be in love and also be the best of friends. Ten or fifteen years after they married they could still say to each other, "What would I ever do without you?" and mean it.

Now he was finding out.

Everything grated on him this New Year's, even Mrs. Ryan with her knitting and chocolate munching. He had offered her the night off but she refused, saying that after the mess with the substitute nurse she didn't feel right about leaving. He knew she was sincere, but her attitude only irritated him, probably because of his own residue of guilt.

Barbara was passing the holiday in New London, chaperoning a party for fifty teen-age friends of her son's. Ken had begun the weekend with her but left after what she told Colin on the phone had been "an awful row, the worst yet."

"What started it?"

"He came back as if nothing had happened. After my letter I assumed he would come back to collect his clothes and make some other arrangements to live away from the house. But he said nothing, didn't even mention my letter."

"And . . . ?"

"So I brought it up and asked him what he was doing. He said he was making himself at home. I asked him if he'd read my letter and he said, 'Oh, that. We'll have to talk about it.' When I said there was nothing to talk about he tried what used to work, put his arms around me . . ."

"And what did you do?"

"I slapped him as if he were a stranger, which in a way he is. He assumes I'm still so helplessly attracted to him I'll put up with anything."

"I half-believe you're enjoying this."

She laughed. "You're right in a way. For me it's no small triumph to stand up to Ken."

"In the end what did you say?"

"I played the angry, outraged woman and told him exactly what he wanted to hear so he could storm out on cue. I couldn't believe it was me."

"Are you okay?"

"Never better. You?"

"I rented a video movie to watch tonight."

She laughed. "You're the limit, Colin. Who rents a video to watch on New Year's Eve?"

"Me. Will you be staying there the whole weekend?"

"The boys have me fairly well locked in, between driving them around and just, you know, being with them. I've told them what I'm doing and why, and they seem to understand. If children ever really do. Can you join us?"

"I'm going to stay here, Barbara. I've got a busy week ahead before I come up for the stockholders meeting."

"Won't I see you until then?"

"Doubt it."

"Do you miss me?"

"Yes."

"What a stupid question. I hate people who ask questions like that. I miss you. Isn't that funny? I've only known you most of my life, Colin Draggett, and don't remember ever missing you before. But now I do. Do you really miss me or are you just saying that because you know I want to hear it?"

"I miss you. Period."

"If you did change your mind you could come ice-skating with us tomorrow. Ice-surfing, the boys call it. They've developed this incredibly dangerous sport, Colin, it curdles my blood."

"Ice-surfing?"

"They rig a sail like a small spinnaker on a pole they support on a belt around their waist. Then they catch the wind and tear across the cove on skates at speeds you wouldn't believe."

"I hope you're not planning to try it."

"Never fear. Darling, I have to go now. Call me tomorrow and tell me how you liked the movie."

"Good night, Barbara, and Happy New Year."

"Happy New Year, my love, and thank you."

"For what?"

"For being there when I need you. For being Colin."

"You sure you're okay?"

"I'm fine," she said, beginning to cry. "Oh, damn it, I didn't mean to do that. I'm so sorry."

"That's okay, I understand."

"That's just it, you're the only person who does, and I'm so lucky to have you for my friend. I only wish I could help you the way you help me."

"Barbara, you are helping, believe me."

"It's sweet of you to say that but I know better. I know what a great pain in the ass I can be."

"What would I do without you?" Colin heard himself saying.

"I know you don't mean that, but I like hearing you saying it. Goodnight, Colin, and may both our new years be happy."

He put the phone down and sat for a long time doing nothing. Thinking, but not in any cohesive or constructive way. Was he in love? He didn't think so, not the way he had always been with Joyce and probably still was. Yet he loved Barbara. Perhaps it was the guilt that stood in his way. She had none of her own because for so long she had been far more sinned against than sinning.

But Colin's love still lay helpless in the next room. Alive but not alive, and yet not dead. What was guilt after all, he asked himself, if not the inability to pay one's debts to those one loved? He felt that he could never give back the happiness Joyce had given him. Never. She used to say, "I've got your number, Draggett. You can't fool me."

But he had fooled her for twenty years. Not about his love, which was deep and certain, but about his power to protect her. Paying doctors and round-the-clock nurses wasn't protection. Intravenous feeding and exceeding the minimum legal doses of Demerol wasn't protection. Fucking another man's wife while his own lay dying didn't qualify either . . . He was being too hard on himself there, he knew, but the feeling wouldn't go away.

Joyce had told him once about a childhood story that terrified her, about Billygoat Gruff and the ogre. Billygoat Gruff had to pass over a bridge every day, and the ogre who lived under it ate those who couldn't pay the toll. The kicker was that nobody knew how much the toll was and the ogre wouldn't say.

"I can never see a bridge without remembering that story," she said. "I mean, think of the ogre under the George Washington!"

With his arm around her he had replied fatuously, "You can forget about ogres now that I'm around."

But it hadn't worked out like that in spite of his good intentions. He could pay the doctors and he could pay the nurses but he could not pay the toll. So the ogre came out to eat her after all.

He put the movie on but soon turned the cassette player off and banged around the study looking for a book. A generous scotch relaxed him without cheering him up and he put *The Magic Flute* on the stereo. Who could possibly be depressed while listening to Papageno or the Queen of Night?

Mrs. Ryan looked in and said, "Aren't you going out, Mr. Draggett? It's New Year's Eve."

"Not this year, Mrs. Ryan."

"Aren't you even going to eat?"

"I hadn't really thought about it."

"I'll fix you something."

"No, thanks. You go ahead."

"Will you let me know when you're hungry?"

The telephone interrupted them. It was Mrs. Ryan's doctor son and his family calling from Fort Bragg to wish her a Happy New Year. Colin gathered from the part of the conversation he overheard that Mrs. Ryan was supposed to be passing the holidays with them in North Carolina but had cancelled out to stay with Joyce. Her son apparently complained, because she said, "I know, dolly, and I miss you too, but the Lord needs me here right now. What? In a few more days it will be all over."

A few more days.

When in doubt, work, Colin told himself. The law had been his salvation in more ways than one over the years, and if it now helped take his mind off the confusing and depressing elements in his personal life, once again he would be grateful.

Anthony Shattuck had prepared a file as he always did with a copy of everything pertinent to cases in which Colin had an active interest. With his usual efficiency he had it sent along in the event Colin wanted to refer to anything over the long weekend.

Colin began to read through parts of the Environmental Protection Act and the federal statutes cited in the injunction against Stanton Technologies. The statutes were clear enough and the injunction was simplicity itself. Colin did not know the federal judge who had issued it, but Anthony had clipped a short biography to the cover of the file, knowing he was a stickler for details about his adversaries. More than once he had snatched victory from the jaws of prejudice by exploiting some little-known weakness of the court or the opposition lawyers.

This judge was young, progressive and scholarly, Harvard-educated like Colin, with a reputation for being soft on ethnic minority criminals and tough on federal agents. Colin made a note to assign Gordon Hamilton, a black lawyer on his staff, to work with another attorney named Shapiro and handle all courtroom appearances.

To some, such an assignment might have seemed cynical, and perhaps it was a little, but Cranmer, Fisher & Cleves was paid to win, and Colin knew an articulate young black attorney would make out better with this judge than some white button-down Yalie. It would also cut some ground out from under the elitist image corporate law firms too often tended to project.

The phone rang again an hour or so later when he was busy writing some notes to himself about the case and the upcoming Stanton board meeting. Mrs. Ryan entered to say, "It's for you, Mr. Draggett. It's your mama."

"Maisie?"

"Colin, who was that woman answered your telephone?"

"That was Mrs. Ryan, Joyce's nurse."

"She didn't sound like a nurse."

"Believe it or not, Maisie, she is."

"She sounded like a hooker."

"Where are you?" The background racket made him wonder if she was telephoning from center stage at a rock concert.

"We're working a gig tonight at the 'Pig-in-a-Poke.' "

"You're doing what?"

"We're headlining in Wheeling, West Virginia. Next stop Caesar's Palace!"

"I thought you were on your way to Florida."

"My son, the nit-picker!"

"Are you all right? What's all that noise?"

"Female mud wrestling. We're on next."

"You're on what?"

"Are you deaf? Max and Maisie, our act! Max got us booked here at the 'Pig-in-a-Poke' for the New Year's weekend."

"Is that a nightclub or a sausage factory?"

"It happens to be the biggest rib joint in Wheeling, Mr. Wisenheimer, and that's not all. Max got Walter booked too."

"The Hawaiian?"

"How many Walters do I know?"

"Yes, right, Maisie. Well, Happy New Year. It sounds like you're off to a running start."

"No thanks to you. If I'd paid any attention to your advice I'd still be locked up like Nutsy Catroni in that stuffy apartment listening to the sanitation trucks drive by."

"Who is Nutsy Catroni, Mom?"

"That was before your time."

"I'm the one who wanted you to try Florida, remember?"

"Sure, bag and baggage, anything to get me out of your hair. Well, I'll tell you something, Skeezix, after a lifetime of looking I finally found a man I can get close to."

"Maisie, maybe this is your big chance."

"You'd like that, wouldn't you? Poor me carried off by somebody I hardly know to some place in the middle of nowhere."

"But you know Max pretty well by now, Maisie."

"Who said anything about Max? I'm talking about Walter."

"Walter from Waikiki, the Fearless Firewalker?"

"Walter Hooponopo."

"Of the Honolulu Hooponopos, you said."

"For your information, Mr. Smart Guy, the Hooponopos used to be kings out there. He's the end of the line, like Canarsie."

"You mean he has no children?"

"He's not even engaged."

"But he's firewalking in Wheeling."

"Who told you that?"

"You just said Max got him booked."

"The Pig-in-a-Poke serves five hundred orders of ribs a night, so they got a twenty-foot-long barbeque pit. When Walter walks it, the people here go crazy betting."

"How do you bet? Medium-rare or well-done?"

"You can't stand to see me happy, can you?"

"On the contrary, Mom. I like to know you're enjoying yourself. Are you planning on going to Hawaii with him?"

"Firewalkers are a dime a dozen out there."

"But being a king should give him an advantage, especially if he's fast on his feet."

"My son, the comic. Ha, ha, ha!"

"I try, Maisie, but I'm no match for you."

"It took a Harvard education to figure that out?"

"How did you guess?"

"I'm your mother."

"Amen."

"Nobody's faster than Walter," Maisie said loyally. "He's been in space, you know. He's faster than light. Supertonic."

Here we go, Colin thought. Walter the firewalking astronaut. Whatever he was, Maisie was beginning to sound close to certifiable. "You mean faster than sound," Colin said. "Super*sonic*."

"No. I don't mean that at all. Walter's faster than light. He's an astral projectionist and that's how they escape."

"I believe it."

"No, you don't. You think you know it all, but there are some things you don't learn about in law school, Mr. Einstein, and astral projection's one of them."

There was nothing like a conversation with Maisie to put Colin off-balance, and in a way, cheer him up. Her whacky self-absorption was so complete it was funny. Almost. She never once asked about Joyce or wished him a Happy New Year. He honestly didn't know if she even remembered whether he was married or to whom, or if she cared.

When Mrs. Ryan brought a tray to the study with broiled pork chops, baked potato and a salad, he discovered he was ravenous. He was finishing this off with a bottle of good Sauvignon when the telephone rang again. It was the lawyer Shapiro.

"Sorry to interrupt your holiday, but there are a couple of things I thought might make your New Year happier."

"You're not still at the office, Bruce?"

"As a matter of fact, no. I am not a workaholic, sir, in spite of the reputation I may have earned around C, F, and C. I'm at home feeding my six-month-old son his last bottle of the year."

"What's up?"

"News today from our consulting chemists."

"That was fast."

"They have found virtually every kind of crap from arsenic to zinc in water samples taken from the Thames River, most of it from *other* sources. If you can spare the time I'd like to drop by tomorrow and discuss our game plan with you. Take about an hour."

"Does it have to be tomorrow?"

"No, but it would be helpful. Hamilton and I want to be in court in Hartford bright and early Monday morning, and you should know what we're up to before we go."

"All right. Come on by tomorrow afternoon."

"Before or after the Orange Bowl?"

"Suit yourself."

"Around five okay?"

"Fine."

After he hung up, Colin finished the wine, read for an hour, and packed it in.

New Year's Day dawned gray and dreary and he ran for forty minutes through the slush before feasting on a cholesterol-rich, high-fat, low-fiber breakfast of waffles, sausage and eggs. He needed that.

———— CHAPTER FIFTY-ONE ————

IT WAS the first time in fifteen years that Oklahoma had made it to the Orange Bowl, and at the end of the third quarter, the Sooners were trailing Penn State 13 to 20. With less than five minutes on the clock Oklahoma scored with a forty-yard pass and made the extra point, tying the score at 20–20. The result was that neither Colin nor his two young colleagues could concentrate on Stanton Technologies until the game was over.

As it turned out, the Sooners' defense did not heed Bruce Shapiro's shouted imprecations, and Penn State ran the ball to their twenty-eight-yard line, then went for a field goal to win the game 23–20.

"It could have been worse," Gordon Hamilton said. "The last time Oklahoma played in Miami they lost to Washington by eight points."

Shapiro was crestfallen as he paid off to Hamilton. "To come so far and lose at the last minute," he groaned dramatically. "What did we do, oh Lord, to deserve this?"

"What is this 'we'?" Hamilton asked him.

"I take this defeat very personally," Shapiro remarked. "They started the season as the underdog and then went on to the Orange Bowl. And look how the Sooners came from behind to tie that game. I say they deserved to win."

"Don't you know without a good defense you're history?"

Shapiro threw up his hands. "A good defense? Just because they lost doesn't mean they weren't brilliant."

Colin said, "We're in trouble, Bruce, if you apply that same logic to your work in the courtroom."

Hamilton appealed to Colin as arbiter. "You saw them go down, Mr. Draggett. Did their defense suck or not?"

"It did," Colin agreed. "Now, what about Stanton's?"

"A different equation entirely," Shapiro said. "In fact, we have several lineups to choose from."

"Let's hear," Colin said.

"We've been lucky," he said. "Right, Gordo?"

The other attorney, Hamilton, was a handsome black man with short clipped hair, gold-rimmed spectacles and a manner as calm and ordered as Shapiro's was tense and nervous. He had graduated first in his class from Georgetown and was currently working on a doctorate in jurisprudence at Columbia.

Some years ago Colin had devised a point system at Cranmer, Fisher & Cleves to determine the winability or loseability of any particular case. Positive and negative points were assigned for different factors, such as the degree of culpability or the kind of proof presented or required, the amount of the client's risk, whether he was the plaintiff or the defendant, what statutes were involved, etc. A zero meant an even chance. A minus score implied they would lose and a plus indicated the degree to which they should win.

Colin asked Shapiro how he assessed the score on Stanton and the EPA. "My preliminary workup on Monday gave the client a minus one," he said. "After Ken Fairchild's TV chat, it dropped to a minus four. But the chemistry we got yesterday puts it back in the plus column."

"About a two," Gordon Hamilton said.

Bruce Shapiro was all arms and legs and gestures when he got wound up, as awkward as a pound puppy and just as likeable. He had removed his jacket and rolled back his cuffs when he arrived. His hair looked like it hadn't seen a comb for a while, the knot in his tie was already ten degrees off center and his shirttail was about to pop out. There was, however, nothing sloppy about his thinking.

"For openers we could go for the clean-hands doctrine in equity which says that relief may be denied because of the injurious and unfair conduct of the party seeking it."

"I don't know if that applies to a government plaintiff," Colin said. "Did you check it out?"

Shapiro stopped pacing the room and pointed at Hamilton, who said, *"The People v. Collins, Burns, Dalrymple et al . . ."*

"What was the issue?"

Shapiro answered, "Contempt of Congress. Teamster witnesses who refused to talk or take the Fifth because they didn't want to end up like Jimmy Hoffa."

"They drew one-year sentences," Hamilton said, "but the convictions were overturned when defense was able to show that the House committee was determined to make an example of them."

"That sounds more like malicious prosecution," Colin said. "Is that the case with Stanton? If so, proving it is something else."

"Right," Shapiro agreed. "I said we had options." Again he stabbed a finger in Hamilton's direction. "Tell him the chemistry, Gordo."

"Twelve sites were chosen, all upriver of the Stanton plant, and samples were taken at eight-hour intervals over a two-day period by an internationally recognized chemical-testing firm. The levels of lead, mercury, zinc oxide and several other toxic substances, including pesticides and various arsenicals, were found to be anywhere from three to twenty times higher than maximum acceptable safe levels."

Shapiro said, "And *most* of this poisonous stuff is already in the water *before* it reaches Stanton."

"What else?" Colin said.

"Isn't that enough? If all the fish aren't dead yet it's only because Long Island Sound is so big."

"I'm off sushi since I read the report," Hamilton said.

"I meant, what else do you have?" Colin pressed.

"We also had them take samples of Stanton's effluent right at the pipe that empties into the river. What they got is not good, how could it be? But Stanton is *not* the primary contaminator."

"That doesn't sound too encouraging."

"By itself, no. Except Sheldon Brandt, the EPA lawyer, screwed up. The twelve sites we checked all have much worse reports than Stanton's, and not *one* of those offenders has ever been notified or warned by the EPA."

"Maybe EPA isn't aware."

"Tell him, Gordo."

"Their teams have checked these same sites two or three times this year and their results tally with the outside consultants we hired. In other words," Hamilton continued, "the federal government has known the location and extent of pollution in the river for some time. It has also been aware that Stanton is actually the *least* offensive of the offenders."

"Then how do you explain Stanton being singled out?"

"That's what Gordo's going to ask the judge to ask EPA," Shapiro said.

"It seems fairly obvious to me," Colin said. "There were a couple of routine notices that Ave Stanton ignored, then several more that Hunt Benson also ignored. Somebody in Washington got properly offended and sent Sheldon after them."

"Okay, here's the plan," Shapiro said. "Gordo's going into federal court Monday morning with a motion to lift the injunction based on insufficient proof that Stanton is polluting the river. As back-up he'll have the results we just described as well as the consulting expert who actually did the sampling."

"Suppose the judge denies the motion?"

"Gordo files a cross-complaint claiming EPA harassment. At the same time I'll be filing in Connecticut state courts on behalf of Stanton for damages in excess of a hundred million."

"How did you arrive at such a figure?"

"It's what Adam Walsh estimates sales of Stanton's Graftite will amount to in the first few months. Benson says they would have to suspend production in order to obey the injunction, so they would lose at least that much in sales."

"Then what?" Colin asked them. "Do you expect that to bring this government lawyer to his knees?"

"Doubtful," Shapiro admitted. "He's come too far to back down without looking bad to his superiors."

"But he's bound to be a lot less zealous," Hamilton said, "if he has to defend their testing procedures."

"We'll win in court," Shapiro said, "if Stanton executives will just stay off television from now on."

CHAPTER FIFTY-TWO

Res ipsa loquitur is one of the many Latin phrases one learns in law school and soon forgets. It means "the thing speaks for itself," and it is useful where something can be taken for granted in law. For example, in the case of a serious accident caused by a drunken or hit-and-run driver, criminal negligence is established *res ipsa loquitur.* Nobody has to prove it because the nature of the act speaks for itself.

On the last day of the year, Brian telephoned the body-and-fender shop where he had left the Porsche and they told him his car was not ready. "Why not? What's the hold-up?"

"Takes time to bake the paint," the garage owner said.

"You said I'd have the car for New Year's."

"Well, I was wrong."

"When can I pick it up?"

"Call me Monday. I'll tell you then."

"What do you mean, you'll tell me then? I need the car. I can't wait all week for it."

"Friday's a holiday, and Saturday we only work half a day. So call me Monday."

"Will the car be ready Monday?"

"Maybe. Call about twelve and I'll tell you."

When Brian hung up his palms were clammy with sweat. Was the man telling the truth? Or had the police been around?

He and Fionna went to a New Year's Eve party at the golf club, where he was still so morose after several drinks she said, "If you didn't want to come why didn't you stay home?"

"I'm all right."

"With a face like fried ice? Just because the car wasn't ready when the man said. Brian, how paranoid can you get?"

"It's not the car. It's a whole bunch of things . . ."

"For instance?"

"Never mind."

"That poor man is going to be all right. If the police knew it was you they would have been here before now."

"I suppose . . ."

"Then snap out of it. The glamorous Fairchilds aren't even here and half the board is, so once more you're center stage. But how can you win friends and influence people unless you cheer up?"

"Just get off my back, will you, Fionna?"

"I will if you promise not to make an ass of yourself the way you did at Scheutters' Christmas party."

"I was sick to my stomach."

"Really? I never would have guessed. Make the effort, will you? Go the last mile, Brian. Back me up and a week from now you'll be in the catbird seat." She paused to flash a radiant smile and blow a kiss to the Livingstons as they passed. "I can't do it all by myself," she hissed under her breath. "You've got to hold up your end!"

He managed as the champagne finally took hold, and by the time they left the party at three he was his old self. If he didn't win any friends at least he didn't offend any important people, and one or two he even impressed favorably.

Howie Livingston's wife was heard to comment on how amusing Brian could be when he let his hair down, and even Howie agreed that Brian was exceptionally well informed and lucid expounding on the Common Market's changing relations with Eastern Europe.

ON NEW Year's Day Brian's depression arrived with his hangover, and he moped around the house, puttering in his basement again, banging and filing until Fionna thought she'd go crazy.

"What are you making down there?" she demanded.

"Some things for the boat." To give his explanation credibility he even spent several hours Saturday and Sunday at the boatyard aboard *Ghost,* his sport fisherman. The boat was his only real luxury besides the Porsche, and his only refuge. Sixty-four feet of diesel-driven power, with an immaculate white hull, an eighteen-foot pulpit jutting from the knife-edged prow and twenty-foot outriggers sprouting from the bridge like the feelers of some giant sea snail, *Ghost* was a "lean, mean fishing machine," as Brian liked to say. The boat carried all the latest electronic aids to navigation and fish-finding, a launch as fancy as an admiral's barge, and accommodations for twelve in seignorial comfort. When Brian bought *Ghost* two years earlier at a cost of almost three hundred thousand dollars he did not tell Fionna right away. He waited until he completed a Coast Guard course certifying him as a qualified captain. Then he took her to the Groton boatyard one spring Sunday and proudly showed her his dream come true.

Fionna hated it on sight.

He remembered the conversation that followed as one of the less salubrious moments in their marriage. "I won't ask you how much you paid for it, Brian," she said at first.

He was ready for that objection. "Actually it was a bargain," he began. She said, "It makes me sick."

"Well, there's always Dramamine and those things, Fionna," he said quickly, "and I read about a thing you can tape behind your ear that's supposed to be—"

"I didn't mean seasick, I meant sick thinking about how much you squandered on that boat."

And that more or less set the tone for all future conversations about *Ghost*. Fionna was slightly mollified when she saw how the Hartford bankers and Stanton board members liked to be invited aboard, but she could never look at Brian's boat without thinking of all the lovely things she could have bought with the money.

Ghost had just had her hull scraped and painted, and Brian had written the yard a giant-size check that Sunday. Another thing to annoy Fionna when the bank statement came in. But if the board voted him into the top job this coming Wednesday she wouldn't ever complain about the boat again. If . . . and always his mind returned to the delay on the Porsche repairs and the reasons for it.

Toward sundown he decided to call Fionna at home and ask her to meet him at the golf club for drinks. That usually put her in a good mood and it would probably cheer him up too. As he walked toward the pay telephone in the boatyard he was thinking that for a man who almost never drank he had certainly made up for it lately. All because of Adam Walsh.

She had left a hurried message for him on the answering machine: "I'm at Barbara's, Brian. It's an emergency."

He called the Fairchilds and got the younger of their two sons. "She took Mom and my brother to the hospital," the boy said.

"What's wrong? What happened to them?"

"Nothing happened to my mom," the boy replied, "but Barry totalled himself on the rocks over at Sawyer's Cove."

"He did what?"

"Crashed and burned ice surfing. I was ahead of him and skated around but he couldn't tack in time."

Redfern hurried to the Thames Valley Hospital, where he found Fionna in the main lounge putting on her coat.

"What happened?" he asked her. "Is the boy okay?"

"Yes, but he put a hell of a dent in some rock when he took his spill. Sixteen stitches in his scalp plus a concussion."

"How's Barbara?"

"Holding up."

"Is Ken with her?"

"Of course not."

"Where is he?"

"Where do you think?"

"Does she know he's with Nora?"

"I'll tell you all about it over a drink."

THE GOLF club bar was crowded with friends, some watching television, some playing bridge and others recovering with Bloody Marys from ten days of fairly continuous holiday drinking. Adam Walsh and his wife were at one of the bridge tables, and the sight of him put a knot in Brian's gut. Walsh was laughing, obviously winning and enjoying it, and by the time Brian reached the bar he was grinding his teeth as he ordered for him and Fionna.

"What's the matter with you?" she asked him.

"Nothing."

She made a face, imitating him. "Some nothing. You want nails instead of peanuts to chew, or ground glass or what?"

"Goddamn it, Fionna, I said *nothing*." But she had seen Walsh, too, and caught her husband's glance in his direction. What she saw in Brian's eyes had almost frightened her.

"Brian?"

"What?"

"Why do you hate him so?"

"I don't hate the son of a bitch."

"You don't?"

"Of course I don't!"

"But you knew who I meant."

He seized his drink with such force he spilled it.

"Brian, calm down."

"I have enough to put up with . . ."

"I'm sorry, but if looks could kill, Adam Walsh would have keeled over dead when you walked in."

"You mean I was that obvious?"

She sighed. "You don't know."

"Then I apologize."

"Why can't you tell me what the problem is?"

"It's fairly simple, I just can't stand him."

"Because of the competition he's giving you? You used to thrive on competition. Do you feel the same about Ken?"

"Fionna . . . ?"

"All right. After you win you'll tell me."

"You still think I'll win?"

"It's either you or him, darling. And if you're so sure Walsh can't or won't make it, then it has to be you."

"You're counting Benson out?"

"After the way he handled that EPA situation?"

"And Ken, too?"

"More than ever. And not only because of his TV appearance. Barbara called him from the hospital about an hour ago."

"She called him? At Nora's place?"

"That's right."

"You told me she knew, but how did she get the number?"

"From the telephone book, I expect, or from Petrey."

"That must have been some conversation. Tell me."

"Barbara was half-hysterical about Barry. God, Brian, you never saw so much blood."

"Why didn't she call an ambulance?"

"She did. Then she called me. I got there before the ambulance, so I drove them in her old station wagon."

"What did she say to Ken?"

"His friend answered the phone."

"Nora."

"That's right, Nora."

"And . . . ?"

"Barbara got off to a running start. 'This is Barbara Fairchild and I want to speak to my husband.' 'I'm sorry,' the other one told her, 'you must have the wrong number.' Well, that did it! Barbie said, 'Listen, here, you put Ken Fairchild on right now or I'll have the police at your door in ten minutes. This is a family emergency!' Nora says, 'I'm sorry, he's not here' or something, you know, trying to maintain the fiction, and Barbara explodes. I didn't know she knew some of the words she used."

"What did Ken say?"

"She didn't give him a chance to say much. Barbara loves her kids, you know, and there were some moments there when, frankly, Brian, nobody could have known whether Barry was going to live or die. God, the blood! You couldn't even see the poor kid's face!"

"What did Ken say?"

"From what I gather, he was so angry, and scared, he started blaming her for the accident, for not taking care of the boys. She let him have it then. When he said he was on his way home she told him not to hurry, he had never been around when she needed him and now she didn't need him anymore. 'I told you I wanted you out of my life,' she said, 'and when the board meets this week I'll see that you're out of my company.' "

"It's hard to believe—"

"Brian, I told you Barbara was finished with him weeks ago. After she saw him groping Nora in the hospital." Fionna took a final sip of her drink and held up her glass.

"You want another?" When she nodded he signaled the barman with two raised fingers. "So what's she going to do now? Divorce him?"

"Short of killing a husband, Brian, that's about the only way a woman usually gets rid of one."

____CHAPTER FIFTY-THREE____

BRIAN REDFERN sweated out the hours until he called the garage about the Porsche and was told it was ready. Still nervous but with a growing sense of relief, he went to collect the car Monday afternoon, writing out the check as the garage owner caressed the repaired fender, saying, "We do better work than the factory."

As soon as Brian left the shop the garage owner dialed the state police barracks and asked for Sergeant Otis. The policeman had come by the garage two days after Brian left the Porsche and had taken paint samples, some of which came from the car Brian had struck. He also photographed the Porsche from various angles to show the damage to the right-hand side. These pictures were compared with the damaged Lincoln and placed in the police file.

The garage owner asked if Brian was the man they wanted.

"Too soon to tell," the sergeant said.

"If you ask me, it ain't this fellow," the garage owner said. "Nobody would deliberately scuff up a great car like that."

"Maybe he didn't do it deliberately," Sergeant Otis replied. "Maybe it was an accident and he just panicked."

"Ah, guys like that don't panic. It ain't him, you'll see."

The sergeant thanked him for his cooperation.

When the man in the hospital did not die, the pressure was off Sergeant Otis, so the case went to the bottom of his pile while he spent time on more urgent matters. But that did not mean it was closed. Repairs to the bridge were going to cost the state more than ten thousand dollars, and although the injured driver carried liability insurance, if it could be proved the accident was caused by a criminally negligent third party, the insurance company would not pay and the state would be out of pocket.

It was clearly a hit-and-run accident according to the man who went into the river and according to the skaters who witnessed it. Sergeant Otis had already checked the Porsche's registration. He had a statement from the garage owner, a name, an address and a telephone number. He was only waiting for a laboratory analysis of the paint samples to find out whether one Brian Redfern was the man responsible for the accident.

Brian thought he was home free. His relief was so great after he left the body shop and reached the turnpike that he gave the Porsche the gas and sang to himself as the speedometer zoomed above the speed limit.

He was clocking over ninety when a state police car pulled him over.

The officer was coldly polite as Brian sat fuming. At least he had not had anything to drink, but he was in trouble anyway. His love of speeding had already cost him two very inconvenient suspen-

sions of his driver's license, and he was aware that under tough
Connecticut laws, this time he could lose it permanently.

As the trooper was punching in Brian's license number on his
computer and getting out his summons book, Brian walked back to
the patrol car. "Look," he said, "I'm awfully sorry about this. I just
had the car fixed and wanted to test it for half a mile or so. There
wasn't any traffic, so . . . well, look, I'm in the wrong, I admit it,
but isn't there some way to avoid a ticket?"

The officer looked up from the computer screen, icicles in his
eyes.

Brian saw but failed to read the warning. "It's worth, say, a
hundred not to have it on my record."

"That's all?"

"Two?" It was risky business, he knew, but risk was the business
he was in these days.

"Don't go away."

While Brian waited in the cold for a reply, the officer rolled up
his window and turned away to read the answer on his computer
screen. Then he called in to the East Haven barracks on his radio.

Sergeant Otis came on the radio to confirm that Brian was a hit-
and-run suspect but they didn't yet have the proof they needed to
arrest him. "I do," the trooper said. "He just offered me two hundred to tear up a speeding citation."

"Accept it as a late contribution to our Kiddies Christmas Fund,"
the sergeant said, "and then let him go."

"With or without the citation?"

"That's up to you."

When he got out of his car the officer was as tall as Redfern. A
handsome blond-haired man in his late twenties with an expression
as cold as death. "You said two hundred dollars?"

Brian reached for his wallet. "Here it is," he said, taking out two
fifties and a hundred.

The trooper slipped the bills into his breast pocket. "If I thought
you were giving me money not to write you a citation, I would
place you under arrest, explain the *Miranda* rules and take you
down to the barracks and lock you up. But since it's the holiday
season and I'd just as soon avoid the hassle I'm going to act like
the subject never came up and consider this a donation to our
children's fund."

"I appreciate that, Officer. That's fine."

"Wait in your car and I'll be with you in a moment."

Brian impatiently returned to the Porsche. The trooper's cynical use of the children's fund didn't fool him.

Within five minutes the trooper came to the Porsche, returned Brian's registration and driver's license and said, "Hold it down to fifty-five on my highway."

"Thanks again," Brian said as he started the engine.

"Just a moment," the policeman said, and handed him the summons he had just written out charging Brian with reckless driving and exceeding the speed limit by forty miles an hour.

"What the hell is this?"

"What does it look like?"

"But I thought we had a—"

"You thought we had a what?"

"Nothing," Brian muttered, and gunned the engine, leaving the policeman standing there. Only after he had returned to his car did the officer crack a smile.

Brian's annoyance was so great it was all he could do to keep within the speed limit the rest of the way home. He played over the humiliating scene in his mind as he recalled "that supercilious son of a bitch handing me the ticket that could lose me my license!"

The relief bordering on euphoria he had felt earlier had been wiped out. At home Fionna came straight to the garage. "It looks okay," she said while he pressed the button to close the overhead door.

"They did a good job."

"And no questions."

He shook his head.

"Feel better?"

"Yes and no." He told her about the cop who had taken his money and then given him a ticket. She burst out laughing.

"Not so damned funny," he said, though he did see the humor in it as he now recounted the story.

"It's not the end of the world if you lose your license. By this time next week you'll have a company limo and driver."

"I wish I was as sure about it as you are."

"Don't worry. I even put the word out through the wives that I was the cause of your little illness at the Scheutters' party."

"You?"

"I said you had a touch of food poisoning from some eggnog I made with bad eggs."

"And they believed you?"

"Why not? They all know I'm an idiot in the kitchen."

"You don't miss a trick, do you, Fionna?"

"I can't afford to, the way you've been behaving lately. And don't forget I've got as much at stake here as you, Brian. In two days I expect all we've been working for to have paid off. I can't say it's been easy but I do know it will have been worth it."

For the moment at least Fionna's assurance and enthusiasm were a wonderful elixir, lifting him above his preoccupation with the Porsche, the audit, the board meeting, even with Walsh himself. "Just let me take over," he kept praying to whatever gods were listening, "and everything's going to be all right."

In New York that same Monday Colin was conducting a frustrating last-minute telephone poll of the directors. Although the EPA injunction was the very thing he had needed to convince Hunt Benson to remain as president, ironically the other directors argued that Hunt's rather inept handling of it was reason enough for him to retire.

Howie Livingston said, "Christ, Colin, if the guy can't deal effectively with an outfit like the EPA, how can he run Stanton Technologies? His preoccupation right now is making Walsh a tour guide at the annual meeting. Can you beat that?"

Lydell Cummings said he thought Benson was over his head and should step aside before even worse things happened.

Nate Sawyer said, "I'd like to go along with you, Colin, but you can't give me one good reason to take Hunt over Walsh."

"Go with Brian Redfern then," Colin said, shifting options.

"I don't know. I grant you Brian's clever, but he still lacks maturity, judgment. He may impress the Koreans or the peasants down in Patagonia but lately he impresses me less every time I see him. You probably heard how he made a spectacle of himself at the Scheutters' Christmas party."

"Nate, that can happen to anybody with a few too many aboard. And you know Brian barely touches the stuff. That's probably why he got so smashed so easily."

"Maybe, maybe not. I don't know what else he was taking, but it wasn't just bad eggnog as his wife would have us believe."

Admiral Scheutter did not mention the Christmas party at all, which omission was significant in itself. He simply said his vote was going to Walsh because none of the other candidates had demonstrated sufficient leadership qualities.

Rog Devere in Boston said, "Walsh is head and shoulders above the others. Just look at his track record."

"I'm familiar with it, Rog," Colin said.

"Well, there you are."

His track record was exactly what they were going to have to show Livingston, Colin was convinced, or Walsh was on his way to becoming Stanton's CEO.

Sweet-spoken Dr. Louisa Mae Barton told Colin how much she had enjoyed his visit, how she liked meeting Mrs. Fairchild, how the directors she had talked to were so charming and knowledgeable . . .

. . . and how she admired Adam Walsh.

Colin could not reach Fairchild, who was at the hospital visiting his son, but he did get through to Brian Redfern to apprise him of the latest head count.

"What are we going to do, Colin?"

"It's time, I think, we had a heart-to-heart with Livingston and let him in on the facts of life about Walsh."

"You really think that's wise?"

"It's the only move we have left unless we want to see Adam take over Stanton Technologies."

"Hold off, Colin."

"Why? The whole board except ourselves is in love with him, so the sooner we take him out the better."

"I agree with you," Brian said. "Literally," he added beneath his breath.

"Please don't start off on those tangents again. We had quite enough trouble with your man Mr. Quirk."

"Sorry, but you know how I feel."

"I know how we all feel, Brian."

"We agreed it's risky to let anyone else in on this. Even Howie Livingston. He's smart but he's got a short fuse and he does tend to run off at the mouth."

"He won't talk for the same reasons we don't."

"Okay . . . but won't the effect be the same if we tell him five minutes before the board meeting? I say do it then." He needed to buy time but not tell Colin why.

"I don't see that it makes much difference."

"Then let's wait, Colin. Look how that EPA business changed all the odds unexpectedly. The board meeting's still two days off."

"Are you expecting a miracle?"

"Colin, you never know."

"If you've got some other crazy idea up your sleeve, Brian, forget it. Don't multiply our troubles."

"Howie's been touting Walsh pretty loudly these last few months, Colin. It won't be easy for him to back down."

"But easier than making an ex-convict president. At the moment they think they know all there is to know and their minds are made up. No Benson, no Fairchild . . ."

". . . and no Redfern," Brian finished.

"Without Walsh you'd virtually have to be their choice unless they reconsider keeping Hunt on."

"Are you so sure Ken's out of the running?"

"Barbara's so upset and determined to divorce him he'll be lucky to keep his job."

"So can we hold off telling Howie until before the meeting?"

Colin finally agreed. "So many bad things have happened around there lately, maybe we are due for a miracle. Anyway, I suppose another forty-eight hours can't be that critical." He badly wanted to believe that, even though he realized he now was operating on hope in carrying things to the brink.

When he hung up he was also far from satisfied that affairs at Stanton were under control, but he hoped that once Howie Livingston knew the truth about Walsh on Wednesday—if that became necessary—they would either keep Benson on or elect Brian Redfern president of Stanton Technologies.

AFTER LISTENING to Colin, Brian had reached his own inescapable conclusions. As long as Walsh remained part of the equation Brian could not be optimistic or even hopeful. He was convinced that telling Howie Livingston the truth about Walsh would not put an end to Walsh's ambitions at all, only enlarge his circle of victims. Walsh himself had made that clear enough at Wes Scheutter's

Christmas party when he told Brian that he could put them all in jail and walk free with three or four million dollars in his pocket.

Thinking this way, the rage Brian felt over Walsh getting away with it was enough to rekindle all the impulses that had prompted the Oyster River attack. Only now, cold sober and without the sustaining power of the pills he had been taking, his planning was, he was sure, more rational, more comprehensive.

He knew how it had to be done.

There was no longer any question in his mind about where or when. He was only a little vague about whether to go ahead on his own or take Ken Fairchild into his confidence before working out the last of the details.

He thought briefly of using Quirk again, but after turning that possibility over in his mind, he decided the Englishman's current problems with the authorities made him too great a risk.

Still uncertain about Fairchild, he tried to telephone, and when he failed to reach him decided it was probably for the best. Ken had already shown a lack of resolve after his mugging and would probably react coolly to Brian's decision even though he had once been in essential agreement. He decided to keep Fairchild out of it.

He went again to his basement workshop to finish filing and sawing while Fionna watched television upstairs. At one point she heard him jumping up and down on something and called to ask what in God's name he was doing.

"Stress tests," he called back, and she closed the kitchen door before returning to a television film.

He had been had by Quirk to the tune of fifty-five thousand pounds. He was disappointed with Ken Fairchild and he was frustrated by his own attempt to take care of Walsh on the Oyster River Bridge. But now he was ready to finish Adam Walsh without any help from Quirk or any advice from Fairchild or warnings from cautious Colin.

The idea of doing it alone also gave him a kind of special satisfaction and lift. Pride of authorship was enhanced by the chance to play the pivotal role in an event he alone had conceived.

This time there would be no mistake, no snow to obscure his visibility, no witnesses to his success.

____ CHAPTER FIFTY-FOUR ____

TUESDAY, THE day before the stockholders meeting, Ma Benson really earned his nickname driving everyone up the wall with his fussy attention to details and his difficulty resolving problems of basic organization.

Colin drove up to New London that morning with his mind mainly filled with what Barbara had told him the previous evening, but even he was not beyond Benson's reach because of the cellular telephone in his car.

"Colin, I don't have a copy of your remarks to the stockholders! I have everyone's except yours."

"That's probably because I didn't send you one, Hunt."

Colin had never heard him sound quite so peevish and distraught, but after his mishandling of the EPA business Hunt was properly terrified of putting the wrong foot forward again.

"Don't worry," Colin told him, "my remarks will be as you requested, a little bit about Avery, a brief review of the company's legal picture including the good news on the EPA injunction—"

"Good news?"

"We went into court yesterday, Hunt, and got the injunction withdrawn."

"Why wasn't I told? Why wasn't it on television?"

"The judge only gave the order yesterday afternoon. And you know how television is. They tend to carry the bad news."

"Don't they have to give us equal time?"

"Just count your blessings, Hunt. You still have to clean up your backyard or they'll issue another injunction."

"I'll be long gone."

"You never know."

"Will you be here in time for lunch, Colin?"

"No, I'm stopping to eat on the way."

"Please make it by three. I'm calling everyone together to go over tomorrow's schedule. Adam Walsh will be leading the first tour, Fairchild the second . . ."

"You told me, Hunt." At least a dozen times, Colin thought.

"I did? I didn't tell you about the mistake I found in the annual reports, did I? A picture of the evaporators in Building Two is captioned 'Acid baths in Building One.'"

"Do you really think someone will notice it?"

"*I* noticed it."

"Well, you can't be everywhere at once, Hunt."

"Some of our managers wanted to get out of guiding the stockholder tours, but I set them straight on that."

"I'm sure you did, Hunt."

"Until now you and Adam are the only ones who agree with me. I'm really pleased about your quashing that injunction, Colin. You will be here by three, won't you?"

"I'll do my best."

"I wouldn't insist except that so many things tend to go wrong, you know. We're expecting at least four hundred shareholders and that many people can be a real problem. Not to mention the tours and questions, which is why I'd like to go over the agenda with you and spend a little time . . ." His voice trailed off.

"I understand, Hunt."

"Well, goodbye then." It was as if he hated to hang up, needing more assurance.

Colin had to shake his head. Hunt Benson carried his insecurities around on his back like a bag of snakes. But this same frightened man had been described only the day before by the EPA lawyer as a modern robber baron, an exploiter of honest workers, a destroyer of the environment and a poisoner of children.

Sheldon Brandt had minced no words. Their meeting began with a stern declaration from him: "I consider the people you serve no better than organized criminals," he told Colin. "Worse in many respects because the long-term damage they do to our nation is greater than all the Mafia godfathers together."

Colin replied calmly, "In two sentences you managed to insult me, my client and all of American industry without taking a breath. Are you always so diplomatic or are you just after my vote?"

"Sarcasm," Brandt shot back, "is the last resort of a guilty conscience." Colin assumed he must have read that somewhere because he doubted Brandt had the wit to invent it.

"Look, Mr. Brandt, I didn't come here to trade insults or debate with you. I came to discuss a client's problem."

Brandt was not having any of that. Shapiro had warned Colin, but he had not really described the man adequately. Brandt rocked back on his chair behind his green metal government-issue desk. One had the impression that he flaunted the furniture like his rumpled suit and wash-and-wear shirt as proof of his humble dedication to public service. The desk was a mass of files, as were two tables, a second desk and the tops of all the file cabinets in the cluttered office.

"Don't think you can come here and cow me the way you do the other small fish," he was saying. "Oh, I know your reputation, Mr. Draggett. We've all heard of Colin Draggett, whose clients figure on Fortune's list of the richest men in the country. Draggett, whose clients screw the consumer, buy politicians and foul the nation with their poisonous waste."

About that time Colin rose and picked up his attaché case.

"Sit down, Mr. Draggett. You came here seeking an accommodation. And I'm the only one who can authorize it."

"Is that so?"

"You want us to get Stanton's injunction lifted."

Colin merely looked back at him without saying anything.

"And you're probably prepared to make it worth my while. Am I right?"

Colin still said nothing but he was amazed at the man's performance. If Sheldon Brandt wasn't after a handout he had to be the most fanatically bigoted so-called liberal Colin had ever met.

"Of course I'm right. Lawyers like you think you own the world. Well, you don't own the law. *I'm* the law. And you can forget the fix because I'm not buyable."

"I'm glad to hear that." And he truly was.

Brandt's secretary entered and handed him a note.

After he read it he made a face and said to Colin, "You have a telephone call. There's a phone in the next office if you want to take it there."

"I'll take the call here if you don't mind," he said, and Brandt pushed the telephone toward him. Colin knew who was on the line before he picked it up. "Hello, Gordo, how did it go?"

"Better than we hoped, Mr. Draggett."

"Did the judge lift the injunction?" Colin asked pointedly, looking at Brandt the whole time.

"It's dead, quashed. No injunction, no fine," Hamilton said. "They have to go back to court again if they want another one."

"That's good news," Colin said, repeating what Hamilton had told him as if to confirm it, and never taking his eyes from Sheldon Brandt. It was only a small victory over an opponent Colin disliked on sight. Meanwhile Colin determined to insure that one way or another Stanton *would* clean up the river while Hamilton and Shapiro took care of the legal details. Colin believed they could eat Sheldon Brandt for breakfast because apart from his ill manners Brandt's technique was not smart. Colin would have felt sorry for him if he hadn't been so damned aggressively offensive. The way the man transformed high principles into vicious personal attacks was hard to take. He was pretty sure the judge would give Brandt hell for wasting the court's time, and the government lawyer would have to do a tap dance to get his next injunction.

When Colin had reached his office door on the way out, Brandt called after him, "You got lucky this time, counselor, but it's only the first round. The gravamen of the government's complaint is still the same."

"But that complaint was dismissed, Mr. Brandt. The ruling says my client is not guilty."

"The judge never said that!"

"The court so ruled. And it was right."

"Rulings can be appealed and overturned," Brandt said, "and your luck won't always hold."

"Luck? How about right? This particular fight is finished because my client intends to comply with government guidelines on effluent control so you will have no cause to harass Stanton Technologies further."

"We'll find it," he muttered.

Colin heard it. "Not unless you fake it. And unless you stop the other polluters further up the river, you're going to be up to your *ass,* sir, in a plethora of disagreeable suits."

"Are you threatening me?"

"No, sir. You were threatening me, I believe. I just let you in on a confidence. There is a difference."

The next day, as Colin rolled along the Connecticut Turnpike thinking about the angry world of Sheldon Brandt, he wished all his problems could be disposed of so easily. Before leaving home he was told again by Dr. Brenner that Joyce could not hang on

much longer. She had not spoken or recognized anyone in days
and once more her fever was running high.

The telephone in the car sounded; Maggie Caruso calling to say
that Anthony Shattuck was already in New London and would hold
Hunt Benson's hand if Colin did not arrive in time for the three
o'clock meeting. She added that Walsh's secretary had called but
said it wasn't urgent. Mr. Walsh would see Colin in New London.

"Anybody else looking for me?"

"You mean besides your mother, Mrs. Fairchild and the usual
collection of clients?"

"I'll call Barbara. What did my sainted mother want?"

"To tell you about her new show business career, which I gather
was launched over the weekend."

"What happened?"

"To quote her, she rolled 'em in the aisles."

"Do you believe it?"

"I never heard her so excited. She said she got onstage and
forgot everything she was going to say until some drunk heckled
her. He reminded her of your father, she said, and as soon as she
began to tell him off people started laughing."

"Did you ask her what she said to make them laugh?"

"Awful things, Colin. You know your mother."

"And they really laughed?"

"No. She said they roared and howled. The more insulting she
became the more they wanted."

"Maybe Maisie's found her calling at last."

"She sounded thrilled. She's been asked to go on television. You
should call her. Here's the number."

He jotted it down as he drove, then dialed it. Maisie wasn't in,
the hotel operator said, she was out jogging.

He called Barbara, who said, "Take your time, darling. It's just
us for lunch. Barry won't be allowed out of the hospital for another
day or two but he's okay, thank God, except for a very nasty cut.
Avery's back at school as of yesterday and Ken is either at the
office or with his lawyers."

For the first time in days Colin was not looking forward to seeing Barbara. They had talked for an hour Sunday night after her
son's accident and after her blow-up with Ken. Then they had
talked two or three times on Monday. She was sorry, she told him,
that she had lost her temper and said all the things she said to

Ken, but they simply came out when he accused *her* of not taking proper care of her children. Just telling Colin about it made her rabid all over again and he had to plead for calm.

"I think I've entered a new stage in my relationship with that man," she said. "After passing from love to tolerance to disgust, I seem to be actively *disliking* him now."

"It's still anger," Colin said.

"Of course it's anger! Wouldn't *you* be angry if you were me? Where was he most of the time when the boys were little? Shacked up with some office tart or out-of-town whore. You're damn right I'm angry, Colin. If you had seen that boy bleeding . . ."

"I know, Barbara. Of course it unnerved you."

"I'm sorry, Colin. You of all people understand. But I just had to get it out of my craw."

"What's for lunch?"

"Eggs Benedict, okay?"

"I should be there in twenty minutes."

"Don't hurry, just come," she said.

"I'm on my way."

"Come safely, please, Colin. Barry's accident was enough to last me for a long, long time."

BARBARA LOOKED unusually pretty when she greeted him at the door. Her hair was pulled back in a soft line and plaited in a thick cue at the nape of her neck, and as usual she wore very little make-up. She was dressed in a cashmere sweater of dark green with a kilt of brown-and-green plaid. Their kiss just inside the door was long, and when they separated at last she said, "My, you're looking serious today, Mr. Draggett."

"I'm on serious business."

"Is that reference to me or to business business?"

"Ah, madame, to tell you that would be to give away the male advantage, to play into your hands, to surrender my hard-won edge in the battle of the sexes."

"Is that how you see it? A battle?"

"Actually its more of an endless war that probably started in paradise when Eve had her first bite of the apple."

She took his hand as they walked through the vast house to the glassed-in veranda overlooking Long Island Sound. "Why would that start a war?"

"To begin with, it was presumably Adam's apple, no pun intended, but he couldn't very well take it back without feeling foolish at best or boorish at worst. Adam probably looked at the world's first woman and thought, She's small and soft and not very muscular. I can easily beat her up and get my apple back. But before he landed the first punch she flashed an irresistible smile and offered to share it. That was the beginning of the war."

Barbara laughed as she led him to the bar and made them each a whiskey and soda. "Colin, really, I don't believe there's any such thing as the battle of the sexes or war or whatever you want to call it."

"Oh, no? Wake up! Eve swished her bottom seductively, tickled his remaining ribs with her exquisite tits and offered to share something that was his to begin with. I mean she took it and when she offered to give part of it back with a smile, he was supposed to be suffused with gratitude and love."

"Was he?"

"Sure. Men are like that."

"And what are women like?"

"Cunning, crafty and full of guile."

"Not trusting, ingenuous and straightforward like men?"

"They can be all that, too. Even more so than men."

"Colin, that's a contradiction in terms."

"It's also a pretty good description of women."

Which made her laugh again. It also brought him a great hug and a kiss as she sat beside him and said, "I'm so glad to see you, darling. These last days without you have been awful."

_____ CHAPTER FIFTY-FIVE _____

THE THREE o'clock meeting of Stanton's top management was held in the main boardroom, with Hunt Benson presiding over the head of the table like a nervous schoolmaster. In fact, the whole atmo-

sphere had something of school about it as he read off the schedule for the following day and indicated to the various managers and
vice-presidents the part each would be expected to play.

Parks, the company controller, said, "I wouldn't be any good as
tour guide, Hunt. I've only been inside the plant twice."

"No problem," Benson replied. "Everything's explained in these
folders"—he held up a small illustrated brochure—"that Mr.
Fairchild's sales-promotion staff had made up for us."

Ken Fairchild was at the meeting, too, sitting at Adam Walsh's
right and enjoying the limelight as various executives, including
Walsh, congratulated him on the spectacular new exhibit just inau-
gurated in Stanton's main entrance hall.

Conceived and produced by Stanton's advertising agency, the
exhibit told the story of the company's high technology accom-
plishments in aerospace and recent military history. Dramatically
lit murals and models of spacecraft, nuclear subs and supersonic
aircraft filled the hall, accompanied by stereophonic music and
sound effects.

Ken told Colin confidentially that it was mainly Nora Hallowell's
work: "She's not just another pretty face, Colin, but the most talented woman I've ever known. Unfortunately, because of all the
fallout with Barbara, Nora doesn't dare show up to take a bow."

"I'm impressed," Hunt Benson was telling the others, "and we're
lucky we got it open in time for the stockholders meeting. It cost
too darn much but I guess we'll be able to keep it around for a few
years." In fact, Hunt had been horrified by the budget, which had
been approved by Avery Stanton shortly before he died.

Brian spent most of the meeting ignoring everybody and glancing at his watch every few minutes. At four o'clock he rose to
leave, saying, "Sorry, Hunt, but I've got calls to make to different
time zones. Catch you later."

"Are you sure you got the schedule straight?" Benson called
after him. "You personally take the Tokyo stock market representatives, Brian . . . at eleven-fifteen right behind—"

"I know, I know. I have it all here," Redfern answered, tapping
his head and disappearing out the door.

Others immediately followed suit and within fifteen minutes less
than half of the original group remained. The meeting broke up
soon after, much to Hunt Benson's dismay. He had wanted to run
through the speeches at least once and he still had not covered the

cafeteria seating for lunch or the airport transportation arrangements. Left alone with only his secretary once again, he was more confused than he had been before the meeting started. Colin asked old Anthony Shattuck to give him a hand while he followed Ken Fairchild out of the room.

It was the first opportunity Colin had to talk to Ken since Barbara dropped her bomb about wanting him out of Stanton Technologies, and Colin was more than a little interested in Ken's reaction. To Colin's surprise, he brushed it off as simply one more predictable lapse on her part.

"She's a little more upset this time, maybe," Ken said with a shrug, as if describing his wife's susceptibility to the flu or the common cold. "You've known Barbara longer than I have."

"You don't think she's serious about wanting a divorce?"

"Sure, she's serious at the moment."

When Colin made no comment Ken added, "Do you know she even hired that Petrey to spy on me? You talked to her, what do you think?"

"She's very angry."

"You know what did it, don't you? She saw me with Nora in O'Hara's when I was supposed to be up in Vermont with my kids."

Normally an attractive and even charming man with an agreeable personality, Ken Fairchild cut a poor figure, Colin thought, as the irritable, injured husband. The Walsh affair seemed to have brought out the worst in all of them.

The two men had now reached the exhibit area, where employees were unloading poster-size display boards featuring excerpts from articles written recently about Stanton.

Colin admired aloud the cleverness of whoever edited the selection, and Fairchild said, "Nora made me keep the references to Walsh."

Even the Newsweek quotes seemed favorable, strung together with strings of ellipses. The reporter had interviewed Sheldon Brandt and quoted him saying some of the same things he had said to Colin, sounding like the vicious fanatic he, indeed, was. Colin had read the original article, and although it was tough on American industry in general, the extensive attention given to Brandt and careless EPA monitoring procedures caused Stanton Technologies to come off looking like a victim of capricious agency harassment, which in fact it largely was. That fact, coupled with

Hunt Benson's planned announcement at the stockholders meeting of a ten-million-dollar clean-up program, would go a long way toward redeeming his reputation.

"Has Walsh pushed you about the second million?" Fairchild asked Colin as they strolled past the exhibits.

"No. He's called a few times and pretended to be annoyed, but it's as I expected. Our first payment pleased him and he seems willing enough to wait."

"You don't think it's an act?"

"Sure it's an act, but it's in his own interest to be a little patient right now because he's beginning to think he actually has a shot at the top spot in spite of us."

"How could he think that? Brian and I made it damn clear he'd never get in except over our dead bodies."

"Maybe that's what he has in mind," Colin said, and Fairchild stared at him in surprise before he laughed.

They had paused before a working model of the main plating room, an exquisitely detailed scale miniature which contained all the glistening metal baths, ladders, catwalks and overhead cranes of the original. When Ken pressed a button everything was set in motion so that one could see how the whole process worked before actually visiting the real thing in the factory.

"Seriously, a lot of people have been telling him he'd make a wonderful company president," Colin told Fairchild. "Maybe he's beginning to believe it's possible."

While they were talking several employees had passed them, tarrying admiringly among the displays, pressing buttons to make the hands-on models go. Colin heard a woman say, "Oh, Mr. Fairchild, isn't this just fascinating?"

He turned to see Celia Walsh with an elderly gray-haired woman. "I'm glad you like it, Mrs. Walsh," Ken said.

"Adam told me it was wonderful but I had no idea," Celia Walsh said. "You must be delighted with the way it turned out."

"I'm very pleased, yes."

"It's one thing to hear about all the wonderful things Stanton makes but quite another to see them displayed in such exciting ways."

"It is interesting," the older woman said.

"Nancy, dear," said Celia Walsh, "I'd like you to meet Mr. Fairchild and Mr. Draggett. Mr. Fairchild works with Adam, and

Mr. Draggett is Stanton's legal counsel. They are dear friends of Adam's." They shook hands in turn as Celia went on, "This is Mrs. Walsh, Adam's mother, who's come to live with us."

"Did you say, Adam's mother?" Colin said, not quite believing what he had heard.

"That's right," Celia Walsh replied, and the elder Mrs. Walsh added with a sweet smile. "Adam's still my little boy even though I know he isn't little anymore."

Fairchild's eyes darted between the woman and Colin and back again as Colin indicated with the barest shift of his shoulders that he was as much in the dark as Ken was. "Welcome to New London," Fairchild said in a forced voice, and Colin could almost hear the rampant questions circling inside his brain, demanding answers. "I hope you enjoy your visit."

"Oh, I'll be staying on," the elder Mrs. Walsh said, looking vaguely at Celia. "Won't I?"

"Yes, dear, you most certainly will."

"My husband died, you see," the old lady said, "and Celia and my son Adam have been so kind to have me."

"Not at all," Celia Walsh said gently.

Under ordinary circumstances this would have been the moment to exchange another platitude and go their separate ways. But both Ken and Colin had to know more. At least probe a little.

"Where did you live before moving to Connecticut?" Ken asked the older woman.

"Santa Barbara, California," Celia answered for her.

"I couldn't manage alone. Thank God for Adam."

"You are fortunate," Fairchild said, not knowing what else to say, short of what the hell is going on, ladies?

For weeks they had puzzled over the other anomalies of Walsh's peculiar circumstances. First a wife who said she had known her husband since childhood. Then O'Connell, the lawyer of impeccable reputation from the Securities and Exchange Commission, who claimed to have gone to Princeton with him. Now, to confuse and baffle them further, they had met a pleasant, attractive woman in her late seventies who said Adam Walsh was her son.

Very neat, Colin reflected, except he is not Walsh but an ex-con named Wadjewska with a record as long as my arm.

Like a malignant spirit, Walsh appeared behind them then, giving his wife a peck on the cheek and asking, "Like it?"

"It's very educational," his mother, or whoever she was, said.

"That's the idea," Walsh replied. "We want each visitor to have a clear perception of what we do as soon as he or she arrives." He turned to the two men. "You met my mother?"

"We met," Colin said.

Walsh put his arm around the older woman, giving her a strong hug. "Nancy's gone through some tough times lately and we're glad she could come stay with us. New London's not Santa Barbara, but it's not so bad when you get used to it."

"It's very nice," the old woman said.

"It can be," Walsh said to Fairchild and Colin. "When the sun shines and things are running smoothly, New London can be a very attractive place. Right, guys?"

"Better than Terre Haute," Ken muttered, but Walsh merely laughed at the dig. As they took their leave and turned toward Fairchild's office, Colin saw again on Walsh's face the merest suggestion of that old enigmatic smile from the prison photographs. The faintest sign that he knew something no one else did, a secret he found vastly amusing.

The instant Fairchild closed the door, he blurted angrily, "Am I hallucinating or what?"

"God knows, Ken. First the wife, then O'Connell, and now a mother from Santa Barbara."

"They can't all be involved in the same elaborate conspiracy," Fairchild said. "Or can they?"

"Let's say it's highly unlikely."

"As unlikely as their telling the truth?"

"What can I say?" Colin answered. "I make no sense of it. But somehow I have the feeling these people are on the level, strange as it seems . . ."

"That made his day, us running into a woman he says is his mother. He's laughing up his sleeve!"

"She says it, too," Colin reminded him.

"Maybe he's the world's greatest hypnotist," Ken said.

"He's certainly got enough people under his spell."

"Goddamn it, Colin, there's got to be a rational explanation. He's not some kind of magician, for God's sake!"

"Are you sure?"

"I'm not sure of a damn thing about that guy anymore."

"I'll say this. If I had not seen his prison file . . . if I had not actually flown to Terre Haute and talked to the prison psychiatrist and the warden . . . I would think we had made a dreadful mistake accusing an innocent man."

"Innocent? He's got my father-in-law's blood on his hands! When we confronted him in Ave's office he denied nothing!"

"True. But he didn't admit anything either. He just laughed at us and then conned us into extracting a million dollars from the company to buy him off."

"The way you say that makes *us* sound like the bad guys."

"Sorry," Colin told him, "I was only reporting the facts. You and I know we agreed to do it that way, but it's Brian who would have a tough time explaining what that money was for if the auditors ever picked it up."

"What are we going to do?" Ken said in a voice that now carried more desperation than anger.

Colin explained that their last-ditch response was to bring Livingston in on Walsh's prison history when he arrived.

"That keeps Walsh off the roster as CEO. But we still have to pay the son of a bitch out."

"Having him in with us might make it easier."

"You mean tell him about the million we paid Walsh?"

"Tell him everything. I don't like it either, but Howie's a banker, remember, and a cautious one. If the word got out about Walsh, and the Stanton stock tumbled, Howie would stand a good chance of losing his job. At the very least he'd have a bad time trying to explain to his board in Hartford how he got taken."

"So you think he'll go along?"

"I do." I hope, Colin silently added to himself.

"That nice little old lady," Fairchild said, shaking his head.

"What about her?"

"She even looks a little like Walsh."

"A little," Colin agreed.

"I can't wait to meet the rest of the family."

CHAPTER FIFTY-SIX

THE STANTON corporate by-laws stipulated that all stockholders be duly and officially notified of a meeting to be held at company headquarters on the first Wednesday in January every year unless the day was a holiday.

Thus shortly after ten on the morning of January sixth over four hundred stockholders assembled in New London to hear how the company was doing. Like all corporations, Stanton Technologies always tried to put on its best face for these gatherings. The fleet of company Lincolns bussed arrivals from the Groton airport to the main plant, where each stockholder was served coffee and croissants and given an annual report and souvenir kit with his or her name on it.

In the past the meetings had been orchestrated and dominated by the company founder and resident genius, Avery Stanton. He had announced sales-and-profit figures, signaled new research projects and declared the latest quarterly dividend.

Lesser executives restricted themselves to reporting on the progress of their respective divisions while trying to present their own roles in the best possible light. But they were only Avery Stanton's chorus. He was the one people wanted to hear from, a man universally respected by scientists and financiers alike because his original inventions invariably made piles of money. Hunt Benson had no such charisma to back him up.

Most of those present were people who owned a small number of shares in many companies but who accounted for less than ten percent of the outstanding shares of Stanton Technologies. Ninety percent was represented by the Stanton Foundation, money-market funds such as those run by Howie Livingston and Lydell Cummings, and a handful of individuals like Barbara and Colin.

A stage had been set up at one end of the company cafeteria where the directors and top management flanked Hunt Benson, who sat like a pink-cheeked Buddha, pouting and frowning at the crowd as people found their seats. The first two rows were reserved for special foreign guests, including a group of European bank representatives and a delegation of Japanese.

Poster-size photographs of products and operations adorned the walls, and above the stage floated a globe similar to the one Colin had seen in Hunt Benson's office, only bigger.

Hunt repeatedly glanced from the crowd to the speech he clutched in his lap, rattling the pages nervously each time he adjusted his glasses and peered out at the faces watching him.

Brian Redfern arrived late, pulling on his jacket as he came through the door. Ordinarily an immaculate dresser, this morning he showed soiled cuffs and a sweaty collar as he mopped perspiration from his brow with a grease-spotted handkerchief.

He sat next to Colin on the platform and glanced over at the Stanton president, who was anxiously riffling the pages of his speech. "You think Ma Benson's afraid his talk will get away from him?" Brian whispered. Colin had never seen him so unkempt or so jumpy, and suspected he was taking something. He wanted to tell Brian to change his shirt and pull himself together but there was no opportunity to speak to him alone. How could the man do this, Colin asked himself, on this of all days?

In spite of the dull and uninspiring delivery of Benson's prepared text, the crowd seemed pleased. Colin could only attribute this to the large fourth-quarter dividend he announced at the end.

Colin gave the promised eulogy on Avery Stanton, as well as a short homily on the reciprocal legal and moral responsibility of government and industry, referring to the withdrawal of the EPA injunction and Stanton's commitment to a clean environment. And inasmuch as Benson had completely forgotten to mention the ten-million-dollar clean-river program, Colin used it for his own punch line.

Fairchild's speech about expanding American markets was short, light and informative, while Redfern's international review was uncharacteristically uneven and discursive, not at all befitting a potential chief executive officer. Colin knew that Brian could be both articulate and witty when he was in good form, and again could not imagine why he was so disheveled or what had given him such a bad case of nerves this day when he should have been at his very best.

The real applause came when Adam Walsh took the floor, his reputation having preceded him from the securities analysts dinner, the pages of the *Wall Street Journal* and the New York *Times,* and the fact that various insider financial newsletters had given him most of the credit for Stanton's succulent fourth-quarter dividend.

Walsh was, indeed, a refreshing change from Hunt Benson, whose halting delivery had made everyone fidget. Using no prepared speech or note cards, leaning his tall figure only occasionally on the big podium, Walsh delivered a condensed version of the same speech Colin had heard him give at the New York dinner, updating the research items that had won him headlines.

The cryogenic crystal SCX-312 was being subjected to further laser tests, he said, which promised a major breakthrough for the superconductor industry in the year to come. The Hot Rock energy source had been offered to the U.S. Defense Department for secret experimental work in the Arctic, and Stanton's new Graftite product line was already back-ordered for nearly a year.

"In case you're wondering about the sudden popularity of Graftite, I can only say that anything this big"—he indicated the podium he was leaning on, which was in fact unusually large and apparently made of oak—"that weighs no more than a candy wrapper . . ." To everyone's astonishment, he picked it up with one hand and waved it easily above his head. His audience broke into applause.

"A product this light that can be molded, bent, extruded, sawed or twisted into anything from a tank to a tennis racket is bound to find an unlimited world market the moment users also discover it is virtually indestructible."

He lowered his voice as he put down the podium and continued, "We have so much confidence in it that we are offering our customers an unlimited product guaranty. If Graftite fails, that is to say if it breaks, rots, buckles or burns, we replace it."

He finished to loud applause. The managers who followed knew they had been upstaged by Walsh's performance, and tried to get on and off as fast as they could. Hunt Benson took the floor again at the end to field questions.

There were two or three corporate gadflies, the sort who buy a few shares in a company just to criticize management, but their questions bounced harmlessly off a man like Benson. Either he answered them obscurely or he complimented the heckler on bringing up the theme and then proceeded to talk about the company's contribution to the space program or the modern American kitchen.

One question, however, stopped the meeting dead, and left Hunt Benson speechless until Colin took the microphone and rescued him. It came from a nice little old lady who was worried about the future of the company. "Could you please tell me," she said in a small voice amplified by the echoing public address system, "if you plan to continue as president? And if not, who will take your place?"

Before Benson's awkward silence could go on too long, Colin said into the microphone, "As company legal counsel, madame, perhaps I can give you the clearest answer," not knowing quite what answer he would give or how clear he could be.

But Colin tended to be fast on his feet, and he was counting on that to get him through. He thought of Maisie forgetting all her lines on stage until a drunk started heckling her. If Crazy Maisie could do it, who was he to fail?

He explained that under the company by-laws, Mr. Benson had succeeded upon Mr. Stanton's decease only as president pro-tem until today's meeting when the stockholders would either confirm him for a term of two years or elect another candidate.

"But who are they?" she said. "The other candidates?"

"Several names have been put forward as possible CEO's," he said, "but there's no official list."

"Could you tell me who they are?" she persisted.

"All part of the regular Stanton team here today." He turned to the seated executives and directors behind him. "Mr. Kenneth Fairchild," he said, "vice-president in charge of sales and advertising, whose broad experience and distinguished career speaks for itself." Ken nodded to the crowd.

There was applause, and already Colin knew he had made a major mistake by inadvertently organizing a popularity contest. But it was too late and he had to push on. "Mr. Brian Redfern," he said, "whose skilled direction of Stanton International contributes importantly to our profit picture." Less applause for Redfern, but loud enough to bring a nervous smile to Brian's face. He finished by mentioning Walsh, but he had barely uttered his name when the whole place was on its feet applauding.

"With friends like you . . ." Fairchild remarked sourly, deliberately leaving the phrase unfinished. "Christ, Colin, anyone would swear you were on his side."

The applause continued until Walsh rose and bowed.

"Who am I to be uncharitable?" Redfern muttered. "It's his last hurrah." Colin assumed his reference was to their intended meeting with Livingston, where he would dash Walsh's hopes forever.

After the racket died down Hunt Benson took the microphone again to announce the pre-lunch company tours. "Each group will be escorted by a different company executive. Please find your name on the list and the name of your tour group leader." A hum of conversation and a rustling of papers followed as people checked to see where they were supposed to go.

"Please form in the corridors," Benson said. "The first group will be escorted by Mr. Walsh, the second will follow with Mr. Fairchild. Our research director, Dr. Henderson, will take the third, and so on. Find your number in the hallway . . ." He droned on as the crowd began to drift out of the cafeteria. "Stay with your group. Do not wander off on your own as there are many unsafe areas in the plant and . . ." They were no longer paying attention so he shrugged and gave in to the noise.

As Walsh and other company brass filed off the platform Ken Fairchild came to ask Colin if he had spoken with Howie Livingston yet. Colin replied that he had Walsh's file in an envelope under his arm at that moment and was about to talk with Livingston.

"Wait," Brian Redfern said, "until lunch."

"What for?" Fairchild asked. "Tell him now, so he has time to get used to the idea before the board meets."

Hunt Benson was behind them, fussily herding everyone toward the corridor. "Gentlemen, your tour groups are leaving," he said. "Ken, you have the one right behind Adam."

Fairchild winked at Colin as he clapped Benson on the shoulder, saying under his breath, "Yes, Ma."

The crowd milled around the corridor. Colin went looking for Howie Livingston but Howie had already gone ahead with Walsh's first group of European bankers.

Fifteen minutes later Walsh surprisingly reappeared alone, avoiding Hunt Benson. Redfern called out in astonishment, "What the hell are you doing back here?" Walsh looked at Brian as if deciding whether to take offense before he smiled his old crooked, knowing smile.

He said to Colin, "When I saw I'd have to climb up on that catwalk, I bowed out. There's no way you'll get me on something like that." Colin remembered then what the prison warden had said about Walsh's vertigo, a fact he had never thought to pass on to Redfern or anyone else.

"What happened to the group you were escorting?" Colin asked Walsh. "Did they just skip it?"

"No. They waited for Fairchild to catch up to go with him." Walsh flipped open his heavy gold pocket watch attached to the Phi Beta Kappa key and glanced at the time. "They should be back in another twenty minutes."

Brian had gone white. "You say Fairchild went up there first?" He backed away from them, turned suddenly and sped down the hallway, disappearing into the crowd.

"What got into him?" Walsh asked as his eyes followed Brian. "Afraid he'll miss something?"

Colin pushed his way through the crowd but when he reached the far end of the corridor Brian had disappeared. An assistant convoying a clutch of Japanese motioned toward a door further down, saying, "Tell Brian he's scheduled to take this group in about five minutes so please not to get lost."

Colin hurried outside to the executive parking lot in time to see Redfern running toward the sprawling main plant building where the plating rooms were housed.

"Brian! What's wrong?" he shouted. "What's going on?" But Redfern neither answered nor looked back. Instead he sprinted toward the side doors a hundred yards distant. There he stopped and tried to open one, but found it locked. He kicked at it, gave up, then ran along the side of the building to another door further on. He jerked it open, running inside as the door closed behind him.

Although Colin had no idea what had happened, somewhere in his limbic subconscious he feared the worst. He found himself breaking into a run now, pounding over the icy pavement toward the door Brian had entered and ducking inside after him.

The place hit his senses like a hammer with its acrid smells, shimmering, ghostly light, and vaporous burning baths of acid. The intense heat and the clanging, echoing noise enveloped him like a blanket from hell as he paused to look around for Redfern.

Nearby Dr. Henderson's tour group stood around on the wet concrete floor watching an extruded roll of Graftite emerge like a glittering golden ribbon from its titanium bath. Further along another group loitered, desultorily following their guide who was pointing at the giant electric cranes passing above.

Then Colin made out Brian's lithe frame directly beneath the cranes, waving and shouting, although his words could not be heard above the metallic clamor of the place. His eye also found the steel ladder beyond him and followed it upward. High above the titanium bath the first tour group was picking its way gingerly across the catwalk with Ken Fairchild in the lead.

As the catwalk was only wide enough for them to pass one abreast between the rails, they were strung out Indian file, moving slowly as Redfern continued his now frantic gestures from below. At first no one on the catwalk saw him. Then one of the guests at the end realized he was trying to get their attention and prodded the man in front of him. They both paused and looked down at Brian but obviously could not hear a word he was saying.

He was telling them to stop—that much could be gathered from his manic hand signals. But the others, perhaps ten in all, continued forward behind Fairchild, who had almost reached the middle of the catwalk. The two at the end sensed some emergency and began calling to the others, but again, no one's voice carried above that appalling racket. One hurried forward and touched the man ahead of him, pointing down at Brian and shouting in his ear. He in turn looked down before he got the attention of the next man in front, and so on down the line.

The message took forever to work its way from one to the other, and while it was being passed along, Brian started up the ladder. Finally the last man turned and saw him, nodded to the one behind him, and reached out to get Ken Fairchild's attention.

Ken felt the tug on his sleeve and turned. Colin saw his face clearly. Curiosity, puzzlement and surprise were there as Fairchild glimpsed Brian coming up the ladder. Then astonishment as the steel plates gave way beneath him and he reached out futilely for the guard rail to keep from falling.

Colin thought he heard his scream pierce the sound of the plating room, but it may have been his own voice cutting through the din.

Time came to a stop as Ken Fairchild seemed to drop in slow motion, to fall the distance between the catwalk and the deadly bath awaiting him.

He struck the surface with a splash that sent hissing globules of bright molten metal in all directions. After a horrifying moment the shimmering metallic bath returned to normal, the enormous weight of the surface tension once more turning it into a steamy golden mirror.

For what seemed an eternity but was probably no more than a few seconds everyone was too shocked to move while a siren alarm shrieked and an emergency gong clanged. Like the frozen frame of a film stopped in mid-projection, the place appeared to be in a state of suspended animation.

Colin recalled as a child seeing for the first time the scene of a high-dive film run backward. After the dive the turbulent pool miraculously came together to become calm as the diver erupted from the water again feet first and ascended in a perfect arc to the diving board. Now Colin wanted it to happen in real life.

But this couldn't be real life, he reminded himself. It was some mad nightmare, some grim, impossible hallucination.

Then the worst thing of all happened. Something so awful, so unnerving and unexpected, the unattenuated horror of it would be etched in Colin's brain forever.

The depth of the titanium bath was only about three feet, and suddenly, in a cruel travesty of the reverse swimming pool dive, its roiling, glittery surface was broken from beneath by a human head.

The rest of the figure rose from the golden deep like some incredible creature out of a science-fiction film . . . Titanium Man, his arms raised in a plea or benediction.

Ken Fairchild was perfectly recognizable beneath the film of metal that covered him, a moving, living, life-size statue.

Every hair was in place. His tie, the West Point ring on his finger, the buttons on his vest, even the flaps on his jacket pockets gleamed golden in the pale industrial light.

The shining apparition stood uncertainly for a moment, as if posing to see how the others liked the effect. Then he staggered blindly toward the edge of the bath like a man with soap in his eyes. Before he reached it he collapsed and slowly sank beneath the surface without a ripple or a trace, as if he had never been.

___ CHAPTER FIFTY-SEVEN ___

A PARAMEDIC and the company doctor, with all their gadgets, could not help. By the time they were able to grapple Ken Fairchild's body from the titanium bath his heart had stopped and the doctor pronounced him dead on the plating-room floor.

Work ceased and a stunned crowd gathered to stare at the body as the paramedic packed away his respirator. There had been accidents in the plating room before, but never a serious one. An employee found a tarpaulin to cover the glistening, gilded body, but everyone continued to stand around exchanging exclamations of shock and horror long after the fatal fall. Except Brian Redfern. He had vanished and no one seemed to know where he had gone.

Hunt Benson asked Colin, "Will you call Ken's wife?"

"Call Barbara?"

"You're the closest to the family," he said.

Indeed, he was. How would Barbara take it? If Colin felt guilt, what would she feel? And who would tell her boys, and Nora Hallowell?

He could say . . . What could he say? There's been a terrible accident. But had there been an accident? His mind raced as he silently imagined a succession of empty phrases to soften the shock of sudden death. Something happened at the plant, he could say, stretch it out. Something bad happened. Or . . . ?

A terrible accident. Missed his footing on the catwalk and fell. Happened so quickly. The floor gave way. A faulty steel plate, an oxidized rivet no one had noticed. It was over in seconds. He never felt a thing.

Except the most excruciating pain as he burned and suffocated beneath the surface of his molten metal tomb.

Adam Walsh put an arm on Colin's shoulder. "If you'd rather not do it, Colin, I can go," he offered.

"No, I will deal with it."

"I suggest you do it now, then," Walsh said, "so you can tell her in person before she hears it from some stranger."

He was right, but Colin wasn't thinking of that. As he looked at Walsh what had been a blur seemed to snap into focus. His mind's eye had been backing up, seeing again and again the flooring give way the instant Ken Fairchild put his weight on it and the expression of stunned disbelief as he reached for the rail.

A terrible accident? Or a carefully planned trap that caught the wrong victim? The instant the question exploded in his mind Colin knew the answer.

But did anyone else?

Did Walsh?

Could he guess or should Colin take him aside and tell him he had just escaped with his life, on account of his vertigo? Which Brian didn't know about.

"Are you all right?" Walsh asked him, concern in his voice. "I know he was your special friend. You sure you're okay?"

"Yeah . . . where's Brian?"

As the horrified and bewildered stockholders were being herded out, Adam Walsh became the one who took over. Propelling a shaky Hunt Benson ahead of him, Walsh suggested that members of the board and some of the top executives go immediately to the board room. There he chaired a brief meeting even though he was not a board member. The election was officially suspended and Hunt Benson remained in place as president until the board could meet again in a month's time.

Fairchild's body was taken to a New London funeral home, a made-over Victorian monstrosity on Lighthouse Avenue that boasted ample parking, a coffin salesroom and a recently added cement block slumber wing with piped-in organ music. How the industry of death cherished its euphemisms. Were these embalming centers called homes or parlors in the mistaken belief that they could cloak their cold purpose or disguise their grisly function?

In any case, that was where Ken Fairchild ended, this man who had survived the Vietnam War and a mugging in New York. By noon that day his titanium-bathed body lay on a porcelain slab in the funeral home basement, a source of golden wonder to the chief mortician.

All efforts to cleanse the body had failed because metal salts had penetrated the skin. Either they would have to show a gilded mummy called Kenneth Fairchild or they must close the casket.

When Colin left to drive to Barbara's he noticed that Brian's

Porsche was not in its regular parking spot, where it had been earlier in the day. He called Brian's home and got Fionna.

"But, Colin, isn't he at the meeting?"

"He left after the accident."

"What accident?"

Colin told her what had happened. Unconsciously, he supposed he was trying to get the story right before seeing Barbara.

"Oh, Christ, Colin! *No.* First her father, now this . . ."

"I'm on my way to Barbara's. I want to catch her before she leaves for the shareholders luncheon."

"Oh, good Lord, yes! Don't let her go there cold."

"If Brian shows up ask him to call me at her place."

"Shall I come over, too?"

"I don't know, Fionna. Maybe she'll need you. I really don't know what to say."

"I just can't believe it."

"Nobody can."

"What got into Brian? Does he know what happened?"

"Yes."

"Then why did he leave? That's not like him."

"Have him call me, Fionna."

"I'll come over. Barbara will have to tell the boys at school and she's going to need heavy back-up for that."

A weeping maid let Colin in and took him to Barbara in the library. The news had arrived only minutes before. Her eyes were moist and she had a handkerchief twisted in her fingers, but she was not crying.

"Did you see it happen, Colin?"

"Yes."

"The man who called said he was . . . electrocuted."

"He fell into one of the electroplating baths."

"Fell, or was pushed?"

"Why do you say that?"

"I don't know . . . was it really an accident?"

"Yes. I saw it. He was leading the first tour group and as they crossed over the plating bath, one of the steel mesh panels in the flooring gave way. Ken grabbed for the rail and missed. Nobody pushed him, Barbara."

She shook her head. "His friend Yancy was afraid something would happen after that awful man came to see me."

"What man?"

"Her husband."

"Nora Hallowell's husband came to see you?"

"One night a month or so ago."

"Why didn't you tell me?"

"I was going to, Colin, but then something came up and later on it no longer seemed so important."

"What did he want?"

"He was desperate and drunk. In love with his wife and threatening to kill Ken. I was frightened of him." And she began to cry, softly at first and then gradually giving way until her whole body shook. "Was it my fault?"

Eventually her crying tapered off as she groped for something to dry her eyes. Colin handed her his own handkerchief because the damp bit of lace she clutched in her fingers was inadequate to her tears.

"I didn't love Ken anymore, not for a long time. I won't pretend I did. But I still . . . well, I married him . . . he's the father of our children . . . and he could be so . . . so likeable, at his best even loving. Oh God, I have to tell the boys, but I can't do it by phone. I'll drive to the school and see them there . . ."

"Do you want me to go with you?"

"I don't know. Maybe I do. But I'm the one who has to tell them their father is dead. You can't do that for me." And she broke down again.

So many things were coursing through Colin's mind as he watched Barbara. She seemed more vulnerable than ever, and he wanted to put his arms around her and hold her, make her feel better somehow. But another, deeper instinct told him no. Leave her alone. She had to be feeling some guilt no matter how little reason she had to feel it, and some of that guilt was associated with him. Let her mourn Ken however she can.

"Colin?"

"Yes?"

"Please don't feel bad. About us, I mean."

He said nothing.

"I don't know what I'm doing or what I'm going to do." What seemed so simple an hour ago has suddenly become very complicated. But I love you. I guess that's the main message."

"Would you like to be alone?"

"Yes. No. I don't know. Would you make me a drink, please?" He poured them each a scotch as she asked, "Where is Ken now?"

He told her.

"Should I go there?"

"Later, perhaps."

"I must call his mother."

"Anyone else?"

"She lives with a sister in California. That's his whole family. Then there are friends. Ken had a great many. He was almost as popular with men as with women." A small sound came from her, part laugh, part sob, as she tried to smile and daubed at her eyes again. "He was particularly close to some of his old army buddies. Men who were at the Point with him and in Vietnam."

She had mentioned Yancy, and Colin wondered how he would take the news of Fairchild's death. Not well, he was sure.

And where had Brian gone? Colin felt the need to talk to him as soon as possible. A hundred questions circled in Colin's mind and he knew that Brian was the only one with answers to most of them. His nervous appearance in a grease-spotted shirt, his disjointed speech to the shareholders and his frantic behavior just before Fairchild fell led Colin to only one conclusion.

Brian knew about the faulty catwalk before it gave way, which meant he almost certainly had something to do with it.

Colin's mind was ranging over a further list of terrible possibilities, each one more implausible and/or worse than the other, when the telephone rang. He was bringing ice, and when the maid called him he took the call on the kitchen extension.

It was Fionna. "Colin, can you come over right away?"

"Did Brian get back?"

"Yes. And I'm afraid he's in serious trouble."

"Put him on."

"I don't know if they'll let me."

"Who's they?"

"The police. They came about fifteen minutes after Brian did and I think they want to arrest him. What do I do?"

"I'll be there soon as I can. Tell them his lawyer is on his way. And tell Brian not to say a word, not to answer questions, not a *thing* until I get there. Okay?"

"I understand. But suppose they take him away."

"They'll wait until I arrive. Just do as I say."

"All right, Colin. How is Barb? Is she holding up?"

"She's hurting, I think she'll be okay."

"Hurry, Colin, please!"

"Fionna, let me talk to the policeman."

"There are two of them."

"Put one on the phone."

After a moment a male voice came on. "Sergeant Otis."

"Sergeant, this is Colin Draggett, Mr. Redfern's attorney. Can you tell me what this is all about?"

"No, sir. Not over the telephone."

"I'm on my way there but I don't want him answering any questions until I get there. He has a right to be represented by counsel and I don't want him saying a word until I find out what's going on."

"No problem, sir. Mr. Redfern's already been quite cooperative and forthcoming without any prodding from us."

"Is he under arrest?"

"Not at this point in time."

"I'll be there in fifteen minutes."

Colin did not tell Barbara the full story when he left but merely said Brian had an urgent problem he needed help with. "I'll be back in a couple of hours. Will you be all right?"

She nodded. "I've got to collect myself to call his mother. She's very old and I don't know how she'll take it. There are so many things to think of. When Daddy died Ken took care of everything."

"Don't do anything now unless you feel up to it. There's no rush."

A short, bitter laugh from Barbara. "No, there isn't, is there?"

IT WAS close to three in the afternoon when Colin arrived at Redfern's house. An unmarked state police car was parked in the drive behind Brian's Porsche. All the way over Colin kept thinking how fast they had acted, going after Brian almost as soon as he left the Stanton plant. Someone must have been suspicious and called them. Otherwise how could they possibly have known?

The officer said Brian was not under arrest. Not yet. That could mean there was not sufficient evidence to hold him, but it did not mean they wouldn't find it. Colin shuddered to think of what was in store for them all if Brian actually had, as he had immediately suspected, tried to kill Adam Walsh and missed . . . By the time he had walked the few steps from his car to the front door he had to admit to himself that he was sure that was exactly what had happened.

Colin could identify easily enough with Brian's frustration but he could not accept his twisted reasoning. He and Fairchild had been against paying Walsh from the start, yet until now Colin had been satisfied that their fantasies of violence ended with the embarrassing arrest of Oliver Quirk. Their idea of solving their corporate problem by recruiting Luther Yancy or Quirk had been as unwise as it was ineffective. When it failed, Brian must have decided to take matters into his own hands and concoct a scheme to kill Walsh and make it look like an accident.

Now he understood that was why Brian had insisted he wait before showing Howie Livingston Walsh's prison record. If everything had gone according to Brian's plan, Walsh would have been dead "by tragic accident" by the time of the board meeting, and the need to prevent his election past.

Instead, Brian's one-time accomplice and rival lay on the porcelain table at the funeral home. What a series of accidental ironies, Colin thought. First, his own failure to mention Walsh's pathological fear of heights. Again, Brian's decision not to take Ken into his confidence for his final solution. And lastly, Ken innocently taking over from Walsh, which guarantied his death . . .

Fionna answered the door with a great sigh. "Colin, thank God! They're so polite it's scary." She led him into the living room where the two state policemen sat drinking coffee. The younger of the officers was in uniform while the older one wore a neat gray suit. They rose to introduce themselves. "I'm Sergeant Otis," the older man said.

Colin nodded but did not shake hands. He sat next to Brian, who had a drink in his hand and looked awful. His eyes had developed huge circles since the morning, his tie was askew and his hair mussed as if he'd been carousing for a week.

"Okay," Colin said to the sergeant in his best voice of authority, "what's this all about?"

"We're just here to ask Mr. Redfern some questions," Otis said mildly, "in connection with an investigation we're running."

"If you don't mind, I'd like a few words with Mr. Redfern alone. Then you may ask your questions in my presence."

"Fair enough, sir," Sergeant Otis replied. "We can wait outside until you're ready."

"That won't be necessary," Fionna told them. "Come into the kitchen for another coffee."

The moment Colin was alone with Brian behind a closed door he said, "What have you told them?"

"Colin, I panicked."

"Did they read you the *Miranda* rules?"

"Oh, that."

"Yes, that. Did they tell you that you had the right to remain silent?"

"I think so, but I wasn't paying much attention after what happened this morning. Ken, Jesus Christ, if only I'd . . ." and he broke down. Pain of guilt, remorse, hysteria, whatever he was suffering, wracked his body as he clutched his head in his hands.

Colin asked no questions for a while, then when Brian began to pull himself together again he said, "Listen, Brian, I'm not interested in what you've done or whose fault Ken's fall was. We can sort all that out later. Right now just tell me what they know."

"Nothing. I don't know . . . how can you tell with them? When they drove up I went into a flat spin. I heard a couple of buzz words, you know, like 'investigation' and 'accident,' and I told them sure it was an accident and they asked how it happened. I told them, you know, that when the group was crossing the catwalk in the plant that, well, you know, they move that thing all the time and some parts of it wear out and must have caved in. So I was trying to explain that to them . . ."

"What else did you tell them?"

"Well, that's the whole point, Colin. Christ, I said I didn't have anything to do with it. I mean, there were fifty other people in the plant when it happened and—"

"All right, all right. Back up a little. Did they tell you why they had singled you out for questioning about it?"

"That's just it. They looked a little puzzled and then started with a whole different bunch of questions until I realized we were talking about two different accidents."

"I don't understand."

"Well, I thought naturally they were investigating what happened at the plant this morning. But they hadn't even heard about that until I told them. They're investigating a car accident on Christmas Eve where some guy drove off the Oyster River Bridge."

"Why ask you about a car accident?"

"Because I banged up my Porsche that same day and didn't report it. The guy who went into the river said he was sideswiped by a car like mine. I mean, it could have been anybody's—"

"Was it yours?"

"Look, Colin, there's no way they could ever hang that on me—"

"As your lawyer, Brian, I must know the truth. What you tell me is entirely confidential, but I can't help unless I know. *Was* it you?" Colin demanded. "Tell me yes or no."

And Brian told him.

____CHAPTER FIFTY-EIGHT____

THE STATE police would like to have arrested Brian that day on the hit-and-run charge but they had no case. Their evidence was spotty: some paint found on the damaged Lincoln that could have come from Brian's Porsche, or it could have come from a BMW, a Mercedes or an Audi. No one could positively identify the car because of the heavy snow falling at the time of the accident, and no one had seen the driver's face.

Brian told them he had not been anywhere near the Oyster River Bridge and that his Porsche had been banged up by some wild-driving kids who clipped him coming off the turnpike. The fiction was partly substantiated because the garage owner had also confirmed that was what Brian had told him the day he brought the car in for repairs.

So there would be no charges brought against Brian Redfern for leaving the scene of an accident or for reckless or drunken driving. The state police were forced to accept his version of events even though it was clear from Sergeant Otis's look that he didn't believe a word of it.

The matter might have ended there except for two unrelated factors. Brian's initial panic at seeing the police car had caused him to protest too much, and his denials that he had anything to do with a fatal accident at Stanton Technologies aroused suspicions before the police even knew there had been an accident.

Sergeant Otis, a patient investigator with a keen nose for the truth, was immediately curious about why Redfern felt so compelled to clear himself of something no one was accusing him of.

Otis was also annoyed because he had no hit-and-run case against Redfern, and he called the New London city police as well as his own office to see if any complaint had been received on a Stanton factory accident. None, he was told, so he had to let it go.

But early the following morning, as he was preparing his final report on the Oyster River incident, recommending that the file be closed because they had no perpetrator and no apparent chance of finding one, a fellow sergeant handed Otis a complaint file.

"Isn't it the one you were asking about yesterday?"

"Bingo," Otis said.

"The guy who filed this," the other officer said, "was real pissed off. So after work last night he went out with his pals to let off a little steam. They talked him into coming down here."

What Otis read made him give a soft, contented whistle. The workman was responsible for the maintenance of equipment in the plating room and he took pride in his work. After Fairchild's death he felt he was being unfairly blamed by the plant safety engineer for the poor condition of the catwalk flooring. He decided to see the floor for himself, and what he found angered him enough to come to the police.

Eighteen of the cotter pins that held a single panel of steel mesh in place had been filed or sawed almost through. Thus the moment anyone stepped on the plate, the fragile steel threads that sustained it were bound to give way. It wasn't sloppy maintenance, as they were saying, the worker insisted, but sabotage. Somebody had deliberately cut those pins so the thing would fall.

Sergeant Otis read over the man's deposition several times and got permission to pursue the investigation personally. Later that day he obtained a second and more detailed statement from the same man, and sent the mobile state police lab out of Hartford to the Stanton plant, where the telltale cotter pins as well as the steel flooring were bagged as evidence.

Between the second and third day after Ken Fairchild's death the state police team, assisted by detectives from the New London city police department, interviewed several plating-room workers. Among other things, they confirmed that during the week prior to the accident Brian Redfern had been seen on or about the catwalk, complaining to those on the shift that his foreign orders were not being put through fast enough. If he had a beef, they had told him, tell the supervisor.

He had rarely been seen in the plating room before those times. "Except once about two months ago," a burly crane driver told one of the detectives assisting Sergeant Otis. "Him and Fairchild got into a kind of push and shove up there."

"A fight on the catwalk?"

"More like a scuffle, but Fairchild nearly went in."

"Do you know what it was about?"

"They say there was no love lost between them two."

"Who says?"

"It was common knowledge."

"Do you have any idea why?"

"One was married to old man Stanton's daughter, but the other one, Redfern, was the old man's favorite. Figure it out."

When this report was passed along to Otis, he laid it alongside the transcript of his own interview conducted earlier the same day with Mr. Hunt Benson, president of Stanton Technologies . . .

"Thank you for your time, Mr. Benson."

"That's quite all right. What can I do for you?"

"We have evidence to indicate that the accident in your factory the other day was a result of deliberate sabotage."

"Oh, good Lord . . . why would anyone do that?"

"That's what we'd like to know, sir. It could be a disgruntled employee trying to cause trouble. Or somebody you fired wanting to get even. I'd like to check the personnel records on people laid off over the last year or two."

"But that would be . . . murder!"

"Yes, sir. It could be that."

"That's impossible! Why would anyone want to kill someone in our plant? I'm sure you're mistaken, Officer."

"Maybe we are. But a man is dead and we have proof someone deliberately rigged that floor to collapse."

"I just can't believe that could happen at Stanton," Benson said, shaking his head, "but if you say so . . ."

"To the best of your knowledge, sir, would anyone have reason to want to kill Mr. Fairchild, or anyone else in that group?"

"Not a soul. Ken was one of the best-liked men in the firm. Very popular with everyone. Very successful, too."

"He had no enemies?"

"Some people may have been jealous of him. Sour grapes kind of thing. But enemies? No, sir!"

"How did he and Brian Redfern get along?"

"Both very competitive fellows. Brian came straight from Harvard Business School as Avery Stanton's assistant. But Ken Fairchild had the inside track, married to Barbara Stanton."

"Pretty tough to compete with that," Otis agreed. "But did you ever notice any trouble between them? Anything obvious?"

"Well, now that you mention it," Hunt Benson said, at first reluctantly, and then told Otis about the day of Avery Stanton's funeral, and how they had to be pulled apart, right at the cemetery, too.

"Did anyone else see it?"

"There were three or four of us waiting to go back to town. It was a bitter cold day and snowing. Brian knocked Ken down before Adam Walsh or Colin Draggett could stop it . . . Look here, Sergeant, you're not suggesting that Brian had anything to do with Ken's . . . ? Oh, my Lord . . ."

SERGEANT OTIS circled closer by the hour as each small piece of circumstantial evidence pointed more convincingly toward Brian. But he was not the only one looking into the circumstances of Ken Fairchild's death.

Luther Yancy was, as predicted, extremely upset when Colin told him about Ken's accident. "Oh, shit, Mr. Draggett, not the major! I knew it! Goddamn, I *knew* it! It's my fault, I should've moved on that weeks ago."

"Take it easy, Mr. Yancy. It's nobody's fault. Anyway, it's being investigated. The police are proceeding on the basis that it was probably someone with a grudge against the company, so they're going through old personnel files, checking out people who quit under bad circumstances or got fired."

"A waste of time," he said. "It's him."

"Who?"

"The man who's been after the major. He did it—"

"There's no evidence, Mr. Yancy."

"There will be. Wait and see."

Luther Yancy's vengeful entrance into the investigation almost derailed the case Sergeant Otis and the Connecticut state police were scrupulously building against Brian Redfern.

Yancy considered another suspect far more promising than Brian because of an obvious sexual motive. Nora Hallowell's divorced husband was still in love with his ex-wife and had made her life with Fairchild something of a trial. Twice she had obtained court orders to keep him from annoying her, and Yancy was able to secure a copy of her original complaint, which said that Randy Hallowell also had allegedly threatened Ken Fairchild.

When Luther checked out Mr. Hallowell he discovered that Nora's former husband was an alcoholic advertising account-executive who had recently lost his job. Hallowell had also made three trips to New London in the two months prior to Ken's death, and on at least one of those occasions was seen at Ken's office.

The details of all this reached Colin from a surprising source. Maggie Caruso had started keeping company with Dominic Petrey some weeks earlier, after they had renewed their acquaintance in Colin's office. His interpretation of her interest in old Anthony Shattuck had been mistaken. They were simply close friends who shared a deep interest in music, while it was Petrey, the down-at-the-heels, sad-visaged retired cop who attracted Maggie romantically. To each his own, Colin thought, and God bless.

Yancy laid out what he had for Petrey's review before he made his own move on Hallowell. Knowing there was an ongoing investigation into Fairchild's death by the Connecticut State Police, the prudent Petrey persuaded Yancy to pass his information along to them instead of playing homicide detective himself.

At first Sergeant Otis tended to discount Luther Yancy's theory until a search of Fairchild's personal correspondence files revealed a letter from Hallowell, written months before, threatening to kill Ken if he didn't stay away from Nora. Fairchild had ignored it.

But now it appeared important enough, in view of the court record of Hallowell's harassment of his ex-wife and his visits to New London, to shift the focus of the investigation away from Brian Redfern to Randy Hallowell.

*   *   *

KEN FAIRCHILD had barely been in his grave a week when Otis and another detective drove to New York to question the suspect. The New York plainclothesman in charge was a friend of Yancy's who moonlighted for his security firm, so Luther was invited to sit in.

Hallowell admitted to writing the letter but said he was drunk when he did it. He swore he knew nothing about Ken Fairchild's death except what he had read in the papers.

When asked what he was doing in New London he at first denied he'd ever been near the city. Confronted with specific evidence of his presence, such as Fairchild's secretary having identified him from a photograph, he changed his story and admitted he had gone to see Fairchild at his office.

"Why?" Otis asked him. "To threaten him?"

"To tell him to stay away from Nora."

"And what did he say to that?"

"He said he wasn't afraid and to get lost."

"That's the first word out of your mouth I believe," Yancy told him. "The major wasn't scared of anything."

"So you went back to blackmail him again a few weeks later," Sergeant Otis said.

"No. I didn't."

"Didn't what? Go back? Or threaten him again?"

"*None* of those."

"What were you doing in New London the second time?"

"I needed money."

"Where did you expect to get it?" Yancy asked.

"From him. He had plenty."

"Why would he give you any?"

"I said I'd tell his wife about him and Nora."

"Did he come across with any money? I guess not," Yancy answered his own question, his tone contemptuous.

"Is that why you killed him?" asked the local detective.

"I didn't kill anybody."

"Why did you go back to New London again?" Otis said.

"I was sorry for what I'd done. I wented to apologize but he wasn't there. I got drunk and started to get mad all over again."

"Tell us how you did it."

"I swear I didn't do anything. I got pissed and went to see his wife. I was going to tell her the whole story."

"And did you?"

He shook his head. "She already knew."

"Then what?"

"I came home and never went back."

"That's all?"

"That's all."

When the interview was over, Yancy reluctantly agreed with Sergeant Otis and the other policemen that Hallowell was not their man. A low-life and a scumbag he might be, in his boozy desperation to get his wife back, but he was not a murderer. Once Otis had talked to Barbara and confirmed that Hallowell indeed had gone to see her, he drew a line through the man's name.

Whatever small doubts the state police might have entertained about Brian's guilt were dismissed when they discovered that like several other top Stanton executives, Ken Fairchild owned a black Lincoln virtually identical to the one forced off the Oyster River Bridge on Christmas Eve.

Otis reasoned that Brian had tried to kill once and missed because of mistaken identity, then tried again and succeeded. The sergeant's logic was accurate enough as far as it went. It was only that he had incorrectly identified the intended victim.

The very nature of a criminal investigation, it has been said, forces police to put the cart before the horse. They had their victim in Fairchild, and by virtue of Redfern's own suspicious behavior they had developed an interesting profile on him as their prime suspect. Although Yancy's interference and Otis's sense of fairness did cause the sergeant to think momentarily that he might be mistaken, at no point did he imagine Redfern had given them the wrong body.

Also, no one thought it at all significant that Adam Walsh and half a dozen other Stanton executives drove black Lincolns.

When Redfern first came clean with Colin the day the state police arrived to question him about the Oyster River incident, he did not come *entirely* clean. He told Colin about as much as Fionna had discovered on her own, that it was indeed his car at the bridge, but not that he had been trying to kill Adam Walsh.

COLIN STAYED in New London holding Barbara's hand, helping her and the boys get through the funeral and sorting out Ken Fairchild's modest estate. There was no change in Joyce's condition, and he almost despaired at the vicious irony of it all. Fairchild, that model of vigorous, arrogant health, lay cold in his grave while Joyce continued to suffer and Adam Walsh walked free.

Rumors wafting like a bad odor off the state police investigation were not helping Brian Redfern's cause at all.

Fionna surprised Colin. He had been vaguely aware of how hard she had worked and plotted to further Brian's chances for the Stanton presidency. He knew she had pushed all the buttons and pulled all the strings with the directors and their wives. But now her aggressive charm gave way to something less selfish and more admirable as she became protective of Barbara.

She understood perhaps better than anyone that Barbara's great dilemma was how to mourn a man she did not love. Fionna spent hours with her before and after the funeral, fending off unwelcome visitors and helping with the hundred nagging problems that follow in the wake of death. Where to send his clothes or other personal possessions whose value might be nil or only sentimental. What to do with old papers and letters, and what notes to write to whom.

When Fionna was not dedicating herself to Barbara, she protected her husband like a lioness watching an errant cub. It was she who answered the telephone to say whether or not Brian was available. It was she who kept reporters at bay. She would continue to defend him, she told Colin, as long as she thought he was innocent.

"And if he isn't?"

"Then I'd leave him. But do you honestly think he has a chance against all the innuendo and suspicion? Frankly, it's getting to me."

Colin disliked the odds against Brian but said nothing.

"Thank God for Adam," Fionna told him. "Without him neither Barbara nor I could have gotten through this."

"What has he done?" Colin asked, genuinely curious.

"Brian's been a mess since Ken died, and while Hunt fidgets, Adam keeps things going. I don't know why you all dislike him so."

"We just don't want him in the top job."

"You could do worse," she said. "In fact, you are doing worse as long as Hunt Benson's driving the bus."

Colin did not comment on that either, but he knew Fionna was right. Since Fairchild's death, Hunt Benson had become hopeless.

Two days after Ken was killed, the police released a statement saying the death had not been accidental but was caused by a person or persons unknown. After that there were few official announcements. But once Randy Hallowell was discarded as a suspect, Otis zeroed in on Redfern, determined to connect him to the crime.

As the investigation ground on, the rumors multiplied and Brian's name was mentioned in most of them. When Colin asked Walsh about their "agreement," he said, "Why don't we wait a-while, Colin, and see what happens to Brian? Take it one day at a time."

That was the same day Fionna sold her Porsche, cleaned out their joint bank accounts and left town. It was also the day Luther Yancy said, "It's about time," when they arrested Brian Redfern for murder.

———CHAPTER FIFTY-NINE———

COLIN WAS always a little vague about some of the things that happened during the four months between Redfern's arrest and the start of his trial, perhaps because he blocked them out after Joyce died. He tended to think of that time as a kind of black hole in his life, an empty space formed by the collapse of everything around him, with no ponderable surface and where no known laws applied.

The nurses had become so accustomed to Joyce hanging on against all odds that when she slipped away finally, an hour passed before Mrs. Ryan even noticed. It was quite late at night. Colin had come back from dinner at the Gansevoort and was working on a brief in the library when Mrs. Ryan came in and said, "I'm afraid she's gone, Mr. Draggett."

He looked up. "Who?" thinking for a moment that the nurse was referring to a visitor. It took another few moments before he understood what she was telling him. He entered the dimly lit sickroom and went to Joyce's bedside. She looked no different, but when he held her hand he knew this time there was no mistake.

Stone and metal are cold, and ice is cold, unyielding to the touch. But the coldness of death is like no other. Flesh keeps nothing when it dies, no trace or memory of warmth or love or life.

The funeral in February was modest, having been arranged by Joyce herself with Maggie's help. Colin asked himself how he could be shocked or saddened after such a long illness when he should have felt relief and gratitude to the fates that finally took her. Yet the knowledge that Joyce no longer existed stunned him after all.

Colin knelt in the small chapel and listened to the music she had chosen. When it was finished he followed the casket to the hearse, and the hearse to the graveside. To say he missed her would have been a disservice to her memory. He had lived with outrage since the day they diagnosed her illness. But sick or suffering, comatose or smiling, somehow she had always been there for him. Now he had only the void.

UNLIKE THE snowy funerals he had attended recently, the morning he buried Joyce was almost balmy. The capricious New England winter had taken itself elsewhere for a few days and the sun shone from the kind of seamless cerulean sky she loved. "Good sailing weather," she would have said, but it always was with Joyce.

Besides the people from Cranmer, Fisher & Cleves who attended the simple service there were a number of Joyce's and Colin's friends from over the years. Barbara was there, but apart from her formal kiss on the cheek and a small squeeze of reassurance when she greeted Colin, nothing passed between them.

Since Ken Fairchild's death there had been an unacknowledged truce in their affair, a cessation of intimacies. Whether it was permanent or temporary neither of them wished to explore yet, but it seemed necessary if they were to get through the mourning and the scandal after Ken's death.

When Colin left the church he caught a glimpse of Dominic Petrey sitting with Maggie. Several clients were represented as well, including those loyal members of the Stanton board, Wes Scheutter and Nat Sawyer. After they offered their condolences outside the church Adam Walsh took Colin's arm and walked him toward the waiting limousine in such a way he could not shake him off without a scene.

"I'm terribly sorry, Colin," Walsh said.

"What the hell are you doing here?"

"If my presence offends you, I apologize. But you may recall I met Joyce on many occasions and considerd her my friend as I did you, prior to our problem."

"Our *problem*? My wife is dead and you're still working for Stanton. That's my only *problem*."

"I want to talk to you about it."

"This is neither the time nor the place."

"It won't take a minute," he said as he followed Colin into the limousine and nodded to the driver that the cortege could depart. To anyone watching, it looked as though Colin had invited Adam Walsh to share his grief. "I'm sure you know," Walsh said as they pulled away behind the hearse, "that I've persuaded Hunt Benson to stay on a few more months."

"Good for you."

"With Ken dead and Brian on leave from the company until after his trial, we're not exactly overstaffed."

"So you're hanging in there, too? How considerate."

"Someone has to do it. By the way, you don't have to worry about making any further payments to me."

"I wasn't too worried, frankly, in view of Ken's death and the Redfern indictment. What do you want from me, Adam?"

"I'm calling off our agreement."

"Oh? Did you sell your story to the *National Enquirer*?"

"My story remains in your hands as always," he said. "I will never tell it publicly. I give you my word."

"Somehow that doesn't seem like much of a guaranty."

"The million you paid out will also be returned."

That stopped Colin. "Why are you doing this?"

"I don't believe in taking money under false pretenses. My methods may not have met with your approval in the past, but as I told you once, I never took a dime from Stanton I didn't earn."

"Remember who you're talking to."

"Today Hunt Benson announced his projected first quarter earnings," Walsh said, "and the stock closed up three points."

"Based on your forecast?"

He nodded. "That's six dollars over December's high."

"Congratulations."

"There should be some satisfaction in that for you, Colin. You're making money too, in spite of all your trials."

"Talk to Redfern about trials."

"Will you be representing him?"

"I don't practice criminal law."

"I meant your firm."

"Same answer. His case is being handled by a Hartford team with Boston back-up."

"Is he going to beat it?"

"What does it matter? His career's ruined. These days, it's enough to be accused of something without being found guilty."

He smiled his small, mysterious smile. "That's an odd remark coming from you. It almost sounds as if you're on my side."

"Don't mislead yourself. You're here because you elbowed your way aboard. Why don't you show some sense of decency for once and let me bury my wife in peace?"

Walsh looked suddenly ashamed and seemed to shrink into the corner of the seat. "I'm terribly sorry, I really am. Please forgive me. I shouldn't have brought all that up now."

"Forget it," Colin heard himself saying. "Tell me something."

"Whatever I can." He waited expectantly, his expression a stricken mask of contrition.

"I know who you are. But does your wife?"

The smile slowly returned as he leaned forward to answer question with question. "You mean because Celia said she's known me since childhood? Haven't you figured that out?"

"It made us wonder because she seems honest."

"She is. Celia is also fourteen years younger than I am. When Walsh went off to Princeton she was three. She has no memory of me at that time except what I have filled in for her."

"But what about mutual friends or relatives?"

"Mostly dead, or moved away ages ago."

"What about Walsh's mother? She's no fake."

"You realized that, did you? She really is Adam Walsh's mother."

"What I can't believe is how you conned that lovely old lady into the act."

"No con. No act. Her son was killed in a car crash twenty years ago. I tracked her down in Santa Barbara after her husband died last year and she was delighted to see me."

"Why? Are you some kind of doppelganger?"

His smile broadened as he savored Colin's confusion. "No, I just got lucky, Colin. When old Mrs. Walsh remembers anything, poor soul, she remembers me. She suffers from Alzheimer's, you see."

"Why did you bring her here?"

"Except for my wife, who thinks she's known me since she was a little girl, what better reference than my ailing mother?"

"You are one cold-blooded son of a bitch."

"By no means. The old lady is better off with us than in a nursing home, and I rather enjoy the role of dutiful son."

"What about the fake Princeton degree?"

"Not fake, Colin. Only assumed. Walsh did graduate from Princeton Phi Bete"—he touched the key at his vest with affection —"which was one of the things that attracted me to him. That and his premature death. We were almost exactly the same age and looked enough alike. Anyone who knew him even slightly twenty years ago would accept me as the ageing Adam Walsh. Our height, hair color and, of course, our golf. That was the clincher. He wasn't as good as I am but good enough for people to remember him as a golfer."

"O'Connell, the SEC lawyer, talked about your golf."

He laughed. "He even imagines we played in college."

"Why Adam Walsh? Because of the initials?"

"You picked up on that, did you?"

"Avery Stanton did the first time we talked about you."

"In a sense Walsh selected me. He came from a town where I once worked. People kept mistaking me for him."

"Having the same initials was a coincidence then?"

"You could call it a coincidence. I saw it more as an omen, as if someone up there was trying to tell me something."

"So you thought you might as well go all the way."

"Not at first. Except for the golf and his high marks, Walsh was unexceptional. But he was what I needed at that time."

"Why?"

"I'm not entirely sure except that when Adrian Wadjewska was released from prison he had no future I wanted to share. No one who has not been there can imagine what it is to be in prison. A man exchanges his soul for those orange denims the moment he puts them on. The people in charge think they give it back to you when you go out the gate, but that's not possible. So you either learn to cope without it or you find another one, as I did."

Colin turned in the seat to face Walsh. "Adam, that all sounds a little too romantically contrived to me. You broke the law, not once but any number of times, and you were convicted. You did your time like any other convict and got paroled. Then you went right back to being a crook again."

"Wrong."

"No, not wrong. You can't claim that the money you took from Stanton for your ersatz research was legitimate. It was stealing."

"I earned that money, as I've told you. And the studies were based on legitimate data that proved invaluable to the company."

"For which you very generously reimbursed yourself."

Walsh was silent for several minutes. Colin thought he had dismissed the subject and would say nothing further when he began again. "I like you, Colin. You've paid your dues and you played fair with me. In a peculiar way we seem destined to be the sole survivors of this unfortunate experience, so maybe you have a right to know as much as I can tell you. It started the day I walked out of the prison gate in Terre Haute, leaving one kind of security behind but not yet in touch with another.

"My life until then had been all sham and failure, as clever as I knew myself to be. This, I was sure, would be my last chance, and I swore I would die before I failed again."

———— CHAPTER SIXTY ————

DURING HIS last three years in prison he had saved seven thousand dollars. "The way I go through money now," Walsh told Colin with a laugh, "that would carry me about a week. But then it was my whole capital. I had to spend it wisely, find work, and according to the terms of my parole not leave the state of Indiana."

Work for a recently paroled convict is never easy to find, he said, even menial work, and any kind of decent paying job was virtually out of the question for a man like Wadjewska, whose crimes involved violations of trust. He had embezzled funds from a Bakersfield bank, sold shares in an imaginary silver mine, dealt in phantom soybean futures and made a killing on Bolivian offshore oil-drigging rigs. But he was lucky. While at the prison farm he had dealt with wholesalers who bought the farm's surplus produce. One of them was sufficiently impressed by Adrian Wadjewska to offer him a job as truck dispatcher at his main wholesale warehouse in Greencastle, Indiana, Adam Walsh's home town."

"That's where you assumed his identity?"

"I never assumed his identity," Walsh told Colin emphatically, "only his name and the credentials I needed to survive."

"Semantics," Colin said, unconvinced. By then the cortege was crossing the Triboro Bridge and heading for Connecticut.

"Wrong again," Walsh said. "There's a difference. I'm the *only* Adam Walsh now."

Colin could not deny that what Walsh said was true in a way. He had fabricated a new life from a dead man's papers and his own need, a life successful beyond most men's dreams.

"In Greencastle one day," he told Colin, "a woman about my own age came up to me and said, 'Aren't you Adam Walsh?' When I said no, she said, 'I don't believe you. You must be his twin then.' She swore I was him even though she hadn't seen Walsh since high school. So I asked her who Adam Walsh was and we had a coffee while she told me.

"The Walsh family had owned a farm-implement business in Greencastle years before but had sold out and moved away to Chicago. The whole time we were having our coffee she kept looking at me, laughing and shaking her head in amazement."

Colin was looking at Walsh then, too, thinking how far the man had come in such a short time, from prison to the deep comfort of a moneyed lifestyle, thanks to a chance meeting with a stranger in Indiana. Truly, Walsh had to be some kind of genius to have fooled all of them for so long.

"Within the next few months," Walsh was saying, "three or four other people also mistook me for this man and I was, as you can imagine, intrigued. Adrian Wadjewska was free but what good would it do him? Forty-five years old and with little formal education. Nearly fourteen years behind bars since high school. A lot of experience but little he could put on an employment application. Most recent reference? The Indiana State Prison Farm. At the wholesale warehouse he made two hundred and forty dollars a week and was lucky to have the job. No, Adrian Wadjewska wasn't going anywhere."

"So you became Adam Walsh," Colin said.

"Not right away, no. More than one person I met mentioned Walsh had gone to college in the East, but no one remembered where. They all said the Walshes were a little snobbish and always considered themselves a cut above the rest of local society.

"I went to the Greencastle high school and checked their yearbooks until I found Walsh in the class of 1960. He had been class valedictorian, president of the debating club and captain of the swimming team. He was considered the student most likely to make a million dollars"—Walsh smiled at Colin—"and he had indicated Princeton as the college of his choice."

"Did you know the real Walsh was dead?"

"Not then. But I couldn't sleep wondering who this man was that looked so much like me, even to people who hadn't seen him in years. I determined to find out, and one Saturday morning I dropped by the office of the man who owned the farm-implement business to see if he had an address for the Walsh family. He didn't remember them because it was his father who had bought the business, but he was kind enough to check his files."

"And he found where they were?" Colin said.

"Yes and no," Walsh replied. "He gave me the address of a lawyer in Indianapolis who had represented Walsh's father in the sale of his business. I went to see the man, told him I was distantly related to the family and asked if he could put me in touch with Adam. He was surprised and a little suspicious like most lawyers" —Walsh looked at Colin with tolerant amusement—"and he asked me a few questions before he volunteered any information. 'Could you give me Adam Walsh's current address?' I asked him finally, and he answered, 'Sure, Elmhurst Cemetery, outside Chicago.' "

Walsh was looking out at the Bronx high-rises beyond the parkway, the winter sun reflecting from their windows like a thousand points of fire. "I asked the lawyer what happened to him.

" 'Killed in a wreck,' he said, 'in seventy-five or -six. A freight train hit his car at one of those unguarded ding-a-ling country crossings. I'm surprised no one in your branch of the family ever knew about it.'

" 'Our families were never close,' I said. 'Second cousins or something like that.'

"The lawyer said, 'Why are you trying to find them after so many years? Just curiosity?'

" 'I'll tell you. Since I went to work over in Greencastle,' I explained, 'I keep being mistaken for Adam by people who knew the family. So I guess there must be a strong resemblance.'

" 'That would make me curious, too,' the lawyer admitted. 'Too bad. One of those tragic things that happens. He was their only son, their pride and joy, and when the boy was killed the old folks were destroyed. They sold the Elmhurst house and moved out to Santa Barbara, California. That was maybe ten years ago.' "

The following weekend, Walsh said, he drove to Chicago, then out to the western suburb of Elmhurst, where he visited the Walsh grave.

"It was uncanny," he went on to Colin. "He was born only a couple of weeks before I was, in December 1941, but the lawyer had been wrong about the date of the accident. It happened in 1972 when he was only thirty-one years old.

"The cemetery office keeps files of the obituaries of people buried there," Walsh said, "and I asked to see the ones covering Walsh. They confirmed that Adam was Princeton, class of 1965, and listed the family address. Elmhurst is a pretty college town. I drove around awhile and saw the house. The Walshes weren't rich but they were certainly well off."

He told Colin that he had taken a week's vacation in the spring and drove East to New Jersey, where he spent the time in the Princeton alumni-records office and the library.

"You'd be surprised at the detail one can get out of old school newspapers and yearbooks. Sports, gossip, names and pictures. Walsh was known for an antique Chrysler convertible he owned."

"So Edgar O'Connell told me."

"Ed's been a valuable friend," Walsh said.

"How did you fool him?"

"People believe what they want to believe, especially if it flatters their egos. Once I knew enough about Walsh to chance it, I went to his twentieth reunion to see if anyone would spot me as a ringer. It was a beautiful June day and each class assembled under their class banner for the reunion pictures. The Princeton tiger was prancing around the lawn in front of Nassau Hall. I signed in as Adam Walsh and they gave me a name tag and a styrofoam straw hat with my class year—1965—written on the orange-and-black hatband."

Colin was caught up in the man's tale in spite of himself. "Did anyone say, 'Hey, you're not Adam Walsh!' "

"On the contrary, several classmates said, 'Walsh, how are you?' or 'It's about time you showed up for a reunion.' Then there were the questions about what kind of job I had and how big a family, which were hard to answer."

"How *did* you answer them?"

"As vaguely as possible. I think it was there that I first metamorphosed into an economic advisor to the government." He smiled. "Yes, it was at the Princeton reunion, when they asked me what I did. They immediately gathered around and began pumping me about this and that in Washington, and how did I see the economy shaping up for the coming year. Bull or bear and all that."

"And you got away with it?"

"I'm still getting away with it."

"No one tripped you up back then?"

"There was one bad moment. Most of the alumni were there with their wives. I had assumed Walsh was single because I found no mention of a wife either in his obituary or in his alumni records. But Edgar O'Connell said, 'Adam, where is Betty? Why didn't you bring her?' When I started to hem and haw a little, and say something like 'Well, Edgar, it didn't work out, you know?' nearly blowing the whole act, he was looking at me very strangely. But luckily he said, 'I can't believe you sold her, did you?' and I realized he must be talking about Walsh's old car that I'd seen in the yearbook, the 1947 Chrysler New Yorker convertible."

"So you picked up on that and kept it going."

"I did, indeed. I signed up for the reunion golf tournament, won a cup and cultivated the acquaintance of several influential alumni. All golfing executives or professionals. I started caddying as a young kid and was a natural little golfer, though my time in the state's facility did leave me a little rusty."

Colin had to smile. "And one of those golfing executives was Edgar O'Connell?"

"Exactly. Although he wasn't influential, just important to me. He and Walsh weren't close friends at college, you see, but after that first meeting he was satisfied he'd known me for years. And since then we've become the best of pals."

"What did you do after the reunion?"

"Keep in mind, Colin, that I was walking around the quad with my wallet filled with Adrian Wadjewska's ID. As soon as I returned to Greencastle I got a postbox in a nearby town in Walsh's name. I sent for a copy of his birth certificate and his social security number. I got an Adam Walsh driver's license, opened a small bank account in his name and deposited five thousand dollars in an account with Merrill Lynch. On the strength of that I obtained three or four credit cards. Gradually I became Adam Walsh."

"It seems you thought of everything," Colin said.

"My whole future depended on it. That summer I spent the Fourth of July weekend on Mackinac Island, where the Walshes once had a summer home. I visited the house and talked with the neighbors, one of whom was Celia's father. I didn't know her then, of course, but introducing myself to him as Adam Walsh later helped establish my bona fides with her when she came to Connecticut. Her parents had known Adam Walsh well as a young man because he spent all his summers there. I think it was about that time that Adrian Wadjewska disappeared forever, except for his obligatory visits to the parole officer. I even filed income-tax returns in Walsh's name that year on more than fourteen thousand dollars."

"Which Wadjewska didn't earn dispatching trucks."

"No. *Walsh* made it playing golf. Every Friday after work I would get in my car and drive hundreds of miles to Chicago or Cleveland or Indianapolis or Kalamazoo. Wherever there was a golf tournament. I played as Adam Walsh in amateur opens and soon had my handicap posted. I made the money playing Nassau in private foursomes. I'm good, as you know, and I was in demand as a partner. That's how Ave Stanton and I became friends."

Colin nodded and said, "I know," bringing a smile to Walsh's lips. Colin had joined Stanton and Walsh on the links a number of times, and agreed that the man could probably have been a pro. "Didn't Princeton have any record at all of Walsh's death?" Colin asked him.

"The alumni office had crossed him off its mailing list but nobody remembered why. Like Mark Twain, I told them the rumors of my death were greatly exaggerated. They laughed and resurrected me."

Colin said, "Where did you learn about marketing economics, statistical analysis?"

"Study is as good a way as any to pass the time in prison. And I have always done my homework."

"Obviously."

"I'm careful, too. I contribute to my Princeton class-endowment fund and get written up regularly in the alumni news." He chuckled softly. "They've even invited me back to lecture."

CHAPTER SIXTY-ONE

"WHAT ARE you going to do now?" Colin asked Walsh.

"Do? Take it one day at a time, Colin, like you." He was silent for a while as the cortege turned into the gates of the cemetery and followed a winding, tree-lined road to the grave site. Just before the car came to a stop he said, "Only you and I know who Redfern really meant to kill. Tell me, were you aware of his plans?" When Colin said nothing, Walsh answered his own question. "I doubt you were. You're much too sensible a man for murder."

"Am I expected to take that as a compliment?"

Walsh shrugged and gave Colin's knee a friendly pat as he stepped from the car. "Poor Brian," he said. "If he's convicted he'll think it's a terrible miscarriage of justice. But telling the jury he killed the wrong man wouldn't help him much either, would it?"

In fact, Brian Redfern was a mess. After his arrest and Fionna's defection he began to drink fairly steadily, and had other substance-abuse problems, too, so that most of the time he was either wired or half-drunk.

The legal team Colin helped assemble for him was first-rate. In addition to Weinstein, Rourke & Russo, the most prestigious firm of criminal lawyers in Connecticut, the senior man at the defendant's table would be Rufus Markham, an elderly Boston trial lawyer who had been a professor of Colin's many years before at Harvard Law School. Markham was a folksy, deceptive devil in his seventies whose smile could disarm the most hostile witness or melt the heart of the hardest juror. He had a winner's reputation and collected a half-million-dollar retainer fee before taking on Redfern.

Colin tried to see Brian at least once every week or ten days while they were preparing his defense. Not because he felt any closer to him than he ever had, but because he considered him almost as much a victim as Fairchild.

The case abounded in ironies, not the least of which was that Brian ended up broke after all. Between the cost of Fionna's divorce suit and the fees charged by his defense lawyers, Brian was suddenly hard up. He was able to borrow on his Stanton stock to pay his bills, but it was Adam Walsh who helped him hold himself together financially. The further irony was that at first he wanted to blow the whistle on Walsh. Only Colin was able to talk him out of it.

"Bring down the heavens on Walsh," Colin told him, "and you cut your own throat. He's the one who put the money back so Benson's audit doesn't show you embezzled a million dollars from the company."

"We were all in on that," Redfern protested. "Why say I was the one who took the money?"

"Brian, you're not paying attention. Your name was the only name on all the transfer vouchers."

"What are you telling me, Colin? That Adam Walsh is Goody Two-shoes all of a sudden? That I owe the bastard a favor?"

"Maybe you do. He also went up against Hunt Benson when Hunt wanted to stop your salary. Hunt wouldn't listen to me, but Adam persuaded him to keep your checks coming."

"Why should that son of a bitch do anything for me?"

"I don't know, ask him. Probably because he wanted to avoid any investigation into the missing funds that might tempt you to tell the truth about him. Or maybe he feared a suit by you against Stanton for violating your employment contract, I don't know. But then again, I'm being a cynic."

"He's on top," Brian seethed, "while I'm out on bail!"

"You can't blame your *present* situation on Walsh, Brian. Anyway, there's no point in exposing the man. Going public now would be far worse than before because the company shares are worth so much more. You'd end up unable to pay the lawyers you have and then you would be at the mercy of some court-appointed type as your defense counsel."

"How can you say that? The crooked bastard won it all!" But Brian did see Colin's reasoning when his checks continued to come, and he kept his mouth shut about Walsh.

Yet depression dogged him as he puzzled over Fionna's desertion, laced his vodka with enough uppers and downers to get him through each day, and worried endlessly about his uncertain future.

He invariably asked two questions every time Colin saw him: "Why did she walk out on me?" and "Do you think the state's case is really as solid as they claim?"

To the first question Colin knew the answer but wanted to spare Brian. In the beginning Fionna had refused to believe in his guilt for her own reasons. But once the mounting evidence began to erode her faith in his innocence, she rejected the role of faithful wife and began to think about cutting her own losses.

The cool courtesy of Sergeant Otis and his men each time they came to her house had scared her to death and made her aware for the first time of possibly incriminating herself. In her fear she had mentioned the unusual banging and sawing going on in Brian's basement workshop immediately prior to Fairchild's death. When police investigators arrived to search the basement, her panic was complete.

As for how solid the case was against Redfern, Colin wasn't sure, but he knew the state had gone to considerable trouble and expense assembling a cast of expert witnesses and a formidable array of circumstantial evidence. He also knew there was no one better at cutting up witnesses and undermining evidence than that wily old fox Rufus Markham.

"I still don't know how they got a warrant to search my basement," Brian said. "Can't that evidence be challenged?"

"Markham will challenge everything," Colin told him, "but it depends on what the judge allows. They're going to say the hacksaw blade and the file they found in your house match the striations on the sawed cotter pins. And the filings found on your basement floor are the same metal."

"How did they know where to look or what to look for? Don't they have to be specific when they go for a warrant?"

"Otis is a very determined officer. He was looking for the same kind of cotter pin and metal shavings and he found them."

"Weinstein thinks they'll try to introduce the Oyster River incident. Can they do that?"

"Markham is sure he can keep it out," Colin told him, "but there are the employees who saw you fighting with Fairchild."

"We weren't fighting."

"They say you were."

"But that's easy to refute, isn't it?"

"Benson also says he saw you assault Ken at Avery's funeral."

"You were there. I went for Walsh and Ken *stopped* it."

"I'm only telling you what they'll say they saw."

"Jesus, even if it was true, it wouldn't prove murder."

"Not by itself, of course not. But all the little things add up. If people say they saw you fighting or arguing in recent months, and the jury believes them, then motive is presumed. They also have Quirk, who plea-bargained his drug case."

"What the hell can he say?"

"According to Wally Scott, he's already said it and they've agreed to reduce the felony charge against him to a misdemeanor if he'll tell the court how you tried to hire him to kill Ken—"

"That's bullshit. I wanted him to put the fear of God into Walsh, and I never once mentioned anybody's name."

"That's not the story Quirk's telling. And even if he told the truth, you would still look bad."

"Bad enough to convict me?"

"Brian, you need to get used to the idea that you might go to jail if Rufus Markham can't demolish their case. And Dom Petrey won't make that easy."

"Petrey? What's he got against me?"

"He taped you trying to recruit him for the same job."

"That son of a bitch! But it's not admissible, is it?"

"The tape isn't, but it doesn't matter. He's already played it for the state's attorney, so they know what questions to ask if they bring Petrey in as a witness."

"But that's all lies. I wasn't trying to hire someone to kill anybody. Least of all Ken."

"I know that, but Markham has to convince a jury."

Before Rufus Markham joined the defense team, Weinstein had secretly explored the possibility of a plea bargain for involuntary manslaughter if Brian accepted a suspended seven-year sentence, but the prosecutor's office wouldn't deal. "The state thinks it's got a pretty good case," Weinstein warned Redfern.

"What do you think?"

"Let's analyze it," the lawyer had said, but the conclusions he reached were not encouraging. The evidence had been solid enough to take to the grand jury and secure an indictment. And solid enough to schedule an immediate trial, which was expected to last into the summer.

Sherman Weinstein knew how to finesse the state court system and his initial efforts were not in vain. Although he failed to plea-bargain Brian out with a suspended sentence, he did get the charge reduced from first-degree murder to second-degree, which meant that at least his client could be released on bail.

But it was Rufus Markham who really earned his fee. When the state turned over its list of witnesses and showed the evidence it would present, Colin was less than sanguine about Redfern's chances. He was even less certain about Brian's future if he was acquitted, after Luther Yancy paid him a visit just before the trial began.

It was Yancy who had urged Petrey to come forward with his tape recording and it was Yancy who had helped swing the deal for Oliver Quirk in exchange for his testimony.

"Justice sometimes needs a helping hand," Yancy said to Colin, "and I want that bastard Redfern convicted."

"Let's leave that to the jury," Colin said.

"Isn't that what we're doing, Mr. Draggett? Even though everybody knows he killed the major."

Colin answered, "I like to think that's what the trial is for, to determine whether he did or not."

"What's to determine? It's determined as far as I'm concerned. The mother's guilty all the way!"

"We'll see," Colin said.

"I tell you something between us, counselor, and remember what I say. If that sucker walks, he won't walk far. You hear it from the horse's mouth. You hear it from Luther."

"I don't want to hear it, Mr. Yancy. I know how much you thought of Mr. . . . Major Fairchild, but let the law decide."

"I'm willing to leave it to the law," Luther Yancy said, "if they decide right. If they don't, then I'm not."

*　*　*

WEINSTEIN AND Markham felt there was nothing to lose by going for an early court date because of the way Redfern was deteriorating. So the *People vs Redfern* opened to a packed New London courtroom on the third Monday in May.

For Colin the trial was a crash course in metallurgy. Experts on both teams trotted out books of facts only to be contradicted by other experts who came armed with different facts. Colin had always been satisfied to know that a light bulb lights or an airplane flies, and he left the how and why to others. He accepted daily miracles as he accepted friendly jurors, without challenge.

Before the trial he would have included the ingredients of a titanium bath among the arcane, unfathomable mysteries of life. Now he not only knew more than he wanted to know about titanium, he was told by the prosecution that the standard size of steel mesh sheets for deck plates or catwalk flooring was thirty inches by seventy-two, and the gauge was three thirty-seconds of an inch. He learned about different kinds of cotter pins and hacksaws and what they were made of. He learned how sulfuric acid and cyanide were used in electroplating, and how it was probably the high chromic content of the titanium oxide bath that did Ken Fairchild in.

As an experienced corporation lawyer he also knew that just because one side may be telling the truth, it did not mean the other side was lying. Lies are allowed in court if they can be substantiated, while the truth is often barred for lack of proof. With a jury composed of people who had never studied physics or chemistry, almost any verdict they brought in on the Redfern case would have been debatable.

Meanwhile the presumption of innocence was all that mattered while the system winnowed whatever facts it could from all the chaff. Colin always said this sort of thing was what the law made possible at the People's expense. Not a costly and pointless debate as it might at first appear, but a continuing search for the semblance of order that could pass for justice.

The state's case was carefully prepared and meticulously documented. Presumed motive was established by a parade of witnesses who testified to bad blood between Brian Redfern and Ken Fairchild.

Opportunity to commit the crime existed according to those who had seen Redfern coming and going around the plating room and up on the catwalk at odd hours any number of times.

Weinstein was on his feet continuously, challenging the state's witnesses, objecting to questions that elicited only hearsay or answers that were otherwise impossible to ignore.

Some damning testimony came from Petrey, even though his taped conversation with Redfern was inadmissible. And that paragon of probity, Oliver Quirk, immensely enjoyed embroidering his story to include Kenneth Fairchild's name and the fact that Redfern had indeed wanted him killed but, of course, had asked the wrong man.

Old Rufus Markham was polite but effective when he cross-examined these witnesses. He had heard Petrey's tape and knew that at worst Redfern's proposition was ambiguous. And he quickly trotted out Quirk's London criminal record to discredit the Englishman.

"You are not a killer then, Mr. Quirk?"

He shook his head. "Not me, guv, not on your life."

"What is your occupation, sir?"

"Lybor consul'nt."

"That's why you came to the United States?"

"In a manner of speaking."

"Why were you arrested when you arrived?"

"Objection!" from the assistant district attorney.

"I withdraw the question," Markham said as he held up some papers in his hand. "We have that information here. Sorry, your honor. I had forgotten it was a drug bust and that this witness is out on two hundred thousand dollars bail—"

"Objection!"

". . . But I haven't even asked a question . . ."

"Objection, your honor!"

And so it went, with the occasional round going to Markham.

But the prosecution had the metal filings, the hacksaw and the file from Brian's basement as well as the cotter pins, and testimony from a series of outside experts who seemed to link Redfern incontrovertibly to the crime.

At that point Colin was sure the jury would convict.

Then Rufus Markham brought into the courtroom more cotter pins and screws and rivets and nails and files and hacksaw blades than anyone had ever seen before. Whole baskets of them appeared together with bags of metal filings and analyses on each done by unimpeachable expert metallurgists. Each report positively identified certain filings as coming from certain cotter pins, and certain scratches on those cotter pins as being made by certain files and certain hacksaw blades.

So what? everyone wondered. Markham then introduced another group of technicians who had compared the different samples by sawing and filing and measuring the cut metal. They backed their testimony with impressive thermographs, X-rays, metal scan analyses and magnaflux reports, and the thrust of it showed that hundreds of cotter pins from the same factory yielded identical filings, just as more than one saw or file could make the same striations.

Watching the old man's performance, Colin thought Markham might have won with all that scrap metal and expert testimony. At least he had shattered a major state claim by proving conclusively that the tools found in Brian Redfern's basement were not necessarily the same ones used to cut the pins holding up the catwalk.

An acquittal was by no means guarantied because juries, Colin knew, rarely abided by the rules of logic, yet Colin thought he would have rested Redfern's defense if he had been managing it.

Markham and Weinstein chose to call as their last witness the one person Colin had not expected to see in the courtroom.

"Will Mrs. Barbara Stanton Fairchild please take the stand?" the clerk intoned. "Raise your right hand."

Markham apologized in his courtly way to Barbara, to the judge and to the members of the jury for summoning the widow of Kenneth Fairchild to testify. He also made it clear that she was not under subpoena but had come forward voluntarily to testify.

"Only a very few questions, Mrs. Fairchild," Markham said gently. "Were your husband and Brian Redfern good friends?"

"Yes. Particularly in recent months."

"They never fought?"

"Not that I know of."

"Mrs. Fairchild, you are the majority stockholder in Stanton Technologies, are you not?"

"Yes, I am."

"So you, in effect, control the company."

"No, because I don't vote my inherited stock."

"But you did plan to take an active part in the recent Stanton annual meeting when a new chief executive officer was to be chosen, is that not correct?"

"Yes, I did."

"Will you tell us why?"

"To keep my husband from getting the job."

"Why, Mrs. Fairchild?"

"I was planning to divorce him and did not want him running my father's company. I intended to use whatever power or influence I had with the board to keep that from happening."

"The state charges that Mr. Redfern killed your husband to keep him from becoming president of Stanton Technologies."

"That's absurd."

"Was Brian Redfern aware of your intentions?"

"He must have known what I planned to do. His wife and some of the other directors knew. And so did my husband."

"Thank you, Mrs. Fairchild."

In his summation Markham explained, "Unlike a fingerprint, which is unique, or a ballistics test that can accurately match a bullet to the barrel of the firearm from which it came . . . unlike hair samples or blood samples or a host of other indisputable evidentiary proofs, the marks made on metal by a particular saw or file are not unique or even very distinguishable from one another. A dozen similar saws can make the same cuts. A hundred different files can make the same scratches."

Markham touched every point of the prosecution's case, saying of each in turn, "This is proof of nothing and here they've proved nothing and again this other business"—his voice swelled with contempt—"is proof of *less* than nothing. Files and hacksaw blades indeed," he said with disdain. "Who among us does not own a hacksaw or a file, or half a dozen, for that matter? When something needs doing around my house, I do it if I can because I can't afford some high-priced handyman. I had to saw some metal pipe recently for a sprinkling system in our garden. Among a hundred other tools, I own a hacksaw and two sets of files, flat ones and round ones."

Colin listened and thought how good this friendly old Yankee was with his home-style, do-it-yourself bullshit, his down-East accent and his folksy delivery. The jury loved him and never got a glimpse of the shrewd Harvard legal scholar behind the act who charged half-million-dollar retainer fees.

"I submit to you, ladies and gentlemen," Markham said, "that Mr. Redfern committed no crime. A man as prominent as he in a company as important as Stanton Technologies is easy prey. If he is anything, he is a victim . . . first of calumnies, malicious gossip and jealousy at the top, then unfairly accused by zealous police officers and attacked by a sensationalist press.

"But I would not dream of asking you to acquit anyone because they've been given a bad time. I do ask you to acquit an innocent man. Apart from a lack of proof, there is an absurd illogic to the entire situation. One could never seriously entertain the possibility that a man like Brian Redfern, whom Forbes magazine recently called the next president of Stanton Technologies, would kill somebody to get a job he was already in line for. Brian Redfern did not kill Kenneth Fairchild. You heard what Mrs. Fairchild said. They were friends, even more so in recent months, on and off the job.

"And so if Brian didn't kill Kenneth, who did? Was it sabotage by some bitter, angry ex-employee? Or . . . and this I ask you to turn over carefully in your minds . . . *was there a crime at all?*"

He paced slowly back and forth before the jurors, the lapels of his jacket splayed and his thumbs hooked in the pockets of his vest, as though puzzled by his own lines of speculation. At last he said, "The idea has even crossed some minds that this could have been a sick practical joke that backfired. Some person with a perverted sense of humor who rigged that piece of flooring, never imagining the tragic consequences.

"The evidence is so contradictory and confusing that I for one will never be entirely convinced there ever was a crime. Probably we shall never know. But one thing we *do* know. An innocent man sits in this courtroom today accused of something he did not do, of a crime that may not even have taken place. I ask you to confirm him in his innocence!"

Markham's performance made two vital points absolutely clear. The hacksaw found in Brian's basement could have been the one that cut the fatal cotter pins, but so could any of a hundred others from the same factory. And Barbara's surprise appearance had cut the ground out from under the state's cherished motive, that Brian had killed Ken to get him out of the way.

The jury understood it just as they understood the judge's

charge. They could not vote to convict unless they were certain beyond all reasonable doubt that Brian Redfern had cut and filed the pins that held the catwalk floor in place, with a malicious intent to kill Kenneth Fairchild.

Rufus Markham had knocked that certainty over, but they were still left with a dilemma. A juror summed it up after the trial was over. "We didn't believe the state proved its case. But we didn't really think he was innocent either."

It ended when the judge declared a mistrial after the jury could not agree on a verdict.

RELIEVED TO be free but confused by the unexpected outcome, Brian asked Colin, "What happens now?"

"The state will probably drop it. If they couldn't win the first time out, it is less likely they will try a second time."

"But what do I do?"

Colin did not tell him the whole truth. In the time left to him, Redfern would find out for himself that short of conviction, a mistrial due to a hung jury is the worst thing that can happen to any defendant. He is not guilty but he is no longer presumed innocent either. He is consigned to a legal limbo, unpunished and unpunishable, and in Brian Redfern's case, shunned and virtually unemployable as well.

The state attorney general did not feel the People could do any better by going into court again, so all charges against Brian were subsequently dropped.

The Stanton board had agreed to retain him if he had been acquitted, or dismiss him if convicted. When neither occurred, the majority simply voted to accept his resignation.

To settle with Fionna and pay off his lawyers he had sold his stock, his house and his beloved boat. *Ghost* was bought by a Palm Beach banker and Redfern decided to deliver it personally, taking it south through the inland waterway.

He never made it. Underway near Charleston one night he went overboard and drowned. An autopsy disclosed an alcohol level indicating he had been drinking heavily at the time of the accident, if such it was. Colin thought of Luther Yancy the moment he heard the news, and wondered where he was the night it happened.

* * *

THAT SUMMER Maisie Draggett married Walter the Firewalker and settled in Kissimmee, Florida, near her friends Max Dimitri and Esther Kleineman. Walter opened a permanent Life Expansion & Astral Travel Workshop there, taking a limited number of disciples, while Maisie "retired from show business," as she put it. "I'm a queen now," she told Colin, "so it wouldn't be fitting. I get the Hawaiian title from Walter's family."

"That's wonderful, Maisie. How do I address you?"

"Don't get smart with me, buster. And in case you start getting fancy ideas, it doesn't make you anything."

COLIN SPENT the month of August sailing between Martha's Vineyard and Cape Cod. Barbara and the boys joined him for ten days, but Colin kept a careful and discreet distance. He was still unsure of his own feelings, but on the day before they went ashore at New London, Barbara said, "I'm sorry this is over, Colin. Will you invite me again?"

"How about the British Virgins this winter?"

"Aye, aye, captain. But on one condition."

"Agreed."

"That it's just the two of us."

IN SEPTEMBER Hunt Benson finally stepped down as president of Stanton Technologies and went off to Florida to fish.

After the board meeting, Colin was summoned to Avery Stanton's old office by the new president. "I don't intend to change a thing," he told Colin, indicating the panelled walls, leather club chairs and ship paintings. "I'll leave it just as it is."

"I'm glad to hear that," Colin said.

"Stick around and have dinner."

"Next time. I'm expected back in New York tonight. There's a do on at the Gansevoort."

"Is it really the best food in the city?"

"It should be," Colin replied. "It costs enough."

"How do you feel about the outcome today?"

"I expected it."

"Why didn't you do anything to stop it?"

Colin thought the question over for a moment before he answered. "I considered it, but then I decided to do what was best for the company. Does that surprise you?"

"A little, Colin. A little." And the faint, familiar smile played around the corners of Adam Walsh's mouth.